SONG TITLE SERIES

I0552924

SIX CROONERS

FEATURING

MICHAEL BUBLÉ
HARRY CONNICK JR.
TONY BENNETT
NAT KING COLE
BING CROSBY
FRANK SINATRA

JOAN MAGUIRE

Copyright Page

New: Six Crooners

Author: Joan Maguire

National Library of Australia Cataloguing-in-Publication – Publication entry

Creator:	Maguire, Joan, author
Title:	Six Crooners/ Joan Maguire.
ISBN:	9780992596491 (paperback)
Series:	Song title series.
Notes:	Includes bibliography reference
Subjects:	Voyages and travels--Fiction
	Titles of musical compositions--Fiction

Dewey Number: A823. 4

Published with the assistance of CreateSpace and is available through the Print on Demand network and www.songtitleseries.com

This short story book was created and written
by Joan Maguire on 4th March 2011 ©
ISBN: 978-0-9925964-9-1

E-book re-written April 2014©
EIBSN: 978-0-9925964-4-6

The large print book was created in March 2015 © and is available
through the same distributors as the normal book and
www.songtitleseries.com
ISBN: 978-0-9943297-3-8 (large print).

DEDICATION

I would like to dedicate this book and say to thank you to my Earth Angel David and his friends, who inspire and motivate me to achieve things that I never dreamt, were possible.

And to my sister who contracted Nephritis and is alive today because of dialysis and a kidney transplant.

INTRODUCTION

Who could go past some of the world's Crooners to use in a book so in this book Michael Bublé, Harry Connick Jr, Tony Bennett, Nat king Cole, Bing Crosby and Frank Sinatra all contribute some of their song titles to the story. Legally I can not use Lyrics or Music because of Copyright but I can use song titles; in fact, a combined total of 2,916 song titles (Italicized) have been used to make this story possible. Also due to the nature of my books; legally I must place a Reference (exactly as it is down loaded) and Bibliography at the end of the story.

Bingsie grew up as an only child in a very affluent family and had everything he wanted, except love. One Christmas, on a walk around his home town, he stops to look at an empty cottage where a blue eyed stranger talks to him. He goes home to find his parents fighting again, so he leaves.

Leaving his business partner in the head office, he travels the world visiting all of their other business offices. After three years away, he is suddenly summoned back to the head office. But why would they want him back when everything is running smoothly?

Follow the story with Bingsie as he tells a young couple about what he goes through after he walks out on his parents and starts travelling. Meet some of the people he deals with on the way and travel with him through some of his ups and downs in his life, especially after he falls in love with Joanna, but she has a secret and leaves him to go home for family reasons. Will he ever meet her again?

From an old girlfriend he meets in Paris, he learns about two forms of kidney diseases and how the press can turn an innocent action into a nightmare.

When in Ireland, he uncovers a family secret with the help of Donegal, a Leprechaun. But is that all he uncovers from the Leprechauns and what has a stranger, who walks into the tavern and speaks Gaelic to the tavern owner, who then has to translate the message to Bingsie, got to do with him?

Was this stranger the same person who had spoken with him before at the empty cottage and what do the messages that he gave him mean? Is this stranger all he seems to be, or is he someone else?

To find out, grab a drink and sit down and start reading and I hope you enjoy the story and don't forget as I have used the original song titles in whole, there may be places where I could not changed to make it more comprehensible for you, the reader. I apologize to the Irish if my translation is not correct.

ACKNOWLEDGEMENTS

I would like to thank my daughters, Jenny and Kylie for their positive but critical input in the first draft of this book and all the help and support that they have given me throughout the Song Title Series books. With taking their input to mind, I have improved the book.

I would also like to thank my son Peter and his family for their support and help in keeping me grounded.

I would like to thank Kay and Julie for their patience and understanding whilst teaching me and giving me the skills to present my unique books in the best way possible.

I would especially like to thank Marci for her help with the Spanish translations, even though I have used them in a different context.

I would also like to thank everyone else who has helped me bring this book to life and to you for purchasing it.

OTHER BOOKS IN THE SONG TITLE SERIES

CONTENTS

THE LAST STRAW

It was a *foggy day in London town,* a suburb of *San Francisco,* when two young lovers arrived at the *Serenata* Club in the *surrey with the fringe on top.* They were there on their first real holiday since their marriage almost three years ago.

As they walked into the club, they were surprised to see a multitude of people hurrying about doing the different jobs that were allocated to them. Some staff members were hurrying around to *deck the halls* with *the holly and the ivy* and more *silver bells* in addition to those that had already had been hung. Other staff members would jingle bells as they tried to hang them along the halls and around the doors that lead to several other rooms. A few staff members were humming *Away in a manger* quietly amongst themselves.

They also saw hanging from the wall to their left, a *portrait of Jennie* wearing a sad *smile,* just like a *little girl blue* and she was sitting in a big old *rockin' chair.* Next to her picture hung a picture that depicted the scene of a beautiful *city beneath the sea.*

In the far left corner of the room, stood *o fir tree dark and tall,* and it was decorated with *the Christmas tree angel* on top, with lots of colored tinsel and *silver bells* covering the rest of the tree and fake white snow sprayed over all of it. In the middle of the room sat a nativity scene, where in *o' little town of Bethlehem,* the staff had placed *the little drummer boy* at the bottom of what was meant to be Jesus lying in the manger.

Coming softly from the back of the nativity scene were Christmas carols like *Adeste Fideles,* the Spanish version of *O Come All Ye Faithful, Away In A Manger, Silent Night, Holy Night* and *Hark! The Herald Angels Sing.* In the far right corner of the room, a working fountain shaped like *Frosty the snowman* sat and there were actually *three coins in the fountain* bowl that would later be donated to charity. The room gave off *that Christmas feeling* so strongly that it made you want to stay longer.

Along the right wall, stood the reception desk where *Nancy* or *Emily* would greet you and direct you to the room that you wanted to be in, like the dining room, games room or the little café/coffee shop type of room. Behind them hung a very old sign that read *God Rest Ye Merry Gentlemen* and Women.

The last room was where our young lovers wanted to go.

After they had entered the room and sat down at a long table that they shared with another gentleman, he turned to them and said "Oh, *hello young lovers;* let me introduce myself. I am William Thurston Bingwell III, but people call me either Bingsie or just Bing. *Welcome to the club.* I haven't seen you here before, so who are you?"

The man told Bingsie who they were and where they had come from and that they were on holidays.

Bingsie said "Ah! You're the *good King Wenceslas* and *Sierra Sue* and you have travelled all the way on *Route 66* from *Avalon* in *the surrey with the fringe on top* to spend a month here. Ah, yes, it would be nice to capture *that Christmas feeling* with *the first snowfall* that will bring a *white Christmas* to these parts. Where are you going to be staying for the month?"

Sierra Sue said "At the *Chanson De Vieux Carre.*"

A surprised look came over Bingsie's face and then he said "The hotel *Chanson De Vieux Carre* is an excellent place to stay and *the waiter and the porter and the upstairs maid* will look after you very well. You should be able to see the *Bourbon Street Parade* from your window."

"What parade?" asked *Sierra Sue.*

"The *Bourbon Street Parade.* It begins *the twelve days of Christmas* events and during those twelve days of Christmas, there are many places to see, visit and there are plenty of things to do.

I hear that the *Joe Slam and the Spaceship* show is on again this year. You should really try to find time to go and see it because the *Dance of the Sugarplum Fairies* while they are *lost in the stars* is so hilarious, but *Mona Lisa* is such a beautiful *ballerina* that she will captivate you with her *dream dancing* and her *angel eyes.* You want to shout out "*dance ballerina dance* again." once she has finished. The show is that good that *I keep goin' back to Joe's* every year that I'm in town.

Now, *on the sidewalks of New York* Boulevard, and it won't be a *Boulevard of broken dreams,* let me tell you that, you can take your taste bud on a trip *around the world* because they sell delightful cuisine from all countries and they even have food cooked by members of the *French Foreign Legion.*

3

Half an hour's drive south, is the *San Fernando Valley* where the *Muddy Water* Bar and Bistro is open all *night and day* and *the late late show* is *sweet Lorraine* and *Alexander's Rag Time Band. Perfida* is another bar and bistro down there where *sweet Georgia Brown* and *sweet Leilani* sing with the *McNamara's Band.*

I must warn you though, that if you go in there, be careful if the *Sheik of Araby* comes up to you for a *chat* because all he'll want to *chat* about is his *Black Market stuff. It amazes me* that he is still operating in the *Black Market stuff* and that he hasn't been closed down.

But seeing he has nothing but a *cold cold heart* and that *Christmas time is here* again, I'm *s'posin'* that he'll still be doing business with the unsuspecting folks.

I just hope the *pistol packin' mama; Rosaleen* doesn't catch up with him. *She is the sunshine of Virginia* and she can *sing soft, sing sweet, sing gentle* but she can be like an *ill wind* if you upset her. She can make *bad bad Leroy Brown* become a *nature boy* or an *Oompa Loompa* just by the look that comes from *them there eyes. I think you get what I mean?*

Now; if it should *snow,* I'd say *let it snow, let it snow, let it snow* because we could have a really wonderful *winter wonderland.* Going on a *sleigh ride* and snuggling under a *blue velvet* fleecy lined blanket beneath a *blue moon* would *make someone happy.*"

Bingsie's voice changed when he said *"That Christmas feeling* is just an *illusion* that has some people *looking at the world through rose colored glasses* and to an *orange colored sky* but *as time goes by,* they find that their *days of wine and roses* are over. *Looking back* over their lives, they found that *in the cool, cool, cool of the evening, that old black magic* was *a weaver of dreams* and had them falling for a *crazy little thing called love.*

Love and marriage was the next step and then *a child is born.* Before long, they start burning their *bridges* until they become *strangers in the night. The two lonely people* are *lonesome and sorry* when *the party's over* and then they begin to play the game of let's *pretend* we have a happy *home.*

You know there is a saying that goes "To be old and wise, you first have to be *young and foolish.*" I don't know where it came from, but I must say that I think that saying is right for a lot of people *around the world.*"

4

King Wenceslas said "You sound sad, and you look like you *put on a happy face* and *smile* to try and hide your feelings from other people."

Bingsie replied "What do you mean; I sound *triste, blue and broken hearted. You don't know me* and I do not just *smile* and *put on a happy face* for the public to see."

He softened his voice and said "Sorry, I *apologize* for speaking to you that way. You can *call me irresponsible* for my behavior, but *who can I turn to* when I need to *chat* about *the bad and the beautiful* things and my *heartache tonight;* my parents?

My father is now like a *booze hound* with a *cold cold heart. Way down yonder in New Orleans* many years ago, he was *Mary's little boy child* who started his working life *working in a coal mine* but when the mine closed, he found that *there's no business like show business* to take you from *rags to riches.* He became an agent who handled many big stars and it was also the time when he was introduced to my mother, who was writing *Frank Sinatra's monologue.*

They had a *fine romance* and it was *in the wee small hours of the morning* just as *a blossom fell* from the tree that they were sitting under, my father proposed to my mother. Well, *love and marriage* go hand in hand and two years later *a child is born;* me. During *this happy madness* time travelling to *far away places* with my parents, my mother became ill and was sent back to *her home on the range* at *Elijah Rock,* near the *Swanee* River to recuperate.

It was a year later during an *Indian summer* that my father put me on a plane with *Mrs. Robinson,* my nanny and sent me back to *Chicago.*

The moment of truth came to my mother when she telephoned my father and asked "*Where are you? You* said that you would be home two weeks ago."

He told her that he was *in San Francisco* with two clients at the *Factory Music* Theatre as they were auditioning people for their two musicals, *Follow The Music* and *Follow The Music Further.*

Don't worry; *I'll be home for Christmas"* he told her and he was home for Christmas but *everything* in *my little world* came crashing down that year. *Something was missing* between my parents and they started fighting and arguing whenever they were together.

5

My mother told him "*What can I say after I say I'm sorry. I still get jealous* when I know that you're around the young females. I promise that *I'll never be jealous again* but it's just *my foolish heart* and the *loneliness of evening* that makes me think of *somethin' stupid* at the time."

The angry look that came from my father's eyes that was directed at my mother would have melted *Frosty the Snowman.*

As the years went by, I wondered *whatever happened to Christmas; is Christmas only a tree* now. I *always* knew when it was time for my father to be returning from his trips overseas, especially around Christmas, and I used to pray to *let it snow, let it snow, let it snow* because if the snow was too heavy, his plane wouldn't be able to land and mom and I could have a *silent night* and a beautiful *white Christmas* day together.

One Christmas, a few years back, both my parents were unable to get *home.* My mother had to stay in *Manhattan* and my father had to stay in *California,* so I was left *all alone* again and when it was time to eat, I said *"Dinner for one please, James."*

That year, *Christmas day* was *all mine* to do whatever I wanted to do. *I love the winter weather,* so I went for a long walk around town where I heard an unusual *Christmas song* coming from a house where a *grown-up Christmas* party was happening. I heard the *silver bells* from a church spire pealing out; *O Come All Ye Faithful, O Come All Ye Faithful,* come and celebrate the day that the child was born and laid in a *cradle in Bethlehem.* I saw children running through the snow, laughing and calling out "*I wish you a merry Christmas.*" and some would *jingle bells* as they ran. I saw horses with *holly and the ivy* and *silver bells* attached to their harnesses, taking *people* on a *sleigh ride.*

As I stood watching the people and especially the children, I thought to myself "*It's beginning to look a lot like Christmas* to me now and *I'd like to hitch a ride with Santa Claus* as he travels *around the world* on Christmas Eve. Now these are the kind of people *I wanna be around,* not the kind of people who constantly bring me down."

The evening began to get colder and the children headed for the warmth of their respective homes and families, so I decided to wander back to my own place of abode via a different route. *In the evening by the moonlight,* I stopped and stared at *a cottage for sale. I don't know why* I stopped, but I did, and while I was standing there staring at this cottage, someone came up behind me and asked "*Brother can you spare a dime?*" I heard him but I couldn't take my eyes away from one of the cottage windows.

Then he said "These are the *moments to remember;* what you have just seen and heard this *white Christmas* afternoon. You are about to set out on *the longest walk* of your life and *somewhere along the way,* the *summer wind* will blow away *the shadow of your smile* for *when you're smiling,* the *eyes of the seeker* will be opened.

After you've gone, the two lonely people will find that they have been living in *a marshmallow world* that is really a *nowhere with love* missing from it. *Weep they will for the good life* that they once shared together.

Out of nowhere, a sleepin' bee will arouse *a taste of honey* from the *garden in the rain. Anything goes* and you can have it *all or nothing at all.* The choice will be yours to make. *Night and day, come rain or come shine, you'll never know* what life has installed for you. Yep, *that's life* and *she's funny that way. Pennies from heaven* will fill your pockets and your *street of dreams,* but please try to *forget to remember* all past sad *Christmas memories.*

You are a *man alone* now but one day, I do not know *where or when,* you will meet another person with *angel eyes.* They will be where there is an unexpected sighting of *Edelweiss* and where you will *hear me in the harmony* of the music. It will be then that you will *look to your heart to love and be loved* by a *lonely girl. May the good lord bless you and keep you* safe."

I turned to give the man a dollar, but he was walking away, however, he did look back long enough for me to see those *unforgettable* blue eyes and to hear him say *"The best is yet to come."* I still stood staring at that cottage window for a few minutes more, before I continued on my journey *home.*

I was surprised when I got *home* to find that both my parents were there. I walked past my father, who was talking to someone on the telephone, to the drawing room, entered and closed the door behind me.

As I was standing on the other side of the door from my father, taking off my scarf and coat, I overheard him say *"One has my name the other has my heart."*

My heart stood still when I heard my mother say *"Nadie Me Ama,"* I think it means nobody loves me in Spanish and the *once a year day playoff* started between them again.

I heard my mother ask *"How long has this been going on; your own private love* affair?"

7

My father replied "Since the last *St Patrick's Day parade. My girl's an Irish girl,* she's the *Peg o' my heart* and at least we have *something in common,* besides she has been married before."

My mother then said "*Your cheatin' heart* will never change and when she finds out what you're like and leaves you, *come next spring* you'll then want to *come back* to me."

My father laughed and said "*Hey! Jealous lover, me and Mrs. Jones* enjoy doing things and going places that you would never do or go to; like *sailing down the Chesapeake Bay* with the *red sails in the sunset* above our heads to the *Pat A Pan* Café for just a coffee and a *chat* or to the *Firefly* Concert Arena to listen to the *fascinating rhythm* of the *Beale Street Blues* Band when they play their *Waltz For Debbie.*

You think that you're such a *sophisticated lady* wearing all those *baubles, bangles and beads,* but *baby,* you're not; you're just a *poor butterfly* on a *road to nowhere* except *to the ends of the earth* where you will eventually find out that *you're nobody 'til somebody loves you,* really loves you. I think that this is the *night we call it a day. You and I* won't have to *pretend* anymore."

I heard my mother climb the stairs to her room slowly saying "*Someday you'll be sorry* because *you'll never find another love like mine.*" then she started humming *Too-Ra-Loo-Ra-Loo-Ral, Too-Ra-Loo-Ra-Loo-Ral. That's an Irish lullaby* that she used to sing when I was little.

As I was really *scotchin' with the soda,* I thought to myself, "I've got to *get out of town,* get right away from these people." So I took my drink, went upstairs and packed a few things and just as I was about to walk out the front door, my parents asked me where I was going so suddenly.

I stood there with my back to them and said "I'm *leaving on a jet plane. This is always* the way it is at Christmas and I have had enough of your *once a year day,* you're leaving fight. *Once upon a time,* you both loved each other but now *how can you mend a broken heart* and a broken *home. Junco Partner* Ltd wants me to visit all their head offices and I'm going to start doing that as from tonight."

I turned to face them and continued "you know, *I could write a book* on both of you and I expect that it would be an instant best seller. Yes, that's right; *I could write a book* on excuses for not wanting to be a family. I *always* thought that when *a child is born,* it was the parent's responsibility to love and care for that child, not for the child to have to learn and defend for themselves *as time goes by.*

8

I've got the world on a string and *I've got a pocketful of dreams. I've got just about everything* I need; except love. *Can you find it in your heart* to think about me occasionally?

For me, *there'll be no teardrops tonight. Why should I cry over you? I won't cry anymore* because *I'm all cried out* over *the very thought of you,* both of you. *I'm walking* away from here tonight. *I'm through with love* if this is what it's all about; in fact, I actually believe that *you don't know what love is,* real love that is. *I'll be seeing you,* if, or when *I'll be home for Christmas* again will depend on what may happen in the future."

I walked out closing the door behind me, leaving my parents to be *beautiful strangers* to each other. That was three years ago.

Each year my mother writes "*Baby, won't you please come home. You know that you're all I want for Christmas* and *Christmas is a coming soon.* You can *call me irresponsible* for leaving you *alone too long* over the years but now, *because of you* leaving the way you did and the things that you said, I have realized how selfish and *how insensitive* I have become. Once we had gone from *rags to riches,* I thought *the good life* was what I wanted but *I'm never satisfied* with what I have.

After you left, your father and I sat down and for the first time in years, and we had a long and honest *chat* about what we really wanted from life and our marriage.

He told me "*All I need is the girl* who used to *fly me to the moon* with just a *smile,* the girl who would give me her *crazy love* both *night and day.* I miss that girl and I don't want to *lose* her forever. *I've got a pocket full of dreams* that I still want to share with you. *Cherie, I love you* and I don't want to *change partners* ever. I will do *whatever it takes* for you to give me *just one more chance.*"

You know me; *I can read between the lines* when your father talks; however, *maybe this time* he really is sincere in what he is saying. I might be *just in time* to revive a *cold cold heart* and save it from becoming a *heart beyond repair.* Again I ask, *baby, won't you please come home. I love you* and I miss your *smile…* Mother."

Oh! I am so very sorry. You didn't come here to listen to me prattle on and on over a personal and private matter. Allow me to order you some *tea for two.*"

Sierra Sue said "Thank you, you're most kind for the tea, but have you been home at all since you left?"

9

Bingsie replied "No, I haven't. I have been working my way *around the world* slowly, spending time in many places and Christmases in different countries. I only returned to this country two weeks ago and I'm still unsure of what I'm going to do next."

Sierra Sue asked "Please tell us about the places you have travelled to. Except for when my husband had to go away to study while he was in training to become a chef and Head Chef, neither of us has been any further than a few miles from our own town until now. It would be nice to hear about other places in the world and maybe I could *dream a little dream* of me visiting them one day. Did you ever see any Edelweiss or find your *lonely girl?*"

WHICH WAY TO GO

Bingsie looked at the young couple and said "Before I tell you anything else about myself, please *tell me all about yourself*."

King said "My real name is *Danny Boy* Wenceslas and I got the nickname King because I was the main, Head Chef at the *Laguna Leap* Restaurant on *Wolverton Mountain* until three weeks ago. I don't know if you heard about the wild fires that went through our area.

Well, Mr. *Booker,* the owner of the *Laguna Leap* lost everything on that *Ash Wednesday* and his insurance was not enough for him to start rebuilding right away. He told me that it *maybe September* before he can open again for business and when he does, he will *send for me.*

At this moment, we are on this holiday looking for work. Sue was the staff manager and in charge of the restaurant, so now we are both out of work. We were living in a *caravan* park opposite the restaurant but we did manage to get the *caravan* out *just in time* because the fire came through very fast.

When we got married, we knew that we were *too young* to start a family and there would be *too much* responsibility put on us at that time if we did start a family. When *a child is born,* we want to be able to give it a *home, a house with love in it.* We were saving to buy a place in *Avalon* which is *my kind of town;* actually it's our kind of town because of all the *dear hearts and gentle people* who live there.

It's a fairly small town *but beautiful.* Up there, you can start with a *foggy day* but soon *that lucky old sun just rolls around the heaven all day,* comes out especially *in the good old summertime.* The folks up there make a *tangerine* drink called Whoopee, so after *making Whoopee,* we would *take advantage* of *those lazy-hazy-crazy days of summer* and find a cool spot and have a *lazy afternoon.*

When you stand and look out from the mountain side, the gentle *summer wind* blows through and blows the clouds away and *suddenly there's a valley* where the *blue Gardenia* grows in patches that looks like someone has laid blankets of *blue velvet* down. You know when *spring is here* because the *Skylark* sings down in the valley as the *April showers* begin to fall.

But when the *autumn leaves* begin to cover the ground; it's *just one of those things* that you could never forget. I bet that *when the world was young,* it would have been more beautiful than it is now.

11

I think that I could *climb every mountain* in this world and never see a *paradise* like our mountain and *Avalon. It's magic,* that's what it is."

Sue continued the conversation by saying "*Paradise* is really what *Avalon* is to us. All our hopes and dreams are now *gone with the wind* and the fire, but we don't live in *a marshmallow world,* so if we stick together, we can go *all the way, side by side, to the ends of the earth* if we have to.

I was offered a part time job in an Ice-cream Soda shop called the *Funky Dunky* in the next town called *Jambalaya,* but the pay wouldn't have been enough to pay the site fees for the caravan at the local park and the shop manager wasn't very nice either, so I declined the offer. *What'll I do* now? I'll *smile* and *say my prayer* every day and ask the good Lord to *light the way* for us."

They were interrupted by a sudden crashing sound, someone saying "*Ding dong the witch is dead* finally." and laughter.

A waitress approached their table and softly said "Mr. Bingwell, *Adeste Fideles* is returning your call. Would you like to take it?"

"Thank you, I will take it." said Bingsie and excused himself from the table.

The young couple looked at each other with a quizzical look on their faces when they overheard Bingsie say "That's right, *Laguna Leap* in *Avalon*. Get *Adelita* on it right away and I want more information in two hours, it's important.
What about *The Continental* down by *the sand and the sea* in *Suas Maos?* Well, tell *Dindi* that I want a report on it tomorrow. Yes, I should still be here. How's *Dinah* going with *the girl from Ipanema* who's in *Piel Canela?* Please call me back the instant you have any information from *Adelita*. Goodbye."

As he hung up the phone, Bingsie turned to the waitress and said "*Ay, Cosita Linda,* please tell *Nancy* to set my table for lunch for three people. Thank you."

Bingsie then returned to the table and said "*The three of us* will be dining together at lunch; that is; if you don't mind. I would like to talk to you a bit more, but I would like to finish my story first."

Nancy approached the table and said "Your table is ready Mr. Bingwell. Is that all you require?"

Bingsie looked at the young couple and said "*Have you met Miss Jones?* She has been here since the club was refurbished seven years ago."

The introduction was made and the three of them moved to the dining room.

Over their meals Bingsie continued "As you know the *rags to riches* story of my parents and how *I've got the world on a string* and I don't need anything, well, *for once in my life,* I'm *feeling good* about it.

When I left my parent's place, I moved to *Chicago* for a while. The *girl next door* to my apartment called out one day as I was passing "*Hey there, it's Sunday.* I'm going over to the *Poinciana* Club to listen to the *Wee Baby Blues* band. You look like a *man alone,* so do you want to come? Come on, *pick yourself up* and come on over. Don't be a *stranger in paradise.*"

Well, I went with her and during the evening she asked "*Are you havin' any fun* at all."

Actually I was enjoying myself but when the *Wee Baby Blues* band started playing the *Yellow Dog Blues,* I said to her "*Something makes me want to dance with you.*"

So we did and I did *have a good time* that night.

She then asked "*What are you doing New Years Eve?* There's a party at my place if you want to come."

On the night of the party, I heard a lot of commotion going on next door so I went to her door and found that it was partially opened. I walked in and found her crying and I asked "*Where did everyone go?*"

She looked at me and said "Did you *call the police?*"

"No." I replied

She got a bit angry and shouted "Well someone did and now *the party's over.*"

I said "*Oh, Mary don't you weep.* We can go over to the *Poinciana* Club."

To my amazement she asked "*Mind if I make love to you* first?"

I didn't know what to say and *just in time,* the door opened wider and a female voice shouted *"Maria Elena!* What do you think you are doing and who is this man?"

I introduced myself as the neighbor and said that I heard people here before and then the commotion, before it all went quiet and I heard Mary crying, so I came in to see if *everything* was alright.

Her father looked at her and then at me and calmly said "When we realized that she had run away again, we knew where she had gone and what she was up to. We called the police and came straight here and it looks like we arrived *just in time* to stop *trouble* from happening."

I looked at *Maria Elena* and was just about to ask when she said *"How old am I?"* and her mother answered *"Too young,* even *too young to go steady."*

As she was about to walk out the door with her parents, she stopped and gave me a *smile* and said softly *"I'd love to make love to you. Have yourself a merry little Christmas* and New Year, what's left of it?"

I went back to my apartment and thought about her. She was *too young, but beautiful* for her age. I left the following day for *San Francisco* and our head office. The *solitude* of my work gave me a chance to *straighten up and fly right.* That was an *unforgettable* Christmas and as for *Maria Elena,* if she hadn't been *too young,* we could have had a *beautiful friendship.*

The next day *Bob White* met me at the office and asked if I wanted to take a look at a place down in *New Orleans* called *Alabamy Bound.* It was a bar and grill owned by *the Donovans.* He was *the first Noel* Donovan to open up a place like that down there when they were younger, but now the elderly couple couldn't continue to run it properly, so they put it up for sale.

Bob White and I became Junco Partner Ltd quite a few years ago, but he used to run it virtually on his own until we started acquiring new properties. He didn't want to or liked travelling, so I became more involved. He stays and works local and in the office and I do all the travelling.

We purchased *Alabamy Bound,* refurbished it and hired a popular local band, *Jeepers Creepers* to play there on the weekends. *The blues don't care* who plays them, just as long as they are played right. *Alabamy Bound* Blues bar is a huge success in *New Orleans.*

Out of nowhere, we were offered the San Antonio Rose which we purchased, refurbished and renamed the *New San Antonio Rose.* A young woman named *Mona Lisa Stardust* manages that place so well, that we may be looking for another property in that town. *Mona Lisa Stardust* has two adult children now; one is a *nature boy* who works for an organization that is trying to protect the environment of *the world around us.* He studied and lived in *San Francisco* for four years.

We sat talking one day and he told me "I fell in *l.o.v.e* with a girl I called *Stella by starlight.* She would often say to me "*Te Quiero, Dijiste (magic is the moonlight)* that comes from your eyes when we meet. *I've got you under my skin* and *the touch of your lips* makes me so happy because *you're mine; all mine.*"

One year I wanted to *take her to the Mardi Gras* but when I asked her, she asked "Isn't the *Mardi Gras in New Orleans?*"

I told her it was, and the only answer that she would give me was *Quizas, Quizas, Quizas (perhaps, perhaps, perhaps).*

That year, I changed my mind about going home for Christmas and decided to stay on campus and to surprise Stella by having a *white Christmas* with her. I was walking over to her place, whistling *the Christmas song, O' Holy Night,* when I heard "*You stepped out of a dream* and *thou swell* this *bewitched* heart of mine until *in the wee small hours of the morning.* As *softly as I leave you,* I will remember *the way you look tonight.*"

What I had just heard made me stop and *smile* until I heard the female voice answer "*Tres palabras (without you)* I am *lost* and *solamente una vez (you belong to my heart)* but *Te Quiero, Dijiste (magic is the moonlight)* that comes from your eyes I will keep you in my heart until we are together again."

The smile on my face disappeared when the *unforgettable* voice of my *Stella by starlight* rang in my ears. "*What'll I do?*" I thought "*should I pretend* that I never heard the conversation or should I…*"

Suddenly standing there in front of me with a shocked look on her face was Stella "*Oh, Stardust!* You heard." she said.

"*Yes indeed* I did." I said and turned to walk away but she stopped me by saying "*Don'cha go 'way mad.*" I looked back at her and said "What do you mean *don'cha go 'way mad.* How else am I supposed to feel?

I told my mother that *I'll be home for Christmas* but I changed my plans so that I could have a *happy holiday* with you.

My room mates warned me about you by saying "That *lady is a tramp* and will have you following her *from promise to promise* until it's time for her to *change partners.*"

I told them *"Don't worry 'bout me,* I know what I'm doing."

I took one step closer to her and continued saying "you can stand there with a smirk on your face thinking that *I've got you under my skin.* Your eyes are showing me how *funny* this situation is to you and I'll bet that you'll say before I walk away *"Can't we be friends?"* But I believe that of *all the things you are;* you are *young and foolish* the most.

If you think that hurting people is *funny,* then *this will make you laugh;* I was only using you *until the real thing comes along. I couldn't care less* if *this funny world* you live in, comes crashing down on you. *The party's over between us;* this is *the end of a love affair* that will have you *learnin' the blues* because you'll find that *if you win, you lose. I'm gonna be the first one* not to play your game. *If we never meet again,* that would be fine with me. In fact, I'm going to do better than that; *I'm gonna laugh you right out of my life.*"

I gave her a *smile* and walked away. *Was that the human thing to do?* I don't know, but sometimes *laughing at life* is fine and sometimes you can *send in the clowns* to brighten up a dull day but at *some other time,* you have to take life seriously.

I finished my last year at university and headed back home but *I left my heart in San Francisco* and I knew that *I'll only miss her when I think of her* so I headed *south of the border* on the *Chattanooga Choo Choo* to *Panama* with the *Chattanoogie Shoe Shine boy,* who was going home.

That Christmas, I was *stompin' at the Panama Rumba Azul,* when *ol' MacDonald* asked me if I would like to join the group that was heading for a small isolated village called *Santariffic,* seventy miles down past *De Glory Road.*

I thought why not, *there's a lull in my life* at the moment and maybe the *solitude* and a *silent night* or two in a tent in the rain forest would start my *Humpty Dumpty heart* again. After two months down there, you start to sing their *coffee song; they've got an awful lot of coffee in Brazil,* and I started to miss my *America the beautiful.*

There was an unusual species of birds around the village where we were camped that were named by the villagers, the Sinner birds and the tune they sang was very loud *but beautiful*. They got their name because every time they stole something from somewhere or someone, they would fly into the trees and start singing and the villagers would watch them fly away and shout out, "Go, *sing you Sinners*."

I wrote my mother just before we left the village telling her that *I'll be home for Christmas* and when we did finally leave, I said "*South America, take it away*. I won't be back for a long time."

Yes, *I'll be home for Christmas* this year because here I am. I realized that it was my family and friends that *I wanna be around* at this time of year. The past two Christmases, I missed hearing the young children excitedly saying "*Santa Claus is coming to town* and so is *Rudolph the red-nosed reindeer* leading the other reindeer." I missed hearing and singing *Christmas carols* like *Away In A Manger,* and *Silent Night, Holy Night*. I missed joining my family and friends singing *O' Little Town Of Bethlehem, O' Holy Night, Hark, The Herald Angels Sing* and *God Rest Ye Merry Gentlemen* in church on Christmas Eve and Christmas Day. *I heard the bells on Christmas Day* and now I know that *I wouldn't trade Christmas* with my family again, not even if the *stars fell on Alabama*."

He still travels but doesn't stay away for long periods of time anymore.

Now his sister, *Ave Maria Stardust,* has been travelling to different places in the world, training to manage another one of our properties that is being refurbished at the moment. She will be a very good manager, just like her mother is. After seeing how well *Mona Lisa Stardust* had done, I thought that I would have a *chat* with Bob about the renewal of their contract with us for the next five years.

I had *Georgia on my mind* because they opened their club about the same time as *Mona Lisa* did, but they had not been very successful.

On my last visit to Georgia, I had to have a serious *chat* with them, so I decided to go and visit there next.

Mr. Magic and his wife Nola, manage the *Bayou Maharajah* Club down there. The last time I was down there, I got a *fever* and Nola gave me this medicine and if you didn't have a *spoonful of sugar* after taking it, the sour taste of the medicine would kill your taste buds for two days afterwards.

Anyway, getting back to *Mr. Magic*; he is a *lazy bones* where work is concerned. I really need to have a good *chat* with him every time I go down there.

Getting from the train station to the club is very nerve racking because *the rules of the road* are; there are no rules. I finally reached the club by mid-day but no-one was there like they should have been, so I went looking for them. The *errand boy for Rhythm Firefly* and *Mack the Knife* was coming *from the candy store on the corner* and stopped for a *chat*. He told me where to find him during their *sleepy time down south*.

I cover the water front of the ol' man river and found Mr. Magic right where I was told he would be. He was surprised to see me and when I asked him where his wife was and why they weren't at the club getting ready for that night, he just looked me straight in the eyes and said "*Oh, my Nola, her is gone fishin'* with *Ramblin' Rose, on the banks of the Wabash. Remember that Tarpon that ma blushin' Rosie* caught last visit, well, my son *Mood Indigo* made a great feed out of it."

I heard bells ringing and Mr. Magic continued saying "*hear dem bells?* Well, that means for her to stop fishin' and for me to stop *dream dancing* 'cos it's time to go open the club. *Because of you* and what you told us last time, we get the club ready early. *Her is* real good to *do dat thing* you told us about; you know, planning our day. It's real good 'cos *I got plenty of nuttin'* to do when it's *sleepy time down south* and she *don't fence me in* and nag me. Before, when she's *gone fishin'*, I used to try and learn more from books, but I *ain't gonna study war no more*. Come, we go to the club now."

When we walked inside the club, Nola, *Ramblin' Rose* and *Mood Indigo* were already there and the place was already starting to get busy.

Nola greeted me and turned to her husband and said "*Miss Otis regrets* that she can't sing tonight 'cos she's come down with a *fever* but *Mood Indigo* has arranged for the *Harlem Blues* band to play instead. *The blues don't care* who sings them but *Harlem Blues* are real good 'specially if you don't sing with them."

Mr. Magic looked at his wife and said "*I gotta right to sing the blues* with them. *That ain't right* for you to stop me singing *the Whiffenpoof song*."

The reply Nola gave her husband was "*Some other time* maybe, but tonight we will be busy."

For some reason, *it was a very good year* at their club and I wondered why. *It never entered my mind* that this couple actually took notice of what I had said to them.

"*Are you fer it?*" said Nola "if we get real busy, you may have to help out for a bit.

Ramblin' Rose pulled me to one side and softly said "*When the wind was green* this morning, it meant that *witchcraft* is happening. Everyone will be on the *look out for love*. If you see or think that it's happening to you, just *close your eyes* and say softly twice, *love look away, love look away* or you may end up with a *lover* who lives on *the Boulevard Of Broken Dreams*.

Don't forget, *it's only a paper moon* that shines tonight, so it's *you and the night and the music* that will have some females wanting to get *close to you*. Tomorrow the *witchcraft* will be gone and that *old devil moon* will have been replaced by the sunshine and you'll be feeling like *somethin' stupid* as you try to remember what you had done the night before. *The best thing for you* to do is, *stay* near us or help *Mood Indigo* to greet the patrons with "*Welcome to the Club*." *Mood Indigo* knows what can happen to a *single man* who is a *stranger in paradise,* our *paradise*."

For once in my life I listened to her and I was glad I did, because several women whispered in my ear "I would really love to *love me some you in the still of the night*."

The club closed *in the wee small hours of the morning* and I said to *Ramblin' Rose* "I give my *Thanks to you. If you never come to me* last night and warned me of the *witchcraft, my foolish heart* would have really done *somethin' stupid*."

The following day, all the family was up at *daybreak* and down at the club, cleaning up and getting it ready for that day's trading.

Even today, *it amazes me* how they have turned their lives around. They work so long and hard at the club and in *the other hours,* they relax in their own ways, yet there is still so *much love* between them, especially as a family."

LUCK; WHAT LUCK

A waitress approached the table and inquired if they would like any more drinks.

Bingsie replied "*I will drink the wine,* tea for the lady and a cup of coffee for the gentleman please."

Danny asked "*All these people* who manage your properties, how do you know that they're the right people? We are sitting here talking but *you don't know me* or Sue; we could be the worst people in the world and big con artists for all you know."

Bingsie looked at them for a moment and replied "*You don't know me* either; I could be trying to *take advantage* of you both and your unfortunate situation. However, my intuition very rarely lets me down. There was this one *occasion* though, where I was wrong.

There was this place called *Caboclo De Rio* in Brazil that was run down but both Bob and I could see the potential for it becoming a great place. We refurbished it and we built a coffee shop in one section and called it *Coffee Song, they've got an awful lot of coffee in Brazil* that are different types of beans with different tastes. In another section, we built a restaurant called *Capullito De Aleli* that became the top place to eat for a while and in the rest of the building, we made it into a nightclub called *El Choclo.*

We interviewed potential managers, Marquita Linda was amongst them. She only spent *a moment with me* and *my heart tells me* that I should give her the position even though my intuition was telling me otherwise. I gave Marquita Linda the position and for a while, *everything* was running smoothly until Marquita Linda's husband left her and she started gambling and drinking again. I was informed that she *once* had drinking and gambling problems but both were under control and she had been sober for over two years. Because of her problem, the bills were not getting paid so the suppliers would not supply the stocks needed to run each section to the best of their abilities. The police ended up closing the nightclub down due to continued very loud noises and violence.

It was *adios Marquita Linda* and while I was looking for another manager, a company called *Solamente Una Ves* Ltd approached me with an offer to buy the property, on the condition that the *Capullito De Aleli* Restaurant and staff remained unchanged; that is, if the staff wanted to remain.

The staff did stay and we did sell the property. *Solamente Una Vez* Ltd struggled for three years to keep the business going, but ended up bankrupt and had to sell the property. The site is now a shopping mall.

We learn by *these foolish things* that we do and now I very rarely waste *my time of day* on anything I feel is not worth it. Bob and I also realized that Rio was not a place for us to have a business in."

Bingsie paused while he took a sip of his wine and glanced *out beyond the window* to what seemed to be the beginning of a cold *but beautiful winter wonderland.* He then brought his attention back to Danny and continued "I can see that by the way *you're looking at me,* you think that we only hire females to manage our properties for us, but the fact is; we actually hire married couples. The men are usually busy running the majority of the business and they leave the office and financial business side to their wives. Like Mr. Magic says about his wife 'She's good at that sort of thing'. Was I right with what you were thinking?"

"Yes." said Danny "but shouldn't they both share the responsibilities? It's like *the rules of the road.* If you don't stay on your side, then an accident could happen that could cause arguments."

"*The rules of the road* are one thing." said Sue "but there are really no rules to life. Everybody is taught the rules of life by their families, the *faith of our fathers,* whether it be in a spiritual or non- spiritual way. In your life, *anything goes* and you never know what's going to happen at *anytime, anyday, anywhere* that you happen to be. Life can be *unfair* at times but at *some other time,* it can feel like you're living *on the sunnyside of the street* with the world at your feet.

I remember when I was about seven years old, my father hurt his leg and was unable to stand or walk for long periods and because he was a carpenter, he couldn't work as much. Some weeks, before he got back to proper work, *the pennies from heaven* wouldn't even *get me to the church on time* because we had to walk a long way. There wasn't enough money for gas to be put in the car and what gas there was, my father used it to go to work with. But *come rain or come shine* we still went to church as a family and it didn't matter if we had *all or nothing at all,* there was *such love* coming from all of us individually, that we as a family stayed strong and help each other through *the bad and the beautiful* times."

She looked at Danny and continued "*you can't buy me love* and *I don't want it that way. Because of you,* I know that *the best is yet to come* and it will, in time. *I want a little girl* and a boy but we must first make a home for them.

21

The more I see you and spend time with you, the more *I love you* and when the *September of my years* come creeping up the path, I want you to be able to say to me "*I can't believe that you're in love with me* still."

Yes, Mr. Bingwell, I do believe that *faith can move mountains,* especially if it is re-enforced with love and trust."

"See, Mr. Bingwell, that's why *I love my wife* and I know that as long as we do things together and talk out issues when they arise, I'll have *someone to watch over me* for the rest of my life.

When the time comes, he looked at Sue, *I want a little girl* too, *a baby just like you* but first *I want to be ready,* if possible, to care for her, or him, if a son comes along, in a loving home.

I'm sorry. Please continue your story." said Danny.

Bingsie took another sip of his wine as the waitress placed the cups of tea and coffee on the table in front of them.

Then Bingsie looked at Danny with hopeful eyes and said "*When I fall in love,* I hope it will be with someone like your Sue.

I was just about to fly out to Hawaii, when I received an urgent telephone call from *Cachito* asking me if I could go down there straight away. *Cachito* and her husband *Agua De Beber* manage a property for us in Monterey and oversee another property as well. *A Media Luz* is on the north side, the second property, and *Las Mananitas,* the main property, near the city central.

Instead of hopping on a plane the next day and then having to transfer to another plane the day after that, in another town, I caught the next train to Albuquerque and changed trains there for Monterey.

It was a long two and a half day trip to Mexico and I was very tired when I arrived. I was met at the station by *Tu Mi Delirio,* who was the assistant manager of the *Las Mananitas* but he could only speak broken English and I only knew a little Spanish so he dropped me off to check in and leave my suitcase at the *Las Chiapanecas* Hotel before taking me to see Agua and *Cachito* and find out precisely what the urgent matter was. She could not tell me much but the following day, after Cachito had the full report on what had happened, we all met again to discuss what we would do.

Apparently as Emanuel and *Mexicali Rose* were closing for the night; they manage the A Media Luz, trouble broke out next door in *Hernando's Hideaway* while people were dancing the *Hernando's Jive*. The trouble spilled out on to the street and then into the Luz. Rose still doesn't really know what happened after that, but Emanuel had disappeared and they believed that he may have been killed. Rose and the restaurant were both in a mess and I was needed there because I was one of the owners of the restaurant.

We all went over to the restaurant to see what we could do about getting it back into business again. I phoned Bob and gave him a thorough report and told him that I had taken some photographs of the damage for the insurance company and to see if it would be possible for us to start the repairs straight away.

It took Bob three hours to ring back with the go ahead for us to start the repairs and we were *racing with the clock* to open the restaurant again as quickly as possible.

I looked at Rose and said *"What am I going to do about you?* You are in no fit state to manage the restaurant on your own and until we hear something about Emanuel, you really can't do anything. *It was a very good year* for the restaurant last year, so I think that some time off will do you some good. *Tu Mi Delirio* can step in here as manager for the next month and Cachito has agreed to spend time in both places each week, although it would be a little awkward for her, as she also had to see to her family as well."

Rose seemed glad to not have to worry about the restaurant.

I still had to stay in Monterey for the next two weeks to oversee *everything* and you know the saying, it never rains but it pours; well, *it happened in Monterey*.

On top of everything that had just happened, *Ramblin' Rose* notified me that she was pregnant and the baby was due in five months' time and she needed to take six months maternity leave once the baby was born. She told me *"I want a little girl,* who would be as strong in her convictions and as gentle in her ways, just like her mother was." She asked if I could find someone to relieve her whilst she was away; maybe a trainee manager.

To top that off, I received an unexpected letter from my mother. Again she asked *"Baby, won't you please come home."* She also told me that she had now moved to San Francisco and was still living with my father. They are still having their ups and downs but they are working on them.

He is now more involved in the theatre and she had gone back to work writing dialogue for *Star Turtle 1* which was due in two weeks and *Star Turtle 2,* due in four weeks. She would be having a month's break before starting *Star Turtle 3,* followed four weeks later by *Star Turtle 4.* The idea of each Star Turtle program, was to try and get through to the *sweet bird of youth;* the runaway children and to get them to phone their parents to tell them "*I'll be home for Christmas.*" and try to support them in working out the issues they had with their parents so that they could live in a home and not on the streets.

She also said that "*The very thought of you* travelling and spending Christmas in other places saddens me, but if you must be away from us, then *have yourself a merry Christmas* wherever you are."

That's all I needed; another one of her "*To Whom It May Concern love letters.*" I said to myself "*I'm gonna sit right down* and reply to her letter and tell her that *I've heard that song before* and I may be in the *merry old land of Oz;* Australia, on the other side of the world by then and I hope that she will *have a holly jolly Christmas* without me."

I never did write to her because I had to keep my *mind on the matter* at hand; the restaurant restoration. Two days after the repairs had been completed and the restaurant was reopened, and two days before I was due to leave the country, Emanuel was found on a lonely bush track, walking back to town. He was dehydrated, bruised and tired, but otherwise he was healthy and unharmed.

He told us and the authorities that he had been mistaken for one of the trouble makers and when one of the people who took the trouble makers away recognized him, they stopped the vehicle, opened the door and pushed him out.

He didn't know who the people were or where they took the other captives, but he was happy to be free and off that *lonesome road,* even though it was *in the wee small hours of the morning* when he was found. Mexicali Rose and Emanuel took the rest of the month off and had a good holiday. They are both back working in the restaurant and it is doing better than before.

A week later, after reporting and giving the photographs to Bob, I flew out of San Francisco for *blue Hawaii.* I knew my parents were living in San Francisco and I really wanted to see and speak to my mother, but

I wasn't ready to give her or my father *just one more chance.* I just wanted to *let there be peace on earth* for a while.

I can't remember how long the flight took, but it seemed as if I was in the air for *one night and day* and another *night,* but we finally reached our destination. I went straight from the airport to the *Trade Winds* Hotel, which was situated a stone's throw away from *the sand and the sea.* I made a couple of telephone calls and went for something to eat.

After I had finished dining, I went for a walk along the beach and a wave came rushing to shore, wetting the bottom of my trousers. *Reflections* of my past went rushing through my mind as the *wave* went back out to sea and although I was *glad to be unhappy,* I thought "*I need to be in love* as well." I realized that *I've never been in love before,* not real love. I knew that *I've got the sun in the morning,* the warm and *gentle summer wind* blowing on my face during the day and I've *got the moon in my pocket* for the night but I don't have anyone to share it with. *I left my heart in San Francisco* again, but this time with my mother and now here I was, *in the middle of an island* chain in *blue Hawaii* and I felt that I was the only *lonely one* in the world.

I spent the next few days at the *Trade Winds* Hotel, some hours on business matters and the *other hours* to myself, just trying to work my life out in my mind. *Who can I turn to* for a *chat,* I wondered; maybe to one of the *Angels we have heard on high* spiritual programs.

I wandered slowly down to the dining room and was seated at a table near an opened window that had a great view of the *sand and the sea.*

I was startled when a female voice asked me "Can I sing a *song for you?*" I looked up to see this beautiful woman with *angel eyes* looking at me and her smile was *unforgettable.*

I replied "*Some other time* maybe."

As she turned and walked away, I noticed some Edelweiss on the piano in the corner of the room and the voice and words of the gentleman who had asked me for a dime came back into my head.

I remembered that he said "You will meet another person with *angel eyes* and they will be where there is an unexpected sighting of Edelweiss and where you will *hear me in the harmony* of the music."

My heart stood still for a moment as I watched her walk over to the piano where she picked up the microphone and began to sing the

St Louis Blues. When she had finished singing her bracket of songs, I invited her over for a drink and to my surprise, she accepted. We sat talking for a while and then I said "*Come dance with me* before you have to *sing another song.*"

"Why not," she said "*lets face the music and dance,* but this will be the *last dance* because after tonight I leave for another booking at the *Mele Kalikimaka* Club near *the sand and the sea* in the Hawaii Island city of Honolulu."

The *Mele Kalikimaka* Club was an exclusive member's only club and was our major office in the Hawaiian Island group but I didn't tell her that. The following day, I arrived at the club early and met Mr. *Penthouse Serenade* (pronounced Ser-en-ar-dee) and we completed our business in a quick and orderly fashion. I asked him about that evening's singer at the club and I told him about the previous evening with her.

"Ah, yes. Miss Joanna, she's a delightful entertainer but be careful as I have heard that the *lady is a tramp* or she used to be. You always hear rumors about entertainers, but you never know if the rumors are true. She will be here for the next week, so if you want to stay around, I will formally introduce you to her this evening and say that you are an old acquaintance of the club's owner."

"*It amazes me Penthouse,* on just how quick your mind works and yes, I will be here tonight and for the rest of the week; that is, if I can shuffle my diary." I said.

Penthouse replied "Isn't Mr. White always carrying on about you not stopping for a holiday. Well, tell him in your report that you will be taking the next week off."

"You are right; as always." I said "I will just do that. I'll go back to my hotel now and do the report and I'll see you around six o'clock tonight."

"Very well Mr. Bingwell. I will have a ringside table near the window reserved for you in the *Moon Love* Room." said Penthouse.

During that week I had off, Joanna and I became inseparable and I found that although *you can't lose a broken heart* quickly, you can begin to live again. I also found that *something wonderful happens in summer*.

On our last day together, I said to Joanna, "*I don't like goodbyes* so why don't you *come fly with me* to Australia. I know that you now have a break from any engagements.

I thought about you all last night and I *guess I'm falling for you*. I feel like I'm *dream dancing* on *Happiness Street*. I do believe that *you stepped out of a dream* because *you leave me breathless*. With *the touch of your lips, there goes my heart swinging on a star* again.

Please don't cry and say no now, but *it all depends on you* as to whether you come and I would love *the pleasure of your company* for a while. Please *come fly with me* to *far away places*."

"*The gypsy* inside me says yes." she said. "*The very thought of you* and *the touch of your lips* makes my heart want to sing *joy to the world*."

The following morning, I checked out of the *Trade Winds* Hotel, met Joanna at her hotel and proceeded to the airport for our flight to Sydney, Australia. We only stayed there for a couple of days because unfortunately we had to fly to Hong Kong.

The night before we were to fly out to Hong Kong, Joanna said to me "*I'm a fool to want you, I've got you under my skin* but *I can't help falling in love with you. The touch of your lips* can *fly me to the moon* and now *you're bringing out the dreamer in me*."

I asked her what she meant when she said "*I'm a fool to want you*." but she didn't answer that question but she did say "*I'm always chasing rainbows* that *soon* disappear. *You brought a new kind of love to me* and I know that *I'll never be the same*. I know that *somewhere along the way,* one or both of us will change." She walked over to the opened door and said "*good night my love, pleasant dreams*."

We spent an *unforgettable* day together wandering around the markets and shops in Hong Kong. It was like one of *those lazy-hazy crazy days of summer* and it was also *Valentine's Day* as well. The *little devil* inside me made me race into a shop, leaving her outside, and after I had come back outside and as I handed them to her, I said "*Violets for your furs,* my lady."

Joanna laughed when she took them and said "Oh my goodness. You would think *spring is here* with all these violets around, but the *summer wind* is still blowing as a gentle breeze. My mother used to tell me that *a new town is a blue town* but here it's a violet town. Come on, *you and I* should go and get something to eat and drink; that is if there are any *empty tables* left in the café."

For the rest of the day, we walked, talked and laughed and I felt like she was the one who could *take me back to Toyland* in Macy's;

the one that my mother took me to when I was young and the place I felt the happiest in.

That evening she wore a *blue velvet* dress and had the violets pinned in her hair and she was so beautiful, just like *my sweet lady;* the one that *I have dreamed* about for most of my life. When I saw her, I said to her "*The ruby and the pearl* cannot match your beauty tonight and *I only have eyes for you. The way you look tonight* and the way *thou swell* this heart with that *crazy little thing called love,* makes me want to be *young and foolish* again. I will have to be careful tonight as many men will want to take you away from me."

We were still talking in the cab when the look on her face suddenly changed and I asked what was wrong, thinking that I had said something that had offended her.

She looked at me and said "When I heard the *ring-a-ding, ding* of the door bell, I was trying on shoes." and she lifted her dress to reveal the two odd shoes she was wearing. We both started laughing and that was the time I started calling her *my funny valentine.*

We went to *My Blue Heaven* for an exquisite meal and bumped into *Lady Day,* an old friend, there and then on to *Swingin' On Central* for the rest of the evening. We were enjoying the evening just listening to the music, when a song was starting to be played and Joanna said "*Come dance with me. This song is you.*" and as we danced, she began to sing the song to me and when it finished she whispered the name of the song in my ear. As I had never heard of it before, I asked her what *Besame Mucho* meant.

She spoke softly and said "*Besame Mucho, Kiss Me Much.*"

We danced the rest of the night away and it was *in the wee small hours of the morning* as I was *walkin' my baby back home,* that I realized that I really was *taking a chance on love* with Joanna.

The words "You will hear me in the harmony of the music." came to mind. *I wonder as I wander,* have I heard him in the harmony of the music or was it just my *dumb luck* that my *luck be a lady.* I thought "Trust me to think of *something stupid* like that, especially now that *somebody loves me* and the world is going *my way* for once. *I wanna be around* Joanna for the rest of my life but it is too soon to make any commitments myself, let alone to ask her to make some."

We finally reached her door and she said *"You don't know what love is. Well,* I didn't *until I met you.* The *first time ever I saw your face, you made me love you.* I have never approached anyone to ask them if I could sing a song for them but *something* made me want to sing a *song for you.* When you said *some other time,* I walked away thinking that we would always be *strangers in the night.* When you asked me over for a drink and then we danced, well, *zing went the strings of my heart* and I knew that *you'd be so easy to love* but *it never entered my mind* that I would be here with you now.

I can't say that *I've got a crush on you* because I think that it's more than that. I must *be careful, it's my heart* that's at stake here. You know *I could write a book* about some men, *just the way you are* and the way some men treat women.

Once you've *put your dreams away* for them, you find that they're *kissing a fool* who gets dumped soon afterwards and then they go around telling their mates that the *lady is a tramp. What is there to say* when that happens, how does a *person just like me* defend herself in that situation? You have to put up with *the bad and the beautiful* gossip, usually the bad things that are said and then wait until the *small talk* and innuendoes die down and wait and see just *who's next in line* on the *Boulevard of Broken Dreams.*

I love you, Bingsie and *I wanna be around* you and go *from here to eternity* with you, but I have to *slow down* because *somewhere along the way,* I'll have to leave you for a while to fulfil the commitments that I have already made, both personally and as an entertainer. If *I concentrate on you* too much, then I won't want to go back and that would be bad for both of us.

Oh, I'm not saying that this is the *end of a love affair* because I don't want it to end; I'm just being honest with you and I know that I'll never *cry me a river* when I am with you. *I've got you under my skin* and in my heart and no matter what the future may hold, I will always remember how my *life is beautiful* when I'm with you, and *they can't take that away from me."*

I looked at her and said *"Oh, my dear,* don't you go thinking like that. *There's always tomorrow* and I'll think of a way for you to *stay* with me. When *I see your face before me,* I know that I want to be with you *night and day.* I know that *there will never be another you* for me, so please *don't take your love from me.*

29

Everybody loves somebody and *it had to be you* to be the one to give me a *reason to believe* that I have been *alone too long. Acerate mas (come closer to me)* and *put your head on my shoulder* and *put on a happy face* because *I'm your man* and *I come with love.* It doesn't matter if it's *Sunday, Monday, or always, I wanna be around* you and *I'll bring you a rainbow* everyday to make you happy.

Hey; I've just had an idea; why don't I buy your contract now and then you won't have to say *farewell to arms* that always want to hold you. I am not suggesting that you put up your *love for sale* to me, but once I own your contract, I would give it to you, with no strings attached, and you would be free of any commitments. Don't *answer me* now but think about it, *this is all I ask.*

Now *brush those tears from your eyes* and give me a *smile.* You looked absolutely *wonderful tonight,* odd shoes and all. *Let's just kiss* and say goodnight and *I'll be seeing you* in the morning."

As Joanna raised her head from my shoulder she said "You're right about some things. Yes, I will think about your idea and we can talk about it tomorrow. It was *wonderful tonight* and I thank you for that. I do believe that *love is the tender trap* that can make you feel like you're *living deep in a dream* and *dancing on the ceiling,* but one day you have to come down to earth and wake up and when that happens, you could wake up to a *cloudy morning* in a *brown world.*"

The following morning, I woke up *feeling good,* the *early morning blues* didn't bother me anymore; however, I did think about my conversation with Joanna that I had had with her after *walkin' my baby back home* and I wondered what her answer would be.

I walked over and looking out of my window towards the ocean, I heard a man on the corner yelling out "*Sing you sinners, sing you sinners* for your souls to be saved. You have to sing a *hymn to him,* our saviour." And then my eyes were distracted by Joanna walking back towards our hotel. I thought "*When my sugar walks down the street,* she looks so beautiful."

I was interrupted by the phone ringing so I went to answer it. It was *Haji Baba* enquiring if I was still going to be arriving that day, usually I'm always a day early for all meetings, and I confirmed that I would be. Really, and *for once in my life,* I had forgotten all about the trip to Montenegro, so I hurried down the hallway to Joanna's room and told her to quickly pack as we were flying out in two hours.

We would have time to talk on the plane. Whatever her decision was, I wanted her to come with me and we made the flight *just in time*."

On the plane Joanna said "*It amazes me* as to how you are able to get me on a plane so quickly. If I tried to get a flight, I would have to maybe wait for hours or book in advance."

I told her "Every airline, train or bus company *all over the world* holds a few seats vacant for special travellers. If no-one needs those seats, they use stand-by passengers to fill them. Before we left Hawaii, I purchased you a *Golden Ticket* that allows you priority over everyone else. Now have you made your decision about your future?"

Joanna just sat there quietly for a while. I looked at her and asked "Please *answer me, my love*."

She finally said "Yes, I have, but now is not the time to give it to you. I want to *think it over* a bit longer; that is, if you don't mind. I promise that I will tell you later."

I wanted to say "*I want it now*." but instead I said "*How about tonight* then, once we've settled into our hotel rooms."

The rest of the fight was pleasant, we would chat occasionally but most of the time we both slept.

WHERE TO NEXT

We arrived in Montenegro and went straight to our hotel in the city of Podgorica. I was very surprised to see *Adeste Fideles* waiting for me in the foyer.

Joanna went straight up to her room and I went to find out what had brought Adeste *all the way* over here from the United States. We went into the café that was decorated in a *theme from New York, New York* and we had a general conversation whilst waiting for our coffee to be served.

Adeste asked about Joanna and my reply was *"Wait till you see her,* she is *all things* that a man could want in a woman *and I love her.* If *my romance* with her keeps getting stronger and if I get *my way,* I'll ask her to be my wife at the end of the year."

I knew something was amiss when Adeste looked at me with a serious face and said "Oh, Mr. Bingwell, I'm afraid that I have some serious news for you. A young lady named *Maria- Elena* came into the office and claimed that you spent last Christmas with her and now she is pregnant to you. She claims that she told you that she was *too young* for you, but you stated that it didn't matter because you would take care of her. She claims that the following morning you just left; leaving her to fend for herself as she had no-one to turn to."

"What! Nothing happened between us, it could have, but her parents arrived *just in time* and took her home. Her parents told me that she was *too young* to be on her own and that she continually ran away from home and that they had to call the police all the time to stop the parties that they knew she would have and the trouble that she would get herself into." I said.

Adeste said "I have worked for you and Mr. White for near on six years now and I would not believe the allegations made towards you. I do believe that the *lady is a tramp* and thinks that *there's a gold mine in the sky* that she can tap into by blaming you. Now, what shall we do to clear your name?"

"Firstly, we'll go over to see *Haji Baba* at the *Soliloquy* Restaurant, the one he redecorated *Chicago style. It was a very good year* for him last year, so I don't see any delays with him. Then we'll come back here and *you and I* will work on this issue. The young girls of today and *these foolish things* that they do and the way they try to get away with them is quite *unbelievable.*

Let me rephrase part of my last statement; some of the young girls of today." I told Adeste.

Adeste replied "*The shadow of your smile* leads me to believe that you have a plan brewing in your head."

"I have." I said "that little *girl next door* to where I was living will have her *high hopes* of getting anything from me dashed. All she'll get from me is the *wee baby blues,* in more ways than one. Come on; let's get down to *Haji Baba.*"

I was just about to walk out of the hotel, when Adeste said "Mr. Bingwell, aren't you forgetting something... Miss Joanna?"

"Oh, yes, thank you for reminding me. I'll go right up and tell her that some urgent business has arisen that needs my immediate attention and ask her to occupy herself today. I will ask her to meet us here in the lobby tonight at six so we can all go out to dinner together this evening. I can't wait for tonight, just *wait till you see her* Adeste and then you'll know why I'm feeling so *young and foolish.*"

I went straight up to Joanna's room and quickly explained that *something* unexpected had arisen that needed my immediate attention and that it would probably take most of the day to sort out. I also told her that we would be dining at the club that evening.

Joanna looked at me apprehensively and I said "I know that they *haven't met you yet,* but Adeste and Haji will love you like I do. Remember *somebody loves you* and wants you to *always stay as sweet as you are.* I am sorry that I have to leave you, however, you have a good day and *I'll be seeing you* as soon as I can. If you have any trouble, you can contact me on either of these two numbers. Yes, I know that one of them is my room but *Adeste Fideles* and I have to work there in private. I'll explain later, but now I have to go."

The business with Haji Baba was over in an hour and a half and I booked our table for the evening. Adeste and I returned to the hotel to sort out the other issue but all I wanted to do was see Joanna. I had to keep telling myself "There's a time for business and there's *a time for love* and right now is the business time." As soon as we reached my room, Adeste asked "What is your plan of action to clear your name?"

"To tell the truth, *that's all there is.*" I said. "However, I will be making sure that *with a little bit of luck,* the young lady will realize that I'm not the *candy man* that she thinks I am and will drop the claim against me.

First of all, *I'm gonna sit right down* and write a letter to her parents explaining the situation because I bet, that they don't know what she is up to and to offer to pay for a paternity test to prove that I'm not responsible. We will then go down to the court house and I'll write an Affidavit for you to take back to our lawyers and then I will be contacting *S.M.Blues* Investigators to get them to find and follow Mary. I will give them my authorization for you to act on my behalf.

By the time you leave here, you will know the complete story of what happened. Mary will be really *learnin' the blues* once we go *all the way* with her and prove that I am not the father. *It worries me* as to whether her parents really know about the pregnancy and if they do, how will they cope with her. She really is *too young* and irresponsible to become a mother herself. Now, let's get over to the court house and get this settled once and for all. I have a big date tonight when I'll be holding my whole *world in my arms.*"

As Adeste and I were walking out of the hotel, Joanna was looking down as she was walking in and walked straight into Adeste. Upon looking up, she gave a cute *smile* and said "Oh, I'm sorry. I was looking to see if any *pennies from heaven* had fallen down for me to pick up. It's a good thing I never stood on your foot because you would now be saying *toot toot tootsie! Goodbye.*"

We all started laughing and I introduced her to *Adeste Fideles* and told her that when we return to the hotel, our business would be completed.

As we walked away Adeste was still laughing a bit and said "Your Joanna, she's great, she's *funny* and she seems to have a wicked sense of humour. What does she do for a living?"

I said "*That's my girl* and yes, *she's funny that way,* well, most of the time but at *some other time,* she can be quite serious. *What good does it do* to go around with a chip on your shoulder all the time, like I have done for the past few years? It is surprising *what a little moonlight* can do especially when I was *walking my baby back home* after having an *unforgettable* night of dining and dancing. Even if you are riding *along the Navajo Trail* or just sitting outside alone, the moonlight will light the way for you until the *morning star* disappears and an *orange colored sky* appears bringing the *sunrise in the morning.*

Now, where were we? Ah, yes. Once this Affidavit has been done, I would like you to make this issue a priority and get it settled quickly and smoothly. Whatever you do, do not give them any money at all and I will inform Bob of my directions personally.

Tonight I intend to explain to Joanna the situation, so you will hear the full and complete story then. What was the name of that band that's playing down at the club tonight?"

"The *Stardust Coquette* band and they are supposed to be like our *McNamara's Band*." said Adeste.

Joanna met us in the foyer at our prearranged time so that we could catch a taxi to the restaurant. As we were shown to our table, many men turned and looked at Joanna and I said to her "My eyes can't believe *the way you look tonight, you're sensational. Don't forget* that *I'm your man* and that you have to *save the last dance for me.*"

She looked at me and with a cheeky *smile* on her face she said "Why thank you sir, but *I won't dance* with anyone but you. Well, maybe I might have one or two dances with Adeste if he asks me."

During the course of the meal, I explained in detail the situation that took me away from Joanna that afternoon to both of them.

Adeste softly said to me "Today you have had some sort of contact with *the bad and the beautiful* women in your life and I must agree with you; Joanna is very beautiful and her *angel eyes,* they're well…The town from where I come from, Joanna would be in the class of, *she …blessed be the one* who could be one of the angels from above. She would be the only one who could instantly warm a *cold, cold heart* in anyone. Even a *Cinnamon Sinner,* one of our worst sinners, would turn their face away before her. What sort of entertainer is she?"

I leaned over to Adeste and said "Listen and you will hear."

The band finished playing their song bracket and Joanna finished softly singing the song and turned back to us and said "The *Stardust Coquette* really is Montenegro's version of *McNamara's Band.* I like the way that they add the sound of the *silver bells* into some of the songs."

Adeste looked at his watch and said "I would love to stay for *the late late show,* but I'm afraid I have to go now. I have an early plane to catch in the morning and I must say that it will be *good to be home* tomorrow night."

Joanna said "We should go too. Tomorrow we fly to Rome, don't we?"

I replied "Yes, we do. This is one of the drawbacks of my job; continuous travelling. That's why I'm always *trav'lin' light.*"

When we arrived back at the hotel, Joanna said good night, leaving Adeste and myself to confirm again to what had to be done about my situation once he got back home to the States.

When I saw Joanna the following morning, I asked if she was feeling well because she didn't look it.

Her reply was "I am not used to so many late nights and early mornings in a row so I'm still feeling tired. *That's all* I think it is. I don't think I'm getting a *fever* or anything like that."

I took her hand and as we walked to the taxi, I said "*When in Rome,* you won't have all those late nights because it'll be eight days before we have to say *arrivederchi Roma (goodbye to Rome)*. My business there should only take a couple of days and after that, we can hire a car and go for a picnic *down by the old mill stream* and take a leisurely *walk in the country* and in the evening, we can have a *quiet night of quiet stars*. Now how does that sound to you? Normally by this time of the year, I'm in France. I usually spend part of *April in Paris* to watch their *Easter Parade* but *because of you,* I'm taking time to see more of the places that I visit."

"That sounds like *my ideal* way of spending the day together and *it's alright with me. I'm just a lucky so and so* to have met you. *Once upon a time,* not too long ago, I was a *stranger in paradise* and then *out of nowhere,* came another *stranger in paradise* to show me why *life is beautiful*. When you walked into the club, *love walked in* with you. I was not on the *look out for love* for I often said "*love look away* from me as I sing my *song for the hopeful lover* to hear."

I think that when I saw you, it was *love at first sight*. I instantly became *lost* in *my little world* and when you invited me over for a drink, *my foolish heart* kept saying, "*Tell him he's yours.*" and *maybe this time, taking the chance on love* will mean the beginning of *the good times* for me."

I heard the clock strike ten o'clock and said to Joanna "*Speak softly love, people will say we're in love* if they hear us talking like this continuously. Come on, it's time for you to *come fly with me* to Rome."

As Joanna slept on the plane, I remembered that she hadn't told me what her decision was about her commitments for the future.

I sat there looking at her sleeping and thought, "*If I ruled the world,* I would make you *all mine* and give you everything your heart desired.

36

I've got the world on a string already and now *I've got you under my skin* but I don't want to *lose* you. *I get a kick out of you* when you spontaneously do or say something *funny.*

I often wondered *what is this thing called love* and *when I fall in love,* would I know it. Well, I don't need *witchcraft* to let me know what it is and I know that I have found it in you. Hång on a minute; I think *I'm getting sentimental over you,* so when we reach the *St Louis Blues* Club in *Noche De Ronda,* I will ask you to become my wife. I have to *make her mine* before she has a chance to leave."

Joanna stirred and woke up just as the cabin staff began serving a light meal to all the passengers. As we were eating our meals, we heard the couple in the seats in front of us discussing what things they would do *when in Rome.*

They must have been looking at some travel brochures as the female said "Look it says here that if you visit this side of Rome, you must visit the Trevi Fountain where you throw a coin in for every wish you make. That means for three wishes you have to throw *three coins in the fountain.* I remember when I came here as a little girl with my parents. We visited the coast and *I saw three ships* out on the harbour with their *red sails in the sunset.* My *papa loves Mambo* and the *Jitterbug* so we came over to watch the championships.

I left my heart in San Francisco that year because I wanted to spend *the blessed dawn of Christmas Day, caroling, caroling* with my friends. After the championships were over, my family went up in the hills to spend a *white Christmas* with dad's family. That was a *blue Christmas* for me, even though the *Christmas song* that *the little drummer boy* played was *Jingle Bells,* just for me. He couldn't stay for long because his father had to get back to watch over *the lonely goatherd* further up on the mountain."

She must have pointed to some pictures because she continued saying "*it's these foolish things* here that made me think of that Christmas. Dad wanted to *take me back again* two years later but for some reason we never went back."

The plane touched down in Rome and we went straight to the Hotel *Domenica.*

After we had settled into our rooms, Joanna and I met in the coffee shop and when I sat down I said to her "At least I don't have to go far to get to the restaurant because it's on the top floor of this building.

Actually, the *Non Dimenticar* is an old fashioned type of place where people can go to have a meal, dance and watch a live floor show, like in the olden days. Now what are you going to do while I'm talking business."

With a cheeky tone to her voice, Joanna said "What everyone else does *when in Rome;* shop, shop and more shopping." She gave a little laugh and then said "Now you go and do your business and get it over with and I'll see you here later. Now go and *don't worry about me,* I'll be alright."

As I stood to go, I bent over and gave her a kiss on the cheek and whispered in her ear "*How sweet it is to be loved by you. I'm an ordinary man* and really *I'm a shy guy* and only *once in a blue moon* does something *fantastico* happen for me. *Love walked in* to my life on the day I met you. The first kiss you gave me was a *kiss to build a dream on* and *we are in love, we make a lot of love* and I really believe that *our love is here to stay.*

I am also *lucky to be me* and sometimes I think that *I must be dreaming* because *I found a million dollar baby* singing beautiful songs. *I can't begin to tell you* how happy I am to have *your love* and *I love you so much. Everytime we say goodbye,* I feel sad but *my heart tells me* that *I'll be seeing you* again in a few hours. *If I should lose you,* I know that *I'll never be the same person.* No matter where I am or what I'm doing, you're *always on my mind* and *here in my heart. How can I replace you,* anyway *my heart won't say goodbye,* never."

Joanna interrupted me by saying "*Oh! Ain't that sweet* of you but *I don't like goodbyes* either. Are you crazy, don't think about losing me because I'm not going anywhere but to the shops. Now, get to your meeting so that we can be together again sooner."

Two and a half days later, my business was completed, so Joanna and I decided to have a *lazy afternoon* in the nearby park. We just sat there watching some children fly a couple of kites. Suddenly we heard "*Quando, Quando, Quando.* Where are you boy?" and in front of us was a young boy who seemed to be a bit distressed.

He turned to us and asked "Mister, have you seen a large brown Neapolitan Mastiff dog come running past here recently.

My sister and I think that he was in a fight a few minutes ago with another dog named *Mac the Knife* and we have to find him before the other dog does."

"No." I replied and heard a young girl's voice in the background calling "*Quando, Quando, Quando,* come here boy. I have a treat for you."

The young boy turned his head and gasped "Oh no, there's *Mac the Knife* now. I have to try and find my dog and get him home before he finds him."

Just as the boy left, we looked towards where the boy had been looking and saw this cute little white Italian Volpino dog go running past and Joanna said surprisingly "That's *Mac the Knife;* the bully dog?"

We looked at each other and burst out laughing.

That evening, Joanna and I dined at the *Moonglow* Café and then went sight seeing at night for a while.

As we were making our way back to the hotel, we turned into this narrow, well lit street and Joanna said "I was down here earlier on today and I went into this very unusual shop called *Supercalifragilisticexpialidocious.* It was full of toys, clothes and different nic nacs. There was a *Rudolph the Red-nosed Reindeer* toy that said "*Zat you Santa Claus.*" as you walked past it. I particularly enjoyed looking at a wind-up dresser ornament that was called *Me and Mrs. You* on a *Peroxide Swing.* I bought a *charade* game called *Lullaby Of Broadway* and a jigsaw puzzle called *Santa Claus Is Coming To Town.* It will be a great gift for a young boy I know."

Joanna looked up and said "Look *how high the moon* is tonight." then suddenly buried her face into my arm saying "sorry, *the moon got in my eyes* and *my foolish heart* sank at the thought of *my old flame* and the *moonlight in Vermont.* That was so many, many years ago and I don't know why I had a sudden memory of it."

We walked the rest of the way back to the hotel in silence where we both retired to our rooms.

Joanna seemed very quiet and not herself the following morning as we went on a sight-seeing tour of Rome. That evening, we went up to the *Non Dimenticar* restaurant and over our meal, Joanna said out of the blue and looking out the window "*While shepherds watch their flocks by night* in the high mountain regions, I wonder what they do?

Are there more than one of them with the flock, and during the *silent night* do they feel *lonesome and sorry* for not being able to be with their loved ones that night?"

Stunned by her revelation, I asked her what made her think of something like that and her reply was "Oh, I don't know. It was *just one of those things* that passed through my mind at that moment."

As the evening drew to a close, Joanna looked up at me and said softly, "That really was *some enchanted evening;* in fact, it was *too marvelous for words. I could have danced all night.* Will you always *save the last dance for me?"*

The following day, Joanna and I were about to drive to the country for our picnic, when a bell boy came running up to the car and said "Miss Joanna, there is a very important telephone call for you. Please come with me."

Joanna followed the bell boy inside and returned a few minutes later looking quite upset and got into the car. As we drove she told me that a relative back home on the mainland of the States, had become very ill and if they had not improved in a few days, she wanted to fly home to be with them.

I told her that I would re-arrange my schedule and fly back with her, but she said that wouldn't be necessary because if she did have to fly back home, she would only be spending a few days there and she would meet up with me wherever I happened to be.

We had a wonderful picnic and we went *dancing in the dark,* getting *lost in the stars.* As we drove back to the hotel, Joanna moved closer and snuggled into me and I asked her if she was getting cold. She snuggled more and replied "Not anymore, *I've got my love to keep me warm,* besides *isn't it romantic, just you just me,* plenty of *time and the river* flowing gently beside us as we're travelling. There are no other souls on the road."

I slept in the next day and when I went to Joanna's room to go down to breakfast with her, I was surprised to find that she wasn't there, so I headed to the dining room to wait for her. She was already there when I arrived and was sitting with her back to me, so I quietly walked up behind her and said, "You know what they say, *when in Rome,* do what the Romans do, that is, if you can find out what they're doing."

She jumped and looked at me and I could see that she had been crying. I immediately said "It's your relative, isn't it?"

She replied *"Oh, my dear, something's gone wrong* and I have to fly home immediately and I have to go *all by myself.*

This is one place and something I have to do on my own. I went to the church this morning to pray for help and guidance and while there were many people there, *I couldn't hear nobody pray,* so I hope the Lord answers my prayer quickly and I think he has. I found the answer while I was sitting here.

I'll go back to the States today and tomorrow, you go on to Algiers for your business meeting and then take the *road to Morocco* for your next meeting in Rabat and I will meet you in Madrid in about a week's time and *we'll be together again.* I know that you want an explanation for what's going on but at the present time, I can't tell you so please don't ask. Please let me do this on my own, *this is all I ask* and be there for me when I return.

Life must have *fidgety feet* because *anything goes* with it. One minute you can have a *cold cold heart* and fly around on your own like a *poor butterfly* while you're *laughing on the outside, crying on the inside* and then the next minute, life is blooming like a *Honeysuckle Rose* and you're *feeling good* and *laughing on the outside* as well as on the inside. Then it turns again and throws more challenges at you. It makes you *climb ev'ry mountain* and *cross bridges* until it gets you to where you have to be. Do you understand what I am saying?"

I looked her in the eyes and softly said "*I understand, that's life,* and, well, *she's funny that way* and *impossible* to predict. It's like an *experiment* that you're given to solve and you have to keep going in order to get the answer. They say *the best things in life are free* but you have to work pretty hard and long to get them and sometimes when you think that you're almost there, life changes again. Yes, life, *she's funny that way.*

Right now; you go and pack and I'll get your plane ticket. Remember *I'm your man* and I'll always be here for you. A love like ours only *comes once in a lifetime* and this short separation can only make it stronger. You can go away, knowing that *soon there'll just be the two of us* again."

Well, Joanna caught the early flight and left me on my own and what does a single person do *when in Rome;* they go sight-seeing again for the day. I knew that I was flying out the following day."

"Oh Bingsie." said Sue "I bet you really missed her. You're right you know, when you say *you don't know what love is* until *your lover* has to go away for a while. I found that out when Danny had to go to *Overture* City for six months while he was in training to take over running the kitchen at Laguna Leap. I found that *when your lover has gone,* the best thing to do is keep busy and your mind occupied as much as possible, both *night and day* and stay positive.

Time after time challenges and temptations are placed in front of us and you may end up *standin' in the need of a prayer* for guidance or you may be strong enough to know exactly what you have to do. For me, *meditation* helps but *only you and you alone* will know what you have to do when the time comes."

Then Danny said "*How do ya'll know* what can happen when *taking a chance on love. Take me* for instance, when I was away from Sue for so long, I found that *it gets lonely early* so *in the still of the night,* I would picture Sue standing in the doorway of *that tumbledown shack in Athlone* Road. I would say to myself, *that's my home, that's my girl* and *I wanna be around her* and *I wanna be loved* by her for the rest of my life. Eventually *I want a little girl,* one that's just like Sue. The thought that *somebody loves me* and is waiting for me to come home, made me *straighten up and fly right.* I knew that *I'll only miss her when I think of her* so I used to *pretend* that *the moon was yellow* and that *it's only a paper moon* and would remain that way until Sue and I were together again.

What happened between you and Joanna? I know something must have gone wrong because you are now a *man alone* who looks like he's living on *the Boulevard Of Broken Dreams.*"

Sue said "Living on *the Boulevard of Broken Dreams,* hiding behind *the shadow of your smile* and going on a *sentimental journey* is alright for a while but remember *there's always tomorrow* and you must have faith. *You must believe in spring* because that's when the world brings forth its new beginnings."

I looked at them and thought "*No one will ever know* just how much these two young people love each other and just how much they think alike. They nearly see the world through the same eyes. *God bless the child* who has them as parents because they will never suffer from the *Memphis Blues. I want to be happy* like them but I wish I knew just how to go about it. *If I love again…*"

My thoughts were distracted by Sue saying "Mr. Bingwell, what you and Joanne had for such a short time, well, *is it better to have loved and lost* and not have loved her at all? These days, people are in a hurry to get what they want and they let the good things pass them by. If they only took their time, maybe, just maybe they could get what they really want and have it, maybe for the rest of their lives."

I replied "Sue, I don't really know. If I may continue then you might be able to answer that question for yourself."

Sue nodded yes.

"I was in Rabat at the *Vaya Con Dios* Club waiting in the reception area when *O Tannenbaum* and his wife, another *Sweet Leilani,* greeted me with "Mr. Bingwell, *Welcome to the Club.* A young lady named Joanna rang earlier and said that she would ring back at nine o'clock this evening to see if you are here. Now, when she rings back, do you want to take the call?"

I replied that I would and that I would prefer to take it in his office as it was a private call that I was expecting.

Sweet Leilani gave me a small smile and said "This Joanna, she has you *swinging on a star* and *someday* soon, you will ask her to marry you. Yes."

"Yes. She would be here with me now but she had to go back home for family reasons. *That ole devil called love* has finally caught up with me and I was thinking that *maybe September* would be a good time to propose to her. You know yourself that *love and marriage* go together and how *tender is the night* when you're all alone together."

When Joanna rang she told me that she wanted to stay with her family for another week. I told her that I would fly back to be with her but she insisted that I continue my business trip. She asked where I would be in a week's time and I told her Paris. I usually spend *April in Paris* but this year I'm going to be late. After the phone call, I returned to my table where I was approached by three very well dressed men.

One of the men said hesitatingly "We three Kings..." but another one of the men said "*We three Kings of Orient* are looking for someone to help us with the purchase and running of a club like this in Kiev."

The third man stated "It is situated on the main *road to Moscow*. We often come to Rabat and we have seen how *O Tannenbaum* and *Sweet Leilani* operate this business and we are very impressed. We even offered them a job but they refused to leave here.

We have been waiting for you to come for many weeks but you are a bit later this year. Would it be possible for us to meet somewhere soon to discuss our plans with you?"

I was not really in the mood to entertain these men; however, I did agree to meet with them the following day at the nearby *DO-RE-MI* Restaurant and discuss their ideas over lunch.

Over lunch the following day, I learnt that the three business men had purchased the *Virigold* Club, there in Rabat and were watching the staff at the *Vaya Con Dios* and copying them. They were moderately successful at it but they were not successful enough to make a good viable profit at this club to purchase the other club in Kiev.

I went with them to visit their club to see how their operation was managed and controlled. I also told them that I would have to be in touch with my partner in the States and discuss matters with him as we have never been in partnership with other people before.

That evening I rang Bob and told him about that day's proceedings and asked him to put *Adeste Fideles* on a plane for Madrid with the necessary paper work if we decided to go ahead and partner the three Kings Brothers. I told him that I would need Adeste for at least a fortnight and I also told him that I had a good feeling about this venture but I wanted to go and check out the place in Kiev personally. I asked him to find out all he could about the *Swing Low Sweet Chariot* Club. I told Bob that I would be in Madrid by the end of the week.

I had *Georgia on my mind* that day as well, so I asked Bob if he had heard anything about Ramblin' Rose having her baby yet. He told me that he hadn't, but he would get in touch with her to find out when she was actually due to have her baby.

I thought that I might as well keep busy whilst waiting for Joanna to return. I arranged for the Kings Brothers to accompany me to Madrid where we would meet Adeste and then we would go to Kiev and visit the club there. If everything was as good as they said it was; then negotiations would take place with Bob having the final say. This was how we had conducted all our business in the past and it worked well that way.

I always liked visiting our restaurant in Madrid because it was so unusual. It was called *On The Alamo* and it was like walking into a restaurant that was *deep in the heart of Texas*. The menu was split so that the patrons could choose from local dishes or from traditional dishes of Texas. This year the managers, *Bridges* and Susannah wanted to discuss the prospects of extending the restaurant to include another section that would be in the *theme from New York, New York* and called *Manhattan Night Lights*.

It really sounded interesting and possible to achieve because *there used to be a ball park* in the adjoining block that had relocated to a larger venue.

Adeste was waiting for us at the hotel in Madrid and while I visited *On The Alamo,* Adeste talked more with the Kings Brothers.

When I saw the plans that had been drawn up for the extension, I looked and said *"Oh, Susannah,* the *theme from New York, New York* that you want to use, has been captured to near perfection; even the menu has memories of home. I feel that this would enhance more tourists to eat here. I will certainly get in contact with Bob and suggest that we go ahead with this idea but you will need more staff, so will you be able to cope with that?"

"Yes." said Bridges "once we get the dates and the go ahead, we will start hiring and training the staff a few at a time. That way it will not interfere with the running of this place and we will soon know if the people we hire are capable of doing the duties set for them."

I thought to myself "This is why our businesses do so well. We don't interfere with the way they are run, unless we have to, and we listen to what the managers have to say. Sometimes they come up with good ideas that are well thought out, *some other time,* the ideas are not really viable but compromising can work for both parties involved."

It had been a very busy day for Adeste and myself, so we enjoyed a very quiet casual evening at the *Guadalajara* Café, three blocks down from our hotel. Adeste informed me that Ramblin' Rose had given birth to a daughter, *Ave Maria.* Bob was working on a few projects and was thinking about flying to Paris so we could catch up with each other and sort business out, plus he needed to get *out of town* for a while.

The issue with the young lady with the accusations was settled quickly. Like I had told Adeste, the girl's parents didn't know about the situation but unfortunately the young girl lost the baby.

Two days before he flew out, Adeste told me that he ran into Joanna whilst *waiting for the Robert E. Lee* ferry. Joanna had told him that she had tried several times to phone me without success, so she wrote a letter and was bringing it to the office for us to pass on to you. She seemed very distant and worried. He handed me the letter which I put in my pocket to read later in private, which I did.

In her letter Joanna wrote, "*It's a lonesome old town* tonight and *I'm alone because I love you. All I do is dream of you* and you are *always on my mind. Because you're mine,* it was very hard for me to say *arrivederci Roma,* but my family has to come first with me and it is very hard for me to write this letter to you. I will be staying here with my family until *maybe September.* My agent has found a way for me to honour my contracts starting with the *Poppa Santa Claus* Ball for sick children. *After the ball is over,* I will be going to the *Mardi Gras in New Orleans* for two nights and then I fly to *Indiana* for three festival engagements, the *Friendless Blues, The Days of Wine and Roses* and the *Pocket Full of Miracles.*

Not so long ago, there once was a man who was a *stranger in paradise* and the moment I saw him I knew that he was sent to *make someone happy.* Little did I know that *it was me* that he came to make happy. I knew that I was not *kissing a fool* just by *the touch of your lips. I used to be color blind* when it came to love and would often say *love look away,* but this time *love walked in* and melted this *cold cold heart.* You could *fly me to the moon* and back with just the *whisper of your name* and now *I've got you under my skin.*

I knew that *if I give my heart to you,* I would never be on the *look out for love* again. *It's been a long long time* since I have felt this good but *oh how I hate to get up in the morning* knowing that you're not here with me. *If love is good to me* then *we'll be together* again soon because my *love is here to stay.* Please, I beg of you, *stay where you are,* I'll be alright and I have my family here with me. I will write or ring again soon. All my love… Joanna."

Adeste greeted me the following morning with "Well, good morning. Didn't you sleep well last night because you look like you've been down in the depths of the cellars at the *Perfidia* and found every bottle empty and only *seven and a half cents* left on the floor for you? Come on cheer up."

I told him about the letter and he replied "*Maybe* it's good that she's with her family at the moment because look at all this work that you have to attend to. What time would you have to give to Joanna?"

"Adeste, you're right. Later *I'm going to sit right down* and write back to her and tell her to enjoy her time with her family and not to hurry back until she is ready. Right now, what is the first thing on the agenda for today – after breakfast that is." I replied.

DISTRACTIONS

The first thing on the agenda was to find a place to stay in Kiev, then to book the plane tickets and then to go shopping for some extra warm clothing because I thought that it might be getting colder in Kiev at this time of year. I had never been to that part of the world before but I had heard that *in the good old summertime,* the countryside, the hospitality and the weather felt like a *return to paradise.* But now the *autumn leaves* were beginning to fall which meant in a few months this part of the world could end up being a *winter wonderland.*

I was glad that we were going to Kiev with the Kings brothers because if you *don't know the language* very well, you may get yourself into a *spot* of trouble by being misunderstood.

Just as we were about to leave the hotel, some *thunder* was heard and Adeste said to me "*The rain in Spain* could last for days, so we might be wise to get some warm waterproof clothing as well. I grew up in a small town here in Spain and one of *my favorite things* back then was when the *rain* turned into *snowfall.* As children, we would all say *let it snow, let it snow, let it snow* because we could get together with our friends and go on a *sleigh ride* down the hills. We all had our own sleighs and as teenagers, two other lads and me would cover our sleighs with *silver bells* and ride them through the town making a terrible noise, especially at night to herald *the first snowfall.*

One year, someone told my father about my antics and I received such a harsh punishment that it made me *straighten up and fly right.* At the time you could *call me irresponsible* and I thought the punishment was too severe, but *as time goes by,* you realize that it wasn't and now *looking back,* I think it's *funny* and I also thank my father for giving it to me. One thing I still miss is going to *Christmasland* Park that was situated next to the old church. I wonder if they still have it there during the *white Christmas* period.

I finally went home one year after telling my parents three years in a row that *I'll be home for Christmas* and my sister brought home a half a bag of apples.

At the end of each school year, each student will take into class, *an apple for the teacher* but a few bigger boys played tricks on her. One boy soaked the apple in vodka, another froze the apple and the other gave her a toffee apple. Now I only have a *grown up Christmas* with my wife instead of a family Christmas with my elderly parents, but I have *nobody else but me* to blame for not doing so.

Actually, if it is alright with you and Mr. White, may I make the arrangements and tell my parents that *I'll be home for Christmas this year.*"

My reply to him was "After all the hard work and hours that you have put into the business, you certainly may have the holiday; in fact, if you would like to go back home for a month, I think that we can arrange for you to do that. For some people, it's *the most wonderful time of the year* being with their families at Christmas. Now let's get back to business and our shopping. Where and when do we have to meet the Kings brothers?"

Adeste replied "We are booked on the early evening flight so we have to meet the Kings adjacent to the *Firefly* News agency at the airport at six thirty pm. We would have to leave for the airport at five pm. When we get to Kiev, a limousine will be waiting for us and the driver will also be an interpreter for us if we need him. Until we meet the Kings, I'm not aware of their arrangements."

We met the Kings as planned and boarded our flight. As I sat looking out the window, I noticed how dull the moon seemed to look and I thought to myself *"It's only a paper moon* that's trying to shine on this *silent night.*"

My thoughts then went to Joanna. *"If I could be with you tonight,* you could *fly me to the moon* and we could get *lost in the stars* while we are *dancing in the dark.* It feels like *it's been a long long time* since I last heard your voice. *I've got the world on a string, I've got you under my skin* but I still feel as if I am living on the *Boulevard Of Broken Dreams.* I've come to realize that *you're my everything* and once my business is completed and after Paris, if you can't join me, then I'm *comin' home baby,* to you.

I will sit down tonight and write you telling you of my plans and then wait for you to *answer me my love.* I'll have to get your address off the letter you sent me except I can't recall seeing one on there. You must have put one on there somewhere so that I could write back."

The cabin stewardess broke my thought by asking me if I would like a tea, coffee or an alcoholic drink with the light meal being served.

Adeste looked past me and said "By the look of that moon, it *looks like a cold cold winter* is coming and that means that we will be having a *white Christmas.* If it is too cold, my family will have some trouble to *get me to the church on time* for the service where we will sing hymns and Christmas carols like *A cradle In Bethlehem,* we sing it very much like

48

Away In A Manger, God Rest Ye Merry Gentlemen and *Hark, The Herald Angels Sing*. When the service is over, the children will go *caroling, caroling* for an hour and they will sing *Jingle Bells* and the *Christmas song Jing-A-Ling, Jing-A-Ling* that some townsfolk do the *Christmas waltz* to. Did the town that you come from have their own *Christmas song?*"

I looked at him and said "No. nothing in particular. There were many nationalities and different religions in my town. Some sang *the Christmas song* of their own country or village and some people didn't celebrate Christmas at all. Most people though would light *Christmas candles* for one reason or another but I know that for the majority of the people, it was a *happy holiday* spent together as a family.

If I hadn't met Joanna, I would be having this *Christmas in Killarney,* in Ireland. A few years ago, *I heard the bells on Christmas Day* calling all the *dear hearts and gentle people* who lived in the town to their churches. *There is a tavern in this town* called Killarney *Dream* Tavern owned and run by an elderly Irishman known as *Two Shillelagh O'Sullivan* and on Christmas Day, if you didn't want to have a *Christmas dinner, country style* with other people who lived *on the street where you live,* then he would serve up *an old fashioned Christmas dinner* that was too *marvelous for words.*

After the meal and a few drinks, you would just get to love the people and you get *to love the language* that they speak. Sometimes a foreigner may find it hard to understand but you can still have a few laughs. That is one of my good memories and *they can't take that away from me.* I would love to buy that tavern for myself."

Adeste said surprisingly "*How can you buy Killarney* for yourself? Mr. White may not want to purchase it and who would you get to manage it?"

I replied "I have enough money of my own and I would leave Mr. O'Sullivan in charge of it. One day, I will want to settle down instead of traipsing across the world. I have seen the world so many times but Joanne has made me look at it. When Joanna and I are married, I don't want to have to travel so much. *I want a little girl* or boy or even both but I can't be travelling all the time. Besides it wouldn't be fair on Joanna and the children if I either took them with me, especially when they were ready for school, or if I continually left them home alone. Some marriages fall apart because of that. I think that I could spend many a *white Christmas* in a place of my own. Why do you think that Bob doesn't like travelling too much?

49

If anything and you were willing, you could take over my job; you just about know how to do it all.

Ah, finally. We're arriving in Kiev and I can't wait to get to the hotel for a shower and a good hot cup of coffee before going off to bed. Sometimes I get so tired when I'm travelling."

A female sitting behind me must have heard me for she said to the male sitting beside her "*Te quiero, dijiste (magic is the moonlight)*."

He replied "Do you think that your mother will sing the *Moonlight Serenade* for us tomorrow night?"

She replied "*Quizas, quizas, quizas (perhaps, perhaps, perhaps)*."

He gave a short laugh and said "You always say *Quizas, quizas, quizas (perhaps, perhaps, perhaps)* when you are not sure of something; and that is one thing that I love you for."

After landing, we were taken to our hotel and the Kings brothers had hired a car and had gone to their grandparents place to stay whilst they were in Kiev.

The following day, Louis and Petro Kings took us to the club that they wished to purchase. As we entered the club, I noticed a sign that read "*Welcome To The Club* and may *God rest you Merry Gentlemen* and Women".

We sat in the club and observed the staff and the patrons for a couple of hours and then we all met with Ivan, the third brother, to discuss their ideas back in our hotel room. After they had finished telling me their ideas I said "*The possibility's there;* however, I think that *there'll be some changes* made to enhance your ideas. I would like to go back tomorrow for another look and to meet the owner and staff. Could you arrange that for me please?"

It's easy to remember to do something when it's written down but I forgot to write to Joanna again and I forgot to write it down.

Adeste and I met with the owner and staff of the Swing Low Sweet Chariot and spent a few more hours with them before returning to Madrid.

When we arrived back in Madrid, it was still raining so we decided to take the morning off and go to the *La Golondrina* Halls to see the exhibition that was on because that week was *La Feria De Las Flores (The Festival of Flowers)*.

While we were in there, Adeste said to me "Mr. Bingwell, please wait here a moment, I see two old friends standing under the *Nao Tenho Lagrimas* banner."

He walked over to them and all I heard was "*Yo vendo unos ojos negros* (I see some black eyes) and *Aquellos ojos verdes* (Those green eyes) and *Si, La Feria De Las Flores* (Yes, The Festival of Flowers). Then I heard one of the females say "*Aqui se habla en amor* (love is spoken here)" and she said something else, to which Adeste answered "Si." Suddenly the woman's voice changed and she said before quickly turning away "*No me platiques* (Don't speak to me anymore)."

Adeste returned and told me that they had come down from the village for a week and that they had *come in out of the rain* and they were on their way to see *China Gate* at the movies. I hadn't seen them for years and Clisty, the girl with the black eyes, saw me walking over and asked if we would like to join them. She asked if you were married and I said that you weren't but when she asked if I was married yet and I said that I was, she didn't want to talk to me anymore.

We spent the next hour looking at different trees and flowers and there was even one flower there that I knew and that was the *Roses Of Yesterday,* my grandmother had some growing in her front garden when I visited her as a child. By the time we had finished at the exhibition, the rain had stopped so we headed off for some lunch before returning to the hotel to complete more business and to phone Bob.

Just opposite the *El Choclo* Café, where we were having lunch, a man stood on the corner preaching. I listened to his sermon which was short. He said "*Hark, the Herald Angels* are saying *sing you sinners, sing you sinners*. Sing to our Lord to forgive your sins. Repent for your sins and change your lives from *rags to riches. Sing you sinners;* sing for the good life that you will have once you repent for your sins. Sing you sinners for the Lord said "*You can depend on me* to be there for you. Have faith, trust and believe in me for I will give you a *lush life* when you join me here in heaven."

A woman went over to the man and they stood there talking for a few minutes before they left together.

Back at the hotel, Adeste and I began working on the business at hand although neither of us felt like it. I started researching the costing for the

Manhattan extension to the *On The Alamo* Club and Adeste started researching information for the business in Kiev. He also tried all afternoon to contact Bob, without success. It seemed to bother him a bit because there seemed to be no-one in the office, which was very unusual and the message machine was not switched on. When he did finally manage to get an answer from the office, he had to leave a message for Bob to contact us at his earliest convenience. Bob finally rang and said that he would meet us in Paris in five days' time and he would explain what had been happening in his part of the world.

That morning it started to rain again and Adeste said *"Here's that rainy day* again that will most probably last the week."

With our business in Spain finished, Adeste and I left for Paris two days later on *El Bodeguero* Airlines. It was on the plane while looking through some papers that I found Joanne's letter and re-read it and decided to answer it, right there and then. I had been so caught up in my business dealings that I had forgotten all about Joanna and her situation.

I wrote and apologized for the delay in replying to her letter and explained why. I asked about her and her family. I told her that I loved hearing from her and that I missed her terribly. I also missed *steppin' out with my baby* in her *blue velvet* dress and odd shoes *in the blue of the evening* for an evening of dining and dancing. And after the *last dance,* I missed *walking my baby back home* and having our *goodnight chat* before we both retired for the evening knowing that *we'll be together again* in a few hours.

Oh, how I miss you tonight, especially tonight because I am on my way to Paris. Being with you *under Paris skies* was the one thing that I was looking forward to because it is a beautiful city. I hoped that I would still be spending my days there with my *Mademoiselle De Paris* with our *love in bloom,* but unless you could get back here to me within the next week, then I would be spending my time in Paris alone and *when your lover has gone,* being alone in Paris, is not very good. Remember *I love you* and when you *close your eyes* to sleep, please *dream a little dream of me.*

Oh, I will be staying at the *Ca C'est Lamour* Hotel on the corner of *Chantez Les Bas* and *Cherchez La Femme* Boulevards. It is a very old but beautiful hotel. I will *sleep tite* tonight and will be anxiously waiting to hear from you as to when you will be joining me again. I signed it Love, Bingsie.

I thought that now I've finally written the letter, I would post it once I got off the plane. I searched Joanna's letter for a postal address but there wasn't one anywhere. I asked Adeste if he had seen a contact address for Joanna, but he said he hadn't. He suggested that I contact Bob to see if he could find out her address. I told him that wouldn't be any good because *I'm confessing* that I didn't know her last name, well, I wasn't sure of it. Adeste told me not to worry too much about it because he would contact a few people he knew once we arrived in Paris and get it for me. I put the letter in a pocket in my briefcase and thought no more of it.

As we were landing, I looked out the window and thought "*I love Paris* and because there is so much going on, it can never be called a *lonely town* or city. For people who love walking, there is the opportunity to walk along the river and sit on the banks between the *bridges* and enjoy the wonderful views."

Three hours after we had arrived at our hotel, Adeste and I were walking down *Chantez Les Bas* Boulevard when I heard "Bingsie, *Darling, Je vous amie beaucoup* (I love you very much) still."

I turned to see a very old friend of mine hastily coming behind us and I said
"*Hello Dolly,* how have you been?"

"Fine." she replied. "Do you remember my *sweet Lorraine?* Hasn't she grown into a beautiful young lady since you last saw her?"

I looked at *sweet Lorraine* and said teasingly "*I remember you* when you used to do the *bop kick* and the *one o'clock jump* down at the *One Note Samba* joint and on your way home, you used to *go down Moses* Street singing *Hit that Jive Jack* until you *hit the ramp* that took you to your house."

Sweet Lorraine looked sternly at me and said "Please Bingsie, *don't be that way,* won't you *try a little tenderness* on me now. I am older and not as wild anymore. Are you alone, because I've heard that *at long last love* has come into your life?"

I told her about Joanna and how she had to go back home and that Adeste and I were in town for a while on our own.

Sweet Lorraine said "Then you and Adeste must dine with mother and me tonight at the *Moondance* Restaurant and tomorrow night, you both can be my guests at the *Laugh! Cool Clown* Charity Ball being held in the *Ebony Rhapsody* Room in your hotel. Laugh! Cool Clown holds a ball each year, here in Paris to raise money for research to help find a cure for what really causes different types of kidney diseases, especially for young children suffering from Chronic Nephritis or Haemolytic Uremic Syndrome, HUS for short. *How little we know* about these terrible diseases that a child suffers from.

Research has shown that some children can be cured of it, some can manage it and lead a somewhat normal life and others may need dialysis while waiting for a kidney transplant. Unfortunately other children, like my baby brother die from kidney disease. Adults can suffer from the same disease but it is called Thrombotic Thrombocytopenic Purpura, TTP for short and Nephritis. You can never be *too young* to be diagnosed with a disease."

I looked at Adeste and back to Lorraine and said "I'm sorry. I didn't know that you once had a brother. I know of kidney disease but not the ones that you have mentioned and of course we will attend the ball, on the condition that we pay for our evening."

"Thank you, that's very kind of you. Money is always being raised to keep the research going. Next month, we have a fund raising ball over in England." said Lorraine.

That evening, Adeste and I dined with Dolly and Lorraine and there were a few photographers and reporters at the *Moondance* Restaurant, trying to get interviews with Lorraine. Evidently, it was Lorraine who began the Laugh! Cool Clown Charity in memory of her brother.

The following morning, Adeste and I went about the business that we had come to Paris for. I was just about to phone Bob, when I received a message saying that he would be arriving in Paris in two hours. He would be coming in on *El Bodeguero* Airlines flight fifty nine from Lisbon. I knew that Bob would want to join us for the evening, so I sent Adeste to pick Bob up from the airport while I arranged a room for him at our hotel and I phoned Lorraine to set another place at our table for Bob, if that was possible. She said that she would shuffle a few people around but she would make sure that he would be seated with us.

Finally Bob and Adeste arrived at the hotel. Bob looked frazzled and then said "*Nobody knows the trouble I've seen* in the past few weeks and am I glad to be here away from it. Now, Adeste told me about tonight's event and as we only have a couple of hours before it starts, I'll tell you what has been going on tomorrow. Right now, all I want to do is have a drink, something to eat and a bit of a rest. Where can we go for a drink?"

"Across the road is the *Memphis Blues* Bar and Grill that sells American style food. We can go over there." I replied.

Bob did tell us that the plane from the States had to land in Lisbon due to mechanical problems, so all the passengers travelling to Paris, Germany, Poland and Holland would be transferred onto an *El Bodeguero* plane for the continuation of their journeys, but there would be a two hour wait at the airport before their departure. When they finally got off the plane in Lisbon, the staff at the airport was on strike so they couldn't go anywhere to get anything decent to eat. The skeleton staff that was working took longer to transfer their luggage than they normally would.

We arrived at the ball for pre-drinks and while we were talking to *the Happy Elf,* (a person dressed up who went around telling the guests about the Charity's fundraising goal and answering questions), Dolly and Lorraine came up behind us and Dolly said delightfully, *"Bob White, Darling, Je vous aime beaucoup."*

Bob turned and saw Dolly coming towards him and the look on his face must have given him away for Dolly said *"Don't you remember* that *Christmas in Killarney* Pub in London and afterwards as a group of us were walking home, *a nightingale sang in Berkley Square* and Pippa tried to copy it, but she just made us all laugh instead."

"Dolly, how are you? Yes, *I remember you* and I remember that evening very well. Pippa, I still see her every now and then, but she *don't get around much anymore,* although she still spends *spring in Manhattan* with her niece *Ave Maria,* that's all I know."

Suddenly Dolly said "Excuse me." and hurried off, leaving Lorraine standing with us and we all heard Dolly say "Mademoiselle *Petite Fleur, Darling, Je vous aime beaucoup,* welcome."

I asked Lorraine why her mother addressed everyone with *Darling, Je vous aime beaucoup* and does she have any idea of what it means?

Lorraine replied "You know mother, once she learns something new, she keeps saying it. She has learnt a few more French phrases and speaks them to her acquaintances back home, which makes her feel special. As for what it means, I don't think she really knows.

I know that I'm even unsure of the meaning but I think that *Darling, Je vous aime beaucoup* means Darling, I love you very much. I must really find out and if it does mean that, then I will have to stop her saying that because most times it is inappropriate to say it to people, especially at functions like this. Well, it's time to go in and be seated at our tables so we can get started."

Once the meal was over, Adeste moved closer to me and softly said "*Yo vendo unos ojos negros* and *Aquellos ojos verdes* looking at us from the table two down from us."

The black eyes that he was talking about as my father's but the green eyes belonged to a lady I didn't know. I excused myself from the table and approached my father who said "Hello son. *Have you met Miss Jones?* Actually, *me and Mrs. Jones* are here in Paris because she is auditioning for a part in *La Vie En Rose*." He looked me straight in the eyes and said "Don't worry, *I ain't misbehavin',* your mother has just gone to the Ladies room and will be returning shortly. It is *because of you* that we have sorted ourselves and our marriage out and now when I go away, I take her with me. Your mother is involved with the San Francisco branch of this charity and that is another reason why we are here. Look, here comes your mother now."

I looked to see an older looking *but beautiful* woman walking towards us trying to *put on a happy face. For once in my life* I actually saw my mother for who she really was and *all of me* just wanted to go over to her and put my arms around her. Then my memory flashed back to the cottage for sale and the man who said something about *the two lonely people* who were living in some sort of world that had *nowhere with love in it* or something like that.

Just before my mother reached the table, an *announcement* was made asking everyone to return to their tables and be seated. The entertainer, who was to perform here tonight, cancelled at the last minute so the band *C'est Magnifique* would be playing instead.

The reporters and photographers will now be allowed into the room and the speeches would commence a few minutes later. Once the speeches are over, the band will commence playing for all those who wished to take to the floor.

Finally the speeches were over, the band started playing and the media started taking their photographs and the reporters started their interviews. For some reason, Lorraine seemed to want to stay by my side all night. I didn't think anything of it because we were old friends until the evening was coming to a close and that's when Lorraine said to me "*Don't go* yet. *I hear music* still and I would like to have at least one dance with you tonight so *let's face the music and dance*."

On the dance floor, Lorraine said, "After all these years, you know *I've still got you under my skin* and oh, *how I'd love to love you tonight*."

And then she kissed me. We didn't know but a photographer from the *Morning Star* Magazine happened to be in the room still and took a couple of compromising photos of us on the dance floor.

I asked Lorraine who the entertainer was supposed to be and she replied "A wonderful singer named Joanna Lacy from the States but her agent called and cancelled her without giving us a reason. Joanna has performed at many functions for us and it's a pity she wasn't here tonight; you would have loved her."

I began to wonder if it was my Joanna who she was talking about. Then I remembered the letter that I had written but had not posted.

Over coffee the following morning, Bob related his story to Adeste and me. "After you had asked Adeste to join you in Madrid, I received an urgent phone call from *Mood Indigo* asking for our help to stop a gambling syndicate that had started in the club. Almost at the same time, I received phone calls from *Mona Lisa Stardust* and *Sweet Georgia Brown* requesting the same help. So with Adeste away, I knew that I would have to handle the situation *all by myself* and you know how I hate travelling, especially by plane.

I hired a car and took *Route 66* down to *Perfidia* and when I finally arrived, Sweet Georgia Brown and Rosaleen met me and explained what was going on and how they had handled the situation whilst waiting for me to arrive. We phoned the Sheriff and explained it to them and I told them of the other two phone calls about the same issue that I had received.

The Sheriff came out and spoke to the other staff members and told me that they were unable to help me in the other two places because it was out of their jurisdiction but said they would notify the other county Sheriffs and the Federal Police."

Rosaleen turned to the Sheriff and said "If he is to get to San Antonia via *Route 66, he'll have to go* within the hour."

I said that I had *Georgia on my mind* and that *Mood Indigo* was expecting me. I wouldn't be able to get to San Antonia for at least two more days.

The Sheriff said "We'll inform Georgia and tell them that you're coming and what it's all about and then we'll get the Federal Police to meet you at the San Antonia Police Precinct in three days' time."

So I drove further down Route 66 until I reached the Georgia turn off. I was so glad to reach the Bayou Maharajah Club where *Mood Indigo* was waiting for me. Don't ever let him make you a coffee because it tastes like *Mississippi mud.*

The police soon joined us and said that they would set up a surveillance team and send a detailed report to the Federal Police within the week. I spent the night in Georgia and headed off for San Antonia, early the following day but somehow I missed a turn off for *Route 66.* I saw a farmer on the side of the road so I pulled over and told him that *I'm lost* and could he give me directions back to where I wanted to go. He did better than that; in fact, he gave me directions to San Antonia that took almost half a day's travelling off my time.

It was in *the cool of the day* and twenty miles out from San Antonia when I saw a group of young people *tie a yellow ribbon around the old Oak tree* and I thought to myself "Oh, to be *young at heart* again but *what'll I do when I grow to old to dream. I've got the world on a string* now but that's all I've got. *I ain't got nobody* to share *the good life* with. *Pennies from Heaven* keep falling for me and the company and you as well Bingsie but we have got to get more from our lives than just work. We are going to have to put on more staff and promote the current staff to higher positions.

L.A. is my lady but at the moment, she is one of the biggest *lonesome cities* in the States, especially now I've *lost April,* my dog, she was old and passed in her sleep a few weeks back.

Getting back to my travels, you wouldn't believe it but *the best is yet to come.*

It was the *night of the quarter moon* as I drove into San Antonia and found a motel for the night but even though I was dead tired, I headed for *Mona Lisa's* place.

As I walked into the club, a man approached me and offered to buy me a drink. He also said that he wanted to talk to me about something. I thought that he wanted to report the gambling syndicate to me, so I agreed to him buying me a drink and I sat down at a table near the wall. He started talking to me about different types of games and then he asked me if I would like to place a bet on a game. I asked him how much I had to put down and he replied that *it's all in the game* I choose. I asked him what happened if the owner found out about what he was doing and he replied "Don't worry about that, *Mona Lisa Stardust* won't do anything, she hasn't got the guts to do anything."

I told him at that point of time, I didn't have any money on me but asked if he would be around for the next few days. He told me that he would be and left the table. I finished my drink and headed outside and went around to the back door where I saw *Mona Lisa* standing by a bench. Seeing me at the back door startled her and I told her what had just happened with one of her customers and that is why I came around back.

She told me that one of her wait staff was an undercover police officer who was pretending to be a trainee because they suspected that *Black Market stuff* was also being sold through the club. After agreeing to meet the following day, I slipped back to the motel for a good night's sleep.

The following evening, I went back into the club wearing a police wire and hoping to meet the same gentleman again. He didn't disappoint me and came and sat down at my table. I told him that I was looking for work and could he get some for me. He asked me a lot of questions which I answered with the answers that the police had given me earlier that day, just in case I needed them. He said that he would have to get in touch with his boss who lived in Monterey and would see me here in the club the next night. So I went back the next night and he told me to be in A Media Luz Club on Friday night and speak to *Acertes Mas*.

It was *a rainy night in Rio* when the plane landed and I was met by the Police down there. They knew about the gambling syndicate but were unsure about how big it was until now and also, if they were also dealing in *Black Market stuff* as well.

The Police there had found out that the Sheik of Araby was actually *Acertes Mas* who was trying to get all our clubs closed down so that he could take them over. But until now they didn't have enough proof or evidence to approach him, so it was just a bit of luck that I was the one that his man approached in San Antonia and as I was the owner of the clubs, I could forewarn the managers as to what was going to happen in each place the next day.

I phoned *The Continental* in Suas Maos to find out if anything was happening there and to my relief, nothing was, so I flew to Monterey for my meeting with Acertes Mas.

Well, *it happened in Monterey* during the meeting, when the police raided the club that the Sheik recognized me and said "*It had to be you* that my man approached." so he gave himself up peacefully. He knew that you, Bingsie and I and all our managers and staff could not be messed with now that we knew who he was and what he was trying to do.

When it was over, I phoned the office and asked them to notify everybody about the demise of the syndicate and to tell them that they all did a good job in the way each of them handled the situation. I received a message at the same time about a place you seemed to forget to visit on your travels here... Lisbon.

I caught the next flight to Lisbon and went and saw *Ansiedad* in the *Calypso Blues* Bar and it's a good job that it's in the airport complex and that I had a two hours wait before boarding again for the continuation of the flight here. *It was a very good year* for the *Calypso Blues;* in fact, it was an excellent year for them and they were extremely busy whilst I was there; strike or no strike."

Bob looked at both of us and said "After lunch, let's work to finish all our business and then for the next two days *let's get away from it all*. I'm sure that there are places to see and other things to do here in Paris. Adeste, unless Bingsie needs you, you can begin after lunch."

I told Bob that I didn't need Adeste, so he was free to go and buy something special for his wife, like *the ruby and the pearl necklace* and earring set that I've seen him looking at in the hotel's jewellery shop.

Adeste blushed and said "Yes, that would look good on my wife for *when I take my sugar to tea* or the way she would feel when other women would turn and comment on her beauty when *walking my baby back home. When my sugar walks down the street* I am very proud to be by her side."

A lady approached our table cautiously while looking at a newspaper and said with a French accent "Oui, you are the *Embraceable You* that is kissing the lady in the newspaper's photograph." and she turned it around so that we could all see it. She continued to say *"Maybe you'll be there* with the lady at the *Nature Boy* Benefit this coming *Sunday. Maybe you'll be there,* yes."

My heart stood still when I saw the picture and I said to Bob "I have to get over to the *La Mer* Hotel and see Lorraine about this. If Joanna sees this, she'll think that I don't love her anymore. I have written her a letter but I don't have her postal address or a contact number either but I think Lorraine knows how to contact her."

I hurried out of the *Azure-Te* Café and straight to the La Mer, only to find that Lorraine and her mother had gone shopping at *Les Feuilles Mortes* Boutique and would be gone for most of the day.

I left an urgent message for Lorraine to phone me at my hotel and I went back to the *Azure-Te* Café, arriving there just as Bob was leaving.

We went back to my suite and continued on with our business, finishing about seven o'clock that evening. Just as we finished, Lorraine called and we spoke briefly about the newspaper headline and picture. I asked if I could meet with her about an hour later and she agreed. We met outside the *Amor Amor* building opposite her hotel and we started walking towards the river.

Lorraine said "I don't see why you're so upset about the article. People will talk, so *let them talk*. After a few weeks, it will die down. I don't know why you're interested in finding this Joanna person, but if it helps, I will give you the contact details of her agent because that's how we contact her. Anyway! What's all the fuss over *for the want of a kiss?*"

I stopped and looked at her and said "You're *unbelievable*. If I remember rightly, last night you kissed me and *I'm not at all in love* with you, especially after all these years have passed. It's your *pure imagination* if you're thinking that. As for Joanna, *no I don't want her* to think that because she's not here that I don't love her. I love her and I want to *make her mine* as soon as we are together again. *For once in my life* I have found someone who's *easy to love* and is happy to *be loved by me,* just the way I am. Of all the female acquaintances that I know, *it had to be you* that I got caught with. Now do you understand what I'm saying to you?"

Lorraine looked away and replied "I understand. Yesterday, when we met after being apart for so long, *my foolish heart* took me back to the days when a group of people, who were still *young at heart,* were out for the afternoon and when *a nightingale sang in Berkley Square;* it made them all laugh.

I loved you then and *I wished on the moon* that you would love me too. I used to *stay awake* at nights just thinking about you and how *you'd be so easy to love* and how *you'd be so nice to come home to.* I imagined that *the touch of your lips* on mine would be *a kiss to build a dream on* and *if I had you* then, I would have *someone to light up my life* and *someone to watch over me* until all the *stars fell on Alabama.* Then *this funny world* of mine changed when you moved back to the States to start your business going with Bob. It was that year that *my love went to London* with me but never came home with me."

A blossom fell from the tree that we were standing under as she continued saying "When my little brother became ill, I had to look after him while mother was away on business. The doctors were never really sure what was wrong with Gary until he was admitted to the Children's Renal Ward after I took him to the hospital because he had collapsed and lost consciousness.

When the hospital staff saw how pale he was, the bruises that we couldn't explain how he got, his swollen limbs and his yellowish skin color, they ran quite a few tests and found that Gary had the advanced symptoms of HUS, which had occurred after an infection of the digestive system. He was placed on the Kidney Transplant list and started on the dialysis machine that does the work that the kidneys are supposed to do. I used to call him my *small fry* hero every time he had dialysis. Unfortunately HUS caused some brain damage but he picked up another infection and his tiny body couldn't cope with it and he went to sleep one night and never woke up.

In the Children's Renal Ward, a couple of volunteers used to dress up as clowns and visit the sick children. Gary was learning to talk again then and when he saw them he used to say "Laugh! Cool clown." so after he passed away, I spent the rest of my time trying to find out what I could on Children's Kidney Diseases and to find a way to help other children with the disease.

I found out that money was badly needed for research, so I started this charity up. Gary was nearly three years old when he died. When *a child is born,* you expect them to grow up and be healthy; but it is not always the case as you have learnt in the past few days."

Lorraine looked up at the sky and said "*Oh, you crazy moon* and *Oh, look at me now* while brushing away some tears. *Please be kind* and *try a little tenderness* if you ever come to meet someone who is or has gone through what I and my family have been through.

It's been a long long time since I felt the feelings that I had for you *yesterday* and I wasn't thinking of your feelings for Joanna. Yes, of course I'll help you find her and get this silly thing sorted out. I will contact her agent and get her to come to London for our ball over there and you must come too. Once she's back with you, then you can *get lost in the stars together* forever. Now how does that sound to you?"

"*It's alright with me* and I will be happy to help out with the charity when I can and as for *you're crying on my shoulder,* I think that *it's alright with me* but only every now and then when things get really bad. I know what it can be like when you need someone to talk to and you keep asking yourself "*Who can I turn to;*" to talk about *the bad and the beautiful things* that happens in your life.

Come on, I'll walk you home so you can go and get some *sleep baby sleep* and not stay awake all night. I know that *there's love* out there for you and maybe *love is just around the corner* and waiting for you. You're a bit upset and unsteady on your feet at the moment, so *hold my hand* just until we get back to your hotel."

It was only a few minutes before we reached her hotel and she looked at me and said "Thank you for being there for me tonight. *What a night* it has been and *when I fall in love,* I hope that the man is *exactly like you, warm and willing* to take the time to listen when a person needs to talk. I will phone Joanna's agent as soon as I get to my suite because it will be daytime back home. Thanks again Bingsie. Goodnight."

Over the next two days, Bob and I spent a lot of time with Lorraine visiting many children in hospitals as well as adults in Renal Wards of the hospitals in and around Paris, learning more about Kidney Diseases and just how many *pennies from heaven* are needed to help so many people all around the world. There are even parts of the world where people are dying from many diseases because medical assistance is not available or affordable.

I thought "*I should care* about other less fortunate people than myself, because one day it might strike my own family and I would appreciate the support from them being there to help get the family through a crisis. I am healthy at the moment but what if one of my children or even my wife became ill with an incurable disease. Research may find a cure that could save their lives."

Bob seemed to become very drawn in by the charity, to the extent that he said "*If I ruled the world,* there are two main things that I would like to bring about and that is *peace on earth* and poverty which is the main reason that people can't access proper medical attention."

Lorraine looked surprisingly at Bob and said "The Lord could use some extra help here on earth. He has been trying for such a long time to bring peace to the earth. Poverty is another matter. That one will be a bit harder to solve because Mother Nature has her hand in it. In some countries, people live in so many remote areas that it becomes very difficult to access them and if you can access these areas and people, then there is a language barrier to overcome and you have to gain the trust of those people.

All I do is raise as much money as I can for research and I let all the other organizations do their part to reach the people who need their assistance."

Lorraine told me that she had been in contact with *Cole Capers,* who was Joanna's agent. He had told her that Joanna was on her way overseas and that he would contact her and inform her of the London engagement. He said that he was sure that she would attend because it was my organization booking her.

On their last day in Paris, Adeste, Bob and I were sitting in the hotel's coffee bar, when a bell boy approached me and delivered an urgent letter to me. I looked at the handwriting and knew that the letter was from Joanna; eagerly I opened the letter to see when she was going to join me again.

Instead I read "Dear Bingsie, *The very thought of you* and the time we spent together *when in Rome* was just a *dream* to me now. You did *fly me to the moon* and back several times but *now is the hour* that I come back down to earth and stay down. Every *time I think of you,* I feel so happy *because you're mine* and you could continue to *fly me to the moon* just by me *taking a chance on love* with you, and then I saw the pictures in the newspapers of you and sweet Lorraine and I realized that *this love of mine* could never last because you're *not mine* anymore.

No matter where I am or what I am doing, my family will always come first to me. So I have decided with great difficulty that this is *the end of a love affair* between us and for me it will always be an affair to remember until *polka dots and moonbeams* cover the earth. You were *my first and only lover* who gave me *my kind of love,* so please let me remember you that way. *May I never love again* in the way that *I love you now?*

The memories I have of you will keep me *dream dancing* for many years to come and no matter who comes along for me in the future, *they can't take that away from me.* I will never have to ask myself again "*What is this thing called love.*" for now I know, but *you don't know what love is* until you have experienced it.

Please don't come back here looking for me because I have asked my agent to fill my calendar with overseas engagements. Just *let me sing and I'm happy* and every place I go, I will sing *a song for you. I had the craziest dream* not long after we met and now I know that *dreams can tell a lie. For all we know, somewhere along the way* we may meet again and *to see you* as a friend and *not as a stranger* would be good.

Please be kind Bingsie and let me go and *remember me* the way I was *when in Rome.* Joanna."

The look on my face must have told Bob and Adeste what the letter was about and Adeste said, "Something is wrong, isn't it; it's Joanna?"

I shook my head yes and said "She's left me. She feels that her family needs her more than I do. She's going to continue her singing career. She knows that she doesn't have to keep singing. We could have worked something out but she isn't giving us a chance to."

Bob asked quite hesitantly, "I think I know you well enough, but I have to ask, did you play *the pajama game* with her?"

I replied "No, but I did think about it. Adeste has met Joanna and he'll tell you that she is so *easy to love.*"

"Yes." said Adeste, "she is a no fuss lady with a great *personality, but beautiful* enough to make heads turn. I remember when I first met her and what she said to me as we were leaving the hotel because Joanna bumped into to me and nearly stepped on my foot. She said she was sorry but she was looking for *pennies from Heaven* to pick up and if she had stepped on my foot, I would be singing *toot toot tootsie goodbye.* Her sense of humour is *unforgettable* and she is a woman who could easily get you to *put your dream away for another day.*"

I said, "Yes, *she's funny that way.* I was *lucky to be me* that she loved for a short while and she'll *make someone happy* one day, but unfortunately *it happens to be me* that will miss out on such a beautiful and wonderful thing in life.

Now, the both of you should get moving or you'll miss the plane and Adeste, your wife will not forgive either of us if that happens. I might just catch the *Katusha Bullet* train and take myself to a *Swiss Retreat* so I can sort my life out and see *what I'll do next.* I'll call you in a couple of weeks to let you know what I'll be doing."

With Bob and Adeste on the plane back home, I decided to walk down to the river and try to work out in my head what went wrong between me and Joanna.

The next minute I heard "*Hey there. Stop, the red light is on.*"

I turned to see Lorraine coming. She stopped, looked at my face and said sarcastically, "Boy, you look great today.

You look like you went to bed with the *friendless blues* last night and they're still with you. What's wrong?"

As we walked, I told her about Joanna's letter and said "*Why does it have to be me* again. *I wish I knew* what I do wrong. *Only yesterday* I thought that this time *love is here to stay*. But now it seems to be *congratulations to someone* else for taking away *my heart's treasure*.

Am I angry? Sure, I'm angry because she never gave us a chance. *Am I Blue?* Sure, I'm blue but *the blues don't care about* happiness. Is this madness? I don't know. *Who can I turn to* when I'm alone and when *no one cares* enough to want to listen? *Here comes that heartache again* and *I don't want to be hurt anymore. I don't want to see tomorrow* if this is all I'm going to have to face."

"Bingsie." Lorraine said sternly, "you're *getting nowhere* in this frame of mind. You have to *pick yourself up, straighten up and fly right. You call it madness* but I call it love. Now Joanna should be in London next month, so we have to get you *someone to tell it too.* I would hate for her to see you now because *the way you look tonight* is upsetting. *There once was a man* I knew, who could sum up a situation and work out a solution to it, but tonight I think that that man is lost.

I know; I have a good friend who works at the *Tres Palabras* Retreat. You go back to your hotel, pack and meet me outside my hotel in two hours. *I know that you know* that you need some help now. Go on, get moving, I have some phone calls to make."

I met Lorraine as she instructed me to do. What she had done was to book me on the *midnight flyer* to the retreat and had arranged for me to meet her friend *Carolina in the morning.*

I gave her a hug and said "Thank you. You have done *more than you know* for me over the past week here in Paris. When I see you again, it will be in London."

She looked at me and gave me a wink and said in a funny voice "*Someday sweetheart,* you and I will *get happy* together and maybe you can *fly me to the moon* in your paper plane." then she said seriously "remember *the blues don't care who's got them,* only don't keep them too long. I will see you in London and Joanna should be there as well."

LEPRECHAUN MISCHIEF

Sue reached across the table and touched Bingsie's hand before saying "Bingsie, I'm so sorry. I know that sometimes when things go wrong and you think "*who can I turn to?*" to help sort things out, and the best person could be a stranger, one who is a professional. Even the experts need someone to talk to at times. Was Carolina able to help you?"

Danny said "Some men think that they don't need help, that they can do it on their own but didn't you meet Joanna in London where you were going to propose to her? What happened?"

"Yes." said Sue "What happened, did she say no?"

Bingsie ordered more drinks before continuing. "I spent two weeks at the retreat and then I flew to London and contacted Lorraine. *For sentimental reasons* we decided to meet at the Killarney Pub for lunch the following day.

That *silent night* I laid on my bed thinking about many things. I thought about when I was younger and the time that *a Nightingale sang in Berkley Square,* how our little group of friends would go *jumpin' at Capital Hall* or *jumpin' at Meaners* Place *just for the fun of it* or we would dress warmly and go out for a walk on a *foggy day* and pretend that we had *lost April,* our pet monkey.

I think *I used to be color blind* when it came to love or was it just because I was *young and foolish* and not on the *look out for love*. At the time I think that I only thought of Lorraine as a *little girl* and a *crazy baby*. Oh, I don't mean that in a bad way but *me, myself and I* had plans for the future and *love and marriage* weren't in them at the time.

Then my *reflections* took me to the first time I saw Joanna and the night that I saw her in her *blue velvet* dress. The same night that she became *my funny valentine* because of her odd shoes and the time we shared together *when in Rome*. As I laid there on that *silent night,* I heard Joanna singing and the voice of the man with the *unforgettable* blue eyes saying that I would hear him in the harmony of the music, and it made me think of *how insensitive* I have been lately to the people around me and as soon as I see Joanna again, I will apologize to her. I wondered if it would be the kind of apology that would be *too little too late*."

It was a *foggy day* when I met Lorraine for lunch. I told her about the past couple of weeks at the retreat and how much good it had done me and she told me about the charity ball that was being held on the following Saturday night.

She told me that here in London; there were two sections of the charity that were fund raising together. The first was *Send In The Clowns* that raised money for research and the other was *You Tell Me Your Dream* who raised and used the money to make an incurable child's dream to come true.

She showed me a photo of nine year old twin girls and told me that a *portrait of Jennie* will be hanging in the ball room on the evening and there will also be a *waltz for Debby* danced that evening. Both girls became ill with HUS and Jennie passed away two months ago. Debby was training to be a *ballerina,* when they finally diagnosed her illness but she is beyond treatment to stop her dying.

This year, You Tell Me Your Dream is trying to raise the funds for her to meet a *ballerina* from Russia and a *ballerina* from the States. Debby is so ill that she may not live long enough to see her dream come true. It's quite sad and very hard for the parent's to lose both girls to the same disease within six months of each other.

Debby is quite remarkable actually because she keeps telling her parents that although she will be joining her sister in heaven very soon, one day *we'll be together again* so remember me *dream dancing while the music plays on.*

Lorraine told me that she hadn't heard from Joanna yet, but there were still a couple of days to go. The next few days seemed to drag by and finally Saturday arrived and I was getting excited about seeing Joanna again.

I arrived at the *Blue Gardenia* Ballroom only to be greeted by one sad Lorraine. She told me that she had been given several pieces of bad news that afternoon. The first was that Debby took a turn for the worse and had just passed away and the second was that Joanna's agent called and said that she was not coming but didn't give a reason. Lorraine said that that was not like Joanna at all and felt that something else was going on and she would talk to Joanna when she went back to the States next week. She also said that it looked like it was going to be just me and *you and the night and the music* but no kissing.

On the wall outside the *Blue Gardenia* Ballroom was a *portrait of Jennie* and Debbie together at their last birthday celebration in the hospital and hanging inside was the *portrait of Jennie* and hanging beside her was a portrait of Debbie and when the *waltz for Debby* was played, everyone possible was on the dance floor. Even though the evening was a huge success and we had lots of fun and laughter, I was concerned over Joanna and the newspaper article that needed sorting out and how I still wanted to *make her mine.*

The following day, I contacted Adeste to see if he could find Joanna and explain the full situation to her with the photographs because he was there and knew exactly what had happened.

Over the phone Adeste said to me 'Oh, Mr. Bingwell, *where do I begin.* The other day as I was *waiting for the Robert E. Lee* ferry, I heard Joanna's voice and as I was about to approach her to get her address, I saw through the crowd that she was with another man who had his arm around her.

I heard her say to him "With all these cancellations I haven't any more work here. How could he be so cruel to me? Seeing that I'm free now, yes Steve, I will go to *Tallahassee* with you until I can get more work."

Then another man approached the man who was with Joanna and called him *Steve Lacy* and they walked away with him and a little boy. What do you want me to do Mr. Bingwell; do you want me to find them?"

I felt like I was standing right where the *stars fell on Alabama* and were hitting me on the head and I couldn't say anything at that moment; let alone think so I told him not to do anything until I contact him again. However, if the office needed me, I would be staying at the *Sovereign Lover* Lodge in *Galway Bay*, Ireland as from the following Tuesday. I told him that I needed to think about the future and where I wanted to go and be. I was in shock and it took me awhile to start to think straight again.

I tried to phone Lorraine to see what she knew about this Steve Lacy but she and her mother had already checked out and no-one knew where they were going next. So I packed and caught *my ship* that would take me to *Galway Bay*. I could have flown to Ireland and then caught a train down but I thought that the sea crossing would be good for me at this time.

I was standing on the deck of our steam ship as we were chugging up *Galway Bay* and I had to smile to myself as *I saw three ships* passing with their *red sails in the sunset* of the *orange colored sky* because the ships were named *Spring Is Here, Summer Wind* and *Autumn Leaves*.

69

I wondered if they would name a fourth ship *Winter Wonderland* if they had one.

We arrived at our destination and were taken to the lodge but I soon found myself in the local tavern watching and listening to the conversations of the local townsfolk and travellers.

I heard someone ask *"Who paid the rent for Mrs. Rip Van Winkle?* Her husband would like to thank them because now he can go back to sleep and she will leave him alone for a while longer."

The barkeeper called out "Hey Patrick, did you ever find out *who threw the overalls in Mrs. Murphy's chowder?"*

"No." came the reply "but I bet the Leprechauns had something to do with it. Have you ever had any of Mrs. Murphy's chowder? If you have, then you would be thanking the Leprechauns."

Some laughter rang out from the small group that Patrick was with.

As the afternoon became evening, more locals gathered in the tavern and a barmaid began work. A couple of the young lads must have had a bet on because they charged their glasses and said *"Here's to the losers."* and then one of them said *"I'll take you home again Kathleen."*

To which she replied "Not tonight, my father's coming in and you know what he's like. *Oh! 'tis sweet to think* that you would *get out and get under the moon* with me but you couldn't stand up long enough. It would be me taking you to your mother instead and me walking myself home *with my shillelagh under my arm."*

A small group of musicians gathered in the corner and started playing *Irish Lullaby* and I started humming to it and immediately thought of my mother and my childhood. As I wandered back to the lodge after the tavern closed, I again heard the words *Too-Ra-Loo-Ra-Loo-Ral, Too-Ra-Loo-Ra-Loo-Ral* in my head and my mother wanting to know if *I'll be home for Christmas this year*. I looked up at the sky and noticed that *it's only a paper moon* shining that night.

The following day, I walked around the town and ended up sitting on the grass near a clump of *Honeysuckle Rose* bushes on the banks of the *ol' man river*. I started fiddling and building stuff with the leaves and twigs that were lying around and I heard a soft but unusual voice call out *"Hey there, don't fence me in,* it's not polite."

I stopped and looked around and saw no-one in sight and just as I was about to resume my building again, I heard "Down here mister. *Don't fence me in,* it's not polite."

I couldn't believe my eyes when I saw a little person standing in the middle of the corral I had just built. I shook my head thinking that I was seeing things and then asked "Who and what are you?"

"I'm *dear old Donegal* and I'm one of the wee folk, a leprechaun. Don't tell me that you haven't heard of us?" came the reply.

I really thought that I had lost my mind but replied "Yes, I've heard of you but I only thought you were a myth, a legend."

Donegal answered "*Once upon a time,* we wandered all over the place until some greedy people captured some of us and tried to make us do things that were even impossible for us to do, so we disappeared and only occasionally do we show ourselves. You look like a man carrying all of *Joe Turners blues* around on his shoulders and wanting to change his life from *rags to riches*. Break down the fence and we'll talk about it. What do you say?"

I thought, "Why not. *Who can I turn to* now? There isn't anyone else I can talk to besides I can't get any crazier than I feel now. So I broke down the building and told him everything including the time that the blue eyed man spoke to me."

Donegal said "Umm, I see, I don't really know what can be done now, but I'll meet you back here tomorrow and we'll start working this out. Don't worry, you're not going crazy and *I am* real. My lovely wife, *crazy she calls me* because I always try to help people. Well, I have to go now because we have a very special visitor coming tonight. Now, be here tomorrow so I won't have to come looking for you."

I sat there for about another hour trying to comprehend what had just happened and then I went to the tavern for a strong drink and something to eat. I was sitting enjoying my meal when an elderly gentleman came in and approached the barman saying "Joe, guess who's back in these parts?"

Joe said "How should I know. So many people come and go around here Shamus."

Shamus said "*Dear old Donegal* has been sighted and that means that Earth Angel David and his mates must be here as well. It's been a very long time since they were here; in fact, I think the last time they were here I was courting Mary before she ran off with that sailor."

Joe said hesitantly, "If they are both here, then there is going to be some fun and games going on and I wonder who the person is. If I knew who they were, I'd give them a stiff drink right now."

Shamus said "We'll just have to watch, wait and see but I don't think that we should let it become common knowledge, do you?"

"No." said Joe "we don't want Donegal to get angry with us or we won't get a silent night for the next three months."

I thought it best that I don't tell anyone about my meeting with Donegal and I decided to turn up tomorrow so he wouldn't come looking for me.

I was sitting on the banks of the river when I heard "*Top of the morning to you.* I have thought about what you have told me. Now a few things have come to mind. You were told that your Joanna was heard saying to another man that with all the cancellations she has had, how could he be so cruel; who was she talking about? Who was the other man she was with and *what child is this* or rather I should say, whose child is it?
Do you think that this Joanna could have been married?
Did you listen to the blue eyed man that spoke to you?
Do you want to be in love with someone or do you want to say *I'm thru with love?*
You don't have to answer me now, just think about it and make some enquiries yourself. Because of who and what I am, I know that you are going to Killarney next week and *how can you buy Killarney* Dream Tavern if you don't intend to stay here in Ireland. I will catch up with you next week to find out how you are going."

Donegal asked the questions so quickly and I had trouble understanding him with his accent and before I had the chance to ask him about what I had heard about him and this Earth Angel David, he was gone.

That afternoon, whist sitting in the tavern, I thought about what Donegal had said. Joanna was due in Hawaii next week so I could ring her there and ask her to *let me come home* to her and we could work things out. Had she found someone else because I had left her *alone too long* but I had no way of contacting her without going through her booking agent?

As I went to get up from my table to go and get another drink, two beautiful young ladies walked past and both winked at me and sat down at the table next to mine. One of the young ladies turned to me and said "Hi, my name is Elizabeth and this is my friend Katie. You know, you look like someone who needs some company, so would you like to join us. Tonight *McNamara's Band* will be playing so it will get pretty packed in here."

I got my drink and joined them and we started talking.

Katie asked "*Is it true what they say about Dixie* and how would you *rock-a-bye your baby with a Dixie melody?* "

Elizabeth said "*You must have been a beautiful baby* and a cute little boy as you were growing up because it looks like you still have the *star dust* from the angels in your eyes."

McNamara's Band was completely different to the one here in the States. Their band played all the Irish songs and did a beautiful rendition of *Too-Ra-Loo-Ra-Ral that's an Irish lullaby* that my mother used to sing to me.

Katie kept looking into my eyes and then asked inquisitively "*Did your mother come from Ireland?* "

I replied "My grandmother did but she married a ranch owner from *deep in the heart of Texas*. My mother was born under the *moonlight in Vermont*. My grandparents were making their way back from the local races and it was *twilight on the trail* when my mother came into this world in a hurry. Why do you ask?"

"Because, *when Irish eyes are smiling,* there's a certain look that comes across the face of people.

Would you believe that my father has race horses as well? We have come here for the *Galway Bay* Cup that's on, on Saturday. He has three horses entered; Night and Day, *Thou Swell* and *Waltz For Debby*.

An American comes over every year and brings some horses with him and this year he has brought with him *Deck The Halls, Wild Is Love, My Funny Valentine* and *Just A Gigolo*. I think *Thou Swell* and *Deck The Halls* are in the same race, as are *Waltz For Debby* and *Wild Is Love*. It will be an interesting afternoon. On the Sunday, we go back home to the farm in Killarney." said Katie.

"What a coincidence. I am going to Killarney for a while next week. We might see each other there sometime. I intend to stay for a couple of weeks and then I'll have to go away on business again. I was thinking that *this Christmas* might be just the right year to spend *Christmas in Killarney* but that will depend on my business matters." I told them.

Elizabeth said "Before the races, Katie and I are going bike riding and we would be happy for you to join us."

I laughed and said "I don't think that it's a good idea for me to join you because I never learnt to ride a bike."

"Oh, that's alright." said Elizabeth "we can go for a ride *on a bicycle built for two,* and this way, you can learn to ride without training wheels."

We all laughed and made arrangements to meet on the Saturday morning.

During the ride, Elizabeth and Katie asked me many questions; like what was it like *way down yonder in New Orleans,* and was it true that *where the river Shannon flows* is *where the Morning Glories grow.*

At the races, I met the American horse owner. He told me "*I'm an old cowhand* and learnt about horses while working ranches in my younger days and it's my big winners *I Still Suits Me, Careless Love* and *Nature Boy,* who sired *My Funny Valentine* that have got me where I am today."

Thou Swell won the cup but the *pennies from heaven* came raining down on me when in the last race, the last three horses, *Luck Be A Lady, Lovesville* and *Come By Me* came around the field and finished in that order. I had put a few dollars on those horses as a trifecta.

Katie said "Everybody's had a win today so I know that there is going to be *a hot time in the old town tonight.*"

On the train to Killarney, I thought about the previous day, the bike riding, the races and the good time I had had with both Elizabeth and Katie. But with the thought of Katie, the strange feeling that I had when I first saw Joanna, I was now feeling again. *This can't be love* that I'm feeling for Katie because I'm in love with Joanna, or am I?

Maybe *my foolish heart* was saying *let there be love* and *let's fall in love* with the next *lonely girl* who comes along. *When a woman loves a man,* she would not keep things from him especially contact details if she were to go away for a while. Maybe I'm just thinking *like someone in love* but I'm not in love, maybe it's just an *illusion.*

74

I'll do what Donegal said and then I'll know more of what's going on with Joanna. So over the next week I contacted Joanna's agent who told me that she had her commitments to fulfil in Hawaii and he would pass on my message and get her to contact me. I contacted *Penthouse Serenade* (pronounced Ser-en-ar-dee) who told me that Joanna's agent has cancelled all her overseas bookings. I contacted *Adeste Fideles* and told him what I had just found out and asked him to investigate the matter and find out where Joanna was living.

Then Bob spoke to me and asked me if I would mind being based over that side of the world for about six months as we were going ahead with the Kings brothers in Kiev and there were at least two more properties that he was looking at in Portugal and England. Bob also told me that he was going to hire another person and promote Adeste to handle the affairs of *Perfidia, Serenata* and anything *south of the border*. You know me; *South America, take it away*. That is, if I was willing to stay over in Ireland for a while.

I found this wonderful café down by the river and I went there every day to enjoy the peace and serenity of the town seeing that *I got plenty o' nuttin'* to do at the present time.

On my second day there; two women were sitting at the table next to me, when a third woman with a child sat down with them and said "Something's going to happen around here soon 'cos the wee folk are back in town. When I was out collecting the eggs this morning, an ill wind came blowing through. You know the kind of wind that the wee folk bring with them when they come."

One of the other ladies said "If it's Donegal, then his Angel mate could be with him and if he is, then it will be *anything goes* for the people who are on the *look out for love*."

The first lady who spoke replied "*Isn't it romantic?* But you don't have to be on the *look out for love,* you only have to be *young and foolish* to get the wee folk's attention."

The other lady said "*Speak low* or the wee folk might hear. You only have to be *young at heart* for something to happen. Remember when *me and Mrs. Jones* went to the markets and bumped into *Mr. Santa Claus,* you know the old man living down *Chicago* Lane; the one who in the *early days* had *high hopes* of becoming an actor. Well, he laughed at the wee folk and said that they didn't exist and they taught him a big lesson, didn't they? They took the love of his life away from him and now he says "*I'm the king of broken hearts.*" because he never found love again.

Morgen married an American and moved over there. You know that she's the sister of O'Sullivan who has the Killarney Dream Tavern. Oh, look at the time. I had better go and get a couple of buns, *one* for Danny and *one for my baby* here. See you around soon."

"Is this another coincidental thing that I just heard; my grandmother's name was Morgen O'Sullivan before she married grandfather Bingwell. It must be a coincidence because Mr. O'Sullivan can't be my relative." I thought out loud.

"Why don't you find out?" a little voice said "you never know or learn about important or trivial things unless you ask questions or research for answers."

"Donegal, how did you find me? People suspect that you and your angel friend are around these parts and I have been hearing stories about you and some of the mischief you get up to. Now is it true?" I asked.

Donegal replied "You know how people like to gossip and how it will grow out of all proportions; however, a little bit of it may be true, but don't you worry about that. That last race bought you a few *pennies from heaven,* didn't it? It's surprising what a word or two can do when spoken into the ears of an animal." and he gave a little chuckle and then he continued to say "you know that *crazy little thing called love* can be *the bad and the beautiful.*

The bad side could be, that one person has their *love for sale* and they disappear after a short while, leaving the other person saying *good morning heartache* but the beautiful side is; that *love is the tender trap* that can snare you *anytime, anyday, anywhere* and when it does snare you, you will find that *love and marriage* go together and that true *love is here to stay.*

Now *don't let it go to your head,* but here comes Katie and she has a *fascination* with you. Be careful, *the lady is a tramp.* She'll *let there be love* until you *wrap your troubles in dreams* to dream away and then she'll say *I'm thru with you.* My wonderful wife always says *"You must believe in spring* because this side of the world has a *white Christmas* and its *winter wonderland* is too cold for anything to grow but when *spring is here,* everything new starts to happen and starts to grow." Well, I had better be *gone with the draft* of Guinness in my hand before Katie sees you talking with me."

"Hello there, Bingsie. Who were you talking to?" asked Katie.

"No one." I lied "I must have been talking to myself out loud. Do you have a Library in the town?"

"Yes, but it's only a small one. It mainly covers archives and stuff like that. Why, do you want to go there?" asked Katie.

"Yes, there is some research that I have to do. Would you show me where it is please?" I asked.

"Sure. Do you want to go there now?" asked Katie.

I told her that I did and she took me to the library and showed me around. I also told her that I would catch up with her later down at the tavern. I spent three hours at the library that day and traced my ancestors back in time and it was fascinating reading. I was surprised to find that the tavern owner was my relative but how could I break the news to him. He would think that I wanted something from him.

Another coincidence seemed to be happening because I found out that a cottage that was up for sale just down the road was actually where my grandmother had been born and lived until she married my grandfather. I left the library and found the estate agent and made enquiries about looking over the property with the intentions of purchasing it.

I completely forgot all about meeting Katie and went back to the place I was staying at and sat down that night to work out my finances and future plans.

I knew that I could afford to buy the property and I knew that Bob wanted me to base myself over here, but what about Joanna. Does *the one I love* belong to somebody else or not? With all this confusion going on in my head and heart and now with this new information that I've just found out about, *I can't get started* on anything unless I *straighten up and fly right*. As I stood in front of the agent's door, I said to myself "*From this moment on* it's only going to be *me and my shadow* and Joanna will be a *beautiful friendship* in my past."

I bought the little cottage that day and the best things about it were, it was situated *on the sunny side of the street* and it was also furnished. I contacted Bob and told him about me buying the cottage, so now I was based in Ireland. There was no more information on Joanna or her whereabouts. Bob told me that he had bumped into Lorraine and she hadn't heard from Joanna either.

I was excited that evening because *for once in my life,* I actually had a home, my own place that was *on the sunny side of the street* and not on *the Boulevard Of Broken Dreams. When Joanna loved me, I just found out about love* and what it was like when *taking a chance on love. I've got the world on a string* and I can have *the best of everything,* but no matter what I do or where I go, I *can't buy me love,* not true love. Maybe I've grown accustomed to her face and that's why I can't say *bye, bye baby, goodbye.*

Donegal startled me when he said "*I get a kick out of you,* yep, I really do. *I get a kick out of you* and the way you think and the things you do. Isn't this like the cottage that you stared at once before when you were in the States? Don't *put your dreams away* just yet because they're *too marvelous for words.*

Once I loved this pretty young girl but *one silent night* she said to me "*Shoo shoo baby. Maybe September* I'll sing my *September song* for you." and she walked away. Then when I was passing through here, I met *my kind of girl* and this year it will be one hundred and fifty four years and seven times of the *wee baby blues* since we first heard *the Anniversary song.* We have had our ups and downs, but *in the sweet by and by* you *learn to love* that person more deeply and in a different way. Don't ask me what a different way means because it will depend on who you are and who the other person is. All I know is that between being single and being married, *I like love more,* the love of my wife and kids.

Now have you done anything that I suggested you do since we spoke last time?"

"Yes I have, as you can see. This cottage is where my grandmother grew up and I found out that the owner of the tavern is my grandmother's brother." I replied.

Donegal looked at me, gave a sigh and said "Mickey and Morgen were the youngest two of Martha's eight children. I am pretty proud of what they have achieved in their lives but it was a pity that Morgen moved away from here. The wife's calling me, so I had best be moving but I'll meet you at the café later on today. I suppose you have a lot to do today?"

"I do have a few things to do here first and then I've got to go and get some food and some other supplies and get the phone connected. This place is going to be my home and my office for a while. I'll see you down at the café about lunch time." I told him.

After Donegal left, I rearranged a few of the rooms around, especially the lounge, it was too cluttered for me and I knew that I would fall over or bump into the furniture during the night, if I got up. I made an office in one of the front bedrooms because the sun shone on that room for most of the day. I had all my business done and was at the café at lunch time where I met Donegal and one of his sons, Muldoon and we chatted for a short time about the history and some of the goings on that happened in the town over the past century.

Then Muldoon said "Pa, we had better disappear because *here comes Santa Claus* and Katie and you know how he hates us leprechauns and blames us for ruining his life."

"You're right son; we'll see you again soon, Bingsie and don't forget what I told you about Katie." said Donegal.

Katie and Santa sat down at the table and during the conversation; Santa told me how he got such an unusual name. He told me that his mother had married a Swedish man with the last name of Claus but she also had a *fascination* with American western movies and her favorite being Santé Fe, so she named me Santa Fernando.

I thought about changing my name years ago but it causes a few laughs around Christmas time. *This is always* the way when parents name their children with an unusual name. A few parents don't think about the future and what their children will go through whilst growing up."

Katie said "What happened to you the other evening. You didn't meet me down at the tavern?"

I told her about buying the cottage as a home base for a while but I never told her anything else about the cottage or the other information that I had found out about my heritage. We agreed to meet at the tavern that evening and she left with Santa and I went and did my shopping.

I was really in for a surprise when I got home; I opened my front door to find that all the furniture that I had rearranged was back to where it had been in the first place. Each room was as it was when I first bought the place. I put the food away, made a coffee and sat at the table trying to work out who could have put the rooms back to the way they were. I thought of Donegal but I remembered that he and his son had been talking to me at the café. I decided to rearrange the furniture again before I went to the tavern.

That evening when I met Katie, she had brought her girlfriend Maggie with her. We spent a pleasant evening talking and laughing until the barkeeper called out "*Lights out,* ladies and gentlemen." which meant that the tavern was closing for the evening.

As I said goodnight to the young ladies, Katie whispered in my ear before kissing me on the cheek "I think *I've got a crush on you* and if I had *my way,* I'd like to be with you *night and day.*" She looked at me like *someone in love* and I knew that I had to get out of there real quick or I'd say something that I would later regret.

When I arrived home, the place was still as I had left it. I went into the kitchen and made a sandwich and a cup of coffee and was just about to start eating, when there was a knock on the front door. When I opened the door, no-one was there so I went back to the kitchen to find most of my coffee gone and my sandwich had disappeared.

I decided to go to bed because I felt as if I had just stepped out of a crazy dream. I had just settled into bed, when the phone rang. I wasn't going to answer it but it wouldn't stop ringing so I got up, but when I turned on the lights, they wouldn't work. I went to answer the phone but it wasn't where I had put it, so trying to follow the ringing tone to wherever it was, I fell over the coffee table, walked into a chair and knocked over the magazine rack that in turn knocked over the hat and coat stand scattering its contents all over the floor.

When I finally reached the phone and answered, Bob was on the other end of the line and said "Sorry, did I wake you? I forgot that it's the middle of the night over there."

He asked me if I could go to Madrid because the On The Alamo extension was completed and they would like to officially open the Manhattan Night Lights Restaurant in two weeks. Two days after the opening, could I please fly to Kiev and sign the papers with the Kings Brothers as all the changes had been completed. Ansiedad at the Calypso Blues Bar in Lisbon needs our help to sort out a few small issues and with everything else that had been happening in the past two months, we had forgotten to visit the *St Louis Blues* Club in *Noche De Ronda* in Switzerland.

Bob told me that *it was a very good year* for the *St Louis Blues* Club so there shouldn't be too much to worry about. He said that I should have all the necessary paperwork by the end of the week.

I asked about Joanna, but Bob said that they couldn't find out where she went, who the man was or the child that was with the group. Bob said that he was glad that I was based in Ireland because *you're nearer* to the European offices now and that Adeste was handling both the Americas excellently.

Just as I hung up the phone, all the lights went on and the furniture was back in their original spots again. I thought to myself "This can't be happening. I will have to get Donegal to find out who's responsible and tell them to leave the things as I put them, my grandmother doesn't live here anymore and won't be coming back."

During the following week, there were no more happenings at home, Katie kept her distance down at the tavern but Maggie tried to get closer to me as did Mary but it was Jessica who caught my eye. She walked into the tavern one afternoon wearing a blue dress with a small posy of Edelweiss in her hair but it was those blue *angel eyes* of hers that I noticed first. I thought of the man who had asked for a dime and thought of Joanna. I then began to wonder if this was the person that I was told about and if she was, I would take it *nice 'n' easy* this time.

That night McNamara's Band was playing so I said to Jessica "*Let's face the music and dance.*" and I soon realized that Jessica couldn't dance.

Jessica said "The only time that *I got rhythm,* is when I play *skip to my Lou* with my younger siblings and even then I can be that bad that they tell me to *go tell it to the mountain,* six miles away."

I flew to Madrid and was there for the opening of the Manhattan Night Lights Restaurant and it really did make you feel like you were back in *New York, New York;* in fact, the ambiance of the place was just like *autumn in New York* when the *autumn leaves* stared falling off the trees. It was just like stepping into a place that was built on *a little street where old friends meet* and it was a place that could remind you of *June in January* back home.

I then flew to Kiev and the changes that were made to the Swing Low Sweet Chariot Club were *unbelievable.* The front outside courtyard had a *little Dutch mill* placed in one section and in the other section; it looked like they were preparing for a really *white Christmas.* The inside décor was a mixture of themes from all over the world. Although the *theme from New York, New York* was noticeable, it was intermingled with the *happy holiday* feeling that you would get if you were on the *Isle Of Innisfree.*

You could feel *June in January;* the heat of summer in June with the cold of winter in January. You could also notice that *Christmas is-a comin'* by the way the different rooms were being set up, ready to be decorated.

"There is an extra chill factor in the air and it *looks like a cold, cold winter* is on its way." said Petro Kings.

I said to him with a bit of a smile "If the children here are anything like the children back home, then they would be praying to God to *let it snow, let it snow, let it snow* so that they could get out and *sleigh ride* all day and end up with a *white Christmas.* I can just hear the children in a month's time calling out excitedly "*Santa Claus is coming to town; Santa Claus is coming to town.* We had better start *caroling, caroling* soon."

"In winter and especially around Christmas, Kiev is *my kind of town* because of the children and the way they decorate their sleighs with *silver bells,* the way they *jingle bells* when they are out *caroling, caroling* and the excitement that they show knowing that *Santa Claus is coming to town.* Most children share a pure love, not a *careless love* with their fellow man and they can make you feel *young at heart.*" said Petro.

That night it began to snow and I thought "*Let it snow* for the children." but it was only a brief covering and not enough for the children to have any fun in.

At the airport, I noticed a new poster of an airline stewardess saying "*Come fly with me* and *Out Of This World* Airlines this Christmas."

I caught the plane to Switzerland's Zurich Airport and hired a car and drove sixty six kilometres to Lucerne where I stopped for lunch and then drove the next fifty kilometres to the little town of *Noche De Ronda* which was just over half way between Lucerne and Bern.

I found the *St Louis Blues* Club and sat outside thinking that this is where I was going to propose to Joanna, *when Joanna loved* me and was travelling with me. I pictured her face in my mind and thought "*The memories of you* and the *joy to the world* around me that you brought was *more* than you could imagine. The *touch of your lips,* the way you *put your head on my shoulder* and how you made me feel, made me realize that *you'd be so nice to come home to anytime, anyday, anywhere.* I know that *I'll never smile again* in the way that I did with you and these are the memories that they *can't take that away from me.*

What happened between us, I wish I knew? I guess that it's *too late now* to find out so *I guess I'll hang my tears out to dry*. As many people say, *that's how it goes, that's life* and *she's funny that way. How can you mend a broken heart?* You can't, but you have to *put on a happy face* and carry on with your life. You can only sing the *Beale Street Blues* for so long, but *don't wait too long* to tell yourself the *best is yet to come*."

I only spent three hours at the club so I drove straight back to Zurich and decided to spend the rest of the afternoon and night there. There was one particular bar in Zurich that caught my eye and it was called *Fly Me To The Moon*. They had an unusual way of introducing the entertainment and that was by saying "*Come fly with me* and I will *play a simple melody* for you." I went in and sat down at the bar and was only there for a few minutes when a young lady wearing a small patterned blue dress started walking towards me. As she was getting nearer, I noticed that the dress pattern was really small Edelweiss flowers and that her eyes were an amazing blue color.

The man drinking next to me turned his head and said "Watch out, *the lady is a tramp*. She will offer to take you to the *street of dreams* but she has a *cold, cold heart* and will leave you in the morning *cryin' for the Carolines* sun and *steam heat* to warm you again. *Such love* would even make *little Jack Frost get lost*."

I thought "*When Joanna loved me,* I never had to ask anymore, *where is love* or *what is this thing called love* because she brought it to me and showed me what it was. Now I'm on my own again, it seems that *anywhere I wander,* I seem to be attracting all these women who keep reminding me of her. Wait a minute! This thing with the women has only started happening since I've met Donegal. The stories that I have heard about him must be true. I'll have to have a good talk to him and tell him to stop *that old black magic* or whatever he's doing to me."

After arriving in Lisbon, I went to visit with Ansiedad at the Calypso Blues Bar and we sorted out the issues that he had. Ansiedad asked me if I was in a hurry to leave Lisbon and I replied that I wasn't.

Then he said "I have planned to take the next couple of days off and go to visit a friend who owns the *Bein' Green* Cosy Inn and Motel up at Mt. *Tenderly*."

He asked me if I would like to join him. He told me that his friend, Nick, wanted to sell the Inn and move back home to his parents place because they were elderly and needed him to look after them. He told me that Nick had offered it to him because Nick didn't want the place to change much. Ansiedad thought about Bob and me for buying it if we were interested and that he would be able to manage both properties. He also said *"It was a very good year* last year and the year before at the Calypso Blues and he was confident that the staff he had now would be able to continue running the place well. Just come up with me for the two days and see what you think. *This is all I ask."*

I was only going to go back to Ireland so I decided to go with him. As we were driving up Mt. *Tenderly,* the terrain reminded me of the lyrics of *the song of Raintree County* in the *Blueberry Hill* Territory back home in the States. From the side veranda of the Inn, you could see *all the way* across the valley to the nearest town. It felt like a place that could be *a dreamer's holiday* haven. You could never experience the *next door blues* or be a *stranger in paradise* up there.

As we entered the Inn, I said to Ansiedad "I really like this place. You know, *this could be the start of something big.* Bob did mention to me last time we spoke about owning another place here in Portugal and this would be ideal. The first thing is to find out what Nick has in mind and then the negotiations can start if I feel that we might purchase this establishment. I know that you have grown up here in Portugal, so please tell me more about the history of the area and of the people who live here."

Ansiedad first told me the history of the region and then told me *"Once upon a time, while shepherds watched their flocks* of sheep or herds of goats, they used to play their musical instruments to relieve the boredom and also to make noise warning any predators of their presence. Then as the generations changed, so did the music until the last generation started *pitchin' up a boogie* until the *Pinetop's Boogie Woogie* became popular and that is what you can hear in the background now."

I said "That sounds like *strange music* to me."

Ansiedad looked at me seriously and said *"Because of you* and Mr. White, I have learnt so much about running a business and how to keep building it up, that, if it is possible, I would like to try and manage both places. I know to begin with, it will be a bit hard and I will need to learn time management a bit better but I feel confident in being able to do so."

I listened to the proposal that Nick had to offer and I told him that I would talk to him in about two weeks' time after consulting Bob. I enjoyed being up at the Cosy Inn and was a bit reluctant to leave but I had something personal to work out with Donegal, back in Ireland.

A SECRET UNCOVERED

I flew back to Ireland and I felt peaceful once I spotted my little cottage waiting for me just down the road. I thought to myself "I knew that *you'd be so nice to come home to* and I think that I have finally found *my kind of town* to settle down in for when *the September of my years* come creeping along. I just wished that Joanna was here to greet me." Then *a blossom fell* from the tree that I was walking past and snapped me out of my thoughts and as I drew closer to my place, I could see flowers covering my front yard so I quickened my pace a little.

As I stood at my front gate and looked in, my garden was covered with roses that never usually bloom at that time of year. I saw *the Rose Of Tralee,* in a red shade, surrounded by the *Roses Of Yesterday* to my right and *the Rose Of Tralee,* in a white shade surrounded by *Honeysuckle Rose* to my left. *All the way* along both sides of the path were small bushes of *Honey Hush, Love-wise* and *Lush Life.* The colors in my garden was like being *somewhere over the rainbow* and the fragrance was just wonderful.

I slowly walked up my path to the front door wondering who could have done this beautiful thing for me but when I reached my front door, I instantly knew. I couldn't get in, the lock and door handle were not there; they were gone, they had completely disappeared. As I walked around to the back door, I called out for Donegal because it was something that he and his little wee folk friends would do to me. The back door was the same as the front door, no lock or door handle so I hid my suitcase behind some bushes and headed for the café, calling for Donegal *all the way.*

I reached the café and Donegal was waiting for me. I was a tad angry by the time I reached the café and as I reached Donegal, I said "*When the world was young,* you and your people were accepted for your jokes and the *old black magic* tricks that you played on people, but this time *you did it;* you went too far. I really enjoyed coming home to the roses in my garden but not being able to get into my own home, of *all things,* is another matter. How you managed to remove the locks and door handles from the doors is beyond me.

You and your friends had better put them back and *it had better be tonight* by the latest. *Have I told you lately* that *I've got you under my skin* and *I got it bad and that ain't no good. I'm beginning to see the light* about what the people are saying about you and *you shouldn't do me like you do.* Playing tricks on me and my home is one thing but *the very thought of you* playing with my emotions is another."

85

"Hold on." said Donegal "what do you mean, playing with your emotions?"

My reply to him was "Haven't you been using your *witchcraft* to attract the women with blue eyes and some sort of Edelweiss to me from all over the world?"

"No." said Donegal.

"*It had to be you.*" I said "you're the only one to whom I revealed how I felt *when Joanna loved me* and how I still feel about her. If I had *my way, I'd like to hitch a ride with Santa Claus* just so I could find out where she is and see her for just a moment. Even in Zurich, I was approached by a woman like Joanna but I was warned that *the lady is a tramp,* even so, I wasn't interested in her, so I left."

"*Don't blame me* for that." snapped Donegal "Yes, I do help the *dear lonely hearts* of *the two lonely people* find each other and *I get a kick out of you,* watching as you try to work things out but I work *day in – day out* here in Ireland only. You can blame me for your roses but *don't blame me* for your doors being messed with or your emotional state.

As for the doors, at least nobody could break in. Have you thought that it may be *something you got* that's attracting these women to you? Just think how lucky you are 'cos you can have it *all or nothing at all.* Well, I'll be going now and see if I can find the ones responsible for your doors and get them to rectify the situation."

"Thanks Donegal. I'll go down to the tavern for a while and calm down. *It had better be tonight* that the doors are fixed because it is at my place where I want to sleep and at no-one else's place." I said.

Sue stopped laughing and said "*What a wonderful world* this would be, if any sort of flower blooms *anytime, anyday, anywhere. If I ruled the world,* I think that I would try and find a way to make that happen. I would even pay someone to help me do it."

Danny replied "It would be *nice work if you can get it.* To get flowers to bloom *at your command* would be *too marvelous for words.*"

Sue gave a sigh and said "Yes, it would be good to look out each morning to *where the blue of the night meet the gold of the day* and have nothing but a beautiful colored view with a beautiful fragrance with it; although people with hay fever or other allergies wouldn't think so."

86

Danny looked at his wife and said "*You are my sunshine* every morning." and then he asked me "Do you believe that it is something you have that attracts the women, like Donegal said?"

"*Honestly now, it happens to be me* that you're talking too. Did I believe it? No, not even when I walked into the tavern where the young ladies all shouted out my name and came rushing over to me. I thought that it was great that *everyone is saying hello again* but being surrounded by so many females made me feel uncomfortable.

I think that Paddy, the barkeeper, sensed how I was feeling and told the females to give me a chance to get a drink and catch my breath. He told them to go sit and wait at their table for me. The girls did as he suggested."

Paddy turned to me and said "I've worked here *night and day* for the past ten years, and I have never seen our young females carry on like that before. I have still got a good memory and *I remember you* spending a *white Christmas* here a few years ago, am I right but I can't remember your name."

I introduced myself using my full name and told him that I'm called Bingsie for short.

The look on his face changed and he asked "Haven't you just bought the little cottage down the road that belonged to the O'Sullivan family?"

The look on his face when I told him that I had, would have made you think that it was *the night that heaven fell all the way* to earth and was *sailing down the Chesapeake Bay* to the open sea, leaving only a *handful of stars* and *stardust* behind. He served me my drink and disappeared into another room behind the bar.

Several minutes later, the owner appeared from the back room and motioned me to the bar. He asked me what my full name was again and then he asked me what my grandmother's name was. The look on his face was somewhere between shock and delight when I said Morgen and that I knew that she was his sister.

He invited me to the living quarters out back and said excitedly "I have many questions to ask but how did you find out about me because it is supposed to be a secret? Did Morgen tell you? Do your parents know about me? Look, just *begin the beguine* and tell me your story. Sorry, I'm so excited; I mean start at the beginning and tell me your story of how you found me."

I wasn't sure of what to tell him, especially about meeting Donegal so I didn't mention him and Mickey interrupted me and said "Donegal's been talking to you, hasn't he? *That Sunday, that summer* when Morgen left with her new husband for America, Donegal said to me that *somewhere along the way* and before I pass, I will meet someone like Morgen again and *the more I see you,* the more I see my sister in you.

Now before you continue your story, you must promise me that for the present, no-one must know that we are related except for Paddy, who told me who you were and *the first Noel* O'Shea who is my solicitor. I will have to contact him now that I have found another living relative besides Morgen and your parents, who shouldn't know about me."

I told him about my parents and their *rags to riches* story, about my growing up and the relationship between me and my parents. I told him a little of my business and partnership with Bob and how I was now based in Ireland and I told him about Joanna and how I still felt about her.

Mickey looked at me and said "I know how you feel. *Once I loved* a pretty young lady but one night she came to me and said *"I've been to town* and I met *a fella with an umbrella* at the *Firefly* Theatre and we have *a fine romance* going. *I found a new baby* to spend my *white Christmas* with."

Me and the moon just watched her walk away into the *silent night*. I *lost April* that night but I heard a couple of years later that once they had gone from *rags to riches,* he left her with the *wee baby blues* for a star who was singing in the *Lullaby Of Broadway* show. And as for my pretty young lady; I've heard *the lady is a tramp* now, looking for love both *night and day.*

After I *lost April,* people kept telling me that I'll get over her and *the best is yet to come.* But it never did for me and if you are anything like me, *you'll never find another love* like your first one. *Once in a while,* I wonder what would have happened if I had gone after her on that *silent night.*

A year and a half, after I *lost April,* I ended up marrying Mary and *loves been good to me* for many years. Mary became very ill and passed away *not so long ago.*

In the beginning, our marriage was going well until we had our son; Mickey Jnr. Mary was told that she couldn't have any more children and one night I found her crying under a *blue moon.* It took a while for her to tell me her fears to which I told her "*Oh Mary, don't you weep, nothing ever changes my love for you* and nothing will." It only took *three little words* and a kiss to reassure her that our *love and marriage* was so strong that it would last *only forever* and a day.

Mickey Jnr. was six months old when he caught a virus but he just wouldn't get better and he passed a year later with something to do with his kidneys not working properly. His death devastated us, Mary in particular but *as time goes by* and if your love is strong enough, you support each other through the bad days and you learn to live again.

This tavern became our life saving project. I can't do as much as I used to do and one day, I'll have to sell it. The only thing is that I'm afraid that whoever buys it, will want to knock it down and build one of those big noisy places here. Oh, look at the time. I have kept you here listening to me prattling on instead of you being out there with your lady friends and *jammin' with Lester. I like to riff* with him out there sometimes."

I told Mickey that it was a pleasure talking with him and I hoped that we could do it again soon. Over the next month, I spent more time with Mickey learning more about our family history and I also expanded our business. We purchased the Cosy Inn and Ansiedad was doing a wonderful job in managing both properties; in fact, business at the Cosy Inn was already starting to pick up. I was there for the opening and Ansiedad posted a flyer to Bob that read "*Bing introduces strange music.*" and a note explaining that I was introducing the Pinetop's Boogie Woogie, one of the local songs that the shepherds played.

I investigated a rumour that the *Nice 'N' Easy* Holiday Inn on the Isle of Wight was up for sale and even though it was; I felt that at that time of year, it was not a going prospect. It needed a lot of work to restore it and it couldn't be done quickly. It would be a very nice place to stay during the warmer months but being off the coast of England, the winter weather could cut the place off from supplies for weeks.

While I was there, *I saw three ships* with their *red sails in the sunset* making their way to the protection of Southampton Port. I was also told by some of the locals that the day before had been a really bad *foggy day;* "A real pea souper." said one man.

One afternoon Mickey asked me where I planned to spend Christmas and I replied "I intend to spend *Christmas in Killarney* and maybe have *Christmas dinner, country style* with all the *dear hearts and gentle people* who live around here. I can spend a *white Christmas* anywhere, but when I was here a few years back, *I heard the bells on Christmas Day* and the children shouting "*Here comes Santa Claus, here comes Santa Claus.*"

as they ran to the town square. The townsfolk who walked past me said "*We wish you a merry Christmas.*" and then caught up with the very excited children.

"Aye." said Mickey "*this is always* the case with the little ones and they get more excited with the sound of *silver bells* jingling and the first sight of *Rudolph, the red nosed reindeer.* I know *the best is yet to come* when the children receive their presents and they start to sing *the Christmas song* of the village, for that's *when my heart finds Christmas. I can't help it,* but the children bring *joy to the world* and I *put on a happy face* especially during the *twelve days of Christmas.*

I remember one year when Mary was still with us. We went down to the town square to help decorate the trees with lights but it was too cold to hold the celebrations there, so everyone moved to the Town Hall to *deck the halls* with the *bells of Christmas* and some of the children began *caroling, caroling.*

Mary and I were still at the square when *the little drummer boy,* who was new to the town, wandered up to us and said "Excuse me sir, but *is Christmas only a tree* and *the snowman* this year? My dad told me that *Rudolph, the red nosed reindeer* was sick and that *Santa Claus is coming to town* only if he gets better."

I was taken aback by what this child had said and replied "No, Christmas is not just a tree this year, everyone has gone over to the town hall and *Santa Claus is coming to town* like he always does to bring some gifts that the children have put on their Christmas lists. What is on your list for Santa?"

"I'm *too young* to write a list. Santa only reads a *grown-up Christmas list* and gives you something from that." he said.

I looked down at the little drummer boy and asked "Where are your parents?"

He replied "Daddy is at home, sitting in mammy's *rockin' chair* and mammy left when I was a little boy to visit grandma in heaven and she hasn't come home yet. Before she left, she gave me this drum and said "I won't be *comin' home baby* so be a good boy for daddy. When it's time for you to come to *my blue heaven,* I will *jingle bells* that will say *won't you come home Bill Bailey.* But *when do the bells ring for me* 'cos I want to see my mammy again?"

Mary said to him "You tell me what you want for Christmas and where you live and I'll put you on my Christmas list for Santa Claus."

Bill said excitedly "*Could 'Ja.* I would like to be a bell 'cos *if I were a bell,* my mammy would be able to hear me or a kitten that I could call Cat Ballou to play with because *I get so lonely* at times. Mammy's favorite song was *The Ballad Of Cat Ballou* and daddy plays it all the time. *That's all* I want, but could you ask Santa to bring daddy something to make him smile again. Mammy used to say that *you're never fully dressed without a smile* and I believe her."

Mary said "Now everyone is over in the Town Hall this year, so run along over there and play *your song* and I'll go and finish my list. I hope you *have yourself a merry little Christmas.*"

As Bill went running towards the Town Hall, it began to snow and he called out "*Merry Christmas* to you." and "*let it snow, let it snow, let it snow* so that it will be a *white Christmas.*"

Mary said "*God bless the child* who is a *beautiful dreamer.* May he always stay *young and warm and wonderful.* Now Mr. O'Sullivan, what do you want for Christmas?" There was a long pause before she continued "*Answer me, my love.*"

I took both of her hands in mine, looked her in the eyes and softly said "*All I want for Christmas is you.*"

I never saw much of Mary over the next two days because she spent them baking and shopping. On the third day, she went to Bill Bailey's place to invite the family to the Christmas dinner at the tavern but their place was empty and she assumed that they had moved on.

When she came in to the tavern to inform me that they were gone, Martha Flannigan told Mary that no-one had been living in that property since the previous tenants had moved out five months ago.

The two women sat talking for half of the day and then Martha said to Mary "He sounds like *the littlest angel* to be sent to you and for a reason, but now you have to wait to find out what the reason is. My way of thinking is that love is the thing especially around Christmas. The love of our families, of our fellow man combined with our love and faith in the good lord will never be hidden behind *the shadow of your smile.*

You are a good woman Mary and whenever there's anything happening, good or bad, it's *always you* who is the first to help.

Your Mickey is a good man too; there aren't any *lazy bones* in his body either because most of the time when he's needed, he's there beside you helping."

Mary's reply was "Yes, I'm *lucky to be me* and to have *someone you love,* love you back *just as much as ever* before; even *more* than before Mickey and I got married."

Just as Martha was about to walk out the door to leave, she stopped and turned to me and said "Are you closing early on Saturday and coming to the *Moonlight Serenade* Christmas dance at the Town Hall?"

"Yes." I said.

"Oh good." said Martha "I want to book you in for the *Merry Christmas Polka* now; that is, if it is alright with you Mary."

Mary chuckled and said "It's all right with me just as long as he does *save the last dance for me, the Christmas waltz.*"

Mary looked at me and said "Now *it's beginning to look a lot like Christmas* so I might just finish sprucing up the *O' Christmas tree.*"

After Mary passed, I never put up that *O' fir tree dark* and tall because I don't have time. It's bad enough trying to *get me to the church on time* to sing *God Rest You Merry Gentlemen, Silent Night, Holy Night* and *Hark The Herald Angels Sing.* Mind you the boys' choir usually stands in front of a lovely back drop that is supposed to be *O Little Town Of Bethlehem* and sing *Away In A Manger* and *It Came Upon A Midnight Clear.*

I suppose that you don't go to church. Many of the young ones are always in a hurry to do something or go somewhere that they say "*Think of the time I save* if I don't go to church." but their parents make them go because it is good for both the *body and soul.*"

"*Oh, but I do* go to church, but not as often as I should and I would like to go with you this Christmas if that's alright with you? Now where is this tree of yours and I'll put it up for you. We might as well have a Christmas to remember in a good way." I said.

"Are you sure that you want to do this?" said Mickey.

"Yes, well, where is it?" I replied.

"It's in the back room somewhere *among my souvenirs* and *my favorite things*. *Because of you,* I will have a good Christmas; in fact, *it's beginning to look a lot like Christmas* now and feel like it too. With you around *it's easy to remember* how Christmas should be and I'm beginning to feel *young at heart* again." said Mickey.

As we went into the back room, we heard female voices arguing. One female shouted "Don't shout at me. *You don't know what love is,* you're too *young and foolish* to know; besides your mother always says that you are trouble."

The other female replied "Ok, *what is this thing called love?* Come on, explain it to me. How do you know that I'm not in love with him? At the moment, *the trouble with me is you,* hanging around trying to *steal away* my feller."

The first female said "Your feller. *The very thought of you* being with him makes me feel ill and *the way you look tonight* would frighten a *nature boy* into hiding."

The second female said "A *nature boy* would hibernate if he saw you coming."

Mickey looked at me and said "You go find the tree and I'll go see what all the noise is about."

I found the tree and decorations quite easily, so I put them in the hallway and then proceeded to go out to where Mickey was talking to the females. I heard him say just before I was about to step into view "Katie, Maggie. What are you two arguing about? You're supposed to be friends. So this arguing won't do."

Maggie lowered her voice and said "*Don't blame me.* Katie says that I have *careless love* that would make me look for *anyone to love.* But I don't…"

Katie butted in and said "Oh *willow tree weep for me,* will ya. Maggie, *you don't know what love is* yet. You only have a crush on him and it's *almost like being in love* but wait *until the real thing comes along,* then you'll know what love is. Remember what *Poppa Santa Claus* said after Barney left "*It's easy to remember June in January. Taking a chance on love* when you are both *strangers in the night* is not the wisest thing to do. You have to get to know a person as a friend first and be really sure before you tell yourself *let's fall in love.*"

Ask Mr. O'Sullivan if I'm not right or *ask anyone in love* if they never knew much about the other person they are in love with. Please listen to me, *this is all I ask*."

Mickey said "*If I may* say *a few last words* before we all go inside, *if love ain't there* for both of you, then *come rain or come shine* your relationship won't last. Now come on inside and have a drink, calm down and *put on a happy face* before he sees you. Whoever he is?"

The girls went into the tavern and Mickey came back to me and said "*Because of you,* Maggie is having *a thousand thoughts of you* with hopes that *let there be love* at the end of each thought. I don't know what it is about you, but most of the young ladies, well, *they long to be close to you.*

If my memory serves me right; many years ago, one of *our old home team* mates had the same thing happen to him before he joined the army. Before taking to the field, he used to say jokingly "Today let *luck be a lady*." and at the end of the last match of the season, he beating off the women and I think he joined the army to get away from them. We were bottom of the ladder again that year."

I replied "*This morning* it was just like any other day but *I see it now* as becoming a problem. I need to go home for a while and think about how I am going to sort this mess out. *I'll be seeing you* later this evening or tomorrow. I'll put the tree and decorations up tomorrow."

I was sitting at my kitchen table pondering over the situation over a coffee when I heard "He, he, he. *I get a kick out of you,* yes, I really do. You have got yourself into a right mess, haven't you? Now, how are you going to get out of it?" asked Donegal.

"It's not how am I going to get out of it, but how are you going to get me out of it. Even though you deny it, I still say that *it had to be you* who started all this female stuff or one of your wee folk friends." I replied.

Donegal defiantly said "It wasn't me or one of my friends."

Then I heard "*I get a kick out of you,* Donegal Doughty. I watch the way you try and worm your way out of some situations. *I get a kick out of you* too Bingsie because when you don't know what to do, you ask Donegal."

I looked down to see a small female standing next to Muldoon by the stove.

Donegal said "Oh, hello dear. Bingsie, this is my good wife Geraldine. What brings you here my dear?"

Geraldine replied "The solution to part of his situation. Tomorrow Bingsie, you go to the tavern and set the tree up and decorate the *Rose Room* for the Christmas festivities. Find the girls and get them to help you with the decorations and during the course of the day and in a *tenderly* manner, tell them about your Joanna, how you still feel about her and explain that at present you *ain't misbehavin'* with anyone because it is too soon. Arrange for *Alexander's Ragtime Band* to come here for New Year's Eve and make sure that each female is invited for the evening by saying "*Let's start the New Year right* together as friends. There isn't any reason to stop us from enjoying each other's company."

I replied "What room are you talking about. I have never seen any other rooms at the tavern except for the one out back?"

Geraldine said "Tell Mickey to *look back in your own back yard* and to remember *the days of wine and roses* in *September in the rain* and *the shadow waltz. For sentimental reasons, now is the hour* to put out the *two cigarettes in the dark* and *when the red, red robin comes bob, bob bobbin' along, let's face the music and dance.* Also tell him that *Babs* has finished *Bidin' my time.*

I know that both you and Donegal won't know what I'm talking about but he will. You will find a new adventure and investment tomorrow but it will be in the New Year that you will embark on this new project and it will make Mickey very happy.

Bingsie, now that you are sorted, Donegal, I have to sort you out but not here, so come on home. Bingsie, we do not know who is playing with your emotions, but I have a fair idea who is responsible and it may take a few more months to get it sorted out. So I suggest that with all these females, you try not to be *alone together* for too long; however, I now know why *they long to be close to you. You make me feel so young* just with *the way you look tonight.*"

"Geraldine!" said Donegal "I've never heard you talk like this before. *The very thought of you* thinking like that about someone else after all these years, especially this human, worries me."

Geraldine said "Oh Donegal, don't worry, *you're getting to be a habit with me.* There is *nobody like you to me* and you know that *I only have eyes for you,* but, sometimes *you go to my head* and make me so mad. But *last night when we were young,* and with *the touch of your lips,* I realized

95

again why *I'll be around* for a long time to come. *You do something to me* and now *I'm in the mood for love. I've got you under my skin* and I know that *the best is yet to come* once the children have left home."

She looked up at me and said "Now will you excuse us please, we have some people to meet up near Limerick."

Donegal looked at me and whispered "This is why *I like love more* and *they can't take that away from me.*"

The following day, I went to the tavern and talked to Mickey about the Rose Room that Geraldine had mentioned and I also gave him the message from her. Mickey told me about all the functions that they had held there. It didn't take much talking on my part to get him to agree to open the room up again for the Christmas and New Year period.

I found the girls who were more than willing to help me decorate the room. I found out that *Alexander's Ragtime Band* was playing in Cork, so I went there to arrange for them to play on New Year's Eve if they weren't booked already. I booked them and the *Basin Street Blues* Band as well.

On the way back and travelling down *Route 66,* I noticed how beautiful the countryside was, the Killarney National Park, that had the township parked at its base and the many people riding bicycles and all those things gave me a few ideas and some projects to discuss with Mickey and if he was keen enough, some work for me in the coming year. I could do all this when I wasn't doing my other job with Bob. Even though I had all this on my mind, I still missed Joanna and wished that she was here with me now. I know now how my mother felt when she kept writing and asking "*Baby, won't you please come home* for Christmas."

I still don't know if *the one I love belongs to somebody else* besides *I've got you under my skin* still, even though you're not here.

As we got nearer to Killarney, I thought "Killarney, *the more I see you* and the townsfolk, the more I know that *you're my kind of town* and that *I'll never be the same* if I ever left you for good. This is now my *paradise* and *they can't take that away from me.*"

It was later that evening when I talked to Bob about my plans for Killarney and the tavern for the coming year. I asked him if he had any objections, if I used my own *pennies from heaven* to do it. I told him that I will still be a base for our business and continue working with him.

He replied sleepily "No, I have no objections to what you want to do and if you need any help, you only have to ask. *You're nearer* to all our European properties but they never need your full attention anyway."

After talking with Bob, I thought "Now, *who can I turn to,* to help me with the different projects next year? I know, I'll talk to the girls and if they would like to work for me. I'll train them in the different areas of the businesses and hopefully this *fascination* that they have for me will change."

It was mid-afternoon when I met the girls and put my proposal to them and they happily agreed to work for me. I spoke to them individually to find out what skills that each one had so that I could give them the job that suited them best. It was during one of these sessions that Maggie shyly said "I don't know how I'm going to be able to do it because *I've got a crush on you* and whenever I'm *near you,* I just want to say *let's fall in love.*"

I looked at her and softly said "*If I give my heart to you,* it wouldn't be fair on the other girls but I can't give all my heart to anyone because Joanna still has a part of it and that wouldn't be fair to the other person or me. I'm glad that you have been honest with me and I still would like you to work for me. *How about you,* would you still like to work for me even though *my need for you* would only be as your employer and friend?"

Having sorted Maggie out and with her agreeing to work for me, I again spoke to all the girls together and asked them not to mention my plans to anyone until I tell them to.

Jessica said "*Can't we tell* our families because mine are already asking me why I'm not home as much anymore."

I told them "Tell your families that you are helping Mickey and me to get this place ready for a special *white Christmas.* Your parents already know that Mickey is unable to do it on his own, so that should stop the questions being asked. You are going to have to *teach me tonight,* the *Christmas song* of your town.

I am really glad that you girls have decided to join me in these projects for *if you said no,* then I would have had to start advertising all over Ireland. At least each of these projects can start off as a local community project and next year, I will need to involve more of the townsfolk that you know.

Come on, I'll buy you all a drink and then I'll have to go and talk to

Mickey about some of my ideas and find out what he wants to do about Christmas Day and trading."

Mickey told me the hours he traded that were set down by the Liquor Trading Policies and said that if I wished to trade after these hours, I would need to get him to apply for extra trading hour's extension.

The girls surprised me one morning as they had all got together to decorate one corner of the Rose Room, nearest to the open door with their own version of a Nativity scene. They had built a shelter out of old boxes, pieces of timber and material and in it they had placed *a cradle in Bethlehem*. Above the cradle, they had placed some stars and they had an angel *swinging on a star* and amongst the stars, they had placed a moon. Although *it's only a paper moon,* you would think that they would have had a *blue moon* but *the moon was yellow*.

They had a fan blowing softly on the stars and they told me that it was supposed to be the *summer wind* blowing gently towards heaven and in turn, that would cause the angel to move and *jingle bells* to herald the arrival of Jesus. Katie had brought some straw from home to place on the floor around the cradle but also to hide the surprise for me under.

She said "Listen closely."

I was surprised to hear all sorts of Christmas music coming from somewhere in the room, like *God Rest You Merry Gentlemen, Away In A Manger* and *the Christmas Song* of the village before it became a town.

Out of all the four girls, Mary was the quiet one and she said "When we turn it on, we can leave it to keep playing until we turn it off."

I inquisitively looked at her and asked "*How do you keep the music playing* without touching it?"

Mary replied "It is a self-winding tape recorder. When one side has finished playing, it automatically starts playing the other side. Once you push the repeat button down, it will just play continuously until you stop it."

The girls and I were startled by the sound of Mickey's voice saying "Oh my, *it's beginning to look a lot like Christmas* in here now in more ways than one. It has just started snowing outside, so we should have a decent *white Christmas* as well. Bingsie, you and the girls have done an excellent job of decorating this room but what does that sign say that is leaning against the cradle?"

We all turned to see Mickey standing in the doorway beside another elderly gentleman. As Mary went over to get the sign, Mickey said "Bingsie, I would like you to meet *the first Noel* O'Shea, my solicitor."

The first Noel said "I was born Noel O'Shea but when my son was born, he was named Noel Jnr, and when his wife gave birth to a son, they named him Noel as well. So I am called *the first Noel,* my son is Noel Jnr and my grandson is known as Noel Patrick. I hope that when he has children, they will be all girls."

Mary came back with the sign which read "The Lord says *that you'll never find another love like mine* on this *O Holy night.*"

Mickey handed me a handmade banner and asked me to carefully hang it somewhere safe. Evidently, Mary, his late wife had embroidered "*Have yourself a merry little Christmas.*" on it, but he kept it safely tucked away from all the other decorations.

Mickey said "Girls, *all these things* that you have done for me in the past few days, have got me *feeling good;* better than I have been all year but can I ask you one question, *how do you keep the music playing?*"

I said "I'll explain it to you later. We have finished in here now and I was just about to buy these lovely young ladies a drink."

Mickey said "*Five minutes more* before *lights out,* so Bingsie, could you please come out back before you go home. There are some things that I would like to discuss with you and Noel."

Mickey was sitting by the fire in his favorite chair when I walked into the living room. He motioned me to sit down as he started talking "Bingsie, now as you know, I *don't get around much anymore* but I hear a great deal of news and gossip. When you arrived here in *our town,* no-one really took much notice, except for a couple of our young ladies, but when you purchased our little cottage so quickly, I became suspicious and asked Noel to investigate you. When we spoke and you knew about me being related to Morgen, I couldn't believe it.

I know all about you and the way your company with Bob operates and I'm quite impressed. Last year, *Joe Turner's Blues* Corporation approached me with an offer to buy this place and I turned it down. I have been watching you closely and *I get a kick out of you* as you try to and do handle situations successfully. The message that you brought me from Geraldine confirmed what Noel had told me.

I pray on Christmas Day each year that I will survive another year here so I don't have to sell out to *Joe Turner's Blues* Corporation.

Noel and I have been talking and we have come up with an idea that I would like to put to you now. If *I concentrate on you* now, *the very thought of you* and me running this place together is viable. *The more I see you* and what you have done to the Rose Room, with the help of the girls, makes me feel confident of my decision.

Next year, I would like to make one of my dreams come true; *it's the same old dream* that I had when Mary was alive, I want to do a bit of travelling. Oh, I don't want you to give up your business with Bob and *I'll be around* to take over when you have to go away or Paddy would manage this place well if we are both away. *You do something to me, you make me feel so young* and *because of you, I'll never be the same. You're nearer to me* than anyone else I know so like I said before, if *I concentrate on you* and teach you *my way* of running this place, you will inherit this place when I pass on, *it's the natural thing to do.*

For once in my life, I feel so *young at heart* but *with every breath I take,* more so climbing stairs, I feel my current age in both my *body and soul.* Now, don't answer me straight away. Think about it and let me know of your decision in a couple of days. *This is all I ask.*"

FAMILY LOVE

Over the next week, Mickey, *the first Noel* and I were busy gathering all the paperwork necessary for me to become an Irish citizen. I was lucky because I could have dual citizenship, which meant that I could keep my American citizenship as well. Papers were drawn up to make me sole heir to all of Mickey's fortune and Mickey notified his sister, Morgen, of all his plans.

Morgen's reply to Mickey was "*After you've gone,* he will carry on your business *exactly like you* have. *For all we know,* he will even make it better. I am so happy to know that *that's my home* that he purchased and is living in. You know that Killarney will always be *my kind of town* but *my one sin* was that because of our secret, I could never come back, not even for a holiday."

One morning, Katie came rushing into the tavern very excited because one of her mares, *Maybe September,* had just had a foal and she named it, *September Song.* She said that he was a beautiful colt and hoped that, *with a little bit of luck,* he would follow in the lineage of his sire, *Without A Song* and his sire *Nature Boy* and win many races for her.

Mary came in looking sad, just after Katie had left and when I asked her what was wrong she said "I maybe *young and foolish* and you can *blame it on my youth* but *I've got you under my skin* still; however, I realized in *my sweet hour of prayer,* that *if I give my heart to you* then *my foolish heart* will always have the *yellow dog blues.*"

I took her into the Rose Room and sat her down and said "*Oh Mary don't you weep. This can't be love* that you are feeling because I feel that *it's magic* being put on you by Donegal and his mates. *You must believe in spring* and that the Leprechauns get their *kicks* out of setting a *lonely girl* up for a trip to *Lovesville,* only to find it wasn't the real thing after all. You know what those wee folk can get up to better than I do.

When the world was young, the wee folk would have you *swinging on a star* and they would be able to get away with it. Now, too many people are aware when they are around and what they can get up to. *I wish I knew* how to counteract their magic, but I don't, so *let's spring one* on them. *The night has a thousand eyes,* so let them see us as friends at night and me as your boss during the day. Will you give it a try? *This is all I ask.*"

Mary looked at me and said "I think you may be right.

This can't be love because I've only been *dream dancing* since the Leprechauns have come back to this part of Ireland. *Yes we can, can* be friends and work colleagues at the same time and *you can depend on me* to lose *these foolish things* going around in my head and the misplaced feelings."

I then said to her "Don't hide behind *the shadow of your smile* because *the best is yet to come* for you. Now, have you heard about Katie's new colt, *September Song?* I think that you had better dry your eyes and go find her because she is so excited."

"Thank you." she said *"you showed me the way* that has stopped me from making a fool of myself. Katie did try to tell me but I didn't want to listen to her."

As Mary walked out the door, a stranger walked in and sat down at the bar and said to Mickey "Dia dhuit. (Hello) An bhfuil Gaeilge agat? (Do you speak Irish)?"

Mickey replied "Yes, an feidir liom cabhru leat. (May I help you)? Cad bo mhait leat. (What would you like)? Au maith leat fion, beoir, tae (Do you like wine, beer, tea)?"

The stranger said "B'fhearr liom liomanaid. (I would prefer lemonade)" and started looking around the tavern.

Mickey gave the man his drink and said "An bhfuil tu ag lorg duine eigin. (Are you looking for someone)? Cad is ainm duit, le do thoil. (What is your name, please)?"

The stranger said "Sean is ainm dom. (Sean is my name)" and as he picked up his drink, he said 'Slainte (Cheers). An bhfuil clan agat. (Do you have a family)?"

Mickey replied "Is baolach (unfortunately) only mo deirfiur (my sister) and my deirfiur's garmhac (my sister's grandson)" and he pointed to me.

Sean looked at me and asked "Ceas tu (Where are you from)?"

Mickey replied "Ta se as America (He is from America)."

Sean took a mouthful of his drink, looked at Mickey and then back at me before saying "Ni dhiolann dearmad fiacha. Nil aon tintean mar do thintean fein. Is folamh fuar e teach gan bean. De reir a cheile a thogtar na caisleain. A bean ar do mhian agat is a bean mo chroi. An rud a lionas an tsuil lionann se an croi and nil aon leigheas ar an ngra ach posadh.

Thar gach ni eile, cuimhnigh I gconai, cha d'dhuin doras nach d'fhosgail doras."

He then turned to Mickey and said "Maireann croi eadrom I bhfad. Rinn tue. Ni neart og cur le cheile. Is maith an scanthan suilcharad. Cuimhnigh I gconai, eist moran agus can beagan."

Mickey replied "Gahn mo leithscaal, ni thuigim."

Sean got up and walked to the door saying "Siochan leat. Slan agus beannacht leat."

All Mickey could say was "Tapadh leat (Thank you)."

As Sean passed through the door, I heard "You will go back to *America the beautiful* where you will be given *just one more chance* at *taking a chance on love* with the *gal that got away.* You can have it *all or nothing at all. Somewhere along the way,* I don't know *where or when,* the *two strangers in the night* will be *in love again.* This time you will know *what is this thing called love* and the *second time around* will be better. Please, *have yourself a merry little Christmas* and a *happy New Year* with your new family."

I recognized the voice as the man who once asked "*Brother can you spare a dime.*" and I hurried outside to ask him to explain himself, but he was gone; just like last time, he had disappeared. I went back inside to talk to Mickey, but before I could say anything, Mickey handed me a stiff drink and said "I think you had better sit down while I tell you what he said. It doesn't make sense to me but *here goes.*

To you he said "A debt is still unpaid, even if forgotten. There is no hearth like your own hearth. It is a cold house without a woman. It takes time to build castles. A wife of your choice to you is a woman of my heart. What fills the eye fills the heart and the only cure for love is marriage. Above all else, always remember, no door closed without another opening."

Then he said to me "A light heart lives longest. You did it. There is no strength without unity. A friend's eye is a good mirror. Always remember, hear much and say little."

My reply to what he said was "Excuse me, I don't understand." but all he answered was "Peace be with you. Goodbye and blessings on you." I have never had anyone like him come in here before."

I told Mickey to get himself a stiff drink before I told him what I had heard and my encounter with the man before.

When I arrived home that night, I found two *love letters* in my mail box and Geraldine waiting for me. The letters were from two different women and were unsigned.

Geraldine said, "Even though *I get a kick out of you* for the way you handle situations, *you go to my head* and *you leave me breathless. You're getting to be a habit with me* because *you make me feel so young* whenever I am *near you. Sometimes I'm happy* with my life but at *some other time;* especially when Donegal says *"Don't fence me in,* woman." *I wonder* if *the best is yet to come. The more I see you,* the more *I wish I were in love again. My romance* with Donegal is fading away."

I looked at Geraldine and said "You always say, *you must believe in spring* and *once in a while,* you have to *wrap your troubles in dreams and dream your troubles away.* I think that you have been caught up in the magic or spell that has been either placed on me or the women I come in contact with. Didn't you say that you thought you knew who was responsible for it?"

Geraldine thought for a moment and then replied "Yes, I thought it was Earth Angel David who was responsible but he wouldn't do that to me."

I looked down at her and asked "Are you sure? *You're nearer* to him to know what he'll do and who he'll do it to."

Donegal appeared *just in time* and surprisingly said "Geraldine, I went looking for you *down by the river* and was still looking for you when I decided to drop in on Bingsie while I was passing. I never expected to find you here.

Bingsie, I ran into David earlier and he told me what he had done but it was not him who put the spell on you or the women you come in contact with. He is going to find whoever is responsible and get them to remove it."

Donegal looked at his wife as if he had heard her conversation with me and said "I know *who's sorry now* for the way that I have behaved. I thought that *wild is love* but I was wrong. *You don't know what love is* until you nearly lose it. *When your lover has gone, empty is* the heart until you realize *how insensitive* you have been and want to make amends. I don't want to be *strangers in the night* with you, I still want to *let there be love* between us.

104

Please *don't take your love from me* or the young ones. How will you get along without us?"

Geraldine looked at Donegal and replied "*I get along without you very well* thank you. You think that *because you're mine,* I have to think of you as my *magnificent obsession* and think how I should be *lucky to be me* to be married to you while you go out drinking and playing around with *Miss Thing* or any of the ladies from the *Lullaby Of Broadway* Club.

When we got married over a century and a half ago, I thought we had a *sure thing* going, I thought that after our last anniversary that *that's a plenty* of time for you to have settled down, but when you keep telling me "*Don't fence me in.*" then I feel that *the party's over* between us. There are no *hidden persuasions* behind my love for you."

Donegal quietly said "I know that *I'm never satisfied* with what I have but *you are the sunshine of my life* and *when Irish eyes are smiling* at me, *I surrender, dear* and pray that *you'll never get away from me. Baby, won't you please come home, I'm lost* without you and so are the children."

I said to both of them "Now listen to me, both of you. Many *beautiful moons* ago you said to each other, *let's fall in love* and you did. You worked on your love and marriage both *night and day* and you could say on any cold day "*I've got my love to keep me warm.*" but listen and look at both of you, you're ready to start *the birth of the blues* for your family. You both admit *the best is yet to come* for the pair of you once your children have left home.

You also know that *it's only a paper moon* outside because of the magic that has affected all of us. Nothing ever runs smoothly especially with *love in bloom.* You both know that your *love is here to stay* so the ups and downs in life are *just one of those things* sent to make us stronger. You know *that's life* and *she's funny that way.*"

Geraldine looked at me and said "You're right you know." and then she looked at Donegal and said "*Forgive my heart, the moon got in my eyes* and I do love you but *what now my love,* where do we go from here?"

Donegal took her hand and *tenderly* said "Home, where you belong. *You're mine, you* beautiful woman and *you'll never get away from me* again. *What can I say after I say I'm sorry except the party's over* for me and my other life? I want you to know that I'm proud to be *walking my baby back home.* Come on; let's go home, *I'm in the mood for love;* how about you?"

Geraldine looked at me and said "Wait till I get my hands on David and his mates. They'll need *some travelling music* to take with them to the place I'll be sending them and it won't be to *where the blue of the night meets the gold of the day.*"

After they had gone, *all of me* just wanted to relax and enjoy the peace of a *silent night;* however, that wasn't to be; Bob rang to ask if in the New Year, I could visit the Cosy Inn and see how Ansiedad was handling his dual role as manager of both properties. He said he knew that being Christmas, travel plans would have to be made early. He also said that "*I'll be home for Christmas* but I'm going to spend a few days in the New Year in Miami." and from all the staff, *we wish you a merry Christmas* and a happy New Year."

My reply to Bob was "The same to you. *I'd like to hitch a ride with Santa Claus,* just so I could visit all my loved ones and friends without them knowing. Yes, I'll arrange with Ansiedad to visit him in January."

I sat down and read the letters that I had found in my mail box and I had to laugh to myself as I read "*This is my night to dream* of your *luscious* love. *You fly me to the moon* every time I see *the shadow of your smile.* But *when you're smiling,* and *the way you look tonight,* it makes me believe that *you'd be so easy to love* on *Sunday, Monday or always.* I know that *when my sugar walks down the street,* he's going to a place where the *Beale Street blues* will disappear.

Walking *on the street where you live* and *making believe you're here* walking with me, wants me to find *what is this thing called love* all about. I know that it's just my *imagination* that makes me pretend that we'll be together, but *I can dream, can't I?* You could put love *in the heart of Jane Doe* very easily but we all know that your love is for someone else at the moment, but *where is the one* who has your heart?"

I was late getting down to the tavern the following day because I needed time to try and work my feelings and situation out. At the tavern, the girls were putting their finishing touches to the room.

There was *laughing on the outside* of the tavern as several excited children were running in front of their parents calling out "*Santa Claus is coming to town, Santa Claus is coming to town.* Hey Uncle Thomas, *Santa Claus is coming to town* in two days." In the background, behind the voices of the excited children, sleigh bells could be heard and they sounded just like a *sleigh bell serenade* that a person could do the *Christmas waltz* to.

106

Mickey was discussing the coming Christmas Day mass with Paddy and how they hoped that young Dave would be over his cold so that he could still take the lead vocals in the choir when they sang *God Rest Ye Merry Gentlemen* and *O Little Town Of Bethlehem* because he had such a strong *but beautiful* voice.

I noticed that a double photo frame had been placed near the cash register in a position that it could be seen but it was also partially hidden from the public's view. In *one* side of the frame was a photo of a beautiful woman whom I guessed to be Mary and placed in the other side was a poem, named The Lord's Message. The message read:

God rest ye merry gentlemen
In O little town of Bethlehem
Be Christmas dreaming this silent night
And peace be with you on this O holy night

For I am love and I raise my hand
My love is always at your command
Today a child is born and in him is all of me
I've gone from rags to riches for my sentimental baby

Tender is the night in my shining hour
Only forever will my love grow like a flower
With the faith of our fathers, we'll go all the way
But remember you're all I want for Christmas Day

Mickey saw me reading it and came over and said "My Mary wrote that one year and when she gave it to me she just said *merry Christmas.* Neither of us knew that it would be two years later that she would pass over. The doctors told us that she would live until *maybe September* but I prayed that *if love is good to me,* she would live to see another Christmas with me. The good Lord did grant me that Christmas and a few months more. I can still hear Mary's last words to me when I look at her photo and they were "*Softly as I leave you,* I have no regrets on how my life has been. *I hadn't anyone till you* came along so please always remember *faith can move mountains for you, for me for evermore.*"

She closed her eyes and she went off with the angels to heaven, just like she said she would. I *lost that Christmas feeling* after she passed.

I thought "*It's beginning to look like Christmas* now and it's feeling like it too."

107

In the following few days the tavern grew busier and busier and Christmas Day was the busiest of all. I think that nearly half the townsfolk either came in for a drink or had their Christmas lunch in the Rose Room and enjoyed themselves. In the evening, Mickey made a small speech thanking everyone for coming and he ended with *I wish you a merry Christmas* and then a few local musicians got together and had the patrons singing their *Christmas song* and their own version of a *White Christmas,* which was quite hilarious.

The best part about Christmas Day was when I saw Mickey laughing and singing with all the other townsfolk. I heard him ask one person *"What child is this?"* and then say "Oh, that one. Isn't he the one who married *the girl from Ipanema* and moved to the *Christmas Island* hoping to have a *white Christmas* there?"

That caused a bit more laughter amongst the group and even more laughter rang out when someone else said "Yes, he'll be saying *let it snow, let it snow, let it snow,* forever because he's living in the sun near the Equator."

I looked over to Katie and Mary who were sitting with some friends and I heard Katie say to one of the young men who were with them *"September Song* will win the one year old stakes next year and your horse, *Lean Baby,* will not be able to keep up with him."

Paddy was talking with Jessica and her father, who was commenting on how nice it was to have the room open again, even if it was only for the Christmas period and how many people used to enjoy coming down on the weekend, especially on a *Saturday night.*

Jessica said *"While we're young,* we need to be able to go to places for entertainment that is not too far from home, like you were able to. *Wouldn't it be lovely* if Mickey would allow us to hold a young person's evening here once a month and bring in the *Basin Street Blues* Band with *Lazy Laura."*

Now that has given me an idea to put to Mickey. If he's doing *nothin' new for New Year,* then I will suggest that he *come fly with me* to Portugal when I go to visit the Cosy Inn. I will be able to show him what Bob and I do in our business and how we try and keep each property as they should be. Cosy Inn would be a good place to see because they have a *white Christmas* there like they do here but when *spring is here* I'll be able to bring in more travellers because of the new projects the girls and I are working on.

I think that he would enjoy the break and this will be his first trip that he's been wanting to do for so long. I also think that he would listen to my ideas and want to help us to get started. It would also be a good idea to involve Noel as he would be our legal representative.

When the evening had ended and the tavern was closed, Mickey and I went into his lounge room to find a few presents there for both of us. I gave Mickey the present that I had bought him, a writing set, but there was another present there for him and it was just signed from *Santa Claus*. He opened it to find a brand new camera and a note saying "To remember all the places that you will visit in the coming years." Mickey said "With these gifts *I could write a book* on my holidays."

I also had an extra present from Santa Claus and mine was a painting. In it *I saw three ships* with their *red sails in the sunset* of an *orange colored sky* and the note read "To remind you of your honeymoon." The other present, that Mickey gave me, was keys and half ownership in the tavern.

I went home and found a couple more presents and three letters and two cards there on my kitchen table. One letter was from my mother saying that both her and my father was doing well and she had wished that I had written her saying that *I'll be home for Christmas*. The second one was from Bob with all the paperwork on a new property, in *Swanee,* South Carolina, that he would like to invest in during the early part of the coming year and the third letter was from Lorraine.

I put Lorraine's to one side to read later and I opened the cards that were from *Adeste Fideles* and his family and Donegal and his family. I knew what was in one present as it is hard to disguise a bottle of alcohol and the other present was from Lorraine.

I opened the present and found a photo of Joanna smiling back at me. I opened the letter from Lorraine and she said that she had seen but was unable to talk to Joanna and that I might appreciate the photo that was taken at a charity day concert at *Blueberry Hill,* two years ago. She also said that Bob had been in contact with her and was now getting involved with the *Send In The Clowns* Charity. They were also becoming close friends as well.

Over the week leading up to New Year's Eve, I noticed a change in Mickey; he seemed to be a lot happier, just like he had been given a new lease of life and other people noticed as well and were commenting on it.

Mickey had applied and was granted an extended trading hour's license for New Year's Eve and *Alexander's Ragtime Band* came and played for us, however, the other band for the younger people were unable to attend. Mickey surprised everyone by getting up with *Annabelle* Fitzsimons to dance the *Sweetheart Waltz* with her. I was also surprised to see hiding in a corner, Donegal and his family who had come to join in the celebrations.

I carefully went over to them to wish them a happy New Year and Geraldine said "*I get a kick out of you* at the way you handle situations but I really appreciate the way you handled our situation. *Love is the tender trap* that we all fall in to at some stage of our lives and you were right when you said that you have to work on it both *night and day*. Oh, look at that, *the song is ended* but the little ones are still ringing their *silver bells*. Oh by the way, with *the way you look tonight, you're sensational*."

Donegal said "You were right. I do have *the best of everything* at the moment and *I've got my love to keep me warm. The best is yet to come* and we'll be over tomorrow to help you drink that bottle of whiskey."

Jessica looked towards me with an inquisitive look on her face, so I said goodbye to Donegal and his family and walked over to Jessica's table. As I approached I heard a female say "*What child is this?*" and Jessica asked who I was talking to. "No one." I lied.

Then Jessica said "Mammy has just told us about a little girl, *Tina,* who lives *on the street where you live,* who has just been admitted to hospital in a serious condition. Evidently, it looks like she may be suffering from some sort of renal failure due to her kidneys not working. She may have to be rushed to Belfast Hospital for specialist treatment. You know there are a lot of children here in Ireland who suffers from Kidney diseases and we have to rely on overseas help in the research field. I wish that we could do something to help."

I looked at Jessica and said "Maybe we can. Just leave it with me and I'll have a talk with someone I know. It may take me a week or more but I'll get back to you but don't say anything to anyone just yet."

"*Can't we tell* mammy, she might be able to help as well?" asked Jessica.

"Not at the moment, I wouldn't want to say or do anything *till* I have all the facts right." I told Jessica.

I was really busy over the next week contacting Ansiedad and making arrangements to visit him during January. I contacted Lorraine and asked her to send me enough information to start another branch of her fund raising charity here in Ireland and suggested that we call it *Over The Rainbow*. I had Noel finding out the legalities of starting Over The Rainbow Charity in Ireland. I asked Jessica to research as much as she could on how many people suffered from kidney diseases in Ireland and if there was information on the types of diseases.

Katie was still ecstatic over *September Song* and was gathering information for me as to where and from whom I may hire horses from, for tourists to go on trail rides to see the local country side. Maggie had just returned from her holiday overseas and was busy gathering information on where and from whom we could buy bicycles from, especially bicycles built for two so we could start a bicycle hiring business also for tourists. Mary, funnily enough became my secretary.

She said to me one day "After all what has happened and the way I felt about you in the past few months, *you're nearer* to me now and I don't feel that way about you anymore. I like being your secretary but you do keep me really busy."

I asked Mickey to *come fly with me* to Portugal so that he could see first-hand the different styles of establishments that Bob and I owned and he could also speak to the staff of each place if he had any questions that he needed answers to. Mickey was excited to be travelling and had to arrange to get his passport.

Paddy was asked if he would like to become like an assistant manager of the tavern which meant a few more hours, a little bit more of responsibility and a reasonable pay rise. He jumped at the chance.

It was two weeks later that Mickey and I left for Portugal and Mickey seemed excited and a bit nervous over his first flight.

He was quite impressed with our establishments, especially the Cosy Inn, as we had made very few changes to it but we had improved its tourist attraction. He was also impressed with the way that Ansiedad was able to manage both properties without many problems arising.

On the flight back home, I discussed some ideas with Mickey that I would like to do in the tavern. It would mean doing a few renovations but they would only be to the Rose Room to make it more of a dining/lounge and entertainment room. My idea was to put in a small stage for a band, a bigger dance floor, a few more tables and hire bands to play regularly

111

each weekend. I took Jessica's idea and said that once a month, we could have a Saturday night set aside for the younger people and hire bands that they would like to have entertain them.

Mickey was quiet for a while and then said "*Looking back* to when Mary was with us, we used to do what you have suggested but I'm not that young anymore to be keeping up with the young ones. If you can come up with a reasonable plan on how your ideas would be managed, then I will certainly think hard about it and I would also be discussing it with Noel. Please give me a chance to think about it. *This is all I ask.*"

When I arrived back at the tavern, Mary said that we needed to get ourselves a proper office to do business through. I knew that the one I had at home was not going to be big enough so I asked her to find one and I would look at it for its suitability. I also knew that I had to start training the girls in their respective positions because we would need to employ more people to work with us.

Mary found just the right office for us; it was big enough to handle all of our enterprises. It would also be big enough to use for the Charity headquarters as well. I decided to lease it for six months and asked each of the girls to meet me there for our first meeting and to give updates on the progress of their activities.

When the girls were gathered, Katie said "I'm sorry that I'm not at my best but I've had a long night with *September Song* but he's alright now. There are three neighbours of ours who have a few horses that they would hire out for trail riders but they can't afford all the tack and they are worried about inexperienced riders and the insurance required. Would you like me to look into that for you?"

My reply was "Yes please and when you find it out, let me have a look at it and if it is feasible, we'll set up a meeting with the horse owners and Noel."

Maggie was limping as she came in and headed straight for a seat on a box. She said "I don't know how I did it, but I dropped my bike on my foot and it was nearly a case of *toot, toot, tootsie goodbye*. It will be at least another week before I can get around properly. I did find out that there is a bike supplier in Limerick who would be able to get all the bikes you need and all the accessories. He will deliver them as well. Like the horse riding, you will need insurance for these people as well.

Are you sure that you can afford to do all these ventures at once, or should we ask the Lord "Please *pennies from heaven* are needed here."

I said to the girls "You need not worry about the financial side of these projects as I have enough money to cover them all. Now, next week I am going to put you all on the payroll, it won't be much to start with but as the businesses increase, so will your pay. The only time when you will have to ask the Lord "Please *pennies from heaven* are needed here." is if I can get a Charity that I am working on with Jessica, up and running."

Jessica said "I am having difficulty in getting much information. I wish I had some information to go on or if I could ask mammy for some help." I gave her all the information that I had received from Lorraine and then I said "Jessica, I know that you have a very hard job ahead of you. I have Noel working on it as well and so far he has given me the green light to continue, so now I think that it would be a good time to ask your mother for some help. Would you please set up a meeting for me to talk to your mother about this charity? As she is a head nurse, I'm hoping that we might be able to get the medical profession involved as well.

When I can get this project off the ground, I'll get Lorraine over from America to give us a hand and we'll have some information days set up so that other people can get answers to their questions. *All of me,* yes; every part of me is striving to get each of these projects running successfully and I hope that you will continue supporting me *all the way* through. Not only will you become a boss and have staff working for you but I will do for you as I do with all my other overseas interests, you will receive part ownership in the business and part of the profit each business makes. I know that the businesses are seasonal however I will work something out for that.

Mary and Jessica, your roles will be dealt with in a different way, but you will still be compensated for your work done. You may not have part ownership in a business, but the possibility of all-expense paid travel all over the world is there for you instead.

The girls looked at each other with surprised looks on their faces because they never had any idea that this was my intentions for them before Christmas."

Danny said "So that's why *it was a very good year* for all your properties and why you have so few troubles to work out with them when you visit. It's no wonder that you are *welcome to the club* each time you go there.

I know that I would be sure that you were made *welcome to the club* if I was one of your managers, especially if you treat all your staff that way. But why give your managers a part of your profits?"

Sue looked at him and said "Wouldn't you work better and try to build up and increase the business if you were going to get an extra reward for all your hard work. *It's all in the game* of promoting good business practices."

Bingsie asked if the young couple would like another drink before he continued with his story.

Jessica said to me "I know that a lot of companies and organizations will now be starting to get things ready for the *St Patrick's Day parade,* so I thought that I would approach them now and also the parade organizers and see what has to be done to have a float in the parade. It can't hurt asking. What do you think?"

Katie replied by saying "If we can have something in the parade, why not ride some of the horses. We can decorate them with signs that will advertise our businesses and that we sponsor the charity. Even though Mickey *don't get around much anymore,* he can be a sponsor as well and that will bring him in more business as people will want to talk to him about the charity. The townsfolk will help him as well because he and his late wife, Mary, were always there for other people when they needed help."

Maggie asked "Didn't Mickey's son die because of something to do with kidney disease? We can also decorate some bikes and a few of my friends and I can ride them through the parade. *Come rain or come shine* we will do our best to be allowed to ride our bikes in this parade or the *Easter Parade* or even both.

I think dad knows the man who organizes both parades, so I'll get him to talk to him. Bingsie, would you be willing to talk to him as well, if he wants to know more about what we are trying to do?"

I replied that I would do everything possible to help each of the girls in their quests. *Once in a while,* you have to ask yourself "*Who can I turn to* when I need advice or support or some extra information on a certain matter." and it comes in handy if you know someone to whom you can turn to in those times.

With everyone busy in their own respective jobs, it wasn't long before St Patrick's Day came around.

The girls were granted permission to ride the bikes and the horses in the parade and they had many helpers from the community as well.

114

It seems that St Patrick's Day is a religious day and many Irish people go to church in the morning, however, in *the other hours* of the afternoon and evening, they celebrate the charitable work that is done by missionaries and organizations over the world. Our 'Over The Rainbow' fund raising charity was accepted readily by the townsfolk of Killarney and the nearby towns of Limerick and Cork. Even a few people from the medical profession became involved with the setting up of the charity.

Lorraine said that "When you are ready, *send for me* and I will come over and spend time with anyone who would like further information about the charity and how it is run." Lorraine came over and spent almost three months in Ireland, getting to know the people and Jessica, before heading over to England and France for a quick visit.

Lorraine arranged for Jessica to travel to America to visit the Headquarters of the Charity and to meet different managers of the different sections of the organization. Lorraine told me that Bob and her were getting quite close and he wanted to *come fly with me* on this trip; however, some business at home needed extra attention.

Two months later, before Jessica was due to fly to America, I heard her say to Mary "I am so excited about this trip that you could *fly me to the moon* and back but I think that I would still be up there *lost in the stars*. I know that I will learn a lot and they will *show me* the right way to manage our branch of the organization. I think that we were all lucky to be affected by the Leprechaun's magic when we met Bingsie.

In our own ways, we all learnt *what is this thing called love* is all about but we also got work out of it and I think that everyone is working in something that they love doing. I know that Katie enjoys working around horses and she is also near *September Song*. Maggie is so happy that she can ride her bike for most of the day and get paid for it and well, I have told you how I feel about what I am doing and it is such a worthwhile cause. How do you feel about being Bingsie's secretary especially after the way you felt about him?"

Mary replied "I must admit that now I have had time to think about it and I see Bingsie nearly every day as my boss, you were right when you said to me that *you don't know what love is. It's only a paper moon* that's shining so *this can't be love* that you feel for him. *Somewhere my love* is waiting and I might find him while I am doing this job.

Bingsie is a great boss; he cares for his employees and he respects them. He always takes the time to help you or answer questions if you have them and he doesn't make you feel silly for asking a simple question. I am happy to be his secretary because I love the work that I am doing here in *my kind of town,* my home town."

Sue looked at Bingsie and said "I bet that hearing that made you happy. Knowing that you could *make someone happy,* no, make four people happy just by turning their lives around with friendship and employment, would give you and them great satisfaction."

Danny said "*Perhaps, perhaps, perhaps.* Maybe at *some other time* still to come that one of these young ladies will still be *yearning* for you to become her *lover.* What will you do then Bingsie, especially *when Irish eyes are smiling* at you?"

It's funny that you asked me that question because Donegal asked me the same question and I answered him "I have made it clear to all the girls that I will be a friend and their employer only. My heart is for Joanna and one day I may get to meet her again and then I will know exactly where my heart stands as far as love goes. If she is happy with someone else, then I will be like a singer *without a song* to sing. I will have to accept it and move on."

Ay Cosita Linda approached Bingsie and said "Excuse me Mr. Bingwell; there is a gentleman in the foyer who wishes to talk with you. Are you available to meet with him?"

Bingsie went to the foyer and met with the gentleman who said "Mr. Bingwell, Katie told me that I may find you here. *I'm an old cow hand from the Rio Grande* Ranch and I have been training race horses for many years. Katie's father and I race against each other every year at the Galway Bay Cup race day.

She has been telling me about the work and business that she is doing and I have a half a dozen horses on my ranch that are not any good for racing but would make great trail riding horses that I would be willing to sell to you. I only offer them to you because I know that Katie would look after them properly. If you would be interested in looking them over, then I would make arrangements for you to do so at your convenience."

Just as he was returning to the table where Sue and Danny were sitting, a waitress intercepted him and said "Mr. Bingwell, a Miss *Adelita* is on the phone for you. Do you wish to take it?"

Sue and Danny overheard Bingsie saying "*Adelita,* how are you? That's wonderful news. Yes, I'll look out for him. I will arrange for Bob to meet them. Did you say that Lorraine and Jessica are with him also? That is interesting to know. *Dinah* says that *the girl from Ipanema* is going to be a good manager at *Piel Canela.* Adeste is in the process of finalizing our take-over of the *Pat A Pan* Coffee Lounge at the *Ebb Tide* Resort in *Swanee.* So, both the coffee lounge and the resort were owned by different people. We're lucky to be able to purchase both properties together then. Thank you for your phone call and I will see Bob late this afternoon."

"I'm very sorry for the interruptions; however, business still goes on. Now would either of you like another drink or a snack?" I asked the couple sitting opposite me.

Sue said "Although I would like to hear the rest of your story, I feel that we should be going soon. We couldn't help in overhearing a part of your phone conversation and you are expecting someone so it will not be very polite of us to be here when your visitor arrives."

"No, don't go yet. I would very much like for you to meet Bob. He is my business partner, besides Lorraine and Jessica will be with him. Please allow me to finish my story before they get here." I replied.

"If you insist, then we will stay. I would like another coffee please?" said Danny.

Over the next six months, both the businesses concerning the trail rides with the horses and the bicycle hire became very popular, not only with the locals but also with tourists who had heard about us from as far away as Belfast andDublin. Katie was so busy that we hired two more people to help her and bookings for the trail rides were being made weeks in advance. Maggie had to buy six more bicycles built for two and we also extended her side of the business to incorporate bike tours of the town as well. Those tours became that popular that we employed another two people to help her.

As for Jessica, the Send In The Clowns Foundation provided a little financial assistance and a lot of training for one permanent and two part time people to help her. They also started the *Only Forever* Dreaming Fund Raising Ireland branch. *Only Forever* Dreaming was where they raised money to grant a dying child their dream if it was possible. These extra people allowed Jessica to become the spokesperson for our branch of the foundation and she started to travel all over the world and even spent *April in Paris.*

117

Mary has become an excellent secretary and now has another person working under her. Sometimes she has to travel to take care of some business for me and it was on one of her local travels that she met her new boyfriend. He works for a sailing company in Galway Bay and one afternoon her took her sailing and they had their *red sails in the sunset* on their way back to shore.

She told me one morning that *all the way* home from her last sailing trip she thought "*Isn't it romantic,* sailing out on the bay on a *silent night* with our *red sails in the sunset* and a *pale moon* coming up that will soon be bright enough to light our way. Sam is more of a *nature boy* than any of the lads from around here and I have heard him singing this one particular song and every time I hear it, I think this is *Sam's song.*

One day when I went to the coast for an unexpected meeting, Sam was delivering a boat to some clients and I thought that *when my dreamboat* comes home wouldn't it be a surprise for him to see me here and sure enough, he was surprised and very happy to see me."

Every month, the girls, Noel, Mickey and I have a business meeting to discuss any issues that may arise and may need help on solving. Mary came up with an idea and asked if she could bring to the next meeting for consideration. Mary's idea consisted of finding a place situated on or near the local lake and setting up a boat hire place.

"If we worked out a reasonable proposition, then maybe we could approach Sam's boss for help in setting it up. We could also get him to supply some small boats for us to use in the lake along with all the safety tack that is needed and if people wanted more than just a lake sailing trip, then we could get them to contact Sam's boss.

This way we could expand our business but also expand the businesses in Galway Bay. The hardest part would be finding experienced sailors to come and work for us. Personally, I would love for Sam to come and work for us, however, I don't think that that would be advisable because it would make things awkward for everyone if we stopped seeing each other." she said.

Katie and Maggie loved the idea and then Jessica said "We are all friends and we work together in different sections of this business and I have an idea that I would like to put to you all. This new idea of Mary's has got me thinking. If we could get this sailing business up and running, we could set aside a different day of the year and begin to have a charity day for each one.

We would all have to help one another to prepare for it, but the funds raised would all go to help our community and all people in Ireland that has or is suffering from some sort of kidney disease.

Imagine how a person with that kind of illness would feel if they were able to fulfil a dream of maybe going sailing, riding a horse or even a bike. Naturally, we would have to make sure that the medical profession was included as it would be by their discretion as to whether the person could be involved safely. Would you girls be willing to give it some thought and let me know how you feel?"

Katie said "I don't have to think about it, I love the idea. Before any of us answer, *if I may,* I would like to ask Mr. O'Shea and Bingsie for their input into these ideas that have just been raised."

Noel said "*How sweet it is,* that you four girls who I've known all your lives, have become such fine outstanding citizens. I am very proud to be associated with you. I would have to look into the financial and legal side of setting it up but it is up to Bingsie to have the final say in the matter."

I looked around at each of them and said "*I've got the world on a string* but you girls have got the *love* for your work and all the people around you. I agree with everything that you have suggested and I will ask for you, Noel to begin looking into the details for us. If it all works out, then *love is the thing* from you girls that will make it succeed. Mary, you have a very sensible head on your shoulders by not wanting to bring Sam into it, however, we may be able to work something out that may be to our and his benefit by having him around from the beginning. This will be a new *experiment* for me because I have no knowledge of sailing or even what end of a boat is what. I do know that each end has a name but that's all.

Mickey, you have been sitting there quietly observing and listening, do you have any input on the matters at hand."

Mickey rubbed his eyes as if he was trying to hide the fact that he had tears in them and said "You girls; listening to each of you makes me feel so proud to know you. *You make me feel so young* again and I would be so glad to help each and every one of you to get both of these ideas off the ground. A Leprechaun saying is you *must believe in spring* and that is what you four girls are doing for a lot of people, not only here in Ireland but all over the world.

Jessica, to some people it would feel like *you stepped out of a dream* because I know personally what it is like to be told that you will lose a child to an unknown disease. The fact that you are trying to help an international organization to raise money for research that one day may find cures for many diseases is very commendable and the rest of you, the way you also rally round with ideas to help Jessica, is the best news I have ever heard. I know that *when I grow too old to dream,* I will not be too old to remember this day.

Bingsie, last year *you brought a new kind of love to me* and I had the *hesitating blues* over your proposal for the tavern but now I'm going to say in front of everyone here, you may go ahead with my blessing and do what you have in mind for the tavern, on one condition and that is, every six months you hold a charity function in the Rose Room with all proceedings as well as half of the bar takings on that night going to the Over The Rainbow Charity and the Only Forever Dreaming Foundation.

I will apply for a permanent extended trading license for Saturday nights. Now if there isn't anything else that needs to be discussed here, I would like to be getting back to the tavern so Paddy can go home."

Mickey and Noel left the office but the girls and I stayed to discuss their ideas a bit more. As it was getting near lunch time, I suggested that we all go down to the tavern and I would buy them lunch. Maggie was the first out of the door and held it open for the rest of us and Mary heard someone whistling and said softly "That's *Sam's song.*" and as she stepped out on to the footpath, she saw Sam standing there waiting for her.

Sam walked up to Mary and said "I thought that it was time that I surprised you and came to see where you worked. Killarney is big *but beautiful* and even more so because you are here. *Ev'rytime we say goodbye,* I find that once you've gone, *I miss you* more and *the more I see you,* the more I want to be with you so I have taken a few days off that were owing to me and I've come to see and spend time with you."

Katie said *"Oh! Ain't that sweet.* Bingsie, invite him to join us and we can discreetly gather more information about the boat idea from him. He would be the best person to talk to and I think I know just how to go about it."

Sam joined us and he gave us so much information that we knew that with the right people working with us, we could start the sailing boat hire business if Noel gave us the right answers on the legal side of things. The next few days, Sam spent time with all the girls and became very interested in the charity side of our business.

The night before he was to return home, we all had a meal at the tavern and he surprised us with the same idea as Mary had suggested.

He said "As there is a lake nearby, why don't you get some boats and hire them out to experienced yachtsmen for the day. You could also arrange for a local café or even this tavern to make picnic hampers for the people to take out with them. I have a few mates that would be willing to help you and two of them live here in Killarney. You might even know one of them. His nickname is *Firefly*."

Maggie said "*Firefly*. Has he got brown scruffy hair and a big scar on his left arm?"

"Yes that's him." said Sam "do you know how he got that scar?"

"Yes." said Maggie "he was walking over to our place when he saw some apple trees. He told my two brothers and they said "*Ah, the apple trees* are about to be climbed." and they took off towards them. One of my brothers was being smart and fell out of the tree when a limb broke and Tony (Firefly) broke his fall but was badly cut by the limb and it also broke his arm. My brothers got a thrashing from dad when he found out and Tony had his arm in a sling for nearly six months because they couldn't put it in a cast."

We got the good news from Noel about setting up the sailing business and suggested that we should become a company that incorporates each type of business and seeing that our businesses aimed more for the tourists, that we should also consider approaching travel agents with packages for the tourists.

A few ideas for company names were suggested like, *Don't Fence Me In* Outdoor Activities, *That's A-Plenty* Of Fun and Wake A *Sleepin' Bee*. They actually settled on *The Good Life* Company because tourists were able to have fun and excitement whilst indulging in new types of activities that they had never experienced before.

On top of getting all the business on track again, I was also helping Mickey everyday because Paddy was away on holiday with his family and I was also overseeing the few renovations that were being done at the tavern. Our opening night was going to be a charity night for Jessica and the Over The Rainbow Charity and the Only Forever Dreaming Foundation.

I arrived home very exhausted one night to find a hot meal on my table and a half a glass of Guinness and my immediate thoughts went to

Geraldine. I hadn't seen or heard from them for quite a while. I didn't know if she was still around but I still called out my thanks to Geraldine anyway.

Her little voice came back to me as she said "No, thank you Bingsie. *I get a kick out of you* still but I can see you are a man of honour. You have dealt with many situations very well and what has been done to you was not very nice. I caught up with David and his mates and it seems that James was given the job of sorting Donegal out and to teach him a lesson, so David and James worked together. David said that his work was not finished yet but James, well; he left *without a song* after I had finished dealing with him. I do believe that *you must have been a beautiful baby* because *when you're smiling* you can make everyone believe that on any *Sunday, Monday or always* that *you're nobody till somebody loves you,* even if it is only as a friend."

Donegal came and stood beside Geraldine and said "I can't say that *I get a kick out of you* anymore because I've been watching you and I am impressed with the way that you have work with the young ladies, given them work that they love and looking after the community. Last night *I wished on the moon* that you get what your heart desires and may your next lot of *luck be a lady. If I ruled the world,* I would fill it with people like you. Now did you enjoy the meal that my Geraldine made for you?"

"Yes I did and thank you again Geraldine. Now Donegal, did you enjoy the other half of the Guinness and thank you for leaving me some in the glass?" I asked him

Geraldine looked at him and said "Donegal, you didn't did you?"

He looked at her and smiled and then she said "Right, now; I'll have to sort you out some more. *This way out* now and don't think of making any excuses for your behaviour."

It was a short time after they had left when the phone rang. It was Bob asking if I could make my rounds of our European properties and the one in Hawaii and personally come back to the office as there were issues that needed to be taken care of by me. I told him that I could start doing them within the next couple of weeks once I had everything in order over here in Ireland. I knew that Bob would not *send for me* unless he really needed me there.

DREAMS COME TRUE

It's a small world because evidently Gerald Thomas O'Shea, Sam's boss was Noel's cousin and when he was informed about our new business adventure, he was more than willing to supply us with everything we needed for cost price. He even arranged for Sam to spend two days a week in Killarney to help us get up and running and to make sure that Tony knew the proper ways to get the boats ready as he would be running that part of the business when Sam wasn't there.

Sam also had to make sure that Tony would know what instructions that he would have to give the sailing persons if a *summer wind* suddenly blew up whilst they were out on the lake. If the *summer wind* became too strong, it would suddenly sway the boat and the sailors would have to know how to *slow down* enough to be able to handle the boat safely.

I told everyone that I was going to be away for a few months with my other job and I had left my itinerary with Mary, so they could get in touch with me if they needed to, but I was confident that they would be able to sort out any issues should they arise themselves. I also said that I would be in the States for at least a month working with Bob; however, I would notify them if my plans changed.

At the tavern Mickey, Paddy and I went over a few things concerning what was left to do with the renovations. I noticed that two women had come in to the tavern about half an hour before closing time and sat down at a table near the door to the Rose Room. One of the came over to the bar and ordered a Guinness and two lemonades, one for me and *one for my baby* over there.

Then she said to Mickey "*The way you look tonight* is almost like the way you used to look when Mary was with us. It seems that having Bingsie around has given you a new lease on life."

Two days before I was to fly out, I got the *blues in my shower* that morning because I didn't want to leave my home. I was finishing my coffee and gathering some paperwork for Mickey when I heard, "Please *say it isn't so*. Please say you're not leaving us. *The shadow of your smile* will be missed by a lot of people around here.

If *there's no you* in this place then we will be having many a *silent night* and *it's only a paper moon* that will be shining down on us. *Who can I turn to* for advice when Donegal is playing up?"

I looked down to see Geraldine standing there and she was wiping her eyes with the sleeve of her dress, so I bent down and *tenderly* picked her up and placed her on my table and I said to her "Geraldine, I'm only going away on business for my other job. I have to travel to a few European countries, Hawaii and then to the States. I will be gone about two months but I will be coming back here as this is my home now. I hope that you will look after my place for me whilst I'm away and I hope that you will be here when I get back. I know that you can sort Donegal out when he starts to get into mischief because *there will never be another you* in his life. Now I have to finish getting ready, so come and let me feel *the touch of your lips* on my cheek with a goodbye kiss that will make me *smile* every time I start to miss my Ireland."

Geraldine replied "I thought that you were leaving us for good. It must be great going off to see the world when you want to. Have a good trip and don't forget to *wrap your troubles in dreams* to dream them away plus *you must believe in spring*. Remember before David left, he said his work wasn't finished so I would suggest that *only the lonely girls* will have their *love for sale* and they might want to sell it to you. Aye, I'll look after your place for you and I'll be here when you get back."

Then we both heard "Geraldine, I can hear you but *where are you?*"

As I placed Geraldine back on the floor, Donegal said "Oh, there you are. What were you doing up there on the table? What girls have got their *love for sale?*"

Geraldine said "Donegal, Bingsie is going away for a while on business and I was warning him to be careful because David said before he left that his work wasn't finished. *That's all* we were talking about. I also said that I would keep an eye on his place while he's away, so don't get any ideas of having *that party* for Muldoon in here. I have just thought of an idea; why don't you take Muldoon and the other lads to see *the late, late show* down at *Swinging On Central* near *Moon River*. You know that they're *never young* enough or old enough to want to go there."

Donegal gave a chuckle before saying "Going away on business, eh. That's *nice work if you can get it* so have you any vacancies coming up for me?"

Geraldine gave him a whack on the arm as I replied "Sorry, I'm afraid not. Anyway how would you handle getting on and of planes and walking around very large cities with millions of people and no countryside to hide in? Now, I have to get moving so don't get into too much mischief while I'm away."

I got down to the office *just in time* because everyone was there for the meeting including Sam, Tony and Gerald. It was only a short meeting as everyone had their businesses in order and didn't have any issues to discuss.

I was surprised to find that Mary had a flower in her hair and she told me that *a blossom fell* from a tree that Sam was walking under, so he picked it up and gave it to me just before you came in.

She took me to one side and said "*Isn't it romantic* with the things he does. You were right when you said *this can't be love* that I was feeling for you because *I just found out about love* and it is Sam. *If love is good to me* then I hope it will *never let me go* and I hope that *when my dreamboat* comes home, he'll make me as happy as dad makes my mammy. Thank you for your friendship and being so understanding and patient with me. I won't let you down. I have everything under control here and I have put your itinerary in my diary, so go and have a good trip. We will see you when you get back."

When I walked into the tavern, Mickey saw me and said with a twinkle in his eyes, "Look what Paddy just found. *It's the same old shillelagh* that I used to chase your grandmother around our garden with. I can't remember how many times I got in to trouble for doing it. If you hold *this side up* to the light, you can see the marks that your grandmother put on it one day as she tried to break it. You know *the more I see you,* the more I see your grandmother in you." Then suddenly a familiar voice was heard by Mickey and he turned towards the door and saw Morgen and her husband Tex standing there.

Morgen said "You were in trouble plenty of times. I remembered *last night when we were young,* and we were playing in the back shed, you told me that one day you would *fly me to the moon.* Well, when are you going to arrange that as I want to gather some *star dust* and go *swinging on a star* before I pass."

"Morgen, Tex." murmured Mickey "what are you doing here? Why didn't you tell me that you were coming? Where are you going to be staying but more importantly, how long are you staying?"

Mickey escorted them back to his living room and left Paddy to carry on his usual job. Grandma took my arm as she followed Mickey.

Tex said "I wanted to *take her to the Mardi Gras* but I knew that Morgen has always wanted to come back to Ireland. With Bingsie finding out about you and her, I thought that his parents will soon find out about your secret, so I thought why not fulfil her dream to come and see you. *Love's been good to me* from the first day that I have met your sister."

Morgan turned to me and said "Would you mind if we stayed with you for a few weeks? I would like to meet up with my old friend *Eileen* who used to live down the street, if she is still there. Have you met Donegal and Geraldine?"

Mickey replied "Yes, she's still there, but now *the lady is a tramp*. She has had a long run of bad luck over the past six years and maybe a visit from you might be what she needs. As for Donegal, he has surely put his mark on Bingsie. When Bingsie first arrived here, those Leprechauns and their angel mates really had some fun and games with him but he seemed to end up outsmarting them. Now they're friends. You will most probably see them tonight."

I said to my grandmother, "You are very welcome and of course you may stay with me, however, I fly out tomorrow on business and I will be gone for about two months. You stay at your old place for as long as you want to and give the Leprechauns a run for their money but don't let them change the way I have the place set up. I will catch up with you in the States when I get there."

We sat there chatting for quite a while before we heard Paddy say "Lights out in five minutes. *Goodnight Irene goodnight* Andy."

It was a *foggy day* when I arrived in England and I thought "*This morning it was summer* when I left but it doesn't seem like it now." I had to run an errand for Maggie so I decided to spend the rest of the day in England and revisit some of the places that I had been to in my youth. As I was walking past, a *Nightingale sang in Berkley Square* and I thought of Lorraine. I remembered the night of the ball when we danced the *Waltz for Debbie,* when just about everyone danced the *Waltz for Debbie* and when Lorraine whispered in my ear that Debbie was a brave little girl and that *they can't make her cry* over anything.

I didn't go to Paris but I flew straight to Switzerland and drove to Noche De Ronda. Again I had thoughts of Joanna and I wondered where she was and if she was happy. It seemed a long way to travel for a two hour meeting. Instead of driving all the way back to Zurich, I decided to drive the ninety four kilometres to Lausanne and catch the plane from there to Lisbon and meet up with Ansiedad.

We took a quick trip up to the Cosy Inn and I was really impressed by the way he had organized himself in handling both the Calypso Blues Bar

126

and the Cosy Inn. Both places were running smoothly and were making a profit. Ansiedad had promoted one of his assistant managers to manager to operate one place and he was training another person to take their place as assistant manager.

I then flew to Madrid and visited On The Alamo where Bridges and Susannah were. Since the opening of the Manhattan Night Lights, business had picked up that much that they had to employ four more staff and they had people booking a week in advance to dine there.

The next day, I met with Petro Kings in Kiev and we took a quick visit to the Swing Low Sweet Chariot and while we were sitting in the restaurant section having lunch, Petro raised his glass and said "*Here's to the band* that plays here. They really draw the crowds in and that has made this place more successful than we had imagined."

I flew back to Madrid and then onto Rabat to see Sweet Leilani and O'Tannenbaum at the Vaya Condios. As we were walking past the bar to the office, one of their waitresses was telling the bar staff about something and I heard him reply "*Mucho, mucho, mucho* (a lot, a lot, a lot)." Sweet Leilani turned to me and said "Did you propose to your lady?"

I replied "No, she left me to go home for family reasons and I haven't seen her since. She did write to me but she never put a return address on her letter so I couldn't send a reply. Maybe it was *just one of those things* that happen in life but you can never be sure of *what is this thing called love*. The feeling that it's *almost like being in love* will be *the tender trap* that makes you want to *jingle bells, silver bells* on any *o holy night* of the week."

After leaving Morocco, I paid quick visits to Montenegro and Rome. Rome brought back a lot of memories to me but there was still one place left to visit, and I really was not looking forward to going back there… Hawaii.

Penthouse was waiting for me at the airport when I flew into Hawaii. He told me that it was his day off so he decided to come and meet me.

He asked me if I had been able to contact Miss Joanna and when I told him that I hadn't, he just looked at me with an 'I didn't think so.' look on his face.

I looked at Penthouse and said "Ok, what is it? What rumors have you heard?"

Penthouse replied, "You know that I hear a lot of things, but they may not be true. I have heard that Miss Joanna's agent became jealous when you and she became an item. When she left you in Rome and returned to the States for whatever reason, he found that it gave him the right opportunity to break the pair of you up. Mr. Capers found out that you owned this club and many more, so he started cancelling all her engagements and blamed you for it.

When your picture with Miss Lorraine was in the papers, he used that to cancel all her bookings with that organization as well. He thought that Miss Joanna would turn to him for help and comfort but he was wrong. She actually stopped singing, which was a pity, and went off with someone, but I do not know who he was. I also heard that there was a child involved in the situation as well."

"Like I have said before Penthouse; it amazes me as to how you find these things out. Now have you come up with any ideas on how I might find her? You found the way for me to meet her the first time around and I will always be grateful to you for that." I said.

"I'm afraid that I haven't. If she were still singing, I could find her." was his reply.

I decided to spend a couple of days in Hawaii before heading back here. I contacted the office in Ireland and Mickey, who told me that everything was superb there and that he was enjoying his time with Morgen. Morgen and Tex met the girls and spent time with them.

They were very proud of what you have done over here and especially starting up the charity. They would be heading home in a couple of days. I phoned Bob at the office and told him that I would be there in a couple of days. I flew in San Francisco two weeks ago and spent time in head office and made quick trips down *Route 66* with Adeste to Georgia, San Antonia and Perfida.

Now that is my story.

Now, I have something to tell you and ask you. "Mr. Booker no longer owns the Laguna Leap Restaurant. Like you said, his insurance was not enough to cover the cost of repairs and he was unable to borrow the money to do it. I'm afraid that he will not be sending for you to go back to work for him."

A sad and disappointed look came over the faces of Sue and Danny and then he looked at her.

She looked back at him and said, "Maybe it's for the best that we know this now because we can start our life over again somewhere else. I know that it will be hard but we can do it if we stick together. The memories that I have is enough for me and *they can't take that away from me*. I know that at any time I feel cold, I need not worry for *I've got my love to keep me warm*."

"I know that you're right and I'm so glad that *you're mine, you* beautiful and wise woman. But it's hard knowing that we may never bring our children up in *Avalon*, but *that's life*." said Danny.

"*That's life* alright, and *Danny Boy* Wenceslas, you know that the good Lord knows what he's doing. Maybe there will be a better opportunity for us around the corner. Bingsie you said that you wanted to ask us something. What is it?" said Sue.

Bingsie asked "Bob and I have just bought a new property and we are starting the renovations next week. It is going to be bigger than it was before because we are building a motel and accommodation for the managers there as well. I have spent these few hours with you and I think that the pair of you would make great managers for the place. If you decide to take the position, it would mean that you will have to travel to a few of our other properties in other countries to learn how we expect our managers to do things. The reason why you would travel to the other places is so that you can learn different ways to run the business. Now, *Danny Boy* and Sierra Sue, do you think that you would like this job?"

Danny and Sue looked at each other and a gigantic smile came across their faces and Danny said "Are you kidding. Of course we'll take it but at the moment we'll have to see if we can get some financial help for the travelling. Would you be able to give us a day or so to arrange that?

Bingsie smiled and said "No, I'm not kidding and your travel, accommodation and training will be paid for by the company. As you have already said that you will take the position, I'm now able to tell you where you will be living…Avalon.

We have purchased the property and it seems that it was a coincidence that we met here today. Bob is coming to meet you with all the necessary paperwork and he will be here shortly. He will also answer any questions that you may have. Adeste will be the other person that you will be working with because I am going to go back to Ireland to live."

Bob said as he stopped beside Bingsie "The Irish don't know what they've done by allowing you to live over there.

129

There again, if all the girls are as beautiful and smart like Jessica here, then maybe Ireland will survive with you there."

They all laughed and Bingsie introduced Bob, Lorraine and Jessica to Sue and Danny.

Bob sat down and discussed the proceedings and signed the necessary paperwork with Danny and Sue. Jessica said that there was a shop next door that she wanted to look at and would be back shortly and Lorraine and Bingsie found another table to sit and have a drink at.

Lorraine reached across the table and put one of her hands over his, looked at him and said "When mother and I left London, I realized that *this can't be love* that I'm feeling for you now because *as time goes by,* people change but their memories don't and it's *these foolish things;* these memories that can sometimes trip you up. I also knew that *somewhere my love* was waiting for me and I think that I've found him. Bob and I have become very, very close; in fact, we're dating seriously and I have to thank you for introducing us to each other in Paris. I ran into Joanna by accident a couple of weeks ago and we had a good long chat. She still loves you very much and knows that you live in Ireland now but is afraid that she has lost you forever. I will give her your address if you want me to so that she can write you again and this time I will tell her to make sure there is a return address on it."

Their conversation was interrupted by people lining up to watch the parade. They heard people saying things like "*Wait 'til the sun shines Nellie.* You've got to be kidding, *Moonburn?* There's no such thing as *Moon Love,* What do you mean *one for my baby,* she's not my baby and *Mona Lisa Baby baby all the time.*"

Then someone shouted "*Here comes the big parade* starting with the *parade of the wooden soldiers.*"

Just as everyone started to clamour around the windows, Lorraine said "Today I feel like being *a weaver of dreams* and for you *this time the dreams on me.*"

Bingsie was just about to ask her what she meant when he heard the song Besame Mucho and Sue saying "Look at that float, aren't those flowers Edelweiss."

Bingsie swung round and saw Joanna wearing a *blue velvet* dress with a *blue gardenia* in her hair, sitting on a throne, high up on the float that was covered with Edelweiss. Although she would *wave* to the crowd, in her *angel eyes* she looked like a lonely girl. He remembered the stranger from the tavern telling him that *there is always one more time.*

Lorraine turned to him and said "What are standing here for, you fool. You are no longer *strangers in the night* so go and talk to her. The parade finishes two blocks down at the park."

Bingsie raced out the club, but had trouble getting through the crowd and when he finally reached the float, he saw Joanna with the other man.

Joanna saw him and called out to him "Bingsie, what are you doing here? I thought you were in Ireland. Come over and meet my twin brother Steve and his wife *Laura.*"

Bingsie thought "*There goes my heart again.*" as he walked over to her, and he watched her face light up like a candle.

Steve said "So you're the man who has my sister moping around all the time for."

We all went back to the club and was greeted by the staff with "*Welcome to the club,* but I'm afraid that the children are too young to come in."

Bob came out and said "It's alright, I have made arrangements with Ay Costa Linda to use one of the private rooms and she is setting it up now. I know that you are new here Sandra, so you wouldn't have met my partner Bingsie before."

Sandra said to Bingsie "Oh, I do apologize. Mr. White did mention that he had a partner but he said that you were in Ireland and I have just begun my shift so Ay Costa Linda isn't here to inform me of the regular clientele."

In the room, the introductions were made and Joanna, who was holding a little boy, said "This is *little Farley,* my nephew and the little girl is his sister *Mona Lisa.* We have just received some great news that Farley has been given a clean bill of health. He had a kidney disease called HUS and it was discovered early by the doctors so we have managed to get the treatment quickly enough to cure him. He will still have to have yearly check-ups but I don't think he'll mind."

Danny and Sue were also invited to join us, so Bingsie introduced them to Joanna and then said to them, "When you get back and get your restaurant running, I'll make sure that you have a lot of tangerines delivered for *makin' Whoopee* and when I come and visit I want you to say *"Welcome to the Club."* and hand me a glass of that *tangerine* drink that you told me you make."

Sue said "Mr. Bingwell, Bingsie, you will always be *welcome to the club* and I want to thank you for today. Never in my wildest dreams did I ever think that Danny and my dreams would come true. Having faith and believing in the good Lord, helps dreams come true for some people."

Bob said "It's been a long day for the lot of us, so why don't we meet here next Saturday and we'll have a proper celebration. Steve, you, your wife and children are invited, so are you Danny and Sue. I think that this will be enough time for everybody to absorb all the good news that they've heard today. I will even invite Adeste and his wife, Dinah and *Dindi,* who I have promoted to being Adeste's secretary."

Bingsie and Joanna met the following day at the park and she told him "I was sitting in the dressing room of the last place I played, thinking about you, when *my heart stood still* as *the man in the looking glass* said *"Who's sorry now?* You should have had more faith and less of the *hesitating blues.* You were a *stranger in paradise* when you said *"Let's face the music and dance* and *be careful, it's my heart* at stake here." but you didn't think of his heart.

The song is ended on this part of your life; however, *the best is yet to come.* I do not know *where or when* but you will once again meet *the man that got away* and you can make it better for both of you in the *second time around* if you say the *three little words* and mean them. Remember that *softly as I leave you,* you will find that *the days of wine and roses* will begin for you."

I must have blinked because he was gone just like that, but I do remember that I was captured by his incredible blue eyes and his infectious smile. At the time, I didn't understand what he meant and I was also in shock but now I am beginning to understand what he was saying."

Bingsie replied *"If this isn't love* that we share, then we should be honest with each other now. As for me, when I said those *three little words,* I love you, I meant it and I still do love you. *The touch of your lips* and *the very thought of you,* wanted me to make you *all mine.* I knew that *all of me* wanted to be with you at *anytime, anyday, anywhere* and it didn't matter if it was on a *Sunday, Monday or always. I found a million dollar baby,* singing beautiful songs and *you made me love you* right from the start. *I've got the world on a string* but *I only have eyes for you.* Not even the *girl from Ipanema* could come close to you."

132

"*I can't believe that you're in love with me* still, especially after what I have done to you. I've missed *the touch of your lips* and the way you used to hold me so *tenderly*. I used to think that I was living in a dream and I used to say to myself "*I can dream, can't I*." I didn't realize that I hadn't put my return address on the letters, so when I never heard back from you, I thought that you didn't care for me. Then when all my bookings started to be cancelled, I blamed you for it until I found out that Cole was doing it.

The way I found out was, I was actually with the owner of a club where I was performing when Cole rang and cancelled my booking saying that I had a booking overseas and was just about to fly out. Steve and I confronted him and that's when he told me the whole story and that he loved me. He is not my agent anymore and I haven't any bookings coming up, at present.

It was just my luck and *luck be a lady,* that I bumped into Lorraine and when she explained about the photograph I felt very foolish. She asked me to be in the parade because the girl who was supposed to do it became ill and she couldn't find someone else in time. Did she know that you were coming back to the States at this time?" said Joanna.

"Bob must have told her because he sent for me. He asked me to visit all the offices on my back but I needed to be here personally to take care of some business that only I could do. I know that Bob and Lorraine have become very close and Bob knew that it would take me a month to visit all the offices and get back here. I do believe that both of them have become *a weaver of dreams* and are trying to make our dreams come true. What do you think?" Bingsie said.

Joanna's reply was "I think that you may be right. They must have planned it so that you would be back here *just in time* for the parade. They would have thought *that's a-plenty* of time for you and by Bob getting you to visit every office, you would not suspect anything. Oh, my goodness, look at the time. I have to be going because I promised Steve and Laura that I would baby-sit for them tonight as it's their anniversary and they are going out.

Tomorrow, I'm going into the charity's head office and if you want to, you could meet me there and I'll show you around. I know that Lorraine and Jessica will be there. Jessica will make a terrific Ambassador for us over on your side of the world. Yesterday was an *unforgettable* day for me and I won't forget it for a long time to come. Think about coming in to the office tomorrow."

133

Joanna and Bingsie spent nearly all the next three days together. They became inseparable and one evening Bingsie said to her "I know that *I'm in love again* with you. *The way you look tonight, the touch of your lips* and the way *you make me feel so young* makes me want to say "*I surrender dear* to your arms and *never let me go* on this *o holy night.*" You are *my kind of girl* who gives me *my kind of love* so I am going to ask you right now, "*What are you doing the rest of your life?* I have a permanent booking for you to consider; would you marry me and come and live with me in *my kind of town.* You don't have to answer me now, but please think about it, *this is all I ask?*"

Joanna took a few moments before answering "*The more I see you,* the more *you go to my head. If I give my heart to you* completely then it will mean that *I surrender dear* to you and *don't ever go away* without me again. The newspaper photograph described you as "*Embraceable You.*" and you are; you're so *easy to love.* Yes, I will think seriously about it and I promise that I will give you my answer on Saturday."

Saturday night came around and everyone was at the club. After the meal was over, Bob had a few announcements to make. First he welcomed Danny and Sue to the organization and from the reports that he had heard from Mr. Booker, he knew they were the right people for the new restaurant. He then congratulated Steve and Laura on the way that they had stuck together through the trying times with Farley's illness and on their recent wedding anniversary. He acknowledged Jessica for the work that she was doing with the charity and wished her well for the future and he gave his deep gratitude to the other staff members present for all their hard work and support.

Then he announced that he was getting engaged to Lorraine. *If love is good to me,* then *what a wonderful world* it will be to live in. Bingsie would you like to say something to your staff and friends."

Just as Bingsie went to stand, Joanna whispered in his ear and he shouted out "*My baby said yes, yip, yip, de hootie.*"

Everyone just bust out laughing then Bingsie said "Bob we have to work something out. We can't get married at the same time. Joanna has just agreed to become my wife but I'm not sure how this is going to work, I live in Ireland and she lives here."

Steve said "That's easy; just *play a simple melody* and she will follow you anywhere. You can take her back with you and we can always come over for the wedding and have a holiday. It's time that my sister left home for good."

That statement made everyone laugh again.

Adeste said "You can marry her here; I think it takes about a week to arrange the license and all your family and friends can attend as well."

During the evening Bob went to Bingsie and said "I know now how you feel about Joanna and how you must have felt after reading that letter in Paris. I understand now, why you had to get away for a while. *When my sugar walks down the street,* I see how some of the other people stare at her in admiration. I sometimes have to say "*Be still my heart* or you will fall right out of my chest."

Bob heard someone say "That's life for you and she can be funny that way." and then he said "Listen; *do you hear what I hear?"*

The following day Bingsie phoned Mickey to inform him that he and Joanna had become engaged and were going to be married in a fortnight so could he please arrange for Paddy to work so he could fly over for the wedding? Mickey was told that Mary would collect the plane ticket for him and make arrangements for him to be taken to the airport. He then phoned his grandparents and invited them to the wedding and he knew that he should inform his own parents and invite them as well.

The next two weeks flew by as the wedding arrangements were made. The night before the wedding, Joanna was sitting with Bingsie on the front porch of her brother's house and she looked at him and said "*Moonlight becomes you* and *the way you look tonight* and *the touch of your lips* lets me know that you will *love me as if there were no tomorrow.* Are you worried about your parents being at the wedding?"

Bingsie didn't answer so Joanna said "*Answer me, my love.*"

Bingsie said "*You're my thrill* and *you're my welcome* and I want your wedding day to be special for you. What if *it started all over again,* you know, the fights between my parents?"

Joanna replied softly, "I don't believe that they will say or do anything in front of your grandparents or Mickey when they see them at the wedding. It will be a shock for them. Your mother won't embarrass herself in front of Bob and Lorraine for fear of losing her position with the charity. Listen; *do you hear what I hear?"*

Coming from somewhere across the road, both Bingsie and Joanna heard "*Tender is the night* for all lovers. Remember *the rules of the road* are different from the rules of life.

Please be kind to each other and say those *three little words* and mean them. The two lonely people have learnt their lesson and will not cause harm to you anymore. *I wish you love* and both of you *stay as sweet as you are.* You know what the little people would say *"Everytime I feel the spirit,* it will either be an angel or a whiskey." You know what I mean Bingsie. *That's life* and *she's funny that way."*

Joanna said "I know that voice; he's the man in my dressing room mirror. I wonder who he is and how he found us here and who are the little people?"

Bingsie laughed and said "I think he's Earth Angel David and the little people are the Leprechauns. It's a long story and I will tell you about it one day."

It was a garden wedding and the day was bright and sunny. The wedding went smoothly. After the meal, Bingsie's grandparents and Mickey pulled him to one side and his grandfather said "I think that you should warn Joanna about Donegal and Geraldine in the plane going home because she can't change her mind and stay here in America.

I think that we all would like to be at your place when you walk in with Joanna. It will be a big shock to those two wee folk."

Joanna came over and said to Bingsie "There is a man standing over there. Do you know who he is?"

Bingsie looked to where she was pointing and said "*I just can't see for looking* because there is a bright light in the place that you are pointing. Then he heard in his head "*That's what they meant* when they say *let's fall in love.*"

Joanna said "Never mind, he's gone now and she heard in her head "The *song is you, let me love tonight, Sunday, Monday or always.*" Then Joanna looked down at the ground and said to Bingsie surprisingly "*Your socks don't match.*"

And they both broke out in laughter. Little Farley walked over to Bingsie and tugged on his trousers and said "Will you *teach me tonight* how to make Auntie Joanna laugh like that, 'cos she hasn't done it in a long time."

In the plane, on the way back to Ireland Bingsie explained to Joanna about the Leprechauns, especially Geraldine and Donegal. He told her that she would soon get used to them.

136

Joanna said "That's *easy for you to say*. What if they don't agree with me being in your house and start playing tricks on me?"

When they reached Killarney, Bingsie took Joanna to the tavern and left her with Mickey so he could go home and tell Geraldine and Donegal about his new wife. He approached his front door cautiously because he didn't know what could be in store for him. He entered his home and everything was in its place.

"Good your back." said Geraldine "I kept everything neat and tidy, *just as though you were here*. Donegal will be here soon to give you a welcome home."

Donegal popped around the corner of the stove and looked a bit disappointed and he said "*What's new*. Well, where is the lovely wife? David called by and said that you got married. Don't tell me you've lost her already or left her behind."

Bingsie told them that she was down with Mickey and that he was there to tell them that he had just been married. He was not sure how they would take the news.

Donegal said "*Let's start the new year right,* I mean, this being your first year of marriage. *You're nearer* to us than most folk around here and it was sure good to see Morgen again, anyway she told us to look after you and any family that you bring in here and she made us promise to behave and not to play tricks on you any more. Morgen said that if she heard any news of us playing up on you then she would *come by me* once she had passed and would give me a what for. I have seen her temper and I don't want to see it again. Well, everything is in its place and you go get your lovely wife. We will stay away until you call us. We can always meet down by the café if you need to talk."

Bingsie went and brought Joanna home and as she stood by the front door he said to her "You'll never have to ask me if *I'll be home for Christmas* because I always will be. *The way you look tonight* and *the touch of your lips* will always bring me home. Don't worry we won't be interrupted because they won't come until you're ready to meet them and I call them."

The following day down at the tavern, a couple of the regular ladies stopped and spoke to Bingsie. They told him that they had seen his picture in the paper and called him "*Embraceable You*." and walked to their table laughing.

Another lady with a child came in and sat with the other two ladies. She came up to the side bar and asked for two lemonades saying that it was one for her and *one for my baby*."

Paddy told Bingsie that he liked the idea of having a section of the bar area made for families with children and he couldn't wait for the family lounge to be finished.

Mary and Sam came into the tavern for lunch and Bingsie introduced Joanna to them. He asked them how the sailing business was going and Sam said "*I'm never satisfied* with the way the boat ramps and moorings are going. Oh. Don't get me wrong, *sometimes I'm happy* but *some other time* I just want to lose my temper. It is important to secure the boats properly or they will *sway* in the breeze and could get damaged. If you think that *these foolish things* don't matter, then just wait until you start getting the repair bills in."

Bingsie called for a meeting at the office so everyone could meet Joanna and tell her about what they do in the organization.

Katie walked in and said "*I'll never smile again* unless I can get this tooth fixed. My brother accidentally hit me in the mouth with his fitness book and it broke my tooth." She smiled and it was her front tooth that was damaged.

Maggie said that the bike hire was slowing down a bit because the rain had been around for a few days so *in the other hours* when she was not out riding, she was working on new places to visit for when we held a charity day."

The phone rang just as Maggie had finished talking so Mary answered it, and she returned to the meeting with a sad look on her face. Bingsie asked what was wrong and Mary said "You remember that little girl Tina, who got that kidney disease, well Jessica just phoned to say that she won't be in because Tina was in a critical condition in hospital and she was with Tina's parents."

Bingsie said to Joanna "She is a very thin child *but beautiful*. What a waste of a young life."

Sam said "I know what you mean; *I've grown accustomed to her face* seeing that she used to be in here helping Jessica some times."

Katie said "Here I am worried about a tooth and there she is fighting for her life. Just think that *it could happen* to you or me or anybody we know. Any disease isn't going to be choosy. It can hit anybody at any time; it could even be this spring or *some other spring*. We have to do something to help these children and we have to try and do it sooner than later."

Bingsie suggested that they finish the meeting down at the tavern because he felt that everyone could do with a drink.

Joanna said "What can I do to help? *The shadow of your smile* and the distant look in your eyes are telling me that you have gone through this before. Am I right?"

Bingsie was quiet and Joanna said "Please *answer me, my love*. What can I do to help?"

That evening at home, Bingsie said to Joanna "If *I concentrate on you,* will you be able to be our function coordinator for the tavern. The Rose Room will be ready for its first function next month. It will be a charity dance for Tina. Now, I really think that you would benefit by Geraldine's help so may I call her and introduce you to her."

As the days hurried by, Joanna with the help of Geraldine, and at times Donegal, managed to get two bands to volunteer their services for the night. Geraldine suggested that they get a singer too. Joanna said that she would sing on the night because before she married Bingsie, she used to be a singer and she often sang at functions for the Send In The Clowns Charity, the one that Jessica and Bingsie organization was a branch of.

Joanna asked Geraldine "I have heard that you have an old village song. I would like to learn the words so could you *teach me tonight.*"

That first charity night was *unforgettable* with the townsfolk supporting them. Some of the townsfolk also became involved in the other businesses which brought in many tourists.

*　　*　　*　　*　　*

Jessica continued her work with the Over The Rainbow Research branch whilst her fiancée joined her with the Only Forever Dream Fund Raiser and between them they were able to make six children's dreams come true and two adult's dreams come true.

Mary's horse, September Song, won his first race and the next twenty races after that. Her side of the business became very popular with trail rides all throughout the year.

Because of their popularity, Maggie's bicycles built for two tours were being booked by overseas travel agents three to four months in advance.

Mary and Sam now have twin girls but she is still Bingsie's secretary. Sam still works in Galway Bay but only for a few days each month but most of the time, he gives sailing lessons down on the lake.

Noel O'Shea retired leaving his son to carry on the business.

Mickey retired and started travelling and on his last trip to America, he went for Morgen's funeral.

Paddy still works at the tavern regularly keeping everyone in line.

Bob married Lorraine, but he still works local and will only fly if he has too.

The rest of the staff at Junco Partner were all doing well. Danny and Sue have made a sleepy little town into a popular, relaxing, tourist retreat.

Joanna and Bingsie became well known for their charity work and their work at the tavern. Bingsie still travels to the offices for his other job but he spaces them out so that he is home more often. He is always home for Christmas.

Joanna still sings at some of the functions and has turned down other singing engagements as it would take her away from home for long periods of time.

Geraldine and Donegal stayed and helped Joanna for a couple of years until Earth Angel David and his mates came back to town. When David left so did the Leprechauns and nobody knows where they went.

So if unusual things start to happen around your place or to you, be careful because it could be those Leprechauns causing mischief or even a mischievous angel.

Who says that an angel has to be good all the time?

REFERENCE AND BIBLIOGRAPHY

MICHAEL BUBLÉ

SPECIAL DELIVERY
THESE FOOLISH THINGS LYRICS
SOFTLY AS I LEAVE YOU LYRICS
DREAM A LITTLE DREAM OF ME LYRICS
I'M BEGINNING TO SEE THE LIGHT LYRICS
MACK THE KNIFE LYRICS
ORANGE COLORED SKY LYRICS

CRAZY LOVE
ALL I DO IS DREAM OF YOU LYRICS
ALL OF ME LYRICS
AT THIS MOMENT LYRICS
BABY LYRICS
CRAZY LOVE LYRICS
CRY ME A RIVER LYRICS
GEORGIA ON MY MIND LYRICS
HAVEN'T MET YOU YET LYRICS
HEARTACHE TONIGHT LYRICS
HOLD ON LYRICS
STARDUST LYRICS
WHATEVER IT TAKES LYRICS
YOU'RE NOBODY TILL SOMEBODY LOVES YOU LYRICS

MICHAEL BUBLÉ MEETS MADISON SQUARE GARDEN (CD/DVD)
CALL ME IRRESPONSIBLE LYRICS
I'M YOUR MAN LYRICS
I'VE GOT THE WORLD ON A STRING LYRICS
LOST LYRICS
ME AND MRS JONES LYRICS
CRAZY LITTLE THING CALLED LOVE LYRICS
EVERYTHING LYRICS
FEELING GOOD LYRICS
HOME LYRICS
SONG FOR YOU LYRICS

CALL ME IRRESPONSIBLE
CALL ME IRRESPONSIBLE LYRICS
I'M YOUR MAN LYRICS
I'VE GOT THE WORLD ON A STRING LYRICS

141

LOST LYRICS
ME AND MRS JONES LYRICS
ALWAYS ON MY MIND LYRICS
COMIN' HOME BABY LYRICS
DREAM LYRICS
EVERYTHING LYRICS
IT HAD BETTER BE TONIGHT LYRICS
THAT'S LIFE LYRICS
THE BEST IS YET TO COME LYRICS
WONDERFUL TONIGHT LYRICS

EVERYTHING PT.2
EVERYTHING (ALBUM VERSION) LYRICS
EVERYTHING (ALTERNATE MIX) LYRICS
THESE FOOLISH THINGS (REMIND ME OF YOU) LYRICS

LET IT SNOW (EP)
CHRISTMAS SONG LYRICS
GROWN-UP CHRISTMAS LYRICS
I'LL BE HOME FOR CHRISTMAS LYRICS
LET IT SNOW LYRICS
LET IT SNOW (LIVE) LYRICS
WHITE CHRISTMAS

LET IT SNOW
CHRISTMAS SONG LYRICS
GROWN-UP CHRISTMAS LYRICS
I'LL BE HOME FOR CHRISTMAS LYRICS
LET IT SNOW LYRICS
LET IT SNOW (LIVE) LYRICS
WHITE CHRISTMAS

IT'S TIME
FEELING GOOD LYRICS
HOME LYRICS
HOW SWEET IT IS LYRICS
MORE I SEE YOU LYRICS
QUANDO, QUANDO, QUANDO LYRICS
SAVE THE LAST DANCE FOR ME LYRICS
SONG FOR YOU LYRICS
TRY A LITTLE TENDERNESS LYRICS
YOU AND I LYRICS
YOU DON'T KNOW ME LYRICS

CAUGHT IN THE ACT
CAN'T BUY ME LOVE LYRICS
FEELING GOOD LYRICS
HOME LYRICS
MORE I SEE YOU LYRICS
SMILE LYRICS
SUMMER WIND LYRICS
YOU AND I LYRICS
YOU'LL NEVER FIND ANOTHER LOVE LIKE MINE LYRICS

MICHAEL BUBLÉ
CHRISTMAS SONG LYRICS
COME FLY WITH ME LYRICS
CRAZY LITTLE THING CALLED LOVE LYRICS
FEVER LYRICS
FOR ONCE IN MY LIFE LYRICS
GROWN-UP CHRISTMAS LIST LYRICS
HOW CAN YOU MEND A BROKEN HEART LYRICS
I'LL BE HOME FOR CHRISTMAS LYRICS
KISSING A FOOL LYRICS
LET IT SNOW, LET IT SNOW, LET IT SNOW LYRICS
MOONDANCE LYRICS
PUT YOUR HEAD ON MY SHOULDER LYRICS
SUMMER WIND LYRICS
SWAY LYRICS
THAT'S ALL LYRICS
THE WAY YOU LOOK TONIGHT LYRICS
WHITE CHRISTAMS LYRICS
YOU'LL NEVER FIND ANOTHER LOVE LYRICS

TOTALLY BUBLÉ
ANYONE TO LOVE LYRICS
GUESS I'M FALLING FOR YOU LYRICS
LOVE AT FIRST SIGHT LYRICS
ME & MRS. YOU LYRICS
PEROXIDE SWING LYRICS
TELL HIM HE'S YOURS LYRICS
THAT'S HOW IT GOES LYRICS

MICHAEL BUBLÉ
FEVER
MOONDANCE
KISSING A FOOL

143

FOR ONCE IN MY LIFE
HOW CAN YOU MEND A BROKEN HEART
SUMMER WIND
YOU'LL NEVER FIND ANOTHER LOVE LIKE MINE
CRAZY LITTLE THING CALLED LOVE
PUT YOUR HEAD ON MY SHOULDER
SWAY
THE WAY YOU LOOK TONIGHT
COME FLY WITH ME
THAT'S ALL

IT'S TIME
FEELING GOOD
A FOGGY DAY (IN LONDON TOWN)
YOU DON'T KNOW ME
QUANDO, QUANDO, QUANDO (DUET WITH NELLY FURTADO)
HOME
CAN'T BUY ME LOVE
THE MORE I SEE YOU
SAVE THE LAST DANCE FOR ME
TRY A LITTLE TENDERNESS
HOW SWEET IT IS (TO BE LOVED BY YOU)
A SONG FOR YOU (DUET WITH CHRIS BOTTI)
I'VE GOT YOU UNDER MY SKIN
YOU AND I

CALL ME IRRESPONSIBLE
THE BEST IS YET TO COME
IT HAD BETTER BE TONIGHT (MEGLIO STASERA)
ME AND MRS. JONES (DUET WITH EMILY BLUNT)
I'M YOUR MAN
COMIN' HOME BABY (DUET WITH BOYZ II MEN)
LOST
CALL ME IRRESPONSIBLE
WONDERFUL TONIGHT (DUET WITH IVAN LINS)
EVERYTHING
I'VE GOT THE WORLD ON A STRING
ALWAYS ON MY MIND
THAT'S LIFE
DREAM

BIBLIOGRAPHY

Special Delivery: http://www.metrolyrics.com/michael-buble-albums-list.html
Crazy Love: http://www.metrolyrics.com/michael-buble-albums-list.html
Michael Bublé meets Madison Square Garden (cd/dvd): http://www.metrolyrics.com/michael-buble-albums-list.html
Call Me Irresponsible: http://www.metrolyrics.com/michael-buble-albums-list.html
Everything pt.2: http://www.metrolyrics.com/michael-buble-albums-list.html
Let It Snow (ep): http://www.metrolyrics.com/michael-buble-albums-list.html
Let It Snow: http://www.metrolyrics.com/michael-buble-albums-list.html
It's Time: http://www.metrolyrics.com/michael-buble-albums-list.html
Caught In The Act: http://www.metrolyrics.com/michael-buble-albums-list.html
Michael Bublé: http://www.metrolyrics.com/michael-buble-albums-list.html
Totally Bublé: http://www.metrolyrics.com/michael-buble-albums-list.html
Michael Bublé: http://en.wikipedia.org/wiki/michael_bubl%c3%a9_discography
It's Time: http://en.wikipedia.org/wiki/michael_bubl%c3%a9_discography
Call Me Irresponsible: http://en.wikipedia.org/wiki/michael_bubl%c3%a9_discography

HARRY CONNICK JR. REFERENCE

IN CONCERT ON BROADWAY
WE ARE IN LOVE
THE WAY YOU LOOK TONIGHT
BÉSAME MUCHO
THE OTHER HOURS
NOWHERE WITH LOVE
HOW INSENSITIVE
COME BY ME
MY TIME OF DAY/I'VE NEVER BEEN IN LOVE BEFORE
ALL THE WAY

145

BAYOU MAHARAJAH
HEAR ME IN THE HARMONY
LIGHT THE WAY
TAKE HER TO THE MARDI GRAS
BOURBON STREET PARADE
MARDI GRAS IN NEW ORLEANS

YOUR SONGS
ALL THE WAY
JUST THE WAY YOU ARE
CAN'T HELP FALLING IN LOVE WITH YOU
AND I LOVE HER
(THEY LONG TO BE) CLOSE TO YOU
BESAME MUCHO (KISS ME MUCH)
THE WAY YOU LOOK TONIGHT
FIRST TIME EVER I SAW YOUR FACE
YOUR SONG
SOME ENCHANTED EVENING
AND I LOVE YOU SO
WHO CAN I TURN TO (WHEN NOBODY NEEDS ME)
SMILE
MONA LISA

WHAT A NIGHT! A CHRISTMAS ALBUM
IT'S THE MOST WONDERFUL TIME OF THE YEAR
WHAT A NIGHT!
CHRISTMAS DAY
HAVE A HOLLY JOLLY CHRISTMAS
O COME ALL YE FAITHFUL
DANCE OF THE SUGARPLUM FAIRIES
LET THERE BE PEACE ON EARTH
WINTER WONDERLAND
IT'S BEGINNING TO LOOK A LOT LIKE CHRISTMAS
SANTARIFFIC
JINGLE BELLS
ZAT YOU SANTA CLAUS
WE THREE KINGS
SONG FOR THE HOPEFUL (FEAT. KIM BURRELL)

CHANSON DU VIEUX CARRE
SOMEDAY YOU'LL BE SORRY
PANAMA
ASH WEDNESDAY

CHANSON DU VIEUX CARRÉ
BOURBON STREET PARADE
PETITE FLEUR
FIDGETY FEET
LUSCIOUS
NEW ORLEANS
I STILL GET JEALOUS
THAT'S A PLENTY
MARDI GRAS IN NEW ORLEANS

OH, MY NOLA
WORKING IN A COAL MINE
WON'T YOU COME HOME, BILL BAILEY?
SOMETHING YOU GOT
LET THEM TALK
JAMBALAYA (ON THE BAYOU)
CARELESS LOVE
ALL THESE PEOPLE
YES WE CAN CAN
SOMEDAY
OH, MY NOLA
ELIJAH ROCK
SHEIK OF ARABY
LAZY BONES
WE MAKE A LOT OF LOVE
HELLO DOLLY
DO DAT THING

HARRY ON BROADWAY, ACT 1
DISC 1
OVERTURE
RACING WITH THE CLOCK
A NEW TOWN IS A BLUE TOWN
I'M NOT AT ALL IN LOVE
I'LL NEVER BE JEALOUS AGAIN
HEY THERE
SLEEP TITE
HER IS
ONCE A YEAR DAY
ONCE A YEAR DAY PLAYOFF
HER IS (REPRISE)
SMALL TALK
THERE ONCE WAS A MAN

FACTORY MUSIC / SLOW DOWN
HEY THERE (REPRISE)
STEAM HEAT
THE WORLD AROUND US
HEY THERE (REPRISE) / IF YOU WIN, YOU LOSE
THINK OF THE TIME I SAVE
HERNANDO'S HIDEAWAY
THE THREE OF US
SEVEN-AND-A-HALF CENTS
THERE ONCE WAS A MAN (REPRISE)
HERNANDO'S JIVE
THE PAJAMA GAME
DISC 2
OH, MY DEAR (SOMETHING'S GONE WRONG)
CAN'T WE TELL
SUCH LOVE
I LIKE LOVE MORE
MY LITTLE WORLD
ALL THINGS
I NEED TO BE IN LOVE
OH! AIN'T THAT SWEET
THE OTHER HOURS
TAKE ADVANTAGE
TAKE HER TO THE MARDI GRAS

OCCASION: CONNICK ON PIANO, VOL. 2
BROWN WORLD
VALENTINE'S DAY
OCCASION
SPOT
I LIKE LOVE MORE
ALL THINGS
WIN
VIRIGOLD
REMEMBER THAT TARPON
LOSE
STEVE LACY
CHANSON DE VIEUX CARRE
GOOD TO BE HOME

ONLY YOU
MORE
THE VERY THOUGHT OF YOU

148

SAVE THE LAST DANCE FOR ME
MY BLUE HEAVEN
YOU DON'T KNOW ME
ALL THESE THINGS
FOR ONCE IN MY LIFE
ONLY YOU (AND YOU ALONE)
MY PRAYER
OTHER HOURS
I ONLY HAVE EYES FOR YOU
GOD NIGHT MY LOVE (PLEASANT DREAMS)

HARRY FOR THE HOLIDAYS
FROSTY THE SNOWMAN
BLUE CHRISTMAS
THE CHRISTMAS WALTZ
I WONDER AS I WANDER
SILVER BELLS
MARY'S LITTLE BOY CHILD
SANTA CLAUS IS COMING TO TOWN
THE HAPPY ELF
I'LL BE HOME FOR CHRISTMAS
I COME WITH LOVE
NATURE BOY
O' LITTLE TOWN OF BETHLEHEM
I'M GONNA BE THE FIRST ONE
THIS CHRISTMAS
NOTHIN' NEW FOR NEW YEAR
SILENT NIGHT

OTHER HOURS (CONNICK ON PIANO, VOLUME 1)
WHAT A WASTE
SUCH LOVE
TAKE ADVANTAGE
HOW ABOUT TONIGHT
SOVEREIGN LOVER
MY LITTLE WORLD
OH, MY DEAR (SOMETHING'S GONE WRONG)
CAN'T WE TELL
DUMB LUCK
OH! AIN'T THAT SWEET
THE OTHER HOURS
YOUR OWN PRIVATE LOVE

30
I'M WALKIN'
CHATTANOOGA CHOO CHOO
SOMEWHERE MY LOVE
THE GYPSY
IF I WERE A BELL
WAY DOWN YONDER IN NEW ORLEANS
TIE A YELLOW RIBBON ROUND THE OLD OAK TREE
THERE IS ALWAYS ONE MORE TIME
NEW ORLEANS
SPEAK SOFTLY LOVE
JUNCO PARTNER
DON'T FENCE ME IN
DON'T LIKE GOODBYES
I'LL ONLY MISS HER (WHEN I THINK OF HER)

SONGS I HEARD
SUPERCALIFRAGILISTICEXPIALIDOCIOUS
THE LONELY GOATHERD
DING DONG! THE WITCH IS DEAD
MAYBE
PURE IMAGINATION / CANDY MAN
GOLDEN TICKET / I WANT IT NOW
OOMPA LOOMPA
A SPOONFUL OF SUGAR
STAY AWAKE
SOMETHING WAS MISSING
YOU'RE NEVER FULLY DRESSED WITHOUT A SMILE
OVER THE RAINBOW
THE JITTERBUG
MERRY OLD LAND OF OZ
EDELWEISS
DO-RE-MI

COME BY ME
NOWHERE WITH LOVE
COME BY ME
CHARADE
CHANGE PARTNERS
EASY FOR YOU TO SAY
TIME AFTER TIME
NEXT DOOR BLUES
EASY TO LOVE
THERE'S NO BUSINESS LIKE SHOW BUSINESS

A MOMENT WITH ME
DANNY BOY
CRY ME A RIVER
LOVE FOR SALE

TO SEE YOU
LET ME LOVE TONIGHT
TO SEE YOU
LET'S JUST KISS
HEART BEYOND REPAIR
ONCE
LEARN TO LOVE
LOVE ME SOME YOU
MUCH LOVE
IN LOVE AGAIN
LOVED BY ME

STAR TURTLE
STAR TURTLE 1
HOW DO YA'LL KNOW
HEAR ME IN THE HARMONY
REASON TO BELIEVE
JUST LIKE ME
STAR TURTLE 2
LITTLE FARLEY
EYES OF THE SEEKER
NOBODY LIKE YOU TO ME
BOOZE HOUND
STAR TURTLE, PT. 3
NEVER YOUNG
MIND ON THE MATTER
CITY BENEATH THE SEA
STAR TURTLE, PT. 4

SHE
SHE
BETWEEN US
HERE COMES THE BIG PARADE
TROUBLE
(I COULD ONLY) WHISPER YOUR NAME
FOLLOW THE MUSIC
JOE SLAM AND THE SPACESHIP
TO LOVE THE LANGUAGE
HONESTLY NOW (SAFETY'S JUST DANGER...OUT OF PLACE)

SHE...BLESSED BE THE ONE
FUNKY DUNKY
FOLLOW THE MUSIC FURTHER
THAT PARTY
BOOKER

WHEN MY HEART FINDS CHRISTMAS
SLEIGH RIDE
WHEN MY HEART FINDS CHRISTMAS
(IT MUST'VE BEEN OL') SANTA CLAUS
BLESSED DAWN OF CHRISTMAS DAY
LET IT SNOW! LET IT SNOW! LET IT SNOW!
LITTLE DRUMMER BOY
AVE MARIA
PARADE OF THE WOODEN SOLDIERS
WHAT CHILD IS THIS?
CHRISTMAS DREAMING
I PRAY ON CHRISTMAS
RUDOLPH THE RED-NOSED REINDEER
O HOLY NIGHT
WHAT ARE YOU DOING NEW YEAR'S EVE?

BIBLIOGRAPHY

In Concert On Broadway:
http://www.harryconnickjr.com/us/music/concert-broadway
Your Songs: http://www.harryconnickjr.com/us/music/your-songs
What A Night! A Christmas Album:
http://www.harryconnickjr.com/us/music/what-night-christmas-album
Chanson Du Vieux Carre:
http://www.harryconnickjr.com/us/music/chanson-du-vieux-carre
Oh, My Nola: http://www.harryconnickjr.com/us/music/oh-my-nola
Harry On Broadway, Act 1:
http://www.harryconnickjr.com/us/music/harry-broadway-act-1
Occasion: Connick On Piano, Vol. 2:
http://www.harryconnickjr.com/us/music/occasion-connick-piano-vol-2
Only You: http://www.harryconnickjr.com/us/music/only-you
To See You: http://www.harryconnickjr.com/us/music/see-you

Harry For The Holidays:
http://www.harryconnickjr.com/us/music/harry-holidays
Other Hours (Connick On Piano, Volume 1):
http://www.harryconnickjr.com/us/music/other-hours-connick-
piano-volume-1
30: http://www.harryconnickjr.com/us/music/30
Songs I Heard: http://www.harryconnickjr.com/us/music/songs-
i-heard
Come By Me: http://www.harryconnickjr.com/us/music/come-
me
Star Turtle: http://www.harryconnickjr.com/us/music/star-turtle
She: http://www.harryconnickjr.com/us/music/she
When My Heart Finds Christmas:
http://www.harryconnickjr.com/us/music/when-my-heart-finds-
christmas

TONY BENNETT

ESSENTIAL TONY BENNETT CD
DISC 1
BECAUSE OF YOU: - MONO
BECAUSE OF YOU: - MONO
COLD, COLD HEART: - MONO
COLD, COLD HEART: - MONO
BLUE VELVET: - MONO
BLUE VELVET: - MONO
RAGS TO RICHES: - MONO
RAGS TO RICHES: - MONO
STRANGER IN PARADISE: - MONO
STRANGER IN PARADISE: - MONO
SING YOU SINNERS: - MONO
SING YOU SINNERS: - MONO
BOULEVARD OF BROKEN DREAMS: - MONO
BOULEVARD OF BROKEN DREAMS: - MONO
JUST IN TIME: - MONO
JUST IN TIME: - MONO
IT AMAZES ME
IT AMAZES ME
LOVE LOOK AWAY: - CONDUCTED BY GLENN OSSER,
CONDUCTED BY GLENN OSSER, TONY BENNETT / ARRANGED
AND CONDUCTED BY GLENN OSSER,
TONY BENNETT / ARRANGED AND CONDUCTED BY GLENN
OSSER, ARRANGED, ARRANGED

LOVE LOOK AWAY: - CONDUCTED BY GLENN OSSER,
CONDUCTED BY GLENN OSSER, TONY BENNETT / ARRANGED
AND CONDUCTED BY GLENN OSSER,
TONY BENNETT / ARRANGED AND CONDUCTED BY GLENN
OSSER, ARRANGED, ARRANGED
FIREFLY
FIREFLY
PUT ON A HAPPY FACE
PUT ON A HAPPY FACE
THE BEST IS YET TO COME
THE BEST IS YET TO COME
TENDER IS THE NIGHT
TENDER IS THE NIGHT
ONCE UPON A TIME
ONCE UPON A TIME
I LEFT MY HEART IN SAN FRANCISCO
I LEFT MY HEART IN SAN FRANCISCO
I WANNA BE AROUND
I WANNA BE AROUND
FOR THE GOOD LIFE
FOR THE GOOD LIFE
THIS IS ALL I ASK
THIS IS ALL I ASK
WHEN JOANNA LOVED ME
WHEN JOANNA LOVED ME
RULES OF THE ROAD, THE
RULES OF THE ROAD, THE
DISC 2
WHO CAN I TURN TO (WHEN NOBODY NEEDS ME): -
ARRANGED, ARRANGED, TONY BENNETT / ARRANGED AND
CONDUCTED BY GEORGE SIRAVO / RALPH SHARON TRIO,
TONY BENNETT / ARRANGED AND CONDUCTED BY GEORGE
SIRAVO / RALPH SHARON TRIO, CONDUCTED BY GEORGE
SIRAVO, CONDUCTED BY GEORGE SIRAVO, RALPH SHARON
TRIO, RALPH SHARON
WHO CAN I TURN TO (WHEN NOBODY NEEDS ME): -
ARRANGED, ARRANGED, TONY BENNETT / ARRANGED AND
CONDUCTED BY GEORGE SIRAVO / RALPH SHARON TRIO,
TONY BENNETT / ARRANGED AND CONDUCTED BY GEORGE
SIRAVO / RALPH SHARON TRIO, CONDUCTED BY GEORGE
SIRAVO, CONDUCTED BY GEORGE SIRAVO, RALPH SHARON
TRIO, RALPH SHARON
IF I RULED THE WORLD

154

IF I RULED THE WORLD
FLY ME TO THE MOON (IN OTHER WORDS)
FLY ME TO THE MOON (IN OTHER WORDS)
SHADOW OF YOUR SMILE, THE
SHADOW OF YOUR SMILE, THE

TONY BENNETT/BILL EVANS ALBUM CD
YOUNG AND FOOLISH: - (WITH BILL EVANS, BILL EVANS
TONY BENNETT)
YOUNG AND FOOLISH: - (WITH BILL EVANS, BILL EVANS
TONY BENNETT)
THE TOUCH OF YOUR LIPS
THE TOUCH OF YOUR LIPS
SOME OTHER TIME: - BILL EVANS TONY BENNETT, TONY
BENNETT BILL EVANS
SOME OTHER TIME: - BILL EVANS TONY BENNETT, TONY
BENNETT BILL EVANS
WHEN IN ROME: - (WITH BILL EVANS, BILL EVANS TONY
BENNETT)
WHEN IN ROME: - (WITH BILL EVANS, BILL EVANS TONY
BENNETT)
WE'LL BE TOGETHER AGAIN: - (WITH BILL EVANS, BILL
EVANS TONY BENNETT)
WE'LL BE TOGETHER AGAIN: - (WITH BILL EVANS, BILL
EVANS TONY BENNETT)
MY FOOLISH HEART: - (WITH BILL EVANS, BILL EVANS TONY
BENNETT)
MY FOOLISH HEART: - (WITH BILL EVANS, BILL EVANS
TONY BENNETT)
WALTZ FOR DEBBY: - (WITH BILL EVANS, BILL EVANS
TONY BENNETT)
WALTZ FOR DEBBY: - (WITH BILL EVANS, BILL EVANS
TONY BENNETT)
BUT BEAUTIFUL: - (WITH BILL EVANS, BILL EVANS TONY
BENNETT)
BUT BEAUTIFUL: - (WITH BILL EVANS, BILL EVANS TONY
BENNETT)
DAYS OF WINE AND ROSES: - BILL EVANS TONY BENNETT,
TONY BENNETT BILL EVANS
DAYS OF WINE AND ROSES: - BILL EVANS TONY BENNETT,
TONY BENNETT BILL EVANS
YOUNG AND FOOLISH
YOUNG AND FOOLISH

155

TOUCH OF YOUR LIPS, THE
TOUCH OF YOUR LIPS, THE
SOME OTHER TIME
SOME OTHER TIME
WHEN IN ROME
WHEN IN ROME
WALTZ FOR DEBBY
WALTZ FOR DEBBY

ULTIMATE TONY BENNETT CD
LEFT MY HEART IN SAN FRANCISCO
BECAUSE OF YOU
RAGS TO RICHES
JUST IN TIME
STRANGER IN PARADISE
THE BOULEVARD OF BROKEN DREAMS
I WANNA BE AROUND
THE GOOD LIFE
THE SHADOW OF YOUR SMILE
PUT ON A HAPPY FACE
IF I RULED THE WORLD
SMILE
NIGHT AND DAY
HOW DO YOU KEEP THE MUSIC PLAYING? - (WITH THE RALPH
SHARON TRIO, THE RALPH SHARON TRIO)
MOOD INDIGO
BLUE VELVET
STEPPIN' OUT WITH MY BABY
WHEN JOANNA LOVED ME
WHEN DO THE BELLS RING FOR ME
THE BEST IS YET TO COME

FIFTY YEARS: THE ARTISTRY OF TONY BENNETT CD
DISC 1
THE BOULEVARD OF BROKEN DREAMS
BECAUSE OF YOU
COLD, COLD HEART
BLUE VELVET
RAGS TO RICHES
STRANGER IN PARADISE
WHILE THE MUSIC PLAYS ON
MAY I NEVER LOVE AGAIN
SING YOU SINNERS

JUST IN TIME
LAZY AFTERNOON
CA C'EST L'AMOUR
I GET A KICK OUT OF YOU
IT AMAZES ME PENTHOUSE
PENTHOUSE SERENADE (WHEN WE'RE ALONE)
LOST IN THE STARS
LULLABY OF BROADWAY
FIREFLY: - HIS ORCHESTRA, TONY BENNETT WITH COUNT
BASIE
& HIS ORCHESTRA, COUNT BASIE
A SLEEPIN' BEE
THE MAN THAT GOT AWAY
SKYLARK
SEPTEMBER SONG
TILL
DISC 2
BEGIN THE BEGUINE
PUT ON A HAPPY FACE
THE BEST IS YET TO COME
THIS TIME THE DREAM'S ON ME
CLOSE YOUR EYES
TOOT, TOOT, TOOTSIE! (GOODBYE)
DANCING IN THE DARK
STELLA BY STARLIGHT
TENDER IS THE NIGHT
ONCE UPON A TIME
(I LEFT MY HEART IN) SAN FRANCISCO
UNTIL I MET YOU
IF I LOVE AGAIN
I WANNA BE AROUND
THE GOOD LIFE
IT WAS ME
SPRING IN MANHATTAN
THE MOMENT OF TRUTH
THIS IS ALL I ASK
A TASTE OF HONEY
WHEN JOANNA LOVED ME
I'LL BE AROUND
DISC 3
NOBODY ELSE BUT ME
IT HAD TO BE YOU
I'VE GOT JUST ABOUT EVERYTHING

157

WHO CAN I TURN TO?
WALTZ FOR DEBBIE

TONY BENNETT SINGS FOR LOVERS CD
MY FOOLISH HEART: - (WITH BILL EVANS, BILL EVANS TONY
BENNETT)
MY FOOLISH HEART: - (WITH BILL EVANS, BILL EVANS TONY
BENNETT)
ISN'T IT ROMANTIC
ISN'T IT ROMANTIC
THIS CAN'T BE LOVE
THIS CAN'T BE LOVE
THE TOUCH OF YOUR LIPS
THE TOUCH OF YOUR LIPS
I COULD WRITE A BOOK
I COULD WRITE A BOOK
THOU SWELL
THOU SWELL
BUT BEAUTIFUL: - (WITH BILL EVANS, BILL EVANS TONY
BENNETT)
BUT BEAUTIFUL: - (WITH BILL EVANS, BILL EVANS TONY
BENNETT)
MY HEART STOOD STILL
MY HEART STOOD STILL
LOVER
LOVER
YOU DON'T KNOW WHAT LOVE IS: - BILL EVANS TONY
BENNETT, TONY BENNETT BILL EVANS
YOU DON'T KNOW WHAT LOVE IS: - BILL EVANS TONY
BENNETT, TONY BENNETT BILL EVANS
MY ROMANCE
MY ROMANCE
ALL MINE
ALL MINE
AS TIME GOES BY
AS TIME GOES BY
BRIDGES
BRIDGES
SOME OTHER TIME: - BILL EVANS TONY BENNETT, TONY
BENNETT BILL EVANS
SOME OTHER TIME: - BILL EVANS TONY BENNETT, TONY
BENNETT BILL EVANS

TONY BENNETT - SWINGIN' CHRISTMAS CD
I'LL BE HOME FOR CHRISTMAS
SILVER BELLS
ALL I WANT FOR CHRISTMAS IS YOU
MY FAVORITE THINGS
CHRISTMAS TIME IS HERE
WINTER WONDERLAND
HAVE YOURSELF A MERRY LITTLE CHRISTMAS
SANTA CLAUS IS COMING TO TOWN
I'VE GOT MY LOVE TO KEEP ME WARM: - ANTONIA BENNETT
THE CHRISTMAS WALTZ
O CHRISTMAS TREE

COMPLETE TONY BENNETT/BILL EVANS RECORDINGS CD
DISC 1
YOUNG AND FOOLISH: - (WITH BILL EVANS, BILL EVANS
TONY BENNETT)
YOUNG AND FOOLISH: - (WITH BILL EVANS, BILL EVANS
TONY BENNETT)
THE TOUCH OF YOUR LIPS
THE TOUCH OF YOUR LIPS
SOME OTHER TIME: - BILL EVANS TONY BENNETT, TONY
BENNETT BILL EVANS
SOME OTHER TIME: - BILL EVANS TONY BENNETT, TONY
BENNETT BILL EVANS
WHEN IN ROME: - (WITH BILL EVANS, BILL EVANS TONY
BENNETT)
WHEN IN ROME: - (WITH BILL EVANS, BILL EVANS TONY
BENNETT)
WE'LL BE TOGETHER AGAIN: - (WITH BILL EVANS, BILL
EVANS TONY BENNETT)
WE'LL BE TOGETHER AGAIN: - (WITH BILL EVANS, BILL
EVANS TONY BENNETT)
MY FOOLISH HEART: - BILL EVANS TONY BENNETT, TONY
BENNETT BILL EVANS
MY FOOLISH HEART: - BILL EVANS TONY BENNETT, TONY
BENNETT BILL EVANS
WALTZ FOR DEBBY: - (WITH BILL EVANS, BILL EVANS
TONY BENNETT)
WALTZ FOR DEBBY: - (WITH BILL EVANS, BILL EVANS
TONY BENNETT)
BUT BEAUTIFUL: - BILL EVANS TONY BENNETT, TONY
BENNETT BILL EVANS

BUT BEAUTIFUL: - BILL EVANS TONY BENNETT, TONY
BENNETT BILL EVANS
THE DAYS OF WINE AND ROSES
THE DAYS OF WINE AND ROSES
THE BAD AND THE BEAUTIFUL
THE BAD AND THE BEAUTIFUL
LUCKY TO BE ME: - BILL EVANS TONY BENNETT, TONY
BENNETT BILL EVANS
LUCKY TO BE ME: - BILL EVANS TONY BENNETT, TONY
BENNETT BILL EVANS
MAKE SOMEONE HAPPY: - BILL EVANS TONY BENNETT,
TONY BENNETT BILL EVANS
MAKE SOMEONE HAPPY: - BILL EVANS TONY BENNETT,
TONY BENNETT BILL EVANS
YOU'RE NEARER: - BILL EVANS TONY BENNETT, TONY
BENNETT BILL EVANS, BILL EVANS, BILL EVANS
YOU'RE NEARER: - BILL EVANS TONY BENNETT, TONY
BENNETT BILL EVANS, BILL EVANS, BILL EVANS
A CHILD IS BORN
A CHILD IS BORN
THE TWO LONELY PEOPLE
THE TWO LONELY PEOPLE
YOU DON'T KNOW WHAT LOVE: - BILL EVANS TONY
BENNETT, TONY BENNETT BILL EVANS
YOU DON'T KNOW WHAT LOVE IS: - BILL EVANS TONY
BENNETT, TONY BENNETT BILL EVANS
MAYBE SEPTEMBER: - BILL EVANS TONY BENNETT, TONY
BENNETT BILL EVANS, BILL EVANS, BILL EVANS
MAYBE SEPTEMBER: - BILL EVANS TONY BENNETT, TONY
BENNETT BILL EVANS, BILL EVANS, BILL EVANS
LONELY GIRL: - BILL EVANS, BILL EVANS, TONY BENNETT
BILL EVANS, BILL EVANS TONY BENNETT
LONELY GIRL: - BILL EVANS, BILL EVANS, TONY BENNETT
BILL EVANS, BILL EVANS TONY BENNETT
YOU MUST BELIEVE IN SPRING: - (WITH BILL EVANS, BILL
EVANS TONY BENNETT)
YOU MUST BELIEVE IN SPRING: - (WITH BILL EVANS, BILL
EVANS TONY BENNETT)
WHO CAN I TURN TO?: - BILL EVANS TONY BENNETT,
TONY BENNETT BILL EVANS
WHO CAN I TURN TO?: - BILL EVANS TONY BENNETT,
TONY BENNETT BILL EVANS

DREAM DANCING: - (WITH BILL EVANS, BILL EVANS, BILL
EVANS, BILL EVANS TONY BENNETT)
DREAM DANCING: - (WITH BILL EVANS, BILL EVANS, BILL
EVANS, BILL EVANS TONY BENNETT)
DISC 2
YOUNG AND FOOLISH
YOUNG AND FOOLISH
TOUCH OF YOUR LIPS,
TOUCH OF YOUR LIPS,
SOME OTHER TIME (ALTERNATE, TAKE 7)
SOME OTHER TIME (ALTERNATE, TAKE 7)
WHEN IN ROME (ALTERNATE, TAKE 11)
WHEN IN ROME (ALTERNATE, TAKE 11)

TONY BENNETT - HERE'S TO THE LADIES CD
PEOPLE
I'M IN LOVE AGAIN
SOMEWHERE OVER THE RAINBOW
MY LOVE WENT TO LONDON
POOR BUTTERFLY
SENTIMENTAL JOURNEY
CLOUDY MORNING
TENDERLY
DOWN IN THE DEPTHS
MOONLIGHT IN VERMONT
TANGERINE
GOD BLESS THE CHILD
DAYBREAK
YOU SHOWED ME THE WAY
HONEYSUCKLE ROSE
MAYBE THIS TIME
I GOT RHYTHM
MY IDEAL

**TONY BENNETT - SINGS THE ULTIMATE AMERICAN
SONGBOOK, VOL. 1 CD**
ANYTHING GOES (FROM "ANYTHING GOES")
THE VERY THOUGHT OF YOU
THE WAY YOU LOOK TONIGHT
EV'RYTIME WE SAY GOODBYE
THAT OLD BLACK MAGIC
A FOGGY DAY
I'LL BE SEEING YOU
AIN'T MISBEHAVIN'

IT HAD TO BE YOU
MOONGLOW
SHE'S FUNNY THAT WAY (I GOT A WOMAN CRAZY FOR ME)
YOU GO TO MY HEAD
THEY CAN'T TAKE THAT AWAY FROM ME
YOU'LL NEVER GET AWAY FROM ME
TAKING A CHANCE ON LOVE

TONY BENNETT - SINGS THE ULTIMATE AMERICAN SONGBOOK, VOL. 2 CD
ANYTHING GOES (FROM "ANYTHING GOES") (ALBUM VERSION)
THE VERY THOUGHT OF YOU
THE WAY YOU LOOK TONIGHT
EV'RYTIME WE SAY GOODBYE (ALBUM VERSION)
THAT OLD BLACK MAGIC
A FOGGY DAY
I'LL BE SEEING YOU
AIN'T MISBEHAVIN'
IT HAD TO BE YOU
MOONGLOW
SHE'S FUNNY THAT WAY (I GOT A WOMAN CRAZY FOR ME) (ALBUM VERSION)
YOU GO TO MY HEAD
THEY CAN'T TAKE THAT AWAY FROM ME
YOU'LL NEVER GET AWAY FROM ME (ALBUM VERSION)
TAKING A CHANCE ON LOVE

TONY BENNETT - WHILE WE'RE YOUNG: ORIGINAL RECORDINGS 1950-1955 CD
COLD, COLD HEART
THERE'LL BE NO TEARDROPS TONIGHT
HOW CAN I REPLACE YOU?
TAKING A CHANCE ON LOVE
WALK IN THE COUNTRY
HAPPINESS STREET (CORNER SUNSHINE SQUARE)
I WANNA BE LOVED
CAN YOU FIND IT IN YOUR HEART
CONGRATULATIONS TO SOMEONE
BECAUSE OF YOU
IN THE MIDDLE OF AN ISLAND
STAY WHERE YOU ARE (THIS IS THE MOMENT I PRAYED FOR)
LOVE WALKED IN
ALWAYS

ALONE TOGETHER
I WON'T CRY ANYMORE
HAVE A GOOD TIME
JUST IN TIME
I AM
GONE WITH THE WIND SEE
HERE IN MY HEART
CLOSE YOUR EYES
WHILE WE'RE YOUNG
YOU CAN DEPEND ON ME
IT'S MAGIC
FIREFLY
SMILE
OUT OF THIS WORLD
WITHOUT A SONG
THE BOULEVARD OF BROKEN DREAMS
STRANGER IN PARADISE
COME BACK
I'M ALWAYS CHASING RAINBOWS
TAKE ME BACK AGAIN
RAGS TO RICHES
MY HEART WON'T SAY GOODBYE
ANYWHERE I WANDER
HOW LONG HAS THIS BEEN GOING ON
SOMEWHERE ALONG THE WAY
CINNAMON SINNER
ROSES OF YESTERDAY
WHY DOES IT HAVE TO BE ME?
BLUE VELVET
FROM THE CANDY STORE ON THE CORNER
NO ONE WILL EVER KNOW
HERE COMES THAT HEARTACHE AGAIN
YOUNG AND WARM AND WONDERFUL
I'M THE KING OF BROKEN HEARTS
NOT AS A STRANGER
TAKE ME
COME NEXT SPRING
SOPHISTICATED LADY
I'LL BRING YOU A RAINBOW
CLIMB EVERY MOUNTAIN
ASK ANYONE IN LOVE
THE NIGHT THAT HEAVEN FELL
SING YOU SINNERS

TONY BENNETT - DUETS: AN AMERICAN CLASSIC CD

LULLABY OF BROADWAY: - (WITH DUET, DIXIE CHICKS, TONY BENNETT DUET WITH DIXIE CHICKS)
SMILE: - (WITH DUET WITH BARBRA STREISAND, TONY BENNETT DUET)
PUT ON A HAPPY FACE: - (WITH DUET WITH JAMES TAYLOR, JAMES TAYLOR, TONY BENNETT DUET)
THE VERY THOUGHT OF YOU
SHADOW OF YOUR SMILE: - SPANISH
RAGS TO RICHES: - (WITH DUET, ELTON JOHN, TONY BENNETT DUET WITH ELTON JOHN)
THE GOOD LIFE
COLD, COLD HEART: - (WITH DUET, TONY BENNETT DUET WITH TIM MCGRAW, TIM MCGRAW)
IF I RULED THE WORLD: - (WITH DUET WITH CELINE DION, CELINE DION, TONY BENNETT DUET)
THE BEST IS YET TO COME
FOR ONCE IN MY LIFE: - (WITH DUET WITH STEVIE WONDER, TONY BENNETT DUET)
ARE YOU HAVIN' ANY FUN?: - (WITH DUET WITH ELVIS COSTELLO, TONY BENNETT DUET, ELVIS COSTELLO)
BECAUSE OF YOU: - (WITH DUET, K.D. LANG, TONY BENNETT DUET WITH K.D. LANG)
JUST IN TIME: - (WITH DUET WITH MICHAEL BUBLÉ, TONY BENNETT DUET, MICHAEL BUBLÉ)
THE BOULEVARD OF BROKEN DREAMS
I WANNA BE AROUND: - BONO
SING, YOU SINNERS
I LEFT MY HEART IN SAN FRANCISCO
HOW DO YOU KEEP THE MUSIC PLAYING

K D LANG - WONDERFUL WORLD CD

EXACTLY LIKE YOU: - TONY BENNETT & K.D. LANG
LA VIE EN ROSE: - (WITH FRENCH)
I'M CONFESSIN' (THAT I LOVE YOU): - TONY BENNETT & K.D. LANG
YOU CAN DEPEND ON ME: - TONY BENNETT & K.D. LANG
WHAT A WONDERFUL WORLD: - TONY BENNETT & K.D. LANG
THAT'S MY HOME: - TONY BENNETT K.D. LANG
KISS TO BUILD A DREAM ON
I WONDER: - TONY BENNETT & K.D. LANG
DREAM A LITTLE DREAM OF ME: - TONY BENNETT & K.D. LANG

YOU CAN'T LOSE A BROKEN HEART: - TONY BENNETT
& K.D. LANG
THAT LUCKY OLD SUN (JUST ROLLS AROUND HEAVEN ALL
DAY): - TONY BENNETT & K.D. LANG
IF WE NEVER MEET AGAIN: - TONY BENNETT & K.D. LANG

TONY BENNETT - ALL-TIME GREATEST HITS CD
BECAUSE OF YOU
RAGS TO RICHES
STRANGER IN PARADISE
SING YOU SINNERS
JUST IN TIME
THE BOULEVARD OF BROKEN DREAMS
LOVE, LOOK AWAY
FIREFLY
PUT ON A HAPPY FACE
I LEFT MY HEART IN SAN FRANCISCO: - CONDUCTED BY
MARTY MANNING, RALPH SHARON, ARRANGED, TONY
BENNETT ARRANGED & CONDUCTED BY MARTY MANNING
WITH RALPH SHARON
I WANNA BE AROUND
THIS IS ALL I ASK
WHO CAN I TURN TO (WHEN NOBODY NEEDS ME): -
CONDUCTED BY GEORGE SIRAVO, RALPH SHARON TRIO,
TONY BENNETT ARRANGED & CONDUCTED BY GEORGE
SIRAVO / / RALPH SHARON TRIO, ARRANGED, TONY BENNETT
ARRANGED AND CONDUCTED BY GEORGE SIRAVO / RALPH
SHARON TRIO
THE SHADOW OF YOUR SMILE
SMILE
A TIME FOR LOVE
FOR ONCE IN MY LIFE
SOMETHING
(WHERE DO I BEGIN) LOVE STORY
MAYBE THIS TIME

TONY BENNETT - TOGETHER AGAIN CD
LUCKY TO BE ME: - (WITH BILL EVANS, TONY BENNETT
BILL EVANS)
LUCKY TO BE ME: - (WITH BILL EVANS, TONY BENNETT
BILL EVANS)
MAKE SOMEONE HAPPY: - (WITH BILL EVANS, TONY
BENNETT BILL EVANS)

MAKE SOMEONE HAPPY: - (WITH BILL EVANS, TONY
BENNETT BILL EVANS)
A CHILD IS BORN
A CHILD IS BORN
THE TWO LONELY PEOPLE
THE TWO LONELY PEOPLE
YOU MUST BELIEVE IN SPRING: - (WITH BILL EVANS,
TONY BENNETT BILL EVANS)
YOU MUST BELIEVE IN SPRING: - (WITH BILL EVANS,
TONY BENNETT BILL EVANS)
YOU'RE NEARER: - (WITH BILL EVANS, TONY BENNETT BILL
EVANS, BILL EVANS, BILL EVANS)
YOU'RE NEARER: - (WITH BILL EVANS, TONY BENNETT BILL
EVANS, BILL EVANS, BILL EVANS)
MAYBE SEPTEMBER: - (WITH BILL EVANS, TONY BENNETT
BILL EVANS, BILL EVANS, BILL EVANS)
MAYBE SEPTEMBER: - (WITH BILL EVANS, TONY BENNETT
BILL EVANS, BILL EVANS, BILL EVANS)
LONELY GIRL: - BILL EVANS, BILL EVANS, TONY BENNETT
BILL EVANS, TONY BENNETT BILL EVANS
LONELY GIRL: - BILL EVANS, BILL EVANS, TONY BENNETT
BILL EVANS, TONY BENNETT BILL EVANS
YOU DON'T KNOW WHAT LOVE IS: - (WITH BILL EVANS,
TONY BENNETT BILL EVANS)
YOU DON'T KNOW WHAT LOVE IS: - (WITH BILL EVANS,
TONY BENNETT BILL EVANS)
THE BAD AND THE BEAUTIFUL
THE BAD AND THE BEAUTIFUL
WHO CAN I TURN TO (WHEN NOBODY NEEDS ME)
WHO CAN I TURN TO (WHEN NOBODY NEEDS ME)
DREAM DANCING: - (WITH BILL EVANS, TONY BENNETT
BILL EVANS, BILL EVANS, BILL EVANS)
DREAM DANCING: - (WITH BILL EVANS, TONY BENNETT
BILL EVANS, BILL EVANS, BILL EVANS)
CHILD IS BORN, A
CHILD IS BORN, A
YOU MUST BELIEVE IN SPRING
YOU MUST BELIEVE IN SPRING
YOU'RE NEARER
YOU'RE NEARER
MAYBE SEPTEMBER
MAYBE SEPTEMBER
YOU DON'T KNOW WHAT LOVE IS

YOU DON'T KNOW WHAT LOVE IS
BAD AND THE BEAUTIFUL, THE
BAD AND THE BEAUTIFUL, THE

**TONY BENNETT WITH RALPH SHARON AND HIS
ORCHESTRA AT CARNEGIE HALL: RECORDED LIVE JUNE 9,
1962. CD**
DISC 1
INTRODUCTION / LULLABY OF BROADWAY
JUST IN TIME: - HIS ORCHESTRA
ALL THE THINGS YOU ARE: - HIS ORCHESTRA
FASCINATING RHYTHM
STRANGER IN PARADISE
OUR LOVE IS HERE TO STAY: - HIS ORCHESTRA
LOVE LOOK AWAY
CLIMB EV'RY MOUNTAIN
PUT ON A HAPPY FACE / COMES ONCE IN A LIFETIME
MY SHIP
SPEAK LOW
LOST IN THE STARS: - HIS ORCHESTRA
ALWAYS: - RALPH SHARON, TONY BENNETT / RALPH SHARON
& HIS ORCHESTRA, HIS ORCHESTRA
ANYTHING GOES: - HIS ORCHESTRA
OL' MAN RIVER: - HIS ORCHESTRA
LAZY AFTERNOON: - HIS ORCHESTRA
SOMETIMES I'M HAPPY: - HIS ORCHESTRA
HAVE I TOLD YOU LATELY?
THAT OLD BLACK MAGIC
SLEEPIN' BEE, A
I'VE GOT THE WORLD ON A STRING
WHAT GOOD DOES IT DO
ONE FOR MY BABY (AND ONE MORE FOR THE ROAD)
DISC 2
THIS COULD BE THE START OF SOMETHING BIG
WITHOUT A SONG
TOOT TOOT TOOTSIE (GOODBYE)
IT AMAZES ME: - RALPH SHARON, TONY BENNETT / RALPH
SHARON & HIS ORCHESTRA, HIS ORCHESTRA
RULES OF THE ROAD, THE
FIREFLY: - HIS ORCHESTRA, TONY BENNETT / RALPH SHARON
& HIS ORCHESTRA, RALPH SHARON
BEST IS YET TO COME, THE
IN SAN FRANCISCO, (I LEFT MY HEART)
HOW ABOUT YOU, (I LIKE NEW YORK IN JUNE)

167

APRIL IN PARIS
CHICAGO (THAT TODDLIN' TOWN)
SOLITUDE: - HIS ORCHESTRA, TONY BENNETT / RALPH
SHARON
& HIS ORCHESTRA, RALPH SHARON
I'M JUST A LUCKY SO AND SO: - RALPH SHARON, TONY
BENNETT RALPH SHARON & HIS ORCHESTRA, HIS
ORCHESTRA
TAKING A CHANCE ON LOVE
MY HEART TELLS ME (SHOULD I BELIEVE MY HEART?): -
(WITH RALPH SHARON & HIS ORCHESTRA, HIS ORCHESTRA,
RALPH SHARON)
PENNIES FROM HEAVEN
RAGS TO RICHES: - RALPH SHARON, HIS ORCHESTRA,
TONY BENNETT / RALPH SHARON & HIS ORCHESTRA
BLUE VELVET: - RALPH SHARON, HIS ORCHESTRA, TONY
BENNETT RALPH SHARON & HIS ORCHESTRA
SMILE
BECAUSE OF YOU: - RALPH SHARON, TONY BENNETT
RALPH SHARON & HIS ORCHESTRA, HIS ORCHESTRA
SING YOU SINNERS: - ORCHESTRA
DE GLORY ROAD: - RALPH SHARON, TONY BENNETT
RALPH SHARON & HIS ORCHESTRA, HIS ORCHESTRA

TONY BENNETT ON HOLIDAY CD
SOLITUDE
ALL OF ME
WHEN A WOMAN LOVES A MAN
ME, MYSELF AND I
SHE'S FUNNY THAT WAY
IF I COULD BE WITH YOU (ONE HOUR TONIGHT)
WILLOW WEEP FOR ME
LAUGHING AT LIFE
I WISHED ON THE MOON
WHAT A LITTLE MOONLIGHT CAN DO
MY OLD FLAME
THAT OLE DEVIL CALLED LOVE
ILL WIND
THESE FOOLISH THINGS (REMIND ME OF YOU)
SOME OTHER SPRING
CRAZY SHE CALLS ME
GOOD MORNING HEARTACHE
TRAV'LIN' LIGHT

GOD BLESS THE CHILD: - (WITH DUET, TONY BENNETT DUET
WITH BILLIE HOLIDAY)

TONY BENNETT - COMPLETE IMPROV RECORDINGS CD
DISC 1
LIFE IS BEAUTIFUL
LIFE IS BEAUTIFUL
ALL MINE
ALL MINE
BRIDGES (TRAVESSIA)
BRIDGES (TRAVESSIA)
RELFLECTIONS
RELFLECTIONS
EXPERIMENT
EXPERIMENT
THIS FUNNY WORLD
THIS FUNNY WORLD
AS TIME GOES BY
AS TIME GOES BY
I USED TO BE COLOR BLIND
I USED TO BE COLOR BLIND
LOST IN THE STARS
LOST IN THE STARS
THERE'LL BE SOME CHANGES MADE
THERE'LL BE SOME CHANGES MADE
WHAT IS THIS THING CALLED LOVE / LOVE FOR SALE / YOU'D
BE SO NICE TO COME HOME TO / EASY TO LOVE / IT'S
ALRIGHT WITH ME / NIGHT AND DAY / DREAM DANCING / I'VE
GOT YOU UNDER MY SKIN / GET OUT OF TOWN / WHAT IS
THIS THING CALLED LOVE
WHAT IS THIS THING CALLED LOVE / LOVE FOR SALE / YOU'D
BE SO NICE TO COME HOME TO / EASY TO LOVE / IT'S
ALRIGHT WITH ME / NIGHT AND DAY / DREAM DANCING / I'VE
GOT YOU UNDER MY SKIN / GET OUT OF TOWN / WHAT IS
THIS THING CALLED LOVE
THERE'S ALWAYS TOMORROW
THERE'S ALWAYS TOMORROW
ONE
ONE
MR. MAGIC
MR. MAGIC
DISC 2
THIS CAN'T BE LOVE
THIS CAN'T BE LOVE

BLUE MOON
BLUE MOON
THE LADY IS A TRAMP
THE LADY IS A TRAMP
LOVER
LOVER
MANHATTAN
MANHATTAN
SPRING IS HERE
SPRING IS HERE
HAVE YOU MET MISS JONES?
HAVE YOU MET MISS JONES?
ISN'T IT ROMANTIC?
ISN'T IT ROMANTIC?
WAIT TILL YOU SEE HER
WAIT TILL YOU SEE HER
I COULD WRITE A BOOK
I COULD WRITE A BOOK
THOU SWELL
THOU SWELL

TONY BENNETT - SNOWFALL CD
MY FAVORITE THINGS
CHRISTMAS SONG, THE (CHESTNUTS ROASTING ON AN OPEN FIRE)
SANTA CLAUS IS COMIN' TO TOWN
WE WISH YOU A MERRY CHRISTMAS / SILENT NIGHT, HOLY NIGHT / O COME ALL YE FAITHFUL / JINGLE BELLS / WHERE IS LOVE
CHRISTMASLAND
I LOVE THE WINTER WEATHER / I'VE GOT MY LOVE TO KEEP ME WARM
WHITE CHRISTMAS
WINTER WONDERLAND: - CONDUCTED BY ROBERT FARNON, ARRANGED, TONY BENNETT / ARRANGED & CONDUCTED BY ROBERT FARNON
HAVE YOURSELF A MERRY LITTLE CHRISTMAS
SNOWFALL
I'LL BE HOME FOR CHRISTMAS

BIBLIOGRAPHY

Essential Tony Bennett CD:
http://www.cduniverse.com/productinfo.asp?pid=4726560
Tony Bennett/Bill Evans album CD:
http://www.cduniverse.com/productinfo.asp?pid=7306311
Ultimate Tony Bennett CD:
http://www.cduniverse.com/productinfo.asp?pid=1088202
Fifty Years: The Artistry Of Tony Bennett CD:
http://www.cduniverse.com/productinfo.asp?pid=6783817
Tony Bennett Sings For Lovers CD:
http://www.cduniverse.com/productinfo.asp?pid=7004859
Tony Bennett - Swingin' Christmas CD:
http://www.cduniverse.com/productinfo.asp?pid=7736089
Complete Tony Bennett/Bill Evans Recordings CD:
http://www.cduniverse.com/productinfo.asp?pid=7908918
Tony Bennett - Here's To The Ladies CD:
http://www.cduniverse.com/productinfo.asp?pid=7612289
Tony Bennett - Sings The Ultimate American Songbook, vol. 1
CD: http://www.cduniverse.com/productinfo.asp?pid=8176154
Tony Bennett - Sings The Ultimate American Songbook, vol. 2
CD: http://www.cduniverse.com/productinfo.asp?pid=8098665
Tony Bennett - While We're Young: Original Recordings 1950-
1955 CD:
http://www.cduniverse.com/productinfo.asp?pid=8447032
Tony Bennett - Duets: An American Classic CD:
http://www.cduniverse.com/productinfo.asp?pid=7262585
K D Lang - Wonderful World CD:
http://www.cduniverse.com/productinfo.asp?pid=5309445
Tony Bennett - All-time Greatest Hits CD:
http://www.cduniverse.com/productinfo.asp?pid=1088732
Tony Bennett - Together Again CD:
http://www.cduniverse.com/productinfo.asp?pid=6260241
Tony Bennett with Ralph Sharon And His Orchestra At Carnegie
Hall: Recorded Live June 9, 1962. CD:
http://www.cduniverse.com/productinfo.asp?pid=1088405
Tony Bennett On Holiday CD:
http://www.cduniverse.com/productinfo.asp?pid=1089790
Tony Bennett - Complete Improv Recordings CD:
http://www.cduniverse.com/productinfo.asp?pid=6783909
Tony Bennett - Snowfall CD:
http://www.cduniverse.com/productinfo.asp?pid=6764425

NAT KING COLE

THIS IS NAT "KING" COLE VINYL, LP
DREAMS CAN TELL A LIE
I JUST FOUND OUT ABOUT LOVE
TOO YOUNG TO GO STEADY
FORGIVE MY HEART
ANNABELLE
NOTHING EVER CHANGES MY LOVE FOR YOU
TO THE ENDS OF THE EARTH
I'M GONNA LAUGH YOU RIGHT OUT OF MY LIFE
SOMEONE YOU LOVE
LOVE ME AS IF THERE WERE NO TOMORROW
THAT'S ALL
NEVER LET ME GO

UNFORGETTABLE LP
UNFORGETTABLE
PORTRAIT OF JENNY
WHAT'LL I DO
LOST APRIL
ANSWER ME, MY LOVE
HAJJI BABA
TOO YOUNG
MONA LISA
(I LOVE YOU) FOR SENTIMENTAL REASONS
RED SAILS IN THE SUNSET
PRETEND
MAKE HER MINE

NAT KING COLE AT THE PIANOVINYL, 10", LP
POOR BUTTERFLY - WRITTEN BY - HUBBELL - GOLDEN
BLUES IN MY SHOWER - WRITTEN BY - NAT "KING" COLE
COLE CAPERS - WRITTEN BY - NAT "KING" COLE
THESE FOOLISH THINGS (REMIND ME OF YOU) - WRITTEN BY
MARVELL - STRACHEY - LINK
HOW HIGH THE MOON - WRITTEN BY - MORGAN LEWIS
NANCY HAMILTON
MOONLIGHT IN VERMONT - WRITTEN BY - SUESSDORF -
BLACKBURN
I'LL NEVER BE THE SAME - WRITTEN BY – MOLNECK
SIGNORELLI - KOHN
THREE LITTLE WORDS - WRITTEN BY - HARRY RUBY
BERT KALMAR

UNFORGETTABLE 2 X VINYL, 7", EP, ALBUM, 45 RPM
UNFORGETTABLE - WRITTEN-BY - IRVING GORDON
PORTRAIT OF JENNIE - WRITTEN-BY - GORDON BURDGE, J.
RUSSEL ROBINSON
WHAT'LL I DO - WRITTEN-BY - IRVING BERLIN
LOST APRIL - WRITTEN-BY - DELANGE*, NEWMAN*,
SPENCER*
TOO YOUNG - WRITTEN-BY - SID LIPPMAN, SYLVIA DEE
MONA LISA - WRITTEN-BY - JAY LIVINGSTON, RAY EVANS
(I LOVE YOU) FOR SENTIMENTAL REASONS - WRITTEN-BY -
DEEK WATSON, WILLIAM BEST
RED SNAIL IN THE SUNSET - WRITTEN-BY - HUGH WILLIAMS
(2), JIMMY KENNEDY

SINGS FOR TWO IN LOVE (LP, ALBUM, MONO)
LOVE IS HERE TO STAY
A HANDFUL OF STARS
THIS CAN'T BE LOVE
A LITTLE STREET WHERE OLD FRIENDS MEET
AUTMN LEAVES
LET'S FALL IN LOVE
THERE GOES MY HEART
DINNER FOR ONE PLEASE, JAMES
ALMOST LIKE BEING IN LOVE
TENDERLY
YOU STEPPED OUT OF A DREAM
THERE WILL NEVER BE ANOTHER YOU

BALLADS OF THE DAY (LP)
A BLOSSOM FELL
UNBELIEVABLE
BLUE GARDENIA
ANGEL EYES
IT HAPPENS TO BE ME
SMILE
DARLING, JE VOUS AIME BEAUCOUP
ALONE TOO LONG
MY ONE SIN
RETURN TO PARADISE
IF LOVE IS GOOD TO ME
THE SAND AND THE SEA

THE PIANO STYLE OF NAT 'KING' COLE (10")
LOVE WALKED IN
MY HEART STOOD STILL
STELLA BY STARLIGHT
WHAT CAN I SAY AFTER I SAY I'M SORRY
TAKING A CHANCE ON LOVE
APRIL IN PARIS
I WANT TO BE HAPPY
I GET A KICK OUT OF YOU
I HEAR MUSIC
TEA FOR TWO

JUST ONE OF THOSE THINGS (LP, MONO)
WHEN YOUR LOVER HAS GONE
A COTTAGE FOR SALE
WHO'S SORRY NOW?
ONCE IN A WHILE
THESE FOOLISH THINGS REMIND ME OF YOU
JUST FOR THE FUN OF IT
DON'T GET AROUND MUCH ANYMORE
I UNDERSTAND
JUST ONE OF THOSE THINGS
THE SONG IS ENDED (BUT THE MELODY LINGERS ON)
I SHOULD CARE
THE PARTY'S OVER

THE VERY THOUGHT OF YOU (LP)
THE VERY THOUGHT OF YOU
BUT BEAUTIFUL
IMPOSSIBLE
I WISH I KNEW
I FOUND A MILLION DOLLAR BABY (IN A FIVE AND TEN CENT
STORE)
MAGNIFICENT OBSESSION
MY HEART TELLS ME
PARADISE
THIS IS ALL I ASK
CHERIE, I LOVE YOU
MAKING BELIEVE YOU'RE HERE
CHERCHEZ LA FEMME
FOR ALL WE KNOW
THE MORE I SEE YOU

COLE ESPAÑOL (LP, ALBUM)
CACHITO
MARIA ELENA
PERHAPS, PERHAPS, PERHAPS (QUIZÁS, QUIZÁS, QUIZÁS)
LAS MAÑANITAS (WITH MARIACHIS)
ACERTES MÁS (COME CLOSER TO ME)
EL BODEGUERO (GROCERS CHA-CHA)
ARRIVEDERCHI ROMA (GOODBYE TO ROME)
NOCHE DE RONDA
TU, MI DELIRIO
TE QUIERO, DIJISTE (MAGIC IS THE MOONLIGHT)
ADELITA (WITH MARIACHIS)

SINGS THE BLUES VINYL, LP
A SIDE
JOE TURNER BLUES
FRIENDLESS BLUES
HARLEM BUES
CHANTEZ LES BAS
STAY
BEALE STRRET BLUES
B SIDE
ST. LOUIS BLUES
HESITATING BLUES
MEMPHIS BLUES
YELLOW DOG BLUES
MORNING STAR
CARELESS LOVE

NAT KING COLE'S - GOLDEN HITS VINYL, LP
A SIDE
MONA LISA
TOO YOUNG
ROUTE 66
YOU CALL IT MADNESS
HOME
THE TROUBLE WITH ME IS YOU
B SIDE
NATURE BOY
BECAUSE OF YOU
THAT'S MY GIRL
ALWAYS YOU
LITTLE GIRL
THIS IS MY NIGHT TO DREAM

TO WHOM IT MAY CONCERN (LP)
TO WHOM IT MAY CONCERN
LOVE-WISE
TOO MUCH
IN THE HEART OF JANE DOE
A THOUSAND THOUGHTS OF YOU
YOU'RE BRINGING OUT THE DREAMER IN ME
MY HEART'S TREASURE
IF YOU SAID NO
CAN'T HELP IT
LOVESVILLE
UNFAIR
THIS MORNING IT WAS SUMMER

A MIS AMIGOS VINYL, LP
A SIDE
AY, COSITA LINDA
AQUELLOS OJOS VERDES
SUAS MAOS
CAPULLITO DE ALELI
CABOCLO DO RIO
FANTASTICO
B SIDE
NADIE ME AMA
YO VENDO UNOS OJOS NEGROS
PERFIDIA
EL CHOCLO
ANSIEDAD
NAO TENHO LAGRIMAS

THE MAGIC OF CHRISTMAS (LP, MONO)
DECK THE HALL
ADESTE FIDELES
GOD REST YE MERRY, GENTLEMEN
O TANNENBAUM
O, LITTLE TOWN OF BETHLEHEM
I SAW THREE SHIPS
O HOLY NIGHT
HARK, THE HERALD ANGELS SING
A CRADLE IN BETHLEHEM
AWAY IN A MANGER
JOY TO THE WORLD
THE FIRST NOEL
CAROLING, CAROLING

SILENT NIGHT

EVERY TIME I FEEL THE SPIRIT (LP, ALBUM, MONO)
EVERYTIME I FEEL THE SPIRIT
I WANT TO BE READY
SWEET HOUR OF PRAYER
AIN'T GONNA STUDY WAR NO MORE
I FOUND THE ANSWER
STANDIN' IN THE NEED OF PRAYER
OH, MARY, DON'T YOU WEEP
GO DOWN, MOSES
NOBODY KNOWS THE TROUBLE I'VE SEEN
IN THE SWEET BY AND BY
I COULDN'T HEAR NOBODY PRAY
STEAL AWAY

MORE COLE ESPAÑOL (LP, ALBUM)
LA FERIA DE LAS FLORES
TRES PALABRAS
LAS CHIAPANECAS
ADIOS MARQUITA LINDA
AQUI SE HABLA EN AMOR
VAYA CON DIOS
LA GOLONDRINA
NO ME PLATIQUES
A MEDIA LUZ
GUADALAJARA
SOLAMENTE UNA VEZ
PIEL CANELA

THE CHRISTMAS SONG (LP, ALBUM)
THE CHRISTMAS SONG
DECK THE HALL
ADESTE FIDELES
O TANNENBAUM
O, LITTLE TOWN OF BETHLEHEM
I SAW THREE SHIPS
O HOLY NIGHT
HARK, THE HERALD ANGELS SING
A CRADLE IN BETHLEHEM
AWAY IN A MANGER
JOY TO THE WORLD
THE FIRST NOEL
CAROLING, CAROLING

177

SILENT NIGHT

RAMBLIN' ROSE (LP, ALBUM)
RAMBLIN' ROSE
WOLVERTON MOUNTAIN
TWILIGHT ON THE TRAIL
I DON'T WANT IT THAT WAY
HE'LL HAVE TO GO
WHEN YOU'RE SMILING
GOODNIGHT, IRENE, GOODNIGHT
YOUR CHEATIN' HEART
ONE HAS MY NAME THE OTHER HAS MY HEART
SKIP TO MY LOU
THE GOOD TIMES
SING ANOTHER SONG (AND WE'LL ALL GO HOME)

THE TOUCH OF YOUR LIPS (LP)
THE TOUCH OF YOUR LIPS
I REMEMBER YOU
ILLUSION
YOU'RE MINE, YOU!
FUNNY
POINCIANA
SUNDAY, MONDAY, OR ALWAYS
NOT SO LONG AGO
A NIGHTINGALE SANG IN BERKELEY SQUARE
ONLY FOREVER
MY NEED FOR YOU
LIGHTS OUT

NAT KING COLE SINGS / GEORGE SHEARING PLAYS (LP, ALBUM)
SEPTEMBER SONG
PICK YOURSELF UP
I GOT IT BAD AND THAT AIN'T GOOD
LET THERE BE LOVE
AZURE-TÉ
LOST APRIL
A BEAUTIFUL FRIENDSHIP
FLY ME TO THE MOON (IN OTHER WORDS)
SERENATA
I'M LOST
THERE'S A LULL IN MY LIFE
DON'T GO

NAT KING COLE / PHIL FLOWERS – SINGS VINYL, LP, STEREO
A SIDE - NAT KING COLE
I'M LOST
LET'S SPRING ONE
BEAUTIFUL MOONS AGO
PITCHIN' UP A BOOGIE
B SIDE - PHIL FLOWERS
YOU SHOULDN'T DO ME LIKE YOU DO
LET ME COME HOME
CRAZY BABY
THINK IT OVER
LITTLE DEVIL

THE NAT KING COLE STORY: VOLUME 2 (LP)
UNFORGETTABLE
SOMEWHERE ALONG THE WAY
WALKIN' MY BABY BACK HOME
PRETEND
BLUE GARDENIA
I AM LOVE
ANSWER ME, MY LOVE
SMILE
DARLING, JE VOUS AMIE BEAUCOUP
THE SAND AND THE SEA
IF I MAY
A BLOSSOM FELL

THE NAT KING COLE STORY: VOLUME 3 (LP)
TO THE ENDS OF THE EARTH
NIGHT LIGHTS
BALLERINA
STARDUST
SEND FOR ME
ST. LOUIS BLUES
LOOKING BACK
NON DIMENTICAR
PARADISE
OH, MARY, DON'T YOU WEEP
AY, COSITA LINDA
WILD IS LOVE

LET'S FACE THE MUSIC (VINYL)
SOMETHING MAKES ME WANT TO DANCE WITH YOU

MOON LOVE
THE RULES OF THE ROAD
EBONY RHAPSODY
TOO LITTLE, TOO LATE
LET'S FACE THE MUSIC AND DANCE
DAY IN - DAY OUT
BIDN' MY TIME
WHEN MY SUGAR WALKS DOWN THE STREET
WARM AND WILLING
I'M GOING TO SIT RIGHT DOWN
COLD, COLD HEART

THOSE LAZY-HAZY-CRAZY DAYS OF SUMMER (LP)
THOSE LAZY-HAZY-CRAZY DAYS OF SUMMER
GET OUT AND GET UNDER THE MOON
THERE IS A TAVERN IN THIS TOWN
ON A BICYCLE BUILT FOR TWO
THAT SUNDAY, THAT SUMMER
ON THE SIDEWALKS OF NEW YORK
OUR OLD HOME TEAM
AFTER THE BALL IS OVER
YOU TELL ME YOUR DREAM
THAT'S WHAT THEY MEANT (BY THE GOOD OLD
SUMMERTIME)
DON'T FORGET
IN THE GOOD OLD SUMMERTIME
THOSE LAZY-HAZY-CRAZY DAYS OF SUMMER

TOP POPS VINYL, LP
A SIDE
SOMEWHERE ALONG THE WAY
WALKIN' MY BABY BACK HOME
FAITH CAN MOVE MOUNTAINS
FUNNY
HOLD MY HAND
TEACH ME TONIGHT
B SIDE
I'M NEVER SATISFIED
BECAUSE YOU'RE MINE
THE RUBY AND THE PEARL
A WEAVER OF DREAMS
PAPA LOVES MAMBO
IF I GIVE MY HEART TO YOU

WHERE DID EVERYONE GO? VINYL, LP
A SIDE
WHERE DID EVERYONE GO?
SAY IT ISN'T SO
IF LOVE AIN'T THERE
(AH THE APPLE TREES) WHEN THE WORLD WAS YOUNG
AM I BLUE?
SOMEONE TO TELL IT TO
B SIDE
THE END OF A LOVE AFFAIR
I KEEP GOIN' BACK TO JOE'S
LAUGHING ON THE OUTSIDE (CRYING ON THE INSIDE)
NO, I DON'T WANT HER
SPRING IS HERE
THAT'S ALL THERE IS

THE NAT KING COLE STORY: VOLUME 1 VINYL, LP,
STEREO
A SIDE
STRAIGHTEN UP AND FLY RIGHT
SWEET LORRAINE
IT'S ONLY A PAPER MOON
(GET YOUR KICKS ON) ROUTE 66!
(I LOVE YOU) FOR SENTIMENTAL REASONS
THE CHRISTMAS SONG
B SIDE
NATURE BOY
LUSH LIFE
CALYPSO BLUES
MONA LISA
ORANGE COLORED SKY
TOO YOUNG

SINGS MY FAIR LADY (LP, ALBUM)
WITH A LITTLE BIT OF LUCK
I COULD HAVE DANCED ALL NIGHT
THE RAIN IN SPAIN
ON THE STREET WHERE YOU LIVE
I'M AN ORDINARY MAN
GET ME TO THE CHURCH ON TIME
SHOW ME
I'VE GROWN ACCUSTOMED TO HER FACE
YOU DID IT
WOULDN'T IT BE LOVERLY

HYMN TO HIM

NAT KING COLE AND LESTER YOUNG (LP)
INDIANA
I CAN'T GET STARTED
JUMPIN' AT MEANERS
S. M. BLUES
JAMMIN' WITH LESTER

THE UNFORGETTABLE NAT KING COLE
UNFORGETTABLE
STRAIGHTEN UP AND FLY RIGHT
IT'S ONLY A PAPER MOON
SWEET LORRAINE
MONA LISA
NATURE BOY
TOO YOUNG
ORANGE COLOURED SKY
SOMEWHERE ALONG THE WAY
BALLERINA
WHEN I FALL IN LOVE
ROUTE 66
LET THERE BE LOVE
RAMBLIN' ROSE
WHEN MY SUGAR WALKS DOWN THE STREET
WITH A LITTLE BIT OF LUCK
YOU'RE MY EVERYTHING
REPRISE - UNFORGETTABLE

L-O-V-E (LP)
LOVE
THE GIRL FROM IPANEMA
THREE LITTLE WORDS
THERE'S LOVE
MY KIND OF GIRL
THANKS TO YOU
YOUR LOVE
MORE
COQUETTE
HOW I'D LOVE TO LOVE YOU
SWISS RETREAT

NAT KING COLE SINGS HIS SONGS FROM CAT BALLOU AND OTHER MOTION PICTURES VINYL, LP, MONO
A SIDE
THE BALLAD OF CAT BALLOU - WRITTEN-BY - LIVINGSTON*, DAVID*
BLUE GARDENIA - WRITTEN-BY - RUSSELL*, LEE*
ST LOUISBLUES - WRITTEN-BY - W.C. HANDY*
THE SONG OF RAINTREE COUNTY - WRITTEN-BY - GREEN*, WEBSTER*
IN THE COOL OF THE DAY - WRITTEN-BY - LIAM SULLIVAN (2), MANOS HADJIDAKIS, NIKOS GATSOS*
B SIDE
THEY CAN'T MAKE HER CRY - WRITTEN-BY - LIVINGSTON*, DAVID*
CHINA GATE - WRITTEN-BY - ADAMSON*, HUGHES*
NIGHT OF THE QUARTER MOON - WRITTEN-BY - VAN HEUSEN*, CAHN*
NEVER LET ME GO - WRITTEN-BY - LIVINGSTON*, EVANS*
BEALE STREET BLUES - WRITTEN-BY - W.C. HANDY*
HAJI BABA - WRITTEN-BY - TIOMKIN*, WASHINGTON*

LOOKING BACK VINYL, LP
A SIDE
TIME AND THE RIVER
WORLD IN MY ARMS
AGAIN
LOOKING BACK
MIDNIGHT FLYER
I MUST BE DREAMING
B SIDE
IS IT BETTER TO HAVE LOVED AND LOST
SEND FOR ME
JUST AS MUCH AS EVER
IF I MAY
SWEET BIRD OF YOUTH

SINGS ST. LOUIS BLUES REEL-TO-REEL, 3 ¾ IPS, MONO, 2 TRACK
A SIDE
JOE TURNER'S BLUES
FRIENDLESS BLUES
HARLEM BLUES
CHANTEZ LES BAS
STAY

BEALE STREET BLUES
B SIDE
ST. LOUIS BLUES
HESITATING BLUES
MEMPHIS BLUES
YELLOW DOG BLUES
MORNING STAR
CARELESS LOVE

WELCOME TO THE CLUB (LP)
WELCOME TO THE CLUB
ANYTIME, ANYDAY, ANYWHERE
THE BLUES DON'T CARE
MOOD INDIGO
BABY WON'T YOU PLEASE COME HOME
THE LATE LATE SHOW
AVALON
SHE'S FUNNY THAT WAY
I WANT A LITTLE GIRL
WEE BABY BLUES
LOOK OUT FOR LOVE

AT THE SANDS (LP, ALBUM)
BALLERINA
FUNNY (NOT MUCH)
THE CONTINENTAL
I WISH YOU LOVE
YOU LEAVE ME BREATHLESS
THOU SWELL
MY KINDA LOVE
THE SURREY WITH THE FRINGE ON TOP
WHERE OR WHEN
MISS OTIS REGRETS (SHE'S UNABLE TO LUNCH TODAY)
JOE TURNER BLUES

**THE UNFORGETTABLE NAT KING COLE SINGS THE GREAT
SONGS! VINYL, LP, MONO**
A SIDE
AN AFFAIR TO REMEMBER
YOU'RE MY THRILL
FASCINATION
FAREWELL TO ARMS
I WISH I KNEW
FOR THE WANT OF A KISS

THERE'S A GOLD MINE IN THE SKY
HAPPY NEW YEAR
BE STILL MY HEART
AROUND THE WORLD
I HAD THE CRAZIEST DREAM

NAT KING COLE (LP, MONO)
BALLERINA
RAMBLIN' ROSE
MONA LISA
ANSWER ME, MY LOVE
WALKIN' MY BABY BACK HOME
STAR-DUST
AVALON
ORANGE COLORED SKY
FASCINATION
TOO YOUNG
IT'S ONLY A PAPER MOON
MUCHO, MUCHO, MUCHO
PRETEND
LOVE

THE SWINGIN' MOODS OF NAT KING COLE 2 X VINYL, LP, STEREO, GATEFOLD
A SIDE
TELL ME ALL ABOUT YOURSELF
TANGERINE
WHO'S SORRY NOW
WARM AND WILLING
DON'T GET AROUND MUCH ANYMORE
B SIDE
MY KIND OF LOVE
YOU LEAVE ME BREATHLESS
WHEN YOU'RE SMILING
LONESOME AND SORRY
IN THE GOOD OLD SUMMERTIME
C SIDE
WILD IS LOVE
COQUETTE
WHEN MY SUGAR WALKS DOWN THE STREET
ONCE IN A WHILE
I JUST FOUND OUT ABOVE LOVE

D SIDE
WELCOME TO MY CLUB
I UNDERSTAND
MOON LOVE
LOOK OUT FOR LOVE
YOU STEPPED OUT OF A DREAM

STAY AS SWEET AS YOU ARE VINYL, LP, ALBUM, REISSUE
A SIDE
STAY AS SWEET AS YOU ARE - WRITTEN BY - HARRY REVEL,
MACK GORDON
YOU STEPPED OUT OF A DREAM - WRITTEN BY - BROWN-
KAHN
ANGEL EYES - WRITTEN BY - DENNIS-BRENT
IF I GIVE MY HEART TO YOU - WRITTEN BY - CRANE-GABLER-
JACOBS
ON THE STREET WHERE YOU LIVE - WRITTEN BY - LERNE-
LOEWE
B SIDE
GET ME TO THE CHURCH ON TIME - WRITTEN BY - LERNE-
LOEWE
WHAT IS THERE TO SAY - WRITTEN BY - DUKE-HARBURG
DON'T GET AROUND MUCH MORE - WRITTEN BY - BOB
RUSSEL, DUKE ELLINGTON
PARADISE - WRITTEN BY - GORDON CLIFFORD-NACIO HERB
BROWN
WHEN YOUR LOVER HAS GONE - WRITTEN BY - EINAR ARON
SWAN

THE NAT KING COLE DELUXE SET 3 X VINYL, LP, STEREO
A SIDE
I DON'T WANT TO BE HURT ANYMORE
YOU'RE CRYING ON MY SHOULDER
ONLY YESTERDAY
I'M ALONE BECAUSE I LOVE YOU
DON'T YOU REMEMBER
YOU'RE MY WELCOME
B SIDE
I DON'T WANT TO SEE TOMORROW
BRUSH THOSE TEARS FROM YOUR EYES
WAS THAT THE HUMAN THING TO DO?
ROAD TO NOWHERE
I'M ALL CRIED OUT

186

C SIDE
THE TOUCH OF YOUR LIPS
I REMEMBER YOU
ILLUSION
YOU'RE MINE, YOU!
POINCIANA
D SIDE
SUNDAY, MONDAY, OR ALWAYS
NOT SO LONG AGO
A NIGHTINGALE SANG IN BERKELEY SQUARE
ONLY FOREVER
LIGHTS OUT
E SIDE
AVALON
SHE'S FUNNY THAT WAY
I WANT A LITTLE GIRL
WEE BABY BLUES
WELCOME TO THE CLUB
F SIDE
THE LATE, LATE SHOW
ANYTIME, ANYDAY, ANYWHERE
THE BLUES DON'T CARE (WHO'S GOT 'EM)
MOOD INDIGO
BABY, WON'T YOU PLEASE COME HOME
LOOK OUT FOR LOVE

CLOSE-UP2 X VINYL, LP, GATEFOLD
A SIDE
A BLOSSOM FELL
UNBELIEVABLE
BLUE GARDENIA
ANGEL EYES
SMILE
B SIDE
DARLING, JE VOUS AIME BEAUCOUP
ALONE TOO LONG
IT HAPPENS TO BE ME
IF LOVE IS GOOD TO ME
THE SAND AND THE SEA
C SIDE
SOMEWHERE ALONG THE WAY
WALKIN' MY BABY BACK HOME
FAITH CAN MOVE MOUNTAINS
FUNNY! (NOT MUCH)

187

TEACH ME TONIGHT
D SIDE
I'M NEVER SATISFIED
BECAUSE YOU'RE MINE
THE RUBY AND THE PEARL
A WEAVER OF DREAMS
IF I GIVE MY HEART TO YOU

NAT KING COLE AND THE NAT KING COLE TRIO VINYL, LP, ALBUM
A SIDE
JUST YOU, JUST ME - SAXOPHONE - WILLIE SMITH (2)
DON'T BLAME ME
FOR ALL WE KNOW
SOMETIMES I'M HAPPY - VIOLIN - STUFF SMITH
YOU'RE LOOKING AT ME - SAXOPHONE - WILLIE SMITH (2)
B SIDE
LONELY ONE - TROMBONE - JUAN TIZOL
DON'T LET GO TO YOUR HEAD - SAXOPHONE - WILLIE SMITH
I KNOW THAT YOU KNOW - VIOLIN - STUFF SMITH
BLAME IT ON MY YOUTH - TROMBONE - JUAN TIZOL
WHEN I GROW TOO OLD TO DREAM - VIOLIN - STUFF SMITH
EXACTLY LIKE YOU

NATURE BOY VINYL, LP, ALBUM, REISSUE
A SIDE
NATURE BOY
LAUGHING ON THE OUTSIDE
SPRING IS HERE
TENDERLY
THIS IS ALWAYS
B SIDE
UNTIL THE REAL THING COMES ALONG
THE END OF A LOVE AFFAIR
STAR DUST
WHEN THE WORLD WAS YOUNG

NAT KING COLE, BUDDY RICH & CHARLIE SHAVERS -
ANATOMY OF A JAM SESSIONVINYL, LP, ALBUM, MONO,
REISSUE
A SIDE
BLACK MARKET STUFF (110-0) (INCOMPLETE)
BLACK MARKET STUFF (110-1)
BLACK MARKET STUFF (110-2)

BLACK MARKET STUFF (110-3)
LAGUNA LEAP (111-1)
LAGUNA LEAP (111-2)
LAGUNA LEAP (111-3)
B SIDE
I'LL NEVER BE THE SAME (112-1) - WRITTEN-BY –
SIGNORELLI*, KAHN*, MALNECK*
I'LL NEVER BE THE SAME (112-2) - WRITTEN-BY –
SIGNORELLI*, KAHN*, MALNECK*
SWINGIN' ON CENTRAL (113-1)
SWINGIN' ON CENTRAL (113-2)
KICKS (142 & 143)

**COLE ESPAÑOL - CANTA BOLEROS VINYL, LP, ALBUM,
STEREO**
A SIDE
CACHITO
MARIA ELENA
QUIZÁS, QUIZÁS, QUIZÁS (PERHAPS, PERHAPS, PERHAPS)
LAS MAÑANITAS (WITH MARIACHIS)
ACÉRCATE MÁS (COME CLOSER TO ME)
EL BODEGUERO (GROCERS CHA-CHA)
B SIDE
ARRIVEDERCI, ROMA (GOODBYE TO ROME)
NOCHE DE RONDA
TU, MI DELIRIO
TE QUIERO, DIJISTE (MAGIC IS THE MOONLIGHT)
ADELITA (WITH MARIACHIS)

FROM THE VERY BEGINNING (2XLP)
HONEYSUCKLE ROSE
SWEET LORRAINE
THIS SIDE UP
GONE WITH THE DRAFT
STOMPIN' AT THE PANAMA
EARLY MORNING BLUES
BABS
SCOTCHIN' WITH THE SODA
SLOW DOWN
HONEY HUSH
I LIKE TO RIFF
THIS WILL MAKE YOU LAUGH
HIT THE RAMP
STOP, THE RED LIGHT'S ON

(BEDTIME) SLEEP, BABY, SLEEP
CALL THE POLICE
THAT AIN'T RIGHT
ARE YOU FER IT?
HIT THAT JIVE JACK
THUNDER

DEAR LONELY HEARTS VINYL, LP, ALBUM, STEREO, REISSUE
A SIDE
DEAR LONELY HEARTS
MISS YOU
WHY SHOULD I CRY OVER YOU?
NEAR YOU
YEARNING (JUST FOR YOU)
MY FIRST AND ONLY LOVER
B SIDE
ALL OVER THE WORLD
OH, HOW I MISS YOU TONIGHT
LONESOME AND SORRY
ALL BY MYSELF
WHO'S NEXT IN LINE?
IT'S A LONESOME OLD TOWN

CHRISTMAS WITH NAT KING COLE AND FRED WARING & THE PENNSYLVANIANS VINYL, LP, ALBUM, STEREO
A SIDE
THE CHRISTMAS SONG - WRITTEN BY - M. TORME, R. WELLS
SILVER BELLS - WRITTEN BY - EVANS, LIVINGSTON
O LITTLE TOWN OF BETHLEHAM - ADAPTED BY
[TRADITIONAL] - NAT KING COLE
GOD REST YE, MERRY GENTLEMEN - ADAPTED BY - EDITH
BERGDAHL, NAT KING COLE
WHITE CHRISTMAS - WRITTEN BY - IRVING BERLIN
CAROLING, CAROLING - WRITTEN BY - A. BURT, W. HUDSON
JOY TO THE WORLD - ADAPTED BY [TRADITIONAL] –
NAT KING COLE
B SIDE
WINTER WONDERLAND - WRITTEN BY - BERNARD, SMITH
AWAY IN THE MANGER - ADAPTED BY [TRADITIONAL] –
NAT KING COLE
A CRADLE IN THE BETHLEHEM - WRITTEN BY - A. BRYAN, L.
STOCK
SLEIGH RIDE - WRITTEN BY - ANDERSON, PARISH

ADESTE FIDELES - ADAPTED BY [TRADITIONAL] - NAT KING
COLE

LOVE IS HERE TO STAY VINYL, LP, GATEFOLD
A SIDE
LOVE IS HERE TO STAY
SHE'S FUNNY THAT WAY
THE VERY THOUGHT OF YOU
ANGEL EYES
WELCOME TO THE CLUB
B SIDE
WHEN MY SUGAR WALKS DOWN THE STREET
TENDERLY
THIS CAN'T BE LOVE
THE MORE I SEE YOU
THERE WILL NEVER BE ANOTHER YOU

NAT KING COLE VINYL, LP
A SIDE
NATURE BOY
LAUGHING ON THE OUTSIDE
SPRING IS HERE
TENDERLY
THIS IS ALWAYS
B SIDE
UNTIL THE REAL THING COMES ALONG
THE END OF A LOVE AFAIR
STAR DUST
WHEN THE WORLD WAS YOUNG

I'M IN THE MOOD FOR LOVE VINYL, LP
A SIDE
STRAIGHTEN UP AND FLY RIGHT
WHEN I GROW TOO OLD TO DREAM
COME IN OUT OF THE RAIN
I'M IN THE MOOD FOR LOVE
SOMEBODY LOVES YOU
I FOUND A NEW BABY
B SIDE
PLEASE DON'T CRY AND SAY NO
MISS THING
ON THE SUNNY SIDE OF THE STREET
IT'S ONLY A PAPER MOON
ERRAND BOY FOR RHYTHM

CARAVAN

UNFORGETTABLE VINYL, LP, ALBUM, REISSUE
A SIDE
UNFORGETTABLE
PORTRAIT OF JENNIE
LOST APRIL
ANSWER ME, MY LOVE
RED SAILS IN THE SUNSET
B SIDE
TOO YOUNG
MONA LISA
(I LOVE YOU) FOR SENTIMENTAL REASONS
PRETEND
MAKE HER MINE

BING CROSBY & NAT KING COLE - WHITE CHRISTMAS
VINYL, LP
A SIDE
WHITE CHRISTMAS - BING CROSBY - WRITTEN-BY - I. BERLIN*
I'LL BE HOME FOR CHRISTMAS - BING CROSBY - WRITTEN-BY
B. RAM*, K. GANNON*, W. KENT*
SILENT NIGHT - BING CROSBY - WRITTEN-BY - F. GRUBER*
IRISH LULLABY (TU-RA-LU-RA-LU-RAL) - BING CROSBY -
WRITTEN-BY - SHANNON*
SILVER BELLS - BING CROSBY - WRITTEN-BY - LIVINGSTONE,
EVANS*
GOD REST YE MERRY GENTLEMEN - BING CROSBY -
WRITTEN-BY - TRADITIONAL
B SIDE
JINGLE BELLS - NAT KING COLE - WRITTEN-BY –
TRADITIONAL
SANTA CLAUS IS COMING TO TOWN - NAT KING COLE -
WRITTEN-BY - GILLESPIE*, COOTS*
A HOUSE WITH LOVE IN IT - NAT KING COLE - WRITTEN-BY –
N. LIPPMAN*, W. DEE*
MR. SANTA CLAUS - NAT KING COLE - WRITTEN-BY - COLE*
TAKE ME BACK TO TOYLAND - NAT KING COLE - WRITTEN-BY
- COLE*
THE CHRISTMAS SONG - NAT KING COLE - WRITTEN-BY -
TORME*, WELLS*

V.I.P.-JAZZ 32 VINYL, LP, LIMITED EDITION
A SIDE
THIS WAY OUT
STRAIGHTEN UP AND FLY RIGHT
HONEYSUCKLE ROSE
MAKIN' WHOOPEE
BODY AND SOUL
IT'S ONLY A PAPER MOON
ROUTE 66
BOP KICK
B SIDE
JUMPIN' AT CAPITOL - WRITTEN BY - NADINE ROBINSON
EMBRACEABLE YOU
CALYPSO BLUES
RUMBA AZUL
SWEET LORRAINE
SWEET GEORGIA BROWN
I THINK YOU GET WHAT I MEAN
LAUGH! COOL CLOWN - WRITTEN BY - LEONCAVALLO

WEAVER OF DREAMS 2 X VINYL, LP
A SIDE
DARLING JE VOUS AIME BEAUCOUP
ANGEL EYES
THE SAND AND THE SEA
IF LOVE IS GOOD TO ME
B SIDE
SOMEWHERE ALONG THE WAY
SMILE
FUNNY (NOT MUCH)
A WEAVER OF DREAMS
C SIDE
IF I GIVE MY HEART TO YOU
WALKIN' MY BABY BACK HOME
BECAUSE YOU'RE MINE
A BLOSSOM FELL
D SIDE
TEACH ME TONIGHT
UNBELIEVABLE
I'M NEVER SATISFIED
ALONE TOO LONG

LOVE SONGS CASSETTE
A SIDE
SMILE
L-O-V-E
THAT'S ALL
ANSWER ME MY LOVE
TENDERLY
B SIDE
LOVE IS HERE TO STAY
THERE GOES MY HEART
THE VERY THOUGHT OF YOU
THIS IS ALL I ASK

UNFORGETTABLE CASSETTE, ALBUM
A SIDE
UNFORGETTABLE
BUT BEAUTIFUL
(I LOVE YOU) FOR SENTIMENTAL REASONS
NON DIMENTICAR
B SIDE
DARLING, JE VOUS AIME BEAUCOUP
THE BEST THING FOR YOU
THIS IS ALWAYS
IF LOVE IS GOOD TO ME
THE PARTY'S OVER

THE UNFORGETTABLE CD, ALBUM
RED SAILS IN THE SUNSET
PRETEND
MAKE HER MINE
UNFORGETTABLE
PORTRAIT OF JENNIE
WHAT'LL I DO
LOST APRIL
HAJJI BABA
AVALON
SHE'S FUNNY THAT WAY
I WANT A LITTLE GIRL
WEE BABY BLUES
LOOK OUT FOR LOVE
WELCOME TO THE CLUB
ANYTIME, ANYDAY, ANYWHERE
MOOD INDIGO

WELCOME TO THE CLUB VINYL, LP, ALBUM
A SIDE
WELCOME TO THE CLUB - WRITTEN-BY - NOEL SHERMAN
ANYTIME, ANYDAY, ANYWHERE - WRITTEN-BY - WILEY*,
WASHINGTON*, YOUNG*
THE BLUES DON'T CARE (WHO'S GOT 'EM) - WRITTEN-BY –
VIC ABRAMS
MOOD INDIGO - WRITTEN-BY - BIGARD*, ELLINGTON*,
MILLS*
BABY, WON'T YOU PLEASE COME HOME - WRITTEN-BY –
CHARLES WARFIELD, CLARENCE WILLIAMS
THE LATE, LATE SHOW - WRITTEN-BY - MURRAY BERLIN,
ROY ALFRED
B SIDE
AVALON - WRITTEN-BY - JOLSON*, DE SYLVA*, ROSE*
SHE'S FUNNY THAT WAY - WRITTEN-BY - NEIL MORET,
RICHARD A. WHITING*
I WANT A LITTLE GIRL - WRITTEN-BY - BILLY MOLL,
MURRAY MENCHER
WEE BABY BLUES - WRITTEN-BY - JOE TURNER*, PETE
JOHNSON
LOOK OUT FOR LOVE - WRITTEN-BY - COLIN ROMOFF,
DANIEL J. MEEHAN*

ESPAÑOL VINYL, LP
A SIDE
PERFIDIA
YO VENDO UNOS OJOS NEGROS
MARIA ELENA
SOLAMENTE UNA VEZ (YOU BELONG TOA MY HEART)
CACHITO
TRES PALABRAS (WITHOUT YOU)
AQUELLOS OJOS VERDES
EL BODEGUERO (CROCER'S CHA-CHA)
B SIDE
QUIZÁS, QUIZÁS, QUIZÁS (PERHAPS, PERHAPS, PERHAPS)
NOCHE DE RONDA
ACÉRTATE MÁS (COME CLOSER TO ME)
ADELITA (WITH MARIACHIS)
TE QUIERO, DIJISTE (MAGIC IS THE MOONLIGHT)
EL CHOCLO
PIEL CANELA
CAPULLITO DE ALELI

NAT KING COLE SINGS GREAT LOVE BALLADS VINYL, LP
A SIDE
THREE LITTLE WORDS
THE TOUCH OF YOUR LIPS
IT'S ALL IN THE GAME
FASCINATION
I REMEMBER YOU
I'VE GROWN ACCUSTOMED TO HER FACE
MORE
B SIDE
ONCE IN A WHILE
THE MORE I SEE YOU
THESE FOOLISH THINGS
STARDUST
A NIGHTNGALE SANG IN BERKELEY SQUARE
AROUND THE WORLD
NEAR YOU

THE ONE AND ONLY CD
SWEET LORRAINE
LOVE IS HERE TO STAY
AUTUMN LEAVES
DANCE BALLERINA DANCE
SEPTEMBER SONG
A BEAUTIFUL FRIENDSHIP
FLY ME TO THE MOON (IN OTHER WORDS)
LET THERE BE LOVE
THE SONG IS ENDED (BUT THE MELODY LINGERS ON)
MONA LISA
PICK YOURSELF UP
THE MORE I SEE YOU
JUST ONE OF THOSE THINGS
LET'S FALL IN LOVE
LOVE IS THE THING
STAY AS SWEET AS YOU ARE
LOVE LETTERS
AZURE-TE
SERENATA
THE PARTY'S OVER

CHESTNUTS ROASTIN' CD
THE CHRISTMAS SONG
GOD REST YE MERRY, GENTLEMEN
O LITTLE TOWN OF BETHLEHEM

HARK! THE HERALD ANGELS SING
AWAY IN A MANGER
O COME ALL YE FAITHFUL
O HOLY NIGHT
THE FIRST NOEL
SILENT NIGHT
CAROLING, CAROLING

WELCOME TO THE CLUB CD
WELCOME TO THE CLUB - WRITTEN-BY - NOEL SHERMAN
ANYTIME, ANYDAY, ANYWHERE - WRITTEN-BY - WILEY*,
WASHINGTON*, YOUNG*
THE BLUES DON'T CARE (WHO'S GOT 'EM) - WRITTEN-BY –
VIC ABRAMS
MOOD INDIGO - WRITTEN-BY - BIGARD*, ELLINGTON*,
MILLS*
BABY, WON'T YOU PLEASE COME HOME - WRITTEN-BY –
CHARLES WARFIELD, CLARENCE WILLIAMS
THE LATE, LATE SHOW - WRITTEN-BY - MURRAY BERLIN,
ROY ALFRED
AVALON - WRITTEN-BY - JOLSON*, DE SYLVA*, ROSE*
SHE'S FUNNY THAT WAY - WRITTEN-BY - NEIL MORET,
RICHARD A. WHITING*
I WANT A LITTLE GIRL - WRITTEN-BY - BILLY MOLL,
MURRAY MENCHER
WEE BABY BLUES - WRITTEN-BY - JOE TURNER*, PETE
JOHNSON
LOOK OUT FOR LOVE - WRITTEN-BY - COLIN ROMOFF,
DANIEL J. MEEHAN*

PRÉFERENCES CD
MONA LISA
FOR SENTIMENTAL REASONS (I LOVE YOU)
NATURE BOY
VAYA CON DIOS
MARIA-ELENA
PARADISE
SOLAMENTE UNA VEZ (YOU BELONG TO MY HEART)
QUIZAS, QUIZAS, QUIZAS (PERHAPS, PERHAPS, PERHAPS)
PERFIDIA
STARDUST
ADELITA (WITH MARIACHIS)
LA FERIA DE LAS FLORES
LOVESVILLE

LES FEUILLES MORTES (SUNG IN FRENCH)
THIS MORNING IT WAS
RAMBLIN' ROSE

PENTHOUSE SERENADE CD, ALBUM, REMASTERED
PENTHOUSE SERENADE (WHEN WE'RE ALONE)
SOMEBODY LOVES ME
LAURA
ONCE IN A BLUE MOON (BASED ON RUBENSTEIN'S MELODY
IN F)
POLKA DOTS AND MOONBEAMS
DOWN BY THE OLD MILL STREAM
IF I SHOULD LOSE YOU
ROSE ROOM
I SURRENDER DEAR
IT COULD HAPPEN TO YOU
DON'T BLAME ME
LITTLE GIRL
I SURRENDER DEAR (ALTERNATE TAKE)
WALKIN' MY BABY BACK HOME
TOO MARVELOUS FOR WORDS
TOO YOUNG
THAT'S MY GIRL
IT'S ONLY A PAPER MOON
UNFORGETTABLE

LEGENDS OF THE 20TH CENTRURY CD, SAMPLER, DIGIPAK
STRAIGHTEN UP AND FLY RIGHT
BODY AND SOUL
(GET YOUR KICKS ON) ROUTE 66
BABY, BABY ALL THE TIME
WHEN I TAKE MY SUGAR TO TEA
NATURE BOY
LUSH LIFE
UNFORGETTABLE
CARAVAN
SMILE
SEND FOR ME
WHEN I FALL IN LOVE
THE PARTY'S OVER
STARDUST
LOOKING BACK
ST. LOUIS BLUES
MOOD INDIGO

PERFIDIA
OH, MARY, DON'T YOU WEEP
RAMBLIN' ROSE
FUNNY (NOT MUCH)
THE CONTINENTAL (LIVE)

THE ULTIMATE COLLECTION CD
LET THERE BE LOVE
WHEN I FALL IN LOVE
MONA LISA
UNFORGETTABLE
TOO YOUNG
SMILE
ON THE STREET WHERE YOU LIVE
PRETEND
NATURE BOY
LOVE LETTERS
A NIGHTINGALE SANG IN BERKELEY SQUARE
ANSWER ME
THE PARTY'S OVER
YOU'LL NEVER KNOW
STARDUST
IT'S ALL IN THE GAME
AUTUMN LEAVES
THE MORE I SEE YOU
YOU MADE ME LOVE YOU
BECAUSE YOU'RE MINE
LET'S FACE THE MUSIC AND DANCE

GREAT SINGERS OF THE CENTURY - NAT KING COLE CD
EMBRACEABLE YOU
I JUST CAN'T SEE FOR LOOKIN'
I'M IN THE MOOD FOR LOVE
I DON'T KNOW WHY
COULD- 'JA
EVERYONE IS SAYING HELLO AGAIN
WHAT CAN I SAY AFTER I SAY I'M SORRY
ROUTE 66
OH, BUT I DO
I'D LOVE TO MAKE LOVE TO YOU
I'M A SHY GUY
KATUSHA
YOU'RE NOBODY 'TILL SOMEBODY LOVES YOU
DON'T BLAME ME

I'M THROUGH WITH YOU
SWET LORRAINE
IT' ONLY A PAPERMOON

BIBLIOGRAPHY

This Is Nat "King" Cole vinyl, LP: http://www.discogs.com/nat-king-cole-this-is-nat-king-cole/release/2146081
Unforgettable LP: http://www.discogs.com/nat-king-cole-unforgettable/master/147760
Nat King Cole At The Piano vinyl, 10", LP: http://www.discogs.com/nat-king-cole-nat-king-cole-at-the-iano/release/2706459
Unforgettable 2 x vinyl, 7", EP, album, 45 rpm: http://www.discogs.com/nat-king-cole-unforgettable/release/2059436
Sings For Two In Love (LP, album, mono): http://www.discogs.com/nat-king-cole-sings-for-two-in-love/master/147628
Ballads Of The Day (LP): http://www.discogs.com/nat-king-cole-ballads-of-the-day/master/84535
The Piano Style Of Nat 'King' Cole (10"): http://www.discogs.com/nat-king-cole-the-piano-style-of-nat-king-ole/master/228874
Just One Of Those Things (LP, mono): http://www.discogs.com/nat-king-cole-just-one-of-those-things-and-more/master/147618
The Very Thought Of You (LP): http://www.discogs.com/nat-king-cole-gordon-jenkins-and-his-orchestra-the-very-thought-of-you/master/219888
Cole Español (LP, album): http://www.discogs.com/nat-king-cole-cole-espa%c3%b1ol/master/266157
Sings The Blues vinyl, LP: http://www.discogs.com/nat-king-cole-sings-the-blues/release/2029738
Nat King Cole's - Golden Hits vinyl, LP: http://www.discogs.com/nat-king-cole-nat-king-coles-golden-hits/release/1554554
To Whom It May Concern (LP): http://www.discogs.com/nat-king-cole-to-whom-it-may-concern/master/147759
A Mis Amigos vinyl, LP: http://www.discogs.com/nat-king-cole-a-mis-amigos/release/2505876

The Magic Of Christmas (LP, mono):
http://www.discogs.com/nat-king-cole-the-magic-of-christmas/master/147751
Every Time I Feel The Spirit (LP, album, mono):
http://www.discogs.com/nat-king-cole-gordon-jenkins-conducts-first-church-of-deliverance-choir-every-time-i-feel-the-spirit/master/139844
More Cole Español (LP, album): http://www.discogs.com/nat-king-cole-more-cole-espa%c3%b1ol/master/260127
The Christmas Song (LP, album): http://www.discogs.com/nat-king-cole-the-christmas-song/master/147633
Ramblin' Rose (LP, album): http://www.discogs.com/nat-king-cole-ramblin-rose/master/147626
The Touch of Your Lips (LP): http://www.discogs.com/nat-king-cole-the-touch-of-your-lips/master/147753
Nat King Cole Sings / George Shearing Plays (LP, album):
http://www.discogs.com/nat-king-cole-george-shearing-nat-king-cole-sings-george-shearing-plays/master/147624
Nat King Cole / Phil Flowers – Sings vinyl, LP, stereo:
http://www.discogs.com/nat-king-colephil-flowers-sings/release/1548802
The Nat King Cole Story: Volume 2 (LP):
http://www.discogs.com/nat-king-cole-the-nat-king-cole-story-volume-2/master/147747
The Nat King Cole Story: Volume 3 (LP):
http://www.discogs.com/nat-king-cole-the-nat-king-cole-story-volume-3/master/266156
Let's Face The Music (vinyl): http://www.discogs.com/nat-king-cole-lets-face-the-music/master/228870
Those Lazy-Hazy-Crazy Days Of Summer (LP):
http://www.discogs.com/nat-king-cole-those-lazy-hazy-crazy-days-of-summer/master/266159
Top Pops vinyl, LP: http://www.discogs.com/nat-king-cole-top-pops/release/2249381
Where Did Everyone Go? vinyl, LP:
http://www.discogs.com/nat-king-cole-where-did-everyone-go/release/2084245
The Nat King Cole Story: Volume 1 vinyl, LP, stereo:
http://www.discogs.com/nat-king-cole-the-nat-king-cole-story-volume-1/release/2058574
Sings My Fair Lady (LP, album): http://www.discogs.com/nat-king-cole-sings-my-fair-lady/master/298618

Nat King Cole And Lester Young (LP):
http://www.discogs.com/nat-king-cole-lester-young-the-historical-jazz-session/master/211062
The Unforgettable Nat King Cole: http://www.discogs.com/nat-king-cole-the-unforgettable-nat-king-cole/master/284636
L-O-V-E (LP): http://www.discogs.com/nat-king-cole-l-o-v-e/master/228869
Nat King Cole Sings His Songs From Cat Ballou And Other Motion Pictures vinyl, LP, mono: http://www.discogs.com/nat-king-cole-nat-king-cole-sings-his-songs-from-cat-ballou-and-other-motion-pictures/release/2408054
Looking Back vinyl, LP: http://www.discogs.com/nat-king-cole-looking-back/release/2077049
Sings St. Louis Blues Reel-To-Reel, 3 ¾ ips, mono, 2 track: http://www.discogs.com/nat-king-cole-sings-st-louis-blues/release/1324920
Welcome To The Club (LP): http://www.discogs.com/nat-king-cole-welcome-to-the-club/master/269406
At The Sands (LP, album): http://www.discogs.com/nat-king-cole-at-the-sands/master/147611
The Unforgettable Nat King Cole Sings The Great Songs! vinyl, LP, mono: http://www.discogs.com/nat-king-cole-the-unforgettable-nat-king-cole-sings-the-great-songs/release/2634555
Nat King Cole (LP, mono): http://www.discogs.com/nat-king-cole-nat-king-cole/master/147622
The Swingin' Moods Of Nat King Cole 2 x vinyl, LP, stereo, gatefold: http://www.discogs.com/nat-king-cole-the-swingin-moods-of-nat-king-cole/release/1661900
Stay As Sweet As You Are vinyl, LP, album, reissue: http://www.discogs.com/nat-king-cole-stay-as-sweet-as-you-are/release/1461643
The Nat King Cole Deluxe Set 3 x vinyl, LP, stereo: http://www.discogs.com/nat-king-cole-the-nat-king-cole-deluxe-set/release/1559378
Close-up2 x vinyl, LP, Gatefold: http://www.discogs.com/nat-king-cole-close-up/release/2011062
Nat King Cole And The Nat King Cole Trio vinyl, LP, album: http://www.discogs.com/nat-king-cole-and-the-nat-king-cole-trio/release/1922139
Nature Boy vinyl, LP, album, reissue: http://www.discogs.com/nat-king-cole-nature-boy/release/2037479

Nat King Cole, Buddy Rich & Charlie Shavers - Anatomy Of A Jam Session vinyl, LP, album, mono, reissue: http://www.discogs.com/nat-king-cole-buddy-rich-charlie-shavers-anatomy-of-a-jam-session/release/1116499
Cole Español - Canta Boleros vinyl, LP, album, stereo: http://www.discogs.com/nat-king-cole-cole-español-canta-boleros/release/2692304
From The Very Beginning (2xLP): http://www.discogs.com/nat-king-cole-from-the-very-beginning/master/234175
Dear Lonely Hearts vinyl, LP, album, stereo, reissue: http://www.discogs.com/nat-king-cole-dear-lonely-hearts/release/2025704
Christmas With Nat King Cole And Fred Waring & The Pennsylvanians vinyl, LP, album, stereo: http://www.discogs.com/nat-king-cole-christmas-with-nat-king-cole-and-fred-waring-the-pennsylvanians/release/1819285
Love Is Here To Stay vinyl, LP, gatefold: http://www.discogs.com/nat-king-cole-love-is-here-to-stay/release/2010375
Nat King Cole vinyl, LP: http://www.discogs.com/nat-king-cole-nat-king-cole/release/1511483
I'm In The Mood For Love vinyl, LP: http://www.discogs.com/nat-king-cole-im-in-the-mood-for-love/release/2235362
Unforgettable vinyl, LP, album, reissue: http://www.discogs.com/nat-king-cole-unforgettable/release/2022768
Bing Crosby & Nat King Cole - White Christmas vinyl, LP: http://www.discogs.com/bing-crosby-nat-king-cole-white-christmas/release/2525437
V.I.P.-Jazz 32 vinyl, LP, limited edition: http://www.discogs.com/nat-king-cole-vip-jazz-32/release/2377643
Weaver Of dreams 2 x vinyl, LP: http://www.discogs.com/nat-king-cole-weaver-of-dreams/release/1878052
Love Songs cassette: http://www.discogs.com/nat-king-cole-love-songs/release/382292
Unforgettable cassette, album: http://www.discogs.com/nat-king-cole-unforgettable/release/1451369
Welcome To The Club vinyl, LP, album: http://www.discogs.com/nat-king-cole-welcome-to-the-club/release/2377668

The Unforgettable CD, album: http://www.discogs.com/nat-king-cole-the-unforgettable/release/1931409
Español vinyl, LP: http://www.discogs.com/nat-king-cole-español/release/1685889
Nat King Cole Sings Great Love Ballads vinyl, LP: http://www.discogs.com/nat-king-cole-nat-king-cole-sings-great-love-ballads/release/2235378
The One And Only CD: http://www.discogs.com/nat-king-cole-the-one-and-only/release/1655844
Chestnuts Roastin' CD: http://www.discogs.com/nat-king-cole-chestnuts-roastin/release/2444552
Welcome To The Club CD: http://www.discogs.com/nat-king-cole-welcome-to-the-club/release/2096503
Préferences CD: http://www.discogs.com/nat-king-cole-préferences/release/1652775
Penthouse Serenade CD, album, remastered: http://www.discogs.com/nat-king-cole-penthouse-serenade/release/1620940
Legends Of The 20th Centrury CD, sampler, digipak: http://www.discogs.com/nat-king-cole-legends-of-the-20th-century/release/2074001
The Ultimate Collection CD: http://www.discogs.com/nat-king-cole-the-ultimate-collection/release/1255586
Great Singers Of The Century - Nat King Cole CD: http://www.discogs.com/nat-king-cole-great-singers-of-the-century-nat-king-cole/release/2592093

FRANK SINATRA

CLASSIC SINATRA
I'VE GOT THE WORLD ON A STRING
I GET A KICK OUT OF YOU
THEY CAN'T TAKE THAT AWAY FROM ME
MY FUNNY VALENTINE
YOUNG AT HEART
SOMEONE TO WATCH OVER ME
IN THE WEE SMALL HOURS OF THE MORNING
I'VE GOT YOU UNDER MY SKIN
YOU MAKE ME FEEL SO YOUNG
IT HAPPENED IN MONTEREY
OH! LOOK AT ME NOW
NIGHT AND DAY
WITCHCRAFT

LADY IS A TRAMP
ALL THE WAY
COME FLY WITH ME
PUT YOUR DREAMS AWAY (FOR ANOTHER DAY)
ONE FOR MY BABY (AND ONE MORE FOR THE ROAD)
COME DANCE WITH ME
NICE 'N' EASY

SINATRA REPRISE: THE VERY GOOD YEARS
LAST DANCE
NIGHT AND DAY
I GET A KICK OUT OF YOU
LUCK BE A LADY
WAY YOU LOOK TONIGHT
MY KIND OF TOWN [CHICAGO]
BEST IS YET TO COME - COUNT BASIE ORCHESTRA
FLY ME TO THE MOON
IT WAS A VERY GOOD YEAR
LOVE AND MARRIAGE
I'VE GOT YOU UNDER MY SKIN - COUNT BASIE ORCHESTRA
STRANGERS IN THE NIGHT
SUMMER WIND
ALL OR NOTHING AT ALL
THAT'S LIFE
MY WAY
LADY IS A TRAMP
SEND IN THE CLOWNS
NANCY (WITH THE LAUGHING FACE)
THEME FROM NEW YORK, NEW YORK

FRANCIS ALBERT SINATRA & ANTONIO CARLOS JOBIM
THE GIRL FROM IPANEMA
DINDI
CHANGE PARTNERS
QUIET NIGHTS OF QUIET STARS
MEDITATION
IF YOU NEVER COME TO ME
HOW INSENSITIVE
I CONCENTRATE ON YOU
BAUBLES, BANGLES AND BEADS
ONCE I LOVED

SONGS FOR SWINGIN LOVERS
YOU MAKE ME FEEL SO YOUNG
IT HAPPENED IN MONTEREY
YOU'RE GETTING TO BE A HABIT WITH ME
YOU BROUGHT A NEW KIND OF LOVE TO ME
TOO MARVELOUS FOR WORDS
OLD DEVIL MOON
PENNIES FROM HEAVEN
LOVE IS HERE TO STAY
I'VE GOT YOU UNDER MY SKIN
I THOUGHT ABOUT YOU
WE'LL BE TOGETHER AGAIN
MAKIN' WHOOPEE
SWINGIN' DOWN THE LANE
ANYTHING GOES
HOW ABOUT YOU?

THE VERY BEST OF FRANK SINATRA
STARDUST
FOGGY DAY
LET'S FALL IN LOVE
GIRL NEXT DOOR
OLD DEVIL MOON
WAY YOU LOOK TONIGHT
FLY ME TO THE MOON - COUNT BASIE ORCHESTRA
NICE WORK IF YOU CAN GET IT - COUNT BASIE ORCHESTRA
I GET A KICK OUT OF YOU
COME RAIN OR COME SHINE
PLEASE BE KIND - COUNT BASIE ORCHESTRA
DON'CHA GO 'WAY MAD
THEY CAN'T TAKE THAT AWAY FROM ME
IN THE WEE SMALL HOURS OF THE MORNING
I'VE GOT YOU UNDER MY SKIN
LET'S FACE THE MUSIC AND DANCE
COME FLY WITH ME
MY KIND OF TOWN
LUCK BE A LADY
BEST IS YET TO COME - COUNT BASIE ORCHESTRA
IT WAS A VERY GOOD YEAR
ALL OR NOTHING AT ALL
NIGHT AND DAY
NANCY (WITH THE LAUGHING FACE)
YOUNG AT HEART
LOVE AND MARRIAGE

ALL THE WAY
WITCHCRAFT
(LOVE IS) THE TENDER TRAP - COUNT BASIE ORCHESTRA
SECOND TIME AROUND
POCKETFUL OF MIRACLES
SOFTLY, AS I LEAVE YOU
STRANGERS IN THE NIGHT
SUMMER WIND
THAT'S LIFE
SOMETHIN' STUPID
WAVE
MY WAY
THEME FROM NEW YORK, NEW YORK
PUT YOUR DREAMS AWAY (FOR ANOTHER DAY)

A MAN ALONE & OTHER SONGS OF ROD MCKUEN
MAN ALONE
NIGHT
I'VE BEEN TO TOWN
FROM PROMISE TO PROMISE
SINGLE MAN
BEAUTIFUL STRANGERS
LONESOME CITIES
LOVE'S BEEN GOOD TO ME
EMPTY IS
OUT BEYOND THE WINDOW
SOME TRAVELING MUSIC
MAN ALONE (REPRISE)

GREATEST LOVE SONGS
MY FUNNY VALENTINE
WHAT IS THIS THING CALLED LOVE?
LIKE SOMEONE IN LOVE
I'VE GOT A CRUSH ON YOU
LET'S FALL IN LOVE
YOU'D BE SO EASY TO LOVE
FLY ME TO THE MOON (IN OTHER WORDS)
IN THE BLUE OF THE EVENING
MOONLIGHT SERENADE
I'M GETTING SENTIMENTAL OVER YOU
IN THE STILL OF THE NIGHT
YOU AND THE NIGHT AND THE MUSIC
DON'T TAKE YOUR LOVE FROM ME
I HADN'T ANYONE TILL YOU

MY HEART STOOD STILL
THE VERY THOUGHT OF YOU
THE WAY YOU LOOK TONIGHT
YOU BROUGHT A NEW KIND OF LOVE TO ME
NIGHT AND DAY
COME RAIN OR COME SHINE
ALL THE WAY (W/ CELINE DION)
STRANGERS IN THE NIGHT

SINATRA-BASIE
PENNIES FROM HEAVEN
PLEASE BE KIND
(LOVE IS) THE TENDER TRAP
LOOKING AT THE WORLD THROUGH ROSE COLORED
GLASSES
MY KIND OF GIRL
I ONLY HAVE EYES FOR YOU
NICE WORK IF YOU CAN GET IT
LEARNIN' THE BLUES
I'M GONNA SIT RIGHT DOWN (AND WRITE MYSELF A LETTER)
I WON'T DANCE

SINATRA & COMPANY
AGUA DE BEBER - ANTONIO CARLOS JOBIM
SOMEONE TO LIGHT UP MY LIFE - ANTONIO CARLOS JOBIM
TRISTE - ANTONIO CARLOS JOBIM
DON'T EVER GO AWAY (POR CAUSA DE VOCE) - ANTONIO
CARLOS JOBIM
THIS HAPPY MADNESS (ESTRADA BRANCA) - ANTONIO
CARLOS JOBIM
WAVE - ANTONIO CARLOS JOBIM
ONE NOTE SAMBA (SAMBA DE UMA NOTA SO) - ANTONIO
CARLOS JOBIM
I WILL DRINK THE WINE - FRANK SINATRA
(THEY LONG TO BE) CLOSE TO YOU - FRANK SINATRA
SUNRISE IN THE MORNING - FRANK SINATRA
BEIN' GREEN - FRANK SINATRA
MY SWEET LADY - FRANK SINATRA
LEAVING ON A JET PLANE - FRANK SINATRA
LADY DAY - FRANK SINATRA

THE CAPITOL YEARS
I'VE GOT THE WORLD ON A STRING [TAKE 10]
LEAN BABY [TAKE 4]

I LOVE YOU [TAKE 7]
SOUTH OF THE BORDER [TAKE 9]
FROM HERE TO ETERNITY [TAKE 9]
THEY CAN'T TAKE THAT AWAY FROM ME [TAKE 4]
I GET A KICK OUT OF YOU [TAKE 12] - NELSON RIDDLE
& HIS ORCHESTRA
YOUNG AT HEART [TAKE 12]
THREE COINS IN THE FOUNTAIN [TAKE 4]
ALL OF ME [TAKE 16] - NELSON RIDDLE & HIS ORCHESTRA
TAKING A CHANCE ON LOVE [TAKE 5]
SOMEONE TO WATCH OVER ME [TAKE 20] - NELSON RIDDLE
WHAT IS THIS THING CALLED LOVE? [TAKE 21] - NELSON
RIDDLE
IN THE WEE SMALL HOURS OF THE MORNING [TAKE 13]
LEARNIN' THE BLUES [TAKE 31]
OUR TOWN [FROM THE TV PRODUCTION OUR TOWN]
LOVE AND MARRIAGE [FROM THE TV PRODUCTION OUR
TOWN]
(LOVE IS) THE TENDER TRAP [FROM THE FILM THE TENDER
TRAP]
WEEP THEY WILL [TAKE 11]
I THOUGHT ABOUT YOU [TAKE 10]
YOU MAKE ME FEEL SO YOUNG [TAKE 12] - NELSON RIDDLE
MEMORIES OF YOU [TAKE 16]
I'VE GOT YOU UNDER MY SKIN [TAKE 22] - NELSON RIDDLE
& HIS ORCHESTRA
TOO MARVELOUS FOR WORDS [TAKE 7]
DON'T LIKE GOODBYES [TAKE 4]
(HOW LITTLE IT MATTERS) HOW LITTLE WE KNOW [TAKE 12]
HEY! JEALOUS LOVER [TAKE 6]
YOU'RE SENSATIONAL [SINGLE VERSION]
CLOSE TO YOU [TAKE 4]
STARS FELL ON ALABAMA [TAKE 7]
I GOT PLENTY O' NUTTIN' [TAKE 21]
I WISH I WERE IN LOVE AGAIN [TAKE 9]
LADY IS A TRAMP [TAKE 17]
NIGHT AND DAY [TAKE 5]
LONESOME ROAD [TAKE 7]
IF I HAD YOU [TAKE 10]
WHERE ARE YOU? [TAKE 12] - BILLY JENKINS
I'M A FOOL TO WANT YOU [TAKE 5] - GORDON JENKINS
& HIS ORCHESTRA
WITCHCRAFT [TAKE 14] - NELSON RIDDLE

SOMETHING WONDERFUL HAPPENS IN SUMMER [TAKE 11]
ALL THE WAY [FROM THE FILM THE JOKER IS WILD]
CHICAGO [FROM THE FILM THE JOKER IS WILD]
LET'S GET AWAY FROM IT ALL [TAKE 7] - BILLY MAY
AUTUMN IN NEW YORK [TAKE 3] - BILLY MAY
COME FLY WITH ME [TAKE 6] - BILLY MAY
EVERYBODY LOVES SOMEBODY [TAKE 4]
IT'S THE SAME OLD DREAM [TAKE 5]
PUT YOUR DREAMS AWAY (FOR ANOTHER DAY) [TAKE 4] –
NELSON RIDDLE
HERE GOES [TAKE 2] - BILLY MAY
ANGEL EYES [TAKE 3] - NELSON RIDDLE
EBB TIDE [TAKE 4] - NELSON RIDDLE
GUESS I'LL HANG MY TEARS OUT TO DRY [TAKE 4] –
NELSON RIDDLE
ONLY THE LONELY [TAKE 9] - NELSON RIDDLE
ONE FOR MY BABY (AND ONE MORE FOR THE ROAD)
[TAKE 1][ALTERNATE TAKE] - NELSON RIDDLE
TO LOVE AND BE LOVED [SINGLE VERSION]
I COULDN'T CARE LESS [TAKE 1]
SONG IS YOU [TAKE 6]
JUST IN TIME [TAKE 6] - BILLY MAY
SATURDAY NIGHT (IS THE LONELIEST NIGHT OF THE WEEK)
[TAKE 3] - BILLY MAY
COME DANCE WITH ME [TAKE 10] - BILLY MAY
FRENCH FOREIGN LEGION [TAKE 5]
ONE I LOVE (BELONGS TO SOMEBODY ELSE) [TAKE 5]
HERE'S THAT RAINY DAY [TAKE 21]
HIGH HOPES [FROM THE FILM A HOLE IN THE HEAD]
WHEN NO ONE CARES [TAKE 10]
I'LL NEVER SMILE AGAIN [TAKE 8]
I'VE GOT A CRUSH ON YOU [TAKE 7] - NELSON RIDDLE
& HIS ORCHESTRA
EMBRACEABLE YOU [TAKE 14] - NELSON RIDDLE
NICE 'N' EASY [TALES 11 & 12]
I CAN'T BELIEVE THAT YOU'RE IN LOVE WITH ME [TAKE 3]
ON THE SUNNY SIDE OF THE STREET [TAKE 5] - BILLY MAY
I'VE HEARD THAT SONG BEFORE [TAKE 5]
ALMOST LIKE BEING IN LOVE [TAKE 5] - BILLY MAY
I'LL BE SEEING YOU [TAKE 7]
I GOTTA RIGHT TO SING THE BLUES [TAKE 3]

THE REPRISE COLLECTION
LET'S FALL IN LOVE
YOU'D BE SO EASY TO LOVE
COFFEE SONG (THEY'VE GOT AN AWFUL LOT OF COFFEE IN
BRAZIL)
ZING! WENT THE STRINGS OF MY HEART
LAST DANCE
SECOND TIME AROUND
TINA
WITHOUT A SONG
IT STARTED ALL OVER AGAIN
LOVE WALKED IN
YOU'RE NOBODY 'TIL SOMEBODY LOVES YOU
DON'T TAKE YOUR LOVE FROM ME
COME RAIN OR COME SHINE
NIGHT AND DAY
ALL ALONE
WHAT'LL I DO?
I GET A KICK OUT OF YOU
DON'CHA GO 'WAY MAD
GARDEN IN THE RAIN
NIGHTINGALE SANG IN BERKELEY SQUARE
PLEASE BE KIND
PENNIES FROM HEAVEN
ME AND MY SHADOW - SAMMY DAVIS, JR.
I HAVE DREAMED
AMERICA THE BEAUTIFUL
CALIFORNIA
SOLILOQUY
LUCK BE A LADY
HERE'S TO THE LOSERS
WAY YOU LOOK TONIGHT
MY KIND OF TOWN
BEST IS YET TO COME
FLY ME TO THE MOON
SEPTEMBER SONG
IT WAS A VERY GOOD YEAR
THIS IS ALL I ASK
I'LL ONLY MISS HER WHEN I THINK OF HER
LOVE AND MARRIAGE
MOONLIGHT SERENADE
I WISHED ON THE MOON
OH, YOU CRAZY MOON

211

I'VE GOT YOU UNDER MY SKIN
SHADOW OF YOUR SMILE
STREET OF DREAMS
YOU MAKE ME FEEL SO YOUNG
STRANGERS IN THE NIGHT
SUMMER WIND
ALL OR NOTHING AT ALL
THAT'S LIFE
I CONCENTRATE ON YOU
DINDI
ONCE I LOVED (O AMOR EN PAZ)
HOW INSENSITIVE (INSENSATEZ)
DRINKING AGAIN
SOMETHIN' STUPID
ALL I NEED IS THE GIRL
INDIAN SUMMER
MY WAY
WAVE
MAN ALONE
FORGET TO REMEMBER
THERE USED TO BE A BALLPARK
WHAT ARE YOU DOING THE REST OF YOUR LIFE?
JUST AS THOUGH YOU WERE HERE
LADY IS A TRAMP
EMPTY TABLES
SEND IN THE CLOWNS
I LOVE MY WIFE
NANCY (WITH THE LAUGHING FACE)
EMILY
SWEET LORRAINE
MY SHINING HOUR
MORE THAN YOU KNOW
SONG IS YOU
THEME FROM NEW YORK, NEW YORK
SOMETHING
GAL THAT GOT AWAY/IT NEVER ENTERED MY MIND
LONG NIGHT
HERE'S TO THE BAND
IT'S SUNDAY
MACK THE KNIFE

SONGS FOR YOUNG LOVERS/SWING EASY
MY FUNNY VALENTINE
GIRL NEXT DOOR

FOGGY DAY
LIKE SOMEONE IN LOVE
I GET A KICK OUT OF YOU
LITTLE GIRL BLUE
THEY CAN'T TAKE THAT AWAY FROM ME
VIOLETS FOR YOUR FURS
JUST ONE OF THOSE THINGS
I'M GONNA SIT RIGHT DOWN (AND WRITE MYSELF A LETTER)
SUNDAY
WRAP YOUR TROUBLES IN DREAMS (AND DREAM YOUR
TROUBLES AWAY)
TAKING A CHANCE ON LOVE
JEEPERS CREEPERS
GET HAPPY
ALL OF ME

SINATRA AT THE SANDS
COME FLY WITH ME
I'VE GOT A CRUSH ON YOU
I'VE GOT YOU UNDER MY SKIN
THE SHADOW OF YOUR SMILE
STREET OF DREAMS
ONE FOR MY BABY (AND ONE MORE FOR THE ROAD)
FLY ME TO THE MOON (IN OTHER WORDS)
ONE O'CLOCK JUMP
FRANK SINATRA MONOLOGUE
YOU MAKE ME FEEL SO YOUNG
ALL OF ME
THE SEPTEMBER OF MY YEARS
LUCK BE A LADY
GET ME TO THE CHURCH ON TIME
IT WAS A VERY GOOD YEAR
DON'T WORRY 'BOUT ME
MAKIN' WHOOPEE
WHERE OR WHEN
ANGEL EYES
MY KIND OF TOWN
A FEW LAST WORDS (MONOLOGUE)
MY KIND OF TOWN (REPRISE) - FRANK SINATRA

SEPTEMBER OF MY YEARS
THE SEPTEMBER OF MY YEARS
HOW OLD AM I?
DON'T WAIT TOO LONG

213

IT GETS LONELY EARLY
THIS IS ALL I ASK
LAST NIGHT WHEN WE WERE YOUNG
THE MAN IN THE LOOKING GLASS
IT WAS A VERY GOOD YEAR
WHEN THE WIND WAS GREEN
HELLO, YOUNG LOVERS
I SEE IT NOW
ONCE UPON A TIME
SEPTEMBER SONG

FRANK SINATRA CHRISTMAS COLLECTION
I'VE GOT MY LOVE TO KEEP ME WARM
THE CHRISTMAS WALTZ
SANTA CLAUS IS COMING TO TOWN
THE LITTLE DRUMMER BOY
WE WISH YOU THE MERRIEST
HAVE YOURSELF A MERRY CHRISTMAS
GO TELL IT ON THE MOUNTAIN
THE CHRISTMAS SONG
I HEARD THE BELLS ON CHRISTMAS DAY
I WOULDN'T TRADE CHRISTMAS
CHRISTMAS MEMORIES
THE TWELVE DAYS OF CHRISTMAS
BELLS OF CHRISTMAS
AN OLD FASHIONED CHRISTMAS
A BABY JUST LIKE YOU
WHATEVER HAPPENED TO CHRISTMAS
WHITE CHRISTMAS
SILENT NIGHT

TOP TUNES KARAOKE CDG FRANK SINATRA TT-170
ALL THE WAY (FRANK SINATRA)
COME FLY WITH ME (FRANK SINATRA)
FLY ME TO THE MOON (UPTEMPO VERSION) (FRANK
SINATRA)
FOR ONCE IN MY LIFE (FRANK SINATRA)
GIRL FROM IPANEMA (FRANK SINATRA)
I GET A KICK OUT OF YOU (FRANK SINATRA)
I'LL NEVER SMILE AGAIN (FRANK SINATRA)
IT WAS A VERY GOOD YEAR (FRANK SINATRA)
I'VE GOT THE WORLD ON A STRING (FRANK SINATRA)
I'VE GOT YOU UNDER MY SKIN (FRANK SINATRA)
LADY IS A TRAMP, THE (FRANK SINATRA)

LUCK BE A LADY (FRANK SINATRA)
MY FUNNY VALENTINE (FRANK SINATRA)
MY KIND OF TOWN (CHICAGO IS) (FRANK SINATRA)
MY WAY (FRANK SINATRA)
NEW YORK , NEW YORK (FRANK SINATRA)
SEPTEMBER SONG (FRANK SINATRA)
STRANGERS IN THE NIGHT (FRANK SINATRA)
SUMMER WIND (FRANK SINATRA)
THAT'S LIFE (FRANK SINATRA)
WITCHCRAFT (FRANK SINATRA)
YOU MAKE ME FEEL SO YOUNG (FRANK SINATRA)
YOUNG AT HEART (FRANK SINATRA)

MY WAY: THE BEST OF FRANK
MY WAY
STRANGERS IN THE NIGHT
THEME FROM NEW YORK NEW YORK
I GET A KICK OUT OF YOU
SOMETHIN STUPID (W NANCY SINATRA)
MOON RIVER
WHAT NOW MY LOVE
SUMMER WIND
FOR ONCE IN MY LIFE
LOVE AND MARRIAGE
THEY CANT TAKE THAT AWAY FROM ME
MY KIND OF TOWN
FLY ME TO THE MOON (IN OTHER WORDS) (W COUNT BASIE
AND ORCH)
IVE GOT YOU UNDER MY SKIN
THE BEST IS YET TO COME (W COUNT BASIE AND ORCH)
IT WAS A VERY GOOD YEAR
COME FLY WITH ME
THATS LIFE
THE GIRL FROM IPANEMA (W ANTONIO CARLOS JOBIM)
THE LADY IS A TRAMP
BAD BAD LEROY BROWN
MACK THE KNIFE
LOVES BEEN GOOD TO ME
L A IS MY LADY (W QUINCY JONES AND ORCH)
LETS FACE THE MUSIC AND DANCE
COME RAIN OR COME SHINE
NIGHT AND DAY
THE VERY THOUGHT OF YOU
PENNIES FROM HEAVEN (W COUNT BASIE AND ORCH)

BEWITCHED
AMERICA THE BEAUTIFUL
ALL THE WAY
IN THE WEE SMALL HOURS OF THE MORNING
THE WAY YOU LOOK TONIGHT
THREE COINS IN THE FOUNTAIN
SOFTLY AS I LEAVE YOU
ALL OR NOTHING AT ALL
YESTERDAY
MOONLIGHT SERENADE
SOMEWHERE MY LOVE
MRS ROBINSON
SOMETHING
YOU ARE THE SUNSHINE OF MY LIFE
SEND IN THE CLOWNS
IT HAD TO BE YOU

THE BEST OF EVERYTHING (W QUINCEY JONES AND ORCH)
IN THE WEE SMALL HOURS
IN THE WEE SMALL HOURS OF THE MORNING
MOOD INDIGO
GLAD TO BE UNHAPPY
I GET ALONG WITHOUT YOU VERY WELL
DEEP IN A DREAM
I SEE YOUR FACE BEFORE ME
CAN'T WE BE FRIENDS?
WHEN YOUR LOVER HAS GONE
WHAT IS THIS THING CALLED LOVE
LAST NIGHT WHEN WE WERE YOUNG
I'LL BE AROUND
ILL WIND
IT NEVER ENTERED MY MIND
DANCING ON THE CEILING
I'LL NEVER BE THE SAME
THIS LOVE OF MINE

RING-A-DING DING!
RING-A-DING DING
LET'S FALL IN LOVE
BE CAREFUL, IT'S MY HEART
FOGGY DAY
FINE ROMANCE
IN THE STILL OF THE NIGHT

216

COFFEE SONG (THEY'VE GOT AN AWFUL LOT OF COFFEE IN BRAZIL)
WHEN I TAKE MY SUGAR TO TEA
LET'S FACE THE MUSIC AND DANCE
YOU'D BE SO EASY TO LOVE
YOU AND THE NIGHT AND THE MUSIC
I'VE GOT MY LOVE TO KEEP ME WARM

SINATRA'S SWINGIN' SESSION!!! AND MORE
WHEN YOU'RE SMILING (THE WHOLE WORLD SMILES WITH YOU)
BLUE MOON
S'POSIN'
IT ALL DEPENDS ON YOU
IT'S ONLY A PAPER MOON
MY BLUE HEAVEN
SHOULD I?
SEPTEMBER IN THE RAIN
ALWAYS
I CAN'T BELIEVE THAT YOU'RE IN LOVE WITH ME
I CONCENTRATE ON YOU
YOU DO SOMETHING TO ME
SENTIMENTAL BABY
HIDDEN PERSUASION
OL' MAC DONALD

WHERE ARE YOU
WHERE ARE YOU?
NIGHT WE CALLED IT A DAY
I COVER THE WATERFRONT
MAYBE YOU'LL BE THERE
LAURA
LONELY TOWN
AUTUMN LEAVES
I'M A FOOL TO WANT YOU
I THINK OF YOU
WHERE IS THE ONE?
THERE'S NO YOU
BABY WON'T YOU PLEASE COME HOME
I CAN READ BETWEEN THE LINES
IT WORRIES ME
RAIN (FALLING FROM THE SKIES)
DON'T WORRY 'BOUT ME

FRANK SINATRA SINGS THE SELECT COLE PORTER
I'VE GOT YOU UNDER MY SKIN
I CONCENTRATE ON YOU
WHAT IS THIS THING CALLED LOVE?
YOU DO SOMETHING TO ME
AT LONG LAST LOVE
ANYTHING GOES
NIGHT AND DAY
JUST ONE OF THOSE THINGS
I GET A KICK OUT OF YOU
YOU'D BE SO NICE TO COME HOME TO
I LOVE PARIS
FROM THIS MOMENT ON
C'EST MAGNIFIQUE
IT'S ALL RIGHT WITH ME
MIND IF I MAKE LOVE TO YOU?
YOU'RE SENSATIONAL

BIBLIOGRAPHY

Classic Sinatra: http://www.music-city.org/frank-sinatra/Classic-Sinatra-1338/
Sinatra Reprise: The Very Good Years: http://www.music-city.org/frank-sinatra/sinatra-reprise:-the-very-good-years-1339/
Francis Albert Sinatra & Antonio Carlos Jobim: http://www.music-city.org/frank-sinatra/francis-albert-sinatra-and-antonio-carlos-jobim-2370/
The Very Best Of Frank Sinatra: http://www.music-city.org/frank-sinatra/the-very-best-of-frank-sinatra-6125/
A Man Alone & Other Songs Of Rod McKuen: http://www.music-city.org/frank-sinatra/a-man-alone-and-other-songs-of-rod-mckuen-16276/
Greatest Love Songs: http://www.music-city.org/frank-sinatra/greatest-love-songs-22141/
Sinatra-Basie: http://www.music-city.org/frank-sinatra/Sinatra-Basie-23251/
Sinatra & company: http://www.music-city.org/frank-sinatra/Sinatra-AND-Company-30874/
The Capitol Years: http://www.music-city.org/frank-sinatra/The-Capitol-Years-31812/
The Reprise Collection: http://www.music-city.org/frank-sinatra/The-Reprise-Collection-31823/

Songs For Young Lovers/Swing Easy: http://www.music-city.org/frank-sinatra/Songs-for-Young-LoversSwing-Easy-31850/

Sinatra At The Sands: http://www.music-city.org/frank-sinatra/Sinatra-at-the-Sands-31981/

September Of My Years: http://www.music-city.org/frank-sinatra/September-of-My-Years-31999/

Frank Sinatra Christmas Collection: http://www.music-city.org/frank-sinatra/Frank-Sinatra-Christmas-Collection-34356/

Top Tunes Karaoke CDG Frank Sinatra TT-170: http://www.music-city.org/frank-sinatra/Top-Tunes-Karaoke-CDG-Frank-Sinatra-TT-170-34641/

My Way: The Best Of Frank: http://www.music-city.org/frank-sinatra/My-Way:-The-Best-of-Frank-37926/

In The Wee Small Hours: http://www.music-city.org/frank-sinatra/In-the-Wee-Small-Hours-38715/

Ring-A-Ding Ding!: http://www.music-city.org/frank-sinatra/Ring-a-Ding-Ding!-61161/

Sinatra's Swingin' Session!!! And More: http://www.music-city.org/frank-sinatra/Sinatras-Swingin-Session!!!-And-More-61188/

Where Are You: http://www.music-city.org/frank-sinatra/Where-Are-You-61760/

Frank Sinatra Sings The Select Cole Porter: http://www.music-city.org/frank-sinatra/Frank-Sinatra-Sings-the-Select-Cole-Porter-61766/

BING CROSBY

TOP O' THE MORNING: HIS IRISH COLLECTION. CD
WHEN IRISH EYES ARE SMILING
MACNAMARA'S BAND
GALWAY BAY
TOP O' THE MORNING
ROSALEEN
HOW CAN YOU BUY KILLARNEY?
IT'S THE SAME OLD SHILLELAGH
TOO-RA-LOO-RA-LOO-RAL (THAT'S AN IRISH LULLABY)
THE ROSE OF TRALEE
DEAR OLD DONEGAL
DANNY BOY
ST. PATRICK'S DAY PARADE

I'LL TAKE YOU HOME AGAIN, KATHLEEN
THE DONOVANS
WHERE THE RIVER SHANNON FLOWS
EILEEN
WITH MY SHILLELAGH UNDER MY ARM
MY GIRL'S AN IRISH GIRL
THAT TUMBLEDOWN SHACK IN ATHLONE
TWO SHILLELAGH O'SULLIVAN
THE ISLE OF INNISFREE
WHO THREW THE OVERALLS IN MRS. MURPHY'S CHOWDER?
DID YOUR MOTHER COME FROM IRELAND?
TOO-RA-LOO-RA-LOO-RAL (THAT'S AN IRISH LULLABY)

BING CROSBY & SOME JAZZ FRIENDS CD
YOUR SOCKS DON'T MATCH
MY BABY SAID YES (YIP, YIP DE HOOTIE)
BASIN STREET BLUES: - (WITH CONNIE BOSWELL,
CONNIE BOSWELL)
YES, INDEED! : - (WITH CONNIE BOSWELL, CONNIE BOSWELL)
SOMEDAY, SWEETHEART: - (WITH JOE SULLIVAN
BOBBY SHERWOOD, BOBBY SHERWOOD)
MOONBURN: - (WITH JOE SULLIVAN BOBBY SHERWOOD,
BOBBY SHERWOOD, JOE SULLIVAN)
PENNIES FROM HEAVEN: -LOUIS ARMSTRONG BING CROSBY,
LOUIS ARMSTRONG / BING CROSBY
THE WAITER AND THE PORTER AND THE UPSTAIRS MAID
THE BIRTH OF THE BLUES
BLUE AND BROKEN HEARTED
AFTER YOU'VE GONE
AFTER YOU'VE GONE
PERSONALITY
PINETOP'S BOOGIE WOOGIE
ON THE SUNNY SIDE OF THE STREET
I STILL SUITS ME: - (WITH LEE WILEY)
I AIN'T GOT NOBODY
DEEP IN THE HEART OF TEXAS
WHEN MY DREAMBOAT COMES HOME
GONE FISHIN': - LOUIS ARMSTRONG BING CROSBY, LOUIS
ARMSTRONG / BING CROSBY

EP COLLECTION CD
ROAD TO MOSCOW
IT HAD TO BE YOU
THAT'S A-PLENTY

220

SOMETHING IN COMMON
MOMENTS TO REMEMBER
LOOK TO YOUR HEART
SUDDENLY THERE'S A VALLEY
THE POSSIBILITY'S THERE
LONELINESS OF EVENING SEE ALL
THE LONGEST WALK
SAILING DOWN THE CHESAPEAKE BAY
THE SWEETHEART WALTZ
SING SOFT, SING SWEET, SING GENTLE
THE MOON WAS YELLOW
ME AND THE MOON
PALE MOON
GOT THE MOON IN MY POCKET
CHICAGO STYLE
YOUNG AT HEART
(OH BABY MINE) I GET SO LONELY
MADEMOISELLE DE PARIS
MER, LA
MORGEN (ONE MORE SUNRISE)
UNDER PARIS SKIES
DOMENICA
WHITE CHRISTMAS

**SWINGING ON A STAR: HIS 50 GREATEST HITS OF THE '30S
AND '40S CD
DISC 1**
IT'S EASY TO REMEMBER
OUT OF NOWHERE
JUST ONE MORE CHANCE
AT YOUR COMMAND
DINAH
PLEASE
BROTHER CAN YOU SPARE A DIME?
YOU'RE GETTING TO BE A HABIT WITH ME
THE SHADOW WALTZ
LITTLE DUTCH MILL
LOVE IN BLOOM
JUNE IN JANUARY
SOON THERE'LL JUST BE TWO OF US
RED SAILS IN THE SUNSET
I'M AN OLD COWHAND
PENNIES FROM HEAVEN
SWEET LEILANI

TOO MARVELOUS FOR WORDS
THE MOON GOT IN MY EYES
BOB WHITE (WHATCHA GONNA DO TONIGHT?)
I'VE GOT A POCKETFUL OF DREAMS
ALEXANDER'S RAGTIME BAND
YOU MUST HAVE BEEN A BEAUTIFUL BABY
AN APPLE FOR THE TEACHER
SILENT NIGHT, HOLY NIGHT
DISC 2
ONLY FOREVER
SIERRA SUE
TRADE WINDS
BE CAREFUL, IT'S MY HEART
MOONLIGHT BECOMES YOU
SUNDAY, MONDAY OR ALWAYS
PEOPLE WILL SAY WE'RE IN LOVE
PISTOL PACKIN' MAMA
SAN FERNANDO VALLEY
SWINGING ON A STAR
I LOVE YOU
AMOR, AMOR
I'LL BE SEEING YOU
TOO-RA-LOO-RA-LOO-RAL
DON'T FENCE ME IN
I CAN'T BEGIN TO TELL YOU
MCNAMARA'S BAND
SOUTH AMERICA, TAKE IT AWAY
THE WHIFFENPOOF SONG
GALWAY BAY
FAR AWAY PLACES
DEAR HEARTS AND GENTLE PEOPLE
IT'S BEEN A LONG LONG TIME
NOW IS THE HOUR
WHITE CHRISTMAS

**SWINGIN' WITH BING! BING CROSBY'S LOST RADIO
PERFORMANCES CD
DISC 1**
SWINGING ON A STAR
DON'T FENCE ME IN
BING INTRODUCES 'STRANGE MUSIC'
STRANGE MUSIC
TALLAHASSEE
PEG O' MY HEART

SHOO SHOO BABY
BING CHATS WITH THE ANDREWS SISTERS (NOT USED IN
STORY)
YOU DON'T KNOW THE LANGUAGE
SOUTH AMERICA, TAKE IT AWAY
IT'S MAGIC
THE NIGHT HAS A THOUSAND EYES
BUT BEAUTIFUL
BING INTRODUCES NAT KING COLE (NOT USED IN STORY)
BING CHATS WITH NAT (NOT USED IN STORY)
SAM'S SONG
MY FOOLISH HEART
THEM THERE EYES
TOO LATE NOW
NOT MINE
BING WELCOMES BACK THE ANDREWS SISTERS (NOT USED
IN STORY)
I CAN DREAM, CAN'T I?
SURE THING
BING INTRODUCES FINALE (NOT USED IN STORY)
MAY THE GOOD LORD BLESS AND KEEP YOU
DISC 2
BASIN STREET BLUES
IF THIS ISN'T LOVE
IT'S A GOOD DAY
BING INTRODUCES LOUIS ARMSTRONG (NOT USED IN STORY)
BING CHATS WITH LOUIS (NOT USED IN STORY)
BLUEBERRY HILL
A FELLA WITH AN UMBRELLA
BING INTRODUCES ELLA AND 'DREAMER'S HOLIDAY' (NOT
USED
IN STORY)
A DREAMER'S HOLIDAY
FOR YOU, FOR ME, FOREVER MORE
BING & LOUIS INTRODUCE 'GONE FISHING' (NOT USED
IN STORY)
GONE FISHIN'
LAZY BONES
THE BEST THINGS IN LIFE ARE FREE
THAT'S A-PLENTY
KISS TO BUILD A DREAM ON, A
LOUIS CONGRATULATES BING ON HIS 20TH ANNIVERSARY
(NOT USED IN STORY)

BLUEBERRY HILL
BING CHATS WITH JACK TEAGARDEN (NOT USED IN STORY)
ROCKIN' CHAIR
BING CHATS WITH DINAH SHORE (NOT USED IN STORY)
ROCKIN' CHAIR
FIVE MINUTES MORE
A MARSHMALLOW WORLD
SILVER BELLS

MY FAVORITE IRISH SONGS CD
DANNY BOY
OH! 'TIS SWEET TO THINK
THE ROSE OF TRALEE
DEAR OLD DONEGAL
MACNAMARA'S BAND
WHEN IRISH EYES ARE SMILING
TOO-RA-LOO-RA-LOO-RAL (THAT'S AN IRISH LULLABY)
HOW CAN YOU BUY KILLARNEY?
GALWAY BAY
ST. PATRICK'S DAY PARADE

CHRISTMAS WITH BING CROSBY CD
DO YOU HEAR WHAT I HEAR
HAVE YOURSELF A MERRY LITTLE CHRISTMAS
WHAT CHILD IS THIS / HOLLY AND THE IVY
THE LITTLE DRUMMER BOY
LET IT SNOW! LET IT SNOW! LET IT SNOW!
CHRISTMAS DINNER, COUNTRY STYLE
I WISH YOU A MERRY CHRISTMAS
HARK! THE HERALD ANGELS SING / IT CAME UPON A
MIDNIGHT CLEAR
O HOLY NIGHT
PAT-A-PAN / WHILE SHEPHERDS WATCHED THEIR FLOCKS BY
NIGHT

DEFINITIVE COLLECTION CD
WHERE THE BLUE OF THE NIGHT (MEETS THE GOLD OF THE
DAY)
STARDUST
BLUE HAWAII
PENNIES FROM HEAVEN
SWEET LEILANI
YOU MUST HAVE BEEN A BEAUTIFUL BABY
HOME ON THE RANGE

WHITE CHRISTMAS
SUNDAY, MONDAY OR ALWAYS
SWINGING ON A STAR
TOO-RA-LOO-RA-LOO-RAL (THAT'S AN IRISH LULLABY)
DON'T FENCE ME IN: - ANDREWS SISTERS, ANDREWS SISTERS
ROAD TO MOROCCO: - BOB HOPE, BOB HOPE
IT'S BEEN A LONG, LONG TIME: - LES PAUL
MACNAMARA'S BAND
ALEXANDER'S RAGTIME BAND: - AL JOLSON, AL JOLSON
NOW IS THE HOUR (MAORI FAREWELL SONG)
DEAR HEARTS AND GENTLE PEOPLE
PLAY A SIMPLE MELODY: - FRIEND, GARY CROSBY & FRIEND,
GARY CROSBY
IN THE COOL, COOL, COOL OF THE EVENING: - JANE WYMAN,
JANE WYMAN
OL' MAN RIVER
AROUND THE WORLD (IN EIGHTY DAYS)

**20TH CENTURY MASTERS - THE MILLENNIUM
COLLECTION: THE BEST OF BING CROSBY CD**
SWINGING ON A STAR
I'LL BE SEEING YOU
WHITE CHRISTMAS
PENNIES FROM HEAVEN
IT'S BEEN A LONG, LONG TIME
DEAR HEARTS AND GENTLE PEOPLE
DON'T FENCE ME IN: - THE ANDREWS SISTERS BING CROSBY,
ANDREW'S SISTERS
MACNAMARA'S BAND
PLAY A SIMPLE MELODY: - FRIEND, GARY CROSBY & FRIEND,
GARY CROSBY
FAR AWAY PLACES
CHATTANOOGIE SHOE SHINE BOY
AROUND THE WORLD (IN EIGHTY DAYS)

SOUTHERN MEMOIR CD
ON THE ALAMO
ALABAMY BOUND
WHERE THE MORNING GLORIES GROW
STARS FELL ON ALABAMA
CAROLINA IN THE MORNING
SWANEE
WAY DOWN YONDER IN NEW ORLEANS
GEORGIA ON MY MIND

225

CRYIN' FOR THE CAROLINES
SHE IS THE SUNSHINE OF VIRGINIA
SLEEPY TIME DOWN SOUTH
SAILING DOWN THE CHESAPEAKE BAY
GALWAY BAY, MACK THE KNIFE, THE SURREY WITH THE
FRINGE ON TOP, THE PLEASURE OF YOUR COMPANY
ON THE ALAMO
ALABAMY BOUND
STARS FELL ON ALABAMA
SWANEE
GEORGIA ON MY MIND
SLEEPY TIME DOWN SOUTH ALTERNATE VERSION

ESSENTIAL EARLY RECORDINGS CD
DISC 1
SIDE BY SIDE
NIGHT AND DAY
JUST ONE MORE CHANCE
SWEET GEORGIA BROWN
RED SAILS IN THE SUNSET
DON'T FENCE ME IN
THREE LITTLE WORDS
I FOUND A MILLION DOLLAR BABY
PLEASE PENNIES FROM HEAVEN
SWEET LEILANI
MUDDY WATER
TRADE WINDS
I'M THRU WITH LOVE
BROTHER CAN YOU SPARE A DIME?
TOO MARVELLOUS FOR WORDS
ALONG THE NAVAJO TRAIL
MISSISSIPPI MUD
I SURRENDER, DEAR
YOU'RE GETTING TO BE A HABIT WITH ME
DISC 2
SIERRA SUE
LOVE IN BLOOM
SWINGING ON A STAR
SAM'S SONG
SILENT NIGHT, HOLY NIGHT
ALEXANDER'S RAGTIME BAND
JUST A GIGOLO
THE WAY YOU LOOK TONIGHT
WHITE CHRISTMAS

YOU ARE MY SUNSHINE
I'VE GOT THE WORLD ON A STRING
OUT OF NOWHERE
BOB WHITE (WATCHA GONNA SWING TONIGHT?)
IT'S EASY TO REMEMBER JUNE IN JANUARY
YOU BROUGHT A NEW KIND OF LOVE TO ME SEE ALL
WRAP YOUR TROUBLES IN DREAMS
DINAH
SOON
SUNDAY, MONDAY OR ALWAYS

BING SINGS THE SINATRA SONGBOOK CD
THE LADY IS A TRAMP
YOUNG AT HEART
TOO MARVELOUS FOR WORDS
APRIL IN PARIS
I GET A KICK OUT OF YOU
IMAGINATION
WITCHCRAFT
HIGH HOPES
WHERE OR WHEN
AMONG MY SOUVENIRS, SEPTEMBER SONG, AS TIME GOES
BY
CHICAGO
THE TENDER TRAP
ALL THE WAY
LOVE AND MARRIAGE
YOU GO TO MY HEAD
IT HAPPENED IN MONTEREY
SOUTH OF THE BORDER
SUMMER WIND

CHRISTMAS WITH BING CROSBY CD
HAPPY HOLIDAY
LET IT SNOW! LET IT SNOW! LET IT SNOW!
SANTA CLAUS IS COMING TO TOWN
LET'S START THE NEW YEAR RIGHT
JINGLE BELLS
SILVER BELLS: - (WITH ELLA FITZGERALD)
WHITE CHRISTMAS
I'LL BE HOME FOR CHRISTMAS
SILENT NIGHT
THE FIRST NOEL

227

WHITE CHRISTMAS CD
SILENT NIGHT
SILENT NIGHT
ADESTE FIDELES
ADESTE FIDELES
WHITE CHRISTMAS
WHITE CHRISTMAS
GOD REST YE MERRY GENTLEMEN
GOD REST YE MERRY GENTLEMEN
FAITH OF OUR FATHERS
FAITH OF OUR FATHERS
I'LL BE HOME FOR CHRISTMAS (IF ONLY IN MY DREAMS)
I'LL BE HOME FOR CHRISTMAS (IF ONLY IN MY DREAMS)
JINGLE BELLS: - HIS ORCHESTRA, HIS ORCHESTRA, VIC
SCHOEN, VIC SCHOEN, ANDREW'S SISTERS, ANDREW'S
SISTERS
JINGLE BELLS: - HIS ORCHESTRA, HIS ORCHESTRA, VIC
SCHOEN, VIC SCHOEN, ANDREW'S SISTERS, ANDREW'S
SISTERS
SANTA CLAUS IS COMIN' TO TOWN: - ANDREW'S SISTERS,
ANDREW'S SISTERS, ANDREWS SISTERS, ANDREWS SISTERS,
THE ANDREWS SISTERS BING CROSBY, THE ANDREWS
SISTERS BING CROSBY
SANTA CLAUS IS COMIN' TO TOWN: - ANDREW'S SISTERS,
ANDREW'S SISTERS, ANDREWS SISTERS, ANDREWS SISTERS,
THE ANDREWS SISTERS BING CROSBY, THE ANDREWS
SISTERS BING CROSBY
SILVER BELLS: - (WITH CAROL RICHARDS, BING CROSBY
CAROL RICHARDS, CAROL RICHARDS, CAROL RICHARDS)
SILVER BELLS: - (WITH CAROL RICHARDS, BING CROSBY
CAROL RICHARDS, CAROL RICHARDS, CAROL RICHARDS)
IT'S BEGINNING TO LOOK A LOT LIKE CHRISTMAS
IT'S BEGINNING TO LOOK A LOT LIKE CHRISTMAS
CHRISTMAS IN KILLARNEY
CHRISTMAS IN KILLARNEY
MERRY CHRISTMAS
MERRY CHRISTMAS

VOICE OF CHRISTMAS CD
DISC 1
HAPPY HOLIDAY
SILENT NIGHT
ADESTE FIDELES
SILENT NIGHT

WHITE CHRISTMAS
ADESTE FIDELES
SILENT NIGHT
GOD REST YE MERRY GENTLEMEN
I'LL BE HOME FOR CHRISTMAS
AVE MARIA
WHITE CHRISTMAS
SILENT NIGHT
THE CHRISTMAS SONG
O FIR TREE DARK
THE FIRST NOEL
YOU'RE ALL I WANT FOR CHRISTMAS
DECK THE HALLS / AWAY IN A MANGER / I SAW THREE SHIPS
GOOD KING WENCESLAS / WE THREE KINGS OF ORIENT ARE /
ANGELS WE HAVE HEARD ON HIGH
RUDOLPH THE RED-NOSED REINDEER
THAT CHRISTMAS FEELING
LOOKS LIKE A COLD, COLD WINTER
A MARSHMALLOW WORLD
DISC 2
CHRISTMAS IN KILLARNEY
IT'S BEGINNING TO LOOK A LOT LIKE CHRISTMAS
SLEIGH RIDE SEE ALL
SLEIGH BELL SERENADE
CHRISTMAS IS A-COMIN'
THE FIRST SNOWFALL
IS CHRISTMAS ONLY A TREE
I HEARD THE BELLS ON CHRISTMAS DAY
JINGLE BELLS: - THE ANDREWS SISTERS BING CROSBY,
ANDREW'S SISTERS
SANTA CLAUS IS COMING TO TOWN: - THE ANDREWS SISTERS
BING CROSBY, ANDREW'S SISTERS
THE TWELVE DAYS OF CHRISTMAS
HERE COMES SANTA CLAUS: - THE ANDREWS SISTERS
BING CROSBY, ANDREW'S SISTERS
THAT CHRISTMAS FEELING / I'D LIKE TO HITCH A RIDE WITH
SANTA CLAUS
THE SNOWMAN / THAT CHRISTMAS FEELING / I'D LIKE TO
HITCH A RIDE WITH SANTA CLAUS
POPPA SANTA CLAUS: - THE ANDREWS SISTERS BING
CROSBY, ANDREW'S SISTERS
MELE KALIKIMAKA: - ANDREWS SISTERS, THE ANDREWS
SISTERS BING CROSBY, ANDREW'S SISTERS

SILVER BELLS: - (WITH CAROL RICHARDS, CAROL RICHARDS)
LITTLE JACK FROST, GET LOST: - PEGGY LEE / BING CROSBY
WHITE CHRISTMAS: - (WITH DANNY KAYE PEGGY LEE TRUDY
STEVENS, DANNY KAYE, TRUDY STEVENS)
SNOW: - PEGGY LEE, TRUDY STEVENS PEGGY LEE DANNY
KAYE BING CROSBY, DANNY KAYE, TRUDY STEVENS
WHITE CHRISTMAS
LET'S START THE NEW YEAR RIGHT

BEST OF BING CROSBY: 20TH CENTURY MASTERS/THE CHRISTMAS COLLECTION
IT'S BEGINNING TO LOOK A LOT LIKE CHRISTMAS
ADESTE FIDELES
GOD REST YE MERRY GENTLEMEN
SANTA CLAUS IS COMING TO TOWN: - THE ANDREWS SISTERS
BING CROSBY, ANDREW'S SISTERS
THAT CHRISTMAS FEELING
CHRISTMAS CAROLS / DECK THE HALLS / AWAY IN A
MANGER /
I SAW THREE SHIPS
JINGLE BELLS: - HIS ORCHESTRA, VIC SCHOEN, ANDREW'S
SISTERS
SILENT NIGHT
CHRISTMAS IS A COMIN'
THE FIRST NOEL
I'LL BE HOME FOR CHRISTMAS
HERE COMES SANTA CLAUS: - THE ANDREWS SISTERS BING
CROSBY, ANDREW'S SISTERS
CHRISTMAS SONG, THE (CHESTNUTS ROASTING ON AN OPEN
FIRE)
RUDOLPH THE RED-NOSED REINDEER
SILVER BELLS: - (WITH CAROL RICHARDS, CAROL RICHARDS)
SLEIGH RIDE
HEARD THE BELLS ON CHRISTMAS DAY
WHITE CHRISTMAS

BING CROSBY'S CHRISTMAS CLASSICS CD
WHITE CHRISTMAS
HAVE YOURSELF A MERRY LITTLE CHRISTMAS
WINTER WONDERLAND
WHAT CHILD IS THIS? / THE HOLLY & THE IVY
THE LITTLE DRUMMER BOY
O HOLY NIGHT
THE LITTLEST ANGEL

LET IT SNOW! LET IT SNOW! LET IT SNOW!
HARK! THE HERALD ANGELS
FROSTY THE SNOWMAN
RUDOLPH, THE RED-NOSED RAINDEER
I WISH YOU A MERRY CHRISTMAS
DO YOU HEAR WHAT I HEAR?
PAT A PAN / WHILE SHEPHERDS WATCHED THEIR FLOCK
CHRISTMAS DINNER COUNTRY STYLE
PEACE ON EARTH / THE LITTLE DRUMMER BOY

BING! HIS LEGENDARY YEARS, 1931 TO 1957 CD
DISC 1
WHERE THE BLUE OF THE NIGHT (MEETS THE GOLD OF THE
DAY)
OUT OF NOWHERE
JUST ONE MORE CHANCE
I'M THROUGH WITH LOVE
I FOUND A MILLION DOLLAR BABY (IN A FIVE AND TEN CENT
STORE): - HIS ORCHESTRA, JOHN SCOTT TROTTER,
BING CROSBY / JOHN SCOTT TROTTER & HIS ORCHESTRA
AT YOUR COMMAND
I APOLOGIZE
DANCING IN THE DARK
STARDUST
THE MOON WAS YELLOW
TWO CIGARETTES IN THE DARK: - GEORGIE STOLL, HIS
ORCHESTRA
WITH EVERY BREATH I TAKE
JUNE IN JANUARY
LOVE IS JUST AROUND THE CORNER
SOON
DOWN BY THE RIVER
IT'S EASY TO REMEMBER
RED SAILS IN THE SUNSET
SILENT NIGHT
I GOT PLENTY O' NUTTIN'
I'M AN OLD COWHAND (FROM THE RIO GRANDE)
PENNIES FROM HEAVEN
A FINE ROMANCE
SWEET LEILANI
DISC 2
BLUE HAWAII
TOO MARVELOUS FOR WORDS
IT'S THE NATURAL THING TO DO

THE MOON GOT IN MY EYES
REMEMBER ME
BOB WHITE (WHATCHA GONNA SWING TONIGHT?): - (WITH
CONNEE BOSWELL, CONNEE BOSWELL)
DON'T BE THAT WAY
SWING LOW, SWEET CHARIOT
SMALL FRY: - (WITH JOHNNY MERCER)
I'VE GOT A POCKETFUL OF DREAMS
MEXICALI ROSE
YOU MUST HAVE BEEN A BEAUTIFUL BABY
WRAP YOUR TROUBLES IN DREAMS (AND DREAM YOUR
TROUBLES AWAY)
SOMEBODY LOVES ME
WHAT'S NEW?
SIERRA SUE
TRADE WINDS
ONLY FOREVER
NEW SAN ANTONIO ROSE
HUMPTY DUMPTY HEART
DEEP IN THE HEART OF TEXAS
WAIT 'TIL THE SUN SHINES, NELLIE
WHEN MY DREAMBOAT COMES HOME
WHITE CHRISTMAS
EASTER PARADE

**MERRY CHRISTMAS WITH BING CROSBY AND THE
ANDREWS SISTERS CD**
HAPPY HOLIDAY
JING-A-LING, JING-A-LING: - ANDREW'S SISTERS, HIS
ORCHESTRA, VIC SCHOEN, ANDREWS SISTERS
TWELVE DAYS OF CHRISTMAS: - ANDREW'S SISTERS, THE
ANDREWS SISTERS BING CROSBY
THE FIRST SNOWFALL
I'D LIKE TO HITCH A RIDE WITH SANTA CLAUS: - ANDREW'S
SISTERS
POPPA SANTA CLAUS: - THE ANDREWS SISTERS BING
CROSBY, ANDREW'S SISTERS
YOU'RE ALL I WANT FOR CHRISTMAS
THE CHRISTMAS TREE ANGEL
SANTA CLAUS IS COMING TO TOWN: - THE ANDREWS SISTERS
BING CROSBY, ANDREW'S SISTERS
O FIR TREE DARK SEE ALL
CHRISTMAS CANDLES: - ANDREW'S SISTERS

JINGLE BELLS: - HIS ORCHESTRA, VIC SCHOEN, ANDREWS
SISTERS
CHRISTMAS IN KILLARNEY
WINTER WONDERLAND
HERE COMES SANTA CLAUS: - THE ANDREWS SISTERS BING
CROSBY, ANDREWS SISTERS
LOOKS LIKE A COLD, COLD WINTER
MERRY CHRISTMAS POLKA: - GUY LOMBARDO, HIS ROYAL
CANADIANS, GUY LOMBARDO & HIS ROYAL CANADIANS,
BING CROSBY, THE ANDREWS SISTERS, ANDREW'S SISTERS
MELE KALIKIMAKA: - ANDREWS SISTERS, THE ANDREWS
SISTERS BING CROSBY, ANDREWS SISTERS
IS CHRISTMAS ONLY A TREE
CHRISTMAS ISLAND: - ANDREWS SISTERS

BING CROSBY MEETS AL JOLSON CD
DISC 1
APRIL SHOWERS
WHEN THE RED, RED ROBIN COMES BOB, BOB, BOBBIN'
ALONG
BACK IN YOUR OWN BACKYARD
YOU MADE ME LOVE YOU
WAITING FOR THE ROBERT E. LEE
I'VE GOT THE SUN IN THE MORNING
EARLY DAYS
MA BLUSHIN' ROSIE
CHAT
SWANEE
CHAT
PHILCO COMMERICIAL (NOT USED IN STORY)
A RAINY NIGHT IN RIO
CHAT
ONE I LOVE, THE (BELONGS TO SOMEBODY ELSE)
WHAT AM I GONNA DO ABOUT YOU?
CHAT
LET ME SING AND I'M HAPPY
CHAT
ROCK-A-BYE YOUR BABY WITH A DIXIE MELODY
CHAT
WHO PAID THE RENT FOR MRS. RIP VAN WINKLE?
2ND PHILCO COMMERCIAL (NOT USED IN STORY)
THE ANNIVERSARY SONG
ANNOUNCEMENT
A HOT TIME IN THE OLD TOWN TONIGHT

OH, SUSANNAH
IN THE EVENING BY THE MOONLIGHT/HEAR DEM BELLS
BEAUTIFUL DREAMER
ON THE BANKS OF THE WABASH
CHAT
ALABAMY BOUND
I CAN DREAM, CAN'T I?
TOOT, TOOT, TOOTSIE, GOODBYE
CHAT
I ONLY HAVE EYES FOR YOU
WAITING FOR THE ROBERT E. LEE
BING INTRODUCES IRVING BERLIN (NOT USED IN STORY)
OH, HOW I HATE TO GET UP IN THE MORNING
CHAT
LAZY
CHAT 2
GETTING NOWHERE
ALL BY MYSELF
ALEXANDER'S RAGTIME BAND
EASTER PARADE
GOODNIGHT CHAT
DISC 2
BYE BYE BABY
BING INTRODUCES JOLSON (NOT USED IN STORY)
IS IT TRUE WHAT THEY SAY ABOUT DIXIE

BIBLIOGRAPHY

Top O' The Morning: His Irish Collection. CD:
http://www.cduniverse.com/productinfo.asp?pid=1103868
Bing Crosby & Some Jazz Friends CD:
http://www.cduniverse.com/productinfo.asp?pid=1001689
Swinging On A Star: His 50 Greatest Hits Of The '30S And '40S
CD: http://www.cduniverse.com/productinfo.asp?pid=6499497
EP Collection CD:
http://www.cduniverse.com/productinfo.asp?pid=6211047
Swingin' With Bing! Bing Crosby's Lost Radio Performances
CD: http://www.cduniverse.com/productinfo.asp?pid=6767971
My Favorite Irish Songs CD:
http://www.cduniverse.com/productinfo.asp?pid=1105421
Christmas With Bing Crosby CD:
http://www.cduniverse.com/productinfo.asp?pid=1517996

Definitive Collection CD:
http://www.cduniverse.com/productinfo.asp?pid=6999848
20TH Century Masters - The Millennium Collection: The Best
Of Bing Crosby CD:
http://www.cduniverse.com/productinfo.asp?pid=1104206
Southern Memoir CD:
http://www.cduniverse.com/productinfo.asp?pid=8373096
Essential Early Recordings CD:
http://www.cduniverse.com/productinfo.asp?pid=8373575
Bing Sings The Sinatra Songbook CD:
http://www.cduniverse.com/productinfo.asp?pid=8373095
Christmas With Bing Crosby CD:
http://www.cduniverse.com/productinfo.asp?pid=2181981&styl
e=classical
White Christmas CD:
http://www.cduniverse.com/productinfo.asp?pid=1105628
Voice Of Christmas CD:
http://www.cduniverse.com/productinfo.asp?pid=1104153
Best Of Bing Crosby: 20TH Century Masters/The Christmas
Collection:
http://www.cduniverse.com/productinfo.asp?pid=6292119
Bing Crosby's Christmas Classics CD:
http://www.cduniverse.com/productinfo.asp?pid=7280563
Bing! His Legendary Years, 1931 TO 1957 CD:
http://www.cduniverse.com/productinfo.asp?pid=1103651
Merry Christmas With Bing Crosby And The Andrews Sisters
CD: http://www.cduniverse.com/productinfo.asp?pid=1104731
Bing Crosby Meets Al Jolson CD:
http://www.cduniverse.com/productinfo.asp?pid=6944904

ABOUT THE AUTHOR

I was 59 years old; a mother of three very special and supportive adult children and a grandmother of three wonderful grandsons (I now have five grand-children.) when I started writing my first book whilst watching a Bon Jovi concert DVD. (I am an avid fan, if you can call me that; crazy is more like it.)

I write from the heart and I really enjoyed writing the book so I wrote another using a different artist, and the books kept coming to me and I kept writing them.(with a little help from above)

Because I use different artist/artists song titles I have to be very careful with Copyright so a lot of legal requirements have to be taken into consideration before publishing the books. I also needed a name that would connect my books to each other; so the "Song Title Series" books began.

All my books are short stories; however it depends on how many song titles there are to be used, as to the length of the book. Some artists didn't have enough song titles on their own so I combined them with a few other artists. Other artists had that many song titles that I could have written a novel; but it would have ended up being boring.

Challenges I like, so writing books with various artists are a lot of fun and require careful thinking.

Why should I have all the fun writing the books and not be able to share them with everyone; so I have converted them into large print and E-books so that you can share my fun as well.

Hopefully in the not too distant future; the books will also be available as audio books so that no-one will miss out on my fun and enjoyment of writing these unique books. I hope that you enjoy reading them.

My web site www.songtitleseries.com is the place to visit for updates of new books and a place to purchase other titles in other formats.

236

TESTIMONIALS

After reading through your range of books I felt I must compliment you Joan on the imaginative and entertaining way in which you presented each group and the Musicians in those groups. The way the stories were constructed is a credit to your work ethic. These must have taken considerable time to piece together and it is obviously a work of love for you.

I wish you all the success you truly deserve and look forward to seeing you next time you visit Tamworth.

Peter Harkins
Managing Director Cheapa Music
Country Music Capital Tamworth

The song titles series are books that were intriguing and were hard to believe that these short stories were written within the incorporated song titles of the artists that are mentioned in the titles. I loved what I have read so far and think that anyone with an imagination and love of music as the author you will surely enjoy reading these.

L.K. Brisbane Australia.

Joan Maguire Books are very nice, I enjoy reading them so much, they are hard to put down!! Especially when she does one about Bonjovi and their songs!!!

If I can say, it is worth every penny, when you buy one!!! The Books make nice presents, for a person whom loves to read!!! I can guarantee that you will LOVE these books, because I do!!!!!!!!!

Dawn from Newark, Delaware in the United States of America

I am Susie and would like to tell you guys, how much I am enjoying Joan Maguire's Books!! They are very enjoyable, and they are something that you do not ever want to put down!! I really enjoy these books; I can't wait until the next one that she puts out!!!!!!! I say go to your local book store, today and get one, you will not be disappointed!!!!!

Sue-from the United States of America

237

www.ingramcontent.com/pod-product-compliance
Lightning Source LLC
Chambersburg PA
CBHW072225170626
46813CB00003B/1091